M000031909

EXECUTE ORDER

By
Jett Ward

First Edition Design Publishing
Sarasota, Florida USA

Execute Order
Copyright ©2018 Jett Ward

ISBN 978-1506-906-84-3 PRINT
ISBN 978-1506-906-85-0 EBOOK

LCCN 2018953657

August 2018

Published and Distributed by
First Edition Design Publishing, Inc.
P.O. Box 20217, Sarasota, FL 34276-3217
www.firsteditiondesignpublishing.com

This is a work of historical fiction. Names, characters, businesses, places, events and incidents are the products of the author's imagination and/or based on the authors real life experiences. Any resemblance to actual persons, living or dead, or actual events is purely coincidental. Many of the characters are based off of real people alive and/or dead, will remain anonymous.

-Unmanned Aerial Vehicle - A powered, aerial vehicle that does not carry a human operator ... can be expendable or recoverable, and can carry a lethal or nonlethal payload. Also called UAV.

Part I

FIRST WEEK

August 2011

"Napoleon's army and Hitler's blitzkrieg were once world powers until their defeat by a coalition of smaller countries."
Joint Chief of Staff's advice to the President

"Iran, Hamas, Hezbollah and ISIS –
we are united against American imperialism."
A senior Houthi rebel in Yemen

Islam calls it the Caliphate.
Christianity calls it the Crusades.
Who will be the ruler of the world?

Our military operations in the Middle East were not a success. We brewed hatred and a formidable Islamic army called ISIS.
Secretary of Defense briefing to the Congressional Intelligence Committee

Chapter 1

THE INNOCENT

The mother finished washing her baby and wrapped a clean white towel snuggly around her small body. She held the little girl in her arms, rocking her back and forth. "I love you," she cooed. A tear rolled down her cheek as she caressed the young child. She exposed a breast to place a nipple in the baby's mouth, prompting the freshly cleansed child to begin sucking. Her thoughts drifted to everything she went through that brought her to this stage in her life. Nothing made sense. The only wonderful thing she had left was the living soul in her arms. Like every woman, she yearned for a loving relationship with a caring husband, family of children and a secure house. A little nest every woman in her village desired, until the Americans came and murdered her husband. Tragically, it would never be.

She laid the baby on the table and proceeded to dress her. From a rope stretched across the room, she unclipped a small white cotton blouse and held it against the wiggling frame. The day prior, the Iman gave her a sheet of white virgin cloth, a spool of thread and a single needle. He told her to lay the baby on the folded material, draw an outline, and then cut and stitch the edges together to make a small gown. She also needed to do the same for herself. The cloth felt like cardboard, making it easy to cut and sew, but once she had the gowns complete, she needed to wash the fabric to make it pliable.

Pulling the cloth over the baby scratched the delicate skin causing her to cry. When her baby enters paradise, the cleansing and the pure white cotton will allow for a beautiful beginning— the Iman told her this in preparation for their sacrifice. The two would be together - forever -without the threat of war, starvation or what she already endured. *It has to be this way.*

With her baby fed and clean, she began to prepare herself. She poured a five-gallon drum of cool water into a rusted catch basin, striped off her soiled clothes and started the process of washing her body, using a bar of soap to lather her hair and finishing by scrubbing her feet. The brown murky water in the basin matched the color of her skin, now a slurry of dirt and dried blood. She poured the coffee colored water into a hole in the floor that emptied along the outside wall and repeated the process until the water became clear—her purification now complete. She had to have every part of her body clean for her entry into paradise. *It has to be this way.*

She shook her newly made undergarments, relaxing the fabric until it became pliable enough to dress. She tucked her long black hair underneath a hajib, pulling the fabric across her cheek to hide the thick scar that ran from her ear to above her breast. The goal was to get the marines to regard her as another mother pushing a stroller, versus repulsed by her ugliness. She hated the scar. It reminded her of what could have been, then as quickly taken. If she could draw the marines closer, out from behind their cement barrier, this would be all the better. They all needed to die for what they did. By sacrificing herself, the Iman told her she would meet her husband again in a beautiful place—a paradise. Without him, she and her baby would starve. No righteous man would take her as his wife, since another had already made her a mother. Her sacrifice would ensure her family would always be together. *It has to be this way,* she again chanted in her head.

A soft knock on the locked door forced her out of her solitude, making her wince with the realization this stage in her life was about to end. She picked up her baby, holding the warmth close to her chest. "Please come in." Seeing the Iman enter caused her to tremble. "Is it time?"

He shook his head. "We are still waiting for the final piece. I see you have prepared yourself for your journey." After stepping into the room, he made sure to lock the door behind him. He came to where she stood and held her shoulders at arm's length.

She flinched when his fingers touched her cheek, pushing her hair away from her neckline to expose her ugliness.

"Do not be afraid. You are a very beautiful woman. Your journey is almost over. We will sit together while we wait." He directed her to a wooden bench along the wall. From a large satchel he carried, he removed a Koran wrapped in sacred cloth, opened it and read her a passage.

Chapter 2

LAS VEGAS

Brent Parker threw a frenzy of strikes against the thick leather. Each concussive impact sounded like a fistfight inside his closed garage. His body glistened with sweat as his muscles worked various combinations against the heavy-bag, striking the top -head, middle -torso, before throwing a roundhouse kick that caved in the thick padding. The movement of his feet around the inanimate object was similar to a ballerina, silently sweeping across the cement floor while always keeping a centered balance to strike again. When the skin on his knuckles split, the pain propelled him to hit harder. Heart racing, he longed to release his anguish into the bag. Each impact chipped away at his soul and began to wash away the grief at what he had done. The mental flash of the woman looking up at him made him pause. He didn't know her name or what she did to deserve an execute order. Nevertheless, someone higher up the food chain wanted her dead and he pulled the trigger. His target was a lone woman in the middle of a courtyard, trying to scratch out an existence in a country nobody cared about, located on the other side of the world. Her posture and the way her hair was pulled back, she couldn't have been much older than himself ... mid-twenties, both of them still trying to figure out this world they lived in. Ten seconds before her life ended, she looked up into the sky, as if she knew he was watching her. Their eyes locked together as he zoomed the camera in on her face—*I'm sorry. God, forgive me for what I have done.* Seconds later, the cylindrical spear slammed into her body.

To purge his soul, he threw another series of strikes, causing the bag to slip off its hook and fall from the chain that held it to the ceiling. Brent slumped over, resting his hands on his knees while taking deep breaths to clear his mind of the images. No matter how many punches he threw, her face would forever be ingrained in his mind. Physically he felt better, but mentally he couldn't stop thinking about her—*so young, what could she possibly have done to deserve this.* He shook the thin leather gloves off his hands and went upstairs to the master bath, stepped out of his shorts and into a steamy shower, allowing the hot water to finish his cleansing.

For the remainder of the morning, he sat on his balcony sipping a tumbler of rye bourbon, watching the pulse of the city skyline. Wearing thin grey gym shorts with orange "OSU Wrestling" stamped on the front, the early fall temperature mixed with a northerly breeze caused a briskness to the morning air. From his vantage, lighted beacons of commercial aircraft, stacked one after another, began their final descent from the west toward McCarran International Airport. To the north, he traced the beam of light that shot straight up to the stars from the Luxor Casino.

Every minute another jet descended over the mountains, each one he wondered who the people were inside: businesspersons or thieves, young parents clutching small babies or grandparents holding a bag full of quarters. He allowed his mind to wonder at the intricacy of life and death, and what it all meant.

The adrenaline of flying missions throughout the previous night finally ebbed, causing his eyelids to droop. He went back inside, slid into white linen sheets, and tried another attempt at sleep. His thoughts kept going back to the moment when he launched the missile, counting off seconds before impact. She knelt, entwined her fingers in front of her chest, while looking up into the sky as if praying to her god. With only a few seconds left, her eyes pierced into him until the silent missile made her disappear. Lying in bed with his eyes closed, he couldn't shake her stare. Sleep slowly filled the void, only to be replaced by dreams he couldn't seem to forget.

Most weeks ran a similar routine, with Brent feeling the mental exhaustion of a night spent watching and waiting, the reaper of death, deciding who lived and who died. Despite the physical strain and fatigue, he found himself reliving missions day after day. The face of the woman in the yard haunted him to his core; leaving him paralyzed, yet wide awake. *Pretty sure accountants don't lay awake at night reminiscing a tax audit with the same level of guilt,* he thought.

The excitement of living two blocks from the Vegas strip did not make up for a windowless dark box, watching high-definition video of a human explode. Getting orders to fly UAVs upon graduating from flight school was not his first choice ... nor second. It wasn't even listed on his dream sheet. Less than a month into flying these sterile missions, he found most of the other pilots remained mum about what they did and the few who did talk about it only spoke of the bravado of the kill. No one sought counseling—seeing a shrink placed a black mark on a security clearance, squelching any type of future promotion. If a pilot couldn't handle the pressure, the other pilots said, "Go confess to a priest." To squelch the pain, he found relief by beating on an innocent bag or playing Blackjack at a local casino—one helped him sleep, the other made him temporarily forget by intermixing with humanity. What he did for his country, he tried his best to keep together.

Once settled in, he slept off and on throughout the day until his internal clock said he had enough. The one bedroom multilayer townhouse he sublet kept him anonymous from the outside world. All he had to do was send a check to the owner, everything else stayed in the owner's name. An open main living area sat above the garage, containing a basic kitchen and an adjoining area large enough for a chair and couch. A previous occupant left behind most of the furniture, with only a few wall pictures added to make the place personable. Those he worked with only knew his identity, and rarely did he associate with any of them. Most people had lives during the day, whereas his involved the night— daytime in another country.

At six in the evening, he sipped on a double-shot espresso while he pulled on an olive green flight suit and laced up black leather boots. It was time to do it all over again. With his game face on, he went down a flight of stairs to the garage and climbed into a midnight-black Nissan 370Z convertible. If he couldn't yank and bank a fighter around the sky, he might as well drive one fast car with an open cockpit. Pulling onto the open road, the evening desert felt cool and crisp. For this city, the radiant skyline from the pulsating casino neon made it look like the beginning of the day. Brent took the highway ramp north onto US-95 out of Vegas, leaving the lights behind and pressed down on the accelerator, rocketing the Z as if shot from a catapult.

Forty-five minutes later, he approached the front gates that led into Creech—an obscure military base that tourists who gamble within the metropolis of sin city didn't know existed. As Brent's car approached, a security police officer stepped out from the guard gate. He straightened his gun belt underneath a portly belly and then yanked the black beret diagonally along his brow, partially obscuring the right eye. "Good evening lieutenant. Another night playing pilot."

Brent handed over his military ID. "Officer Johnson, looks like you're dressed to play cops and robbers. Which character are you going to be tonight?" While the officer held his ID longer than needed, Brent tried to bait him further. "I'm curious, how can you even see with that bonnet pulled over your eye like that? I sure hope you never have to shoot someone," he said with a bit of sarcasm.

Johnson flipped the ID back and forth, analyzing every little detail while cars lined up behind Brent, their drivers patiently waiting. "It's a beret. As I told you before, it signifies I'm a member of the special security force who keeps this place safe." After scrutinizing the picture against the driver for the third time, he handed the card back. "Have a peaceful evening in your box— try to drive safely tonight."

Brent tapped the accelerator as he now entered the confines of the reclusive military installation, home to several squadrons of Predator and Reaper UAVs; large Unmanned Air Vehicles capable of carrying a six-pack load of air-to-ground Hellfire missiles. A dozen of these aircraft lined the flight line ramp area. Most were away flying missions on the other side of the world, either providing reconnaissance or targeting terrorists who the senior leadership of the Department of Defense or the Central Intelligence Agency wanted dead.

At 1930 hours, Brent walked toward an eight-foot gate with spiraling razor wire fastened to the top. Once through, he came upon a similar fence, with nothing but concrete between the two layers, followed by a twenty-foot sidewalk that led to a glass-framed steel door—the front entrance to a windowless drab building. Except for the building's small size, and the array of satellite dishes and air-conditioning systems adorning the back patio area, the building resembled a maximum-security prison. Instead of guard towers on each corner, thick steel columns rose twenty feet high with a 'T' at the top containing an array of spotlights and foot long video cameras that watched over the entire structure. Brent scanned his ID against a card reader, initiating a buzz-click, prompting him to enter. Once inside the fenced perimeter, he repeated the same ritual to get inside the building, each step along the sidewalk his face continually recorded and digitally matched.

The first layer inside contained a room with sterile office furniture for any visitors, and a glass partitioned duty office with a sergeant sitting at a desk watching various monitors. A bulletin board along the hallway wall held a flight schedule showing the missions to be flown within the current forty-eight hour period. Parker looked for his name and found *Lieutenant Parker, Box 3 from 2000 to 0600 - Report to* **Room 8** *for mission specific details.* Seeing his name associated with Room 8 caused him to pause. "Room 8," he muttered. "Not again." Last night he killed a woman in cold blood—no name, what she did or if she even had a family.

He first went to Crew Planning to get a preliminary briefing on the country specific details, check-in frequencies and target location. Once he had what he needed to fly the aircraft, he went back into the hallway. The specifics of the mission would come next in briefing room 8. Just the association with this room indicated tonight would be another execution order.

The farther he went into the building's labyrinth, the layers of security intensified. The entire place felt like a prison with square foot beige tiles covering a cement foundation and pastel green cinderblocks made up the walls along the hallway. Every corner had cameras watching corridors with a full security detail waiting to pounce against an unauthorized access.

Upon reaching a steel vault type door with a lighted "8" above, he swiped his ID against a cipher lock and stood back so the camera could get a good look at him. With a swish, the door opened, he stepped inside, and the door hydraulically closed behind him.

A middle-aged man sporting a salt and pepper beard, wearing khaki slacks and a Bermuda shirt sat behind a sparse metal table. A single plain manila folder with a red TOP SECRET stamped on the outside lay on the table in front of him. Brent never knew who these people were, though he was told if they looked in good physical shape, they were most likely military Special Forces intelligence officers, otherwise the person was CIA—a spook. He learned Special Forces grew beards before deploying and CIA were recognizable by their stoic *no bullshit* attitude. For a moment he wasn't sure who this person was. Since they were all visitors to this little outpost, they all had an ID badge with a red "Visitor" across a portrait facial picture, a series of numbers underneath—never their name—and a striped black border along the edges indicating they held a security clearance beyond his. From the paperwork drill he had to fill out to do this job—along with an extensive background check that took several months to complete—he already knew just to be in this room required providing information that included the name of your great-grandfather's dog.

Before anything was discussed, Bermuda man slid a single sheet of paper across the table in front of Brent. It was a non-disclosure statement threatening a life behind four concrete walls if later he said anything about tonight's event. Brent wasn't exactly sure what would happen if he didn't sign the letter, since he had already seen this man's face and knew the approximate target location from the mission brief. Would they take him out back and shoot him, throw him in an isolated prison or toss him on a deserted island in the middle of nowhere. All of the above equaled a career expectancy of zero. Versus chancing the unknown, he scribbled his name and the brief started.

The man removed several pictures from the folder and pushed them across the table in front of Brent—he already knew not to touch anything.

"This building is your target," he said. "The X is your impact point. Keep your Reaper as high and obscure as possible. We do not want to spook anyone until we have confirmation of the person inside."

"We have both done this type of mission before. At thirty thousand feet, the Reaper will be a silent speck. Is there someone near the target location to verify there are actually bad guys inside?"

The man looked up and only smiled.

Brent held his stare, waiting for an answer. The clock above the door clicked off seconds.

"This HVT builds bombs: suicide vests. He is very good at it and needs to go away before another of his creations explodes in a crowded shopping mall. That's all you need to know—no name or where he is from. Your job is to fire your missile when told to do so." The spook looked up and stared at Brent. "Do you have a problem with that?" He waited until Brent looked down at the picture. "These sets of numbers," he pointed to a circle with a set of digits inside—from the circle, a line traversed to the southeast corner of the building, "are your target coordinates. Do you have any other questions?"

Definitely CIA, Brent guessed—stoic with no sense of humor. "The target looks like a mud enclosed apartment building. Entire families could be trying to scratch out an existence, with only one bad guy about to ruin it for everyone."

"That's right. It's called collateral damage for a higher priority. Anyone inside is expendable. Are you still asking a question?"

Brent wanted to reach across the table and choke the cocky bastard. This man could probably sleep with no problem at all, giving the dirty work to someone else to handle. "No sir."

"Is there anything else you'd like to know before we begin?"

"I can assume flying an American military aircraft into another country's airspace has already been coordinated with the State Department and we've been given permission to blow up a building in a sovereign country with who-knows who or what inside." Brent already knew the answer to this statement, but wanted to make sure they both knew what he was getting into. Clear as mud, essentially the United States could do whatever it needed to do in the name of combating terrorism.

Again, seconds ticked off. The spook glanced up at the clock and back at Brent. "It's time to get this rolling." He stood and walked out the door without saying anything further. The briefers rarely divulge any more detail than the bare minimum.

Outside the hardened enclosure, Brent grabbed a cola from the refrigerator, placed a checkmark next to his name and proceeded down the hall to the door marked Box 3. On each side of the hallway, four doors lined the corridor with each having ID scanners similar to the vault. Behind each door was an UAV control room, otherwise called a "black box." Each room had all the controls and instrumentation to fly an individual MQ-9 Reaper anywhere in the world. With the wars in Iraq and Afghanistan, and CIA sanctioned -hits- throughout the world, the rooms were continuously in use.

Scanning his ID, the lock unlatched and he entered a dimly lit room that resembled a darkened computer center with an aircraft's flight deck as the centerpiece. On the far wall, a set of upper and lower computer screens glowed on each side of two control consoles. A high-backed chair stationed in front of the left console remained empty and a system operator sat at the right console. The operator pushed various buttons and monitored readouts as he performed internal system checks prior to the Reaper's handoff.

Brent sat in the left seat and turned up the brightness to the upper screen that displayed the aircraft's attitude, altitude and airspeed against overlaid video footage from the Reaper's nose camera, and then repeated the process on the lower screen showing a moving map plot of the aircraft's location. All the screens were in standby mode, awaiting the handoff from the LRE—launch recovery element—a scaled down module similar to the controls inside this room, although located on the other side of the world, twelve hours different. It might be nighttime in Vegas, though currently morning in the Middle East.

He slewed the two joysticks, one on each side of a computer keyboard, watching how each display changed. The joysticks resembled a high-tech video game controller, except one manually overrode the autopilot automation and the other moved the nose mounted camera. Recognizing intelligence photos he had analyzed moments earlier and the moving map plot of a Reaper's location, he realized this would be a new mission over the CIA's latest terrorist battleground—the city of Ma'rib, the al-Qaeda capital of Yemen.

***

Ali leaned against his Toyota truck, glanced at his watch, and looked out once again at the shimmering landscape. Mornings were his favorite time of day. It always felt like the rebirth of the world as Allah meant it to be. Pure and clean, the earthly smell from the fresh dew. While he surveyed the landscape, the internal timer in his head ticked off another minute. Each mission he worked, timing was the most important factor. The runner scheduled to take the package was already five minutes late— *unacceptable!* Off in the distance a dust cloud formed, indicating a vehicle approaching. He measured the sun, three fingers high along the eastern horizon, internally confirming the time to be past eight o'clock. This land resembled a light brown moonscape contour with shallow crevices, darkened by shadows before the sun cast its beam overhead. The only vegetation was scrub brush that tried to survive in the sandy dirt. His truck sat hidden in a shallow dry wash off to the side of a gravel road, its location marked by a set of GPS coordinates—indicating a turn off highway N5, forty kilometers east from the city of Sana'a, situated in the middle of the Yemen desert.

A slight breeze stirred, making him shiver. His breath misted in the brisk morning air. He cocked his head to the side, listening for an indiscernible sonic vibration of a propeller indicative from one of those infernal American drones. Off in the distance, a locust buzzed and a wasp searched for food, otherwise his surroundings were quiet ... too quiet. His internal clock ticked past ten minutes, already too long in one spot. Every minute spent waiting increased the chance someone took notice of two vehicles meeting in the middle of nowhere—not from the ground, but from the air—and it wasn't the Yemen intelligence agency he worried most about.

He took a sip of water from his canteen and peered off at the brown dust plume that drew closer. He had yet to hear the car's engine, indicating at least another ten minutes of waiting. Once they arrived, the transfer should take only seconds and he would be back moving. He thought about the contents inside the box and the little wafer thin transmitter hidden on the bottom between the layers of cardboard. The GPS tracking device would allow him to follow from a distance to the Chef's location. Ali wanted to find out more as to what the Chef was making—and if needed, to shoot a bullet in his head if this mission became compromised. He hated being a logistic errand boy for an indiscriminate killer. His agency sent him to procure specific items for the Chef, a known bomb maker working for the Houthi rebel group who specialized in making suicide vests. Ali found terrorists to be unpredictable who had a tendency to change the rules halfway through the game—hence the reason for the transmitter. He also detested indiscriminate killing—the only thing it produced was more hatred. His government wanted this Chef to build these bombs and he obediently complied—*no more, no less.* For his personal survival within his own agency, he never questioned an assignment. He just made sure to cover every contingency that could possibly develop. If he died today, the ending of his life became Allah's will. It would be *'In shā'allāh.* Before he took his last breath, he'd also make sure the Chef preceded him. From this final act, his soul would then be clean to enter paradise.

It had already taken him three days to smuggle the micro-detonators and *Semtex* from Iran into the city of Sana'a, and two more to set up the transfer time and place. Everything remained in his control except for the vulnerability of this transfer. For some unknown reason the Chef also requested a bag full of American pennies. This spurred Ali's curiosity and gave him concern that he might be facilitating an unrighteous act. An Iranian intelligence agent, working with terrorists in Yemen, gathering a bag of American pennies in an Islamic country—it had all the ingredients of a suicide mission. A good intelligence agent would eventually put all the pieces together. To survive, Ali demanded obscurity. Unsure why the Chef wanted this unusual request, he fulfilled the order anyway, shipping it to Yemen by FedEx—utilizing American ingenuity—the very country they were at war with.

The intelligence dossier said the Chef now used a young fourth-tier Saudi prince as his logistics runner who Ali would soon meet—when he finally showed for this meeting. Everything about this Saudi angered Ali. Once educated in the United States living an opulent lifestyle of abusing fast cars and sleeping with young teenage girls—pure, innocent and beautiful—a delicate flower that should be impeccant. This prince came to Yemen to follow the footsteps of Awad bin Laden, also a Saudi who started his reign of terror in this country before developing an al-Qaeda network in Afghanistan. Because of Awad, the world had become chaos. Before, America did not care about this region. Now, even his own country was classified as a state sponsor of terrorism, their sanctions crippling Iran's people.

Ali despised the arrogance of Saudi royalty and he harbored no respect for bin Laden. He preferred to slip into a country unnoticed, complete the mission and disappear. He also abhorred the mass murder of innocent people, especially those involving women and children; they were innocent victims in this war. A bomb's destruction caused an outcry of hate, whereas he felt killing a politician provided a more pronounced change to the political landscape.

From the dust plume, a vehicle emerged—a white Range Rover barreling along a road at over eighty kilometers per hour. Ali opened his truck's door and stepped behind the Kevlar door panel to shield his body. His hand gripped the FN assault rifle that laid along the front seat, flicking a lever to full automatic.

Slouching his posture, he looked over his glasses. It appeared as though the vehicle would pass, but at the last second the driver slammed on the brakes causing the Range Rover to slide sideways before stopping a mere meter from Ali's door. Murky dust enveloped the meeting site, reducing visibility to the point where he could only make out silhouettes sitting within the interior. Ali pulled his shirt up over his mouth, trying his best to squint through the grit.

A percussive beat thumped from inside the vehicle. The passenger's window rolled down, blasting a trough of cool air followed by abrasive American rap music that belched from the interior's amplified sound system. "Hey old man, hopefully you weren't waiting long. You better have my package!"

Ali took off his spectacles, cleaning them with a handkerchief he pulled from his pocket, and peered inside the vehicle. His disguise was one of his favorites—a grey haired old college professor with a stooped posture. His stomach protruded over his belt, covered by a dirty white shirt that hid a Kevlar bulletproof vest. Most people found this look to be non-confrontational and underestimated his true intent. The driver he had never seen before—the person sitting in the passenger seat matched the picture of the Saudi prince. Addressing the occupants, he asked in an old fragile voice, "I do not think we have met. May I ask who you might be?"

The driver ignored Ali and proceeded to tap his fingers on the steering wheel to the percussive rhythm. Ali overheard the prince mumble to the driver, "They sent a stupid old man," causing them both to snicker. The prince looked over at Ali. "You do not need to know who we are." When Ali did not move, he continued, "Don't make me get out of this car to show you some respect. Give me the damn package."

Ali let go of the rifle hidden behind him and instead gripped the pistol tucked inside his back waistband. "Your driving is reckless and you are late. Both will cause reasons to be noticed."

Without the driver even looking at him, he said, "Piss off old man, or I'll take you out right now." This caused the prince to snicker

Ali leveled his PSS silent pistol at the driver's head and pulled the trigger, spitting out a 7.62 SP-4 Hollow Point. The bullet punched a half-inch diameter hole into the driver's forehead, snapping the head back before it flipped forward against the steering wheel. Bloody brains splattered the driver's side window, accentuated by a single perforation of the glass. Ali snapped his aim over so the passenger could see straight down the barrel. "I suggest you turn off the noise."

"You killed Ammed! You didn't have to—"

Ali altered his aim by three inches and again pulled the trigger. A bullet sliced a divot across his target's ear before blowing out more skull fragments from the dead driver.

The Saudi grasped the side of his head as if stung. Red crimson blood speckled his white tunic. "You have no idea—" He stopped short when Ali pressed the barrel against the prince's forehead, pushing his head backward.

Keeping his head still, the Saudi fumbled at the radio's controls until he found the mute button and the desert finally became quiet.

"I will ask once. Why are you late?" Ali wanted to blast a hole into this spoiled imbecile's head but held back from pulling the trigger. Killing him was not part of the mission. He didn't want to become any more involved than he already had with this Houthi group. His orders were to provide the Chef what he needed to build his bombs then leave—*no more, no less*. Instead, he pushed the barrel hard enough to leave an imprint in the skin. A pungent smell of urine permeated through the open window. "The one thing you can control in this life is to be on time and to always be respectful to all you meet. Lessons you must learn to survive."

"Yes sir. I'm sorry. I didn't—"

Ali held up his hand to stop the babbling. Reaching inside his own vehicle, he removed a cardboard box. "Take this to the Chef. Next time you make me wait, your life will abruptly end. Now go."

***

The Chef unwrapped the cellophane around the *Semtex*, cut the clay in half and inserted a piece inside the light blue diaper bag that rested on a wooden table. He would have preferred pink to match the baby's gender, but the Iman said the marines would not notice. This little oversight galled him. Building bombs required precision. The minutest detail could be the difference between inert material and a catastrophic explosion. The baby was a girl—the bag should be pink.

From inside a cardboard box, he removed two cylindrical tubes the diameter of a golf pencil and inserted both into the soft plastic explosive. While he waited for his Saudi runner to arrive with the remainder of needed items, he stepped out of his coveralls and began to wash himself with a moist baby towelette he found within the diaper bag. Once he felt clean, he changed into *Gucci* jeans with a pullover *Izod* shirt, and placed a pair of glasses on top of his head with flipped down lenses that he used for close intricate work.

When he heard a vehicle's engine approaching, the Chef went over to the window to peek through a crack. A white Range Rover skidded to a halt in front of his apartment, crushing a rusted red tricycle and flattening a tattered ragdoll. Three families lived at the far end of his building, thankfully away from him, though close enough to keep him safe. Children playing outside kept this apartment from being targeted—social camouflage. With the recent arrival of a young woman and her baby who now lived across the hall, the sound of incessant crying made concentration difficult. Soon she would be gone, replaced by another who would sacrifice her life for a greater cause. They all lived in a nondescript apartment building built out of brick and mud-mortar with a flat wood-beamed roof, nestled on the outskirts of the ancient city of Ma'rib located within the north central province of Yemen.

His young Saudi prince got out from the driver's side and delicately removed a cardboard box. His *keffiyeh* scarf, bloodied on the left side, was now tightly wrapped around his head. The Chef noticed his runner tried to keep the box steady while walking bowlegged, as he proceeded up the steps and into the building.

A half minute later, he heard pounding on the doorframe. "Yaheem, open up, it's me. Hurry!"

The Chef left the window to open the door wide enough for the Saudi to enter.

"*As-salamu alaykum,*" the Saudi said, pushing his way past.

Yaheem, known as the Chef, took a quick look down the hallway to make sure no one heard his given name, before closing the door. "I told you to never say my real name. We do not know who might be listening. You must always call me the Chef - it's my code name - my moniker."

The prince stormed across the room and set the box on a table. "I don't give a shit who might have heard. You sent me to meet a lion. I didn't volunteer to be your fucking errand boy."

Seeing the box made him forgive a spoiled prince's transgression. This prince came from money—the only reason he tolerated the arrogance. With the delivery now complete, he rubbed his hands together in anticipation to what was inside. "Set it over there on the table next to the diaper bag, everything else is ready." Trying to get his runner to calm down, he said, "You were gone longer than expected. What happened?"

"The person you had me meet shot my ear. Here look." He touched the side of his bloody headdress to remove it. "He also blew Ammed's brains all over my car."

The Chef took a step back, his hand covering his mouth to conceal a smile. The ear was severed in half; lower and upper pieces with a bloody trough in the middle—a precise shot by an expert shooter. "What did Ammed do? You must've done something." He didn't care about either of these two's fate. What worried him was whether they had altered the relationship with his supplier. Iran provided the micro-triggers for his vests.

"When we pulled alongside, he shot us both for no reason. Who is he?" His prince paced across the room, at times peeking out the window.

"I never meet them—that's why I have you. The detonators I use are built in Iran. Always reliable versus the garbage your scientists produce. My guess is you met an Iranian Quds agent since we are building bombs in Yemen. All that matters is what's inside the box you carried, and you're still alive." This last part he said without conviction. "You now have a battle scar that you can feel proud of. The girls will think of you as a true warrior."

The prince stopped at the mention of Quds. "You should have told me I was meeting an Iranian assassin—one of Soleimani's henchmen. They've killed several of my uncles. Iran and Arabia have different religious beliefs and worldly concerns. They do not like us. He probably knew I was from royalty—that's why he shot me."

"Your wound looks like a perfect shot. If he wanted to kill you, you would not be here bitching like a little girl. All of your uncles are distant and have many princes by their multiple wives. You are alive because you're an unknown." Yaheem ignored the rest of his babbling while he inspected the box. Slicing open the tape, he removed a bulging burlap sack the size of a pineapple and two smaller boxes, placing each next to the light-blue diaper bag. He untied the burlap string and reached inside, pulling out a handful of pennies. After smelling them, he shoved his hand inside the light blue bag packing the pennies against the *Semtex*.

While Yaheem continued to work, he said, "If I had told you who you were meeting, you would not have gone. I needed what you brought. It's what will complete my masterpiece. Right now Iran is helping us. Their enemy is our enemy, which makes us partners in this war. My guess is you provoked a lion and he bit you. You'll survive and be wiser for it. As for Ammed, I didn't like him anyway and I hated his music. Just like yourself, arrogant and full of himself. The business we're in does not allow for either. I told you not to highlight yourself, and when you do, this is what happens." When he looked up from the diaper bag, he noticed wetness around the young man's crotch, prompting him to shake his head with disgust.

The prince's temper snapped. "Next time, you can get what you need. You seem to forget that I'm a prince from royalty, not your little errand boy."

"Perfect and you can play with volatile explosives." Yaheem placed another handful of pennies around the soft clay inside the diaper bag. His concentration tuned out a continuous dribble of complaints. When the prince stood next to him to get his attention, Yaheem stopped what he was doing. "You will soon meet Allah if you keep ranting about nothing." With the pressure switch now connected, he slit open the smaller box to remove a device no bigger than a golf tee with wires dangling out the cupped end making it look like a large insect. He held it in front of his antagonist's face.

The young Saudi backed away. "I thought you said we were picking up timers—a stopwatch or something."

Yaheem straightened multi-colored spaghetti protruding from two cylindrical tubes. "These two," isolating green and brown wires, "will cause a chunk of *Semtex* to detonate. Snip the wrong wire in the bundle—instantaneous paradise." He held the digital detonator up for the Saudi to look at. "Inside are fiber optic connections—no metal material except for these single copper fibers and a miniature hearing-aid battery to power the unit. It is undetectable to a magnetic anisotropy detector. You could carry it through any international airport without setting off an alarm. Catch," as he faked the toss, causing the Saudi to yelp and back away. "You can drop this from the top of this building and it won't explode. The Iranians make a similar trigger for their nuclear weapons, but on a much larger scale with a much bigger boom," snickering at his own joke. "Before it's inserted into explosive, I will set it to initiate an electrical charge on a cellular signal, internal timer or remotely when a pressure switch is released."

"Next time I'll shoot first and take the package. Then you'll respect me for who I am."

Yaheem laughed at the absurdity, thinking, *young and privileged.* He removed another detonator from inside the box and placed it inside the diaper bag. A device heating on the table was a micro-soldering iron that resembled a space ray gun. He flipped down his glasses and went to work—smoke rings puffed out as he soldered wire connections to the pencil detonators. "I wire two for redundancy - two separate ignition sources - one with a dead-man switch that she'll hold and the other attached to a cellular connection that she doesn't know about. I'll use the second in case our volunteer doesn't have the courage Allah has required of her."

"Is she ready?"

"She is with the Iman preparing her soul for entrance to paradise. Tomorrow she will go to the American embassy. They will never suspect a mother pushing a stroller. We'll explode a vehicle a block away from the main entrance, causing mass confusion. When Marines come out from behind their barricade to assist, she'll give her and her baby's life to our cause. Our outcry against America's arrogance will be heard."

He pushed another handful of coins into the clay mass. "Two kilos of American pennies are packed around the explosive. What better way than to cause destruction with their president -their Lincoln - embedded in everyone's bodies. It's so American. Don't you think?"

Chapter 3

CLEARED HOT

Brent adjusted the volume on his headset to hear the broadcast over the satellite link. "The man you saw enter the apartment is the bomb maker's runner—an accomplice. We think he is meeting our primary target. Wait one ...." The radio went silent with a pause in the transmission. "We have confirmation from a voice match. He's in the eastern-most edge of the building. This is your impact point. Wait for final clearance."

"I have a visual on the building," Parker transmitted back. He had control of a Reaper, call sign Hunter zero-six. The metallic voice over the speaker sounded robotic—impersonal. Most likely, the distant voice came from a CIA operative or a SF member— Special Forces team leader tasked under CIA control. They both had the capability to stream his Reaper's video feed over the encrypted intelligence network onto a ruggedized miniature laptop from an overhead orbiting satellite. While he waited, he scanned the surrounding area, using both thermal and regular optics, looking for anything unusual. Several people were milling about on the opposite end of this ancient city and he found a few indiscernible heat sources in the desert several kilometers away from the target. Otherwise, nothing appeared unusual, except for a small tricycle.

Brent wiped his hands against his leg and re-gripped the camera's control stick. This pause, knowing he was about to fire a missile, caused his heartbeat to quicken. The woman's face from last night's mission flashed through his mind. *Put it aside and focus,* he reprimanded himself. Unsure when he would receive a clearance to shoot, he brought the Reaper's engine back to fifty-seven percent power, an optimum endurance while it turned lazy circles at thirty-thousand feet. At this speed, the aircraft had one hour of loiter fuel remaining before it needed to head back to a runway—referred to as its BINGO fuel point.

He focused back onto the Range Rover and, more importantly, what lay underneath. A vehicle entered the Reaper's viewing area, catching his attention. Keeping the camera locked on the target building, he got up from his seat to get a closer look at the upper monitor. A Toyota truck pulled off to the side road, stopping several kilometers from the outskirts of the village. An old man got out holding binoculars to his face. He was about to say, "Wait," when he heard, "You are cleared hot on the building."

He had also seen the tricycle and doll now crushed underneath the Range Rover. Both meant children were in the area. Forgetting the truck, he zoomed the camera focal to maximum to gain a close up view, looking for any other clue that would preclude a shot, but saw nothing. Hearing the control room door open, Brent saw his Director of Operations step into the room.

The DO came to where Brent sat and leaned over his shoulder, checking the various screens. "What do you have going?"

"OGA has cleared me hot on the eastern corner of the building. I'm hesitant to take the shot. I think there are children inside."

"I'm sure they've already taken that into consideration. It's not your job to question what has already been decided by someone a lot higher than you. Your job is to either fire or get out of the seat. That's an order!"

Brent continued to scan the area to see if a child emerged from the building. *Please, walk out the door.* This whole situation didn't feel right. The pressure of the moment made the two-inch scar above his left cheek burn. He tried rubbing the itching away as his other hand gripped the control stick.

The DO gripped Brent's shoulder. "I said shoot, dammit!"

Brent jerked the camera off target when he shrugged the grip off his shoulder. "Get your hand off me or I'll break it." Turning back to the screen, he refocused the Reaper's video camera onto the eastern edge of the building. *This is your job. Do it,* he said to himself. "Fire laser," he commanded.

"Laser is active and firing," reported the sensor operator, a technical sergeant sitting in the adjoining console. He glanced at Brent. He too had seen the tricycle and ragdoll.

Brent placed his thumb on the pickle button, waiting ... considering the ramifications. No children came running out the front door to stop him from firing. Finding only one option, he pressed down.

The camera view obscured when the solid fuel rocket propellant torched. A missile flew off the rails and into supersonic flight. Five seconds later the motor ran out of fuel, becoming a silent spear. As the rocket smoke dissipated, the building reappeared. When the countdown timer hit fifteen seconds, the missile pierced the apartment roof with twenty pounds of high explosive blasting through the eastern walls. A second later, a secondary explosion obscured the entire building. When the dust settled, a billowing fireball mushroomed toward the Reaper's camera. A super-heated pressure wave punched outward incinerating everything organic within a hundred foot radius.

"What just happened? No way could a single Hellfire cause that much damage." Brent said.

Nobody else spoke as a hushed silence fell across the interior of the Reaper control module.

The DO proceeded to the outer door and turned around. "Don't ever question orders again, like the procedures we follow, no exception. Either toughen up or go find a different job. After the handoff, go home. You're done here."

"Yes sir," Brent huffed, but his DO had already left the room.

***

Ali sat in his truck trying to process the destruction in front of him. Even parked this far away, the concussion from the blast rocked his truck side-to-side. With a UAV orbiting overhead, he knew it would still be recording the destruction. If he moved the truck, he might be its next target. He had seen the high definition video produced from these cameras. As long as he stayed inside the vehicle, he remained an unknown. If anyone walked up to investigate, his FN rifle laying across his lap would end an inquisitive mind.

The explosions caused people to come out of nearby buildings, standing in the decaying streets, gazing at the huge dust cloud that once held an apartment building—most were elderly with aged faces as they mingled and pointed at the destruction. A few old men tried to get close enough for a rescue, but each time the intense heat pushed them back. Off in the distance, a vehicle emerged coming from the same road he entered. Before it came close enough to see inside, it proceeded out into the desert and then stopped several kilometers away. Two silhouettes emerged from the desert floor holding backpacks. They both climbed into the vehicle before it drove away. Ali guessed they were the forward observers who called in the strike. They were members of America's assassination squad, who did not care about the consequences.

He would need to wait while the apartment burned. Embers floated into the heavens as Allah himself watched from above. It would be at least a day before it cooled enough to go inside and sift through the ruble. By then the UAV would have run out of fuel and gone back to whatever hell it came from.

***

Brent left the Operations building shaking his head. He fired up the three-hundred seventy-horse engine underneath the hood of his Z and punched the accelerator causing the wheels to squeal before turning out of the parking lot onto the main road. Only a hint of sunrise illuminated the mountains to the east. With the convertible top down, the cool windy air cleared his head. His thoughts again drifted to the woman looking up at him right before impact, and now images of children with black charred skin. Before he reached the guard shack, another car pulled in behind him with blue flashing lights flicking beams into his interior. A sharp siren broke the stillness of the early morning telling him to pull over.

The officer came alongside with a flashlight beam shining in his eyes.

"I need to see your identification, driver's license, registration and proof of insurance."

Brent recognized the voice coming from the police officer. "Hello Officer Johnson." While handing over the necessary items, he asked, "What's your reason this time?"

"The speed limit is twenty-five on base. I clocked you at thirty-two and I heard your tires screech coming out of the Ops parking lot. I figured it had to be your car—bet you get a lot of tickets with it?" He handed Brent a clipboard. "Sign here, indicating you've received this citation for speeding. Next time I'll charge you with reckless driving if I hear your tires screech again—then you'll have to take the bus and walk in to get inside. Now that would be cool."

Brent scribbled his name on the paper and handed it back. The patrol officer got back in his car and followed close behind until Brent drove past the front gate and off federal property. Once outside the officer's jurisdiction, he floored the accelerator, laying a patch of rubber for twenty feet.

***

The cellphone on his nightstand blared out a country music song, pulling Brent back to reality. He cracked open an eyelid to see who might be calling. The angle of the sun piercing through his shades told him he had only slept for an hour. The caller ID originated from a base number. A call during scheduled crew-rest could only mean bad news. "Hello. Lieutenant Parker," he hesitantly answered.

"This is Colonel Drake, from Creech. Have you seen the international news?"

Brent sat up in his bed, trying his best to sound coherent. Not every day his boss's boss called. "No sir. Should I have?" He crawled out of bed and began pacing around the room. His heart thudded as he looked for the remote control.

"CNN is playing detailed footage of a recent drone strike in Yemen. Several families were killed. The time and place matches your mission from last night. Everything about this mission has been sequestered. Thought you might want to know before the media coverage caught you by surprise. People who are surprised tend to say things. Do you have any questions?"

Brent already signed his life away if he said anything—discussing anything involving the CIA meant going to jail. What he did inside a black box essentially didn't happen. *Either way, I'm fucked.* "I'm not sure what to say."

"I'm calling to remind you to not to say anything to anybody. There will be a full investigation as to why you took that shot. In the meantime, you're off flight status until further notice. I'm told you hesitated before taking the shot, but took it anyway. You'll be getting a full psych evaluation and a board evaluation to determine your decision judgement. You might want turn on your television to see what you did." With the last statement, the conversation disconnected.

After firing missiles over the past month, it was inevitable that this day would come. *When you fire enough missiles, something unintentional will eventually happen.* He kept a running tally of the number of Hellfires fired—forty-three missiles over the past thirty days. With the high definition clarity of the Reaper's camera, he witnessed close up what twenty pounds of explosives can do to a human body - not much was left - people disintegrate into a bloody mist.

Turning on the television, he flipped through the channels until he found one broadcasting news on a recent American drone strike in Yemen. The picture showed a video clip with an *Al-Jazeera* stamp displayed in the upper corner of the screen. Brent didn't have to hear what the commentator said, the images told the story. Bodies covered in white bloody sheets laid alongside a road, a pool of blood soaking into the dirt next to each prone figure. Old women wearing black burkas knelt in a row, wailing over the lifeless forms. The video panned to another area showing a man carrying a small baby as blood dripped from a dangling arm. Brent forced himself to listen.

"… Americans with no regard human decency targeted this apartment. Four families lived inside, children played in this courtyard, now their bodies violated with American pennies." The camera operator panned the area, showing the carnage from the explosion. It focused back on the journalist leaning over and picking up what looked like copper pennies. She held them up for the camera, "This is a disgusting act of US arrogance—attacking a sovereign country in their search to counter terrorism using these to promote their propaganda. A confidential source inside the Yemen government verified this attack came from an American unmanned air vehicle that violated their sovereign airspace. I am told these aircraft are flown from the decadence of Las Vegas, Nevada in the United States—a place known for its sin and debauchery. America is the terrorist, not the innocent families who are now dead. This is Al Jazeera reporting live from Ma'rib, Yemen." The camera swept past the same olive-drab Toyota truck Brent had seen earlier from the Reaper's camera. An old man sat inside, not helping with the recovery, just watching.

Brent turned the television off and stared into a void, his mind numb from what he'd just seen. He feared there were children in the apartment. The decision on whether to kill or not kill rested in his hands. *I'm the one who pressed the button.* His shoulders slumped from the weight of what he had done. The scar on his face began to burn. He went down the stairs to the garage, this time he would not wear gloves. Soon, the snap of fists hitting leather sounded from his closed garage.

***

Ali waited in his Toyota truck throughout the day for the fire and heat to dissipate. When evening finally came, the place still felt like an oven. Smoke rose from charred beams that collapsed and the rubble from the mud-rock walls could still fry an egg. With no water in the area, the fire had to burn itself out before he could begin his search for any evidence. While he waited, he watched several of the local men doing their best to rescue anyone who might have survived. They could only stand the heat for a few minutes before they remerged carrying a burnt body part. His pulse quickened when he saw a man carrying a baby no longer that the length of his forearm. He wrapped the young infant in a white sheet and laid it next to other mounds, some large, most small, while women wailed over the lifeless forms.

As soon as the journalist drove away, Ali got out carrying his FN rifle. He climbed over rubble in search of the Chef's room. There needed to be no evidence linking back to him. Inside the destroyed apartment, he found a couple of wire bundles attached to small cylinders. These he slipped inside his pocket. Scattered everywhere were American pennies and bloody splatters from either the Chef or the prince. Pulverized concrete mixed with charred human tissue fragments littered the floor. He didn't quite understand the science behind DNA, but he figured it would be impossible to distinguish what body part the blood came from or if a person's DNA even survived an incineration. Though the Americans initiated the explosion, Ali knew whatever the Chef was building certainly contributed to the destruction. As far as the Al-Jazeera journalist knew, America brought forth this crime against humanity.

Back outside, he rejoined the mass of grieving. Customary to their Islamic law, the dead women and children were stacked in a row along the road, whereas the men were placed on the opposite side. He knelt down next to the dead baby girl and recited a prayer. "God is the One who supports you, together with His angels, to lead you out of darkness into the light. Allah is most merciful towards his believers." He knelt down and kissed what was left of the infant's forehead, and then looked up into the sky, trying to understand why someone would blow up an entire apartment with families inside. If he wanted the Chef dead, he would have simply shot him—one bullet, one death. *No more, no less.* Why murder innocent women and children? *It makes no sense.* Searching skyward, he prayed, "Though we have not yet met, we will soon. I promise."

Returning to the surrounding chaos, Ali dialed his satellite phone. Once it went through an encryption process, the connection opened at the distant end. "This operation has been compromised. The Americans somehow found the Chef—he is no longer available. They blew up an apartment with families inside. Send me to America and I will take this war to where they live. I will hunt and kill the person responsible."

The distant end reported, "There is already an asset in America who will find the person responsible. If he is unsuccessful, you will have your chance. Until then, make sure what you gave the Chef cannot lead back to us. The Yemen Special Security Force has already been told what happened and who is responsible. They have already started to use this propaganda to our advantage. It's time we sent a message to all Muslims that America's arrogance makes them a terrorist, not us."

For some reason, the timing of what he just heard felt wrong—*too soon, too quick.* He questioned whether his own agency staged the Chef's demise. Everything about this mission seemed contrived, as if adverse propaganda was somehow part of bigger plan and he was just a pawn that supplied the pennies.

Chapter 4

THE CONNECTION

Thomas Rawls, the United States Ambassador to the United Nations, did not like being caught off guard. From across the vast domed room, the Russian delegation entered, led by their ambassador. Seeing Thomas, the Permanent Representative of Russia passed by where he sat, and then stopped and turned around to give a sly smile. "Thomas, I just heard your president did it again. Your country is going to have to stop its witch-hunt—forcing yourself into another sovereign country without United Nations approval. You are making it too easy for us."

Unsure what intentions Vitaly knew about, Ambassador Rawls gave a sterile answer back. "If Russia did not support the Assad regime, we would not be in this mess." What was happening in Syria and the building strength of ISIS continued to be on the forefront of American and Russian controversy.

The Russian chuckled and proceeded to his seat at the front of the voting delegation. As for the other members of the assembly, Thomas did not care about their opinions. He cared only about the five voting members to the delegation. It was his responsibility to make sure he stayed ahead of whatever sinister plan they thought the United States should ... or should not do.

Nevertheless, as soon as the Secretary-General's gavel smacked the lectern to open the general assemblage to any new business, Ambassador Vitaly Churkin took the stage by hitting him broadside with a question to the constituents. "What right does America have to conduct military operations in a sovereign country? This is against the very basis of what this assembly is trying to prevent."

All eyes fell onto Thomas, causing his anger to grow. To gain some time to formulate a nebulous answer, he asked, "Could you please be more specific?" He instantly regretted meeting with his girlfriend this morning versus attending another boring intelligence briefing.

"Yemen ... Your country killed children in Yemen. Haven't you seen the morning news? For this reason, I turn my time to speak over to the representative to Yemen."

He knew he had been set up when the Prime Minister of Yemen proceeded to the lectern. The ambassador fumed—his anger blistered. He scribbled a note to his aid: *I want to see the Secretary of State immediately.* He then leaned over and whispered, "As soon as this son-of-a-bitch is done, make sure my motorcade is ready to leave." He put back on a false smile while turning the volume down on the translation. Whatever Yemen had to say, he could care less about—they did not have a vote to anything important.

The Yemen Ambassador pounded the podium to make his point, causing the people in the room to look up. "The United States conduct is outrageous. They must be stopped—they will be stopped!" This time he pointed his finger directly at the US seating area, prompting the ambassador to turn up the volume to listen to the translation.

"Your warplanes attacked my country without diplomatic clearance. We have yet to receive even a simple apology from your president for the egregious murder of my people. What gives you the right to attack us, to attack the world? We should come to your country and kill your children. Then you will understand what it feels like. General assembly, I demand retribution. I demand a monetary restitution to the families of the deceased and sanctions against America to prevent this from happening again."

That was the bottom line. The prime minister didn't actually care about all the deaths. He wanted money and the US had deep pockets. The remainder of what was said he could care less about. As soon as the general assembly concluded, the ambassador didn't stay for customary handshakes between various country representatives. Instead, his delegation escorted him out of the building through a side door and into a waiting black Cadillac Escalade. Before he could fasten his seatbelt, the motorcade started moving with blue and red lights flashing within the grille.

His chief of staff, sitting in the front seat, handed him a New York Times. "This just hit the newsstand. You might want to look at the front page. There's a picture of a man holding a dead baby. Sure makes us look bad."

"Why was I not given any warning about this? I represent the United States in foreign matters for Christ sake. I should have been briefed on this before some journalist already had an entire article written." The double scotch before the meeting began gave him a pounding headache.

He read the front page and the three full pages in the middle during the sixteen-miles from the United Nations Plaza to the Teterboro Airport. Cars pulled off to the side to allow flashing lights of the motorcade to pass. Once at the airport, the twin engines of the Gulfstream VI were already spinning. By the time he drank his third scotch for the day, the jet lifted from the runway for a short flight to Andrews, located outside the DC beltway.

The Ambassador carried the Times into the Secretary of State's office, slapping it down on her desk. "Madam Secretary, why is it the New York Times knows about a major event in our small world before I do? A simple phone call would have been nice!"

The Secretary got up from behind her desk and sat on the couch that faced into the room. "Thomas, this caught me by surprise as much as it did you. I just got off the phone with the Director of the CIA who said the number four terrorist on our watch list is now dead. The people killed were collateral damage. We'll pay restitution to the Yemen government and it will be all forgotten within a week." She snapped her fingers as if it would all be gone in a second. "You're just the spokesman. We in this white house make decisions. Do not ever forget your placement."

She actually patted his knee, like a mother consoling a child, which made him madder. "You don't have to stand in front of the United Nations assembly while the representative from Yemen fires rounds into my face. Ambassador Churkin is laughing at us. Do you have any idea how embarrassing it is to be blindsided like that—by the Russians? I should have known about it before it happened."

"Calm down Thomas." She got up and stood in front of him, hands on her hips—a teacher lecturing a child. "All I know is that this was a CIA directed execute order. When it involves a sanctioned hit, they tend to keep a tight lid on what they are doing. In the past, leaks have caused a target to disappear before a bomb fell on their head. I hate to say it, but this place is a sieve when it comes to keeping classified information secret. We eliminated another terrorist in this world, that's all that matters."

"You're telling me you were not informed about a US airplane flying into a foreign country to blow shit up without your permission? Who gave this authorization?"

"Every day ... every hour military and clandestine operations happen in this world without first going through the State Department. Formally, nobody will admit giving the authorization—that's not the way these missions work. It's called plausible deniability. Joint Resolution twenty-three signed by Congress gave the CIA a broad swath of legitimacy to hunt known terrorists anywhere in the world. Yemen—specifically Ma'rib—is known for harboring terrorist activity. This mission plopped directly under this congressional umbrella. Sometimes I get a courtesy call, usually after the fact. When I'm president, I'll change how the world revolves. Right now, these are the rules we play with."

"That resolution was written to keep our surgical activity secret, not to blow up an entire apartment building." He was not about to let her disparage what happened.

As the two were talking, madam Secretary's secretary came into the room holding a manila envelope. "This is a preliminary report from the CIA on what they are willing to divulge. I printed it from the classified server."

Madam Secretary took the envelope and returned to her desk chair. Diagonally across the front displayed a red stamp of TOP SECRET. Before her secretary left, she said, "pull a copy and email me the entire version. I'll read it later when I have time. Thank you."

Her secretary hesitated for a moment, and then said, "Yes Madam Secretary," before stepping out the door.

As she read the contents, her eyebrow raised. "It says the actual target was a known bomb maker by the name of Yaheem Rashad. Born in UAE, parents immigrated to England, then came to America to study electrical engineering and micro-circuity at MIT. He later joined a radical Islamic underground and attended a local mosque in the Boston area before feeling the need to help with the Jihad against America. His expertise in making suicide vests placed him on the top ten list of targeted terrorists. It says here he was involved in the suicide bombing in Pakistan last January that killed a hundred and five people— this was during a volleyball match. Recently, two female suicide bombers detonated his explosive belts on the Moscow Metro system at the peak of morning rush hour—this maimed over a hundred people, killing forty. Your attitude would change if this was at a football stadium or on the DC metro?"

"This might justify our actions, but I want to know who had the audacity to fire a missile into an apartment complex. Couldn't we have just shot him? Blowing up an entire apartment is certainly overkill."

"Next time we'll sober you up long enough to go in there and do the dirty work. Thomas, it's cleaner this way ... trust me." She read further along in the report. "It lists a Lieutenant Brent Parker as the person who fired the missile. It doesn't say who gave the actual authorization. It might have been the president as far as we know. I'm certainly not going to go barging into the oval office and challenge him on this subject. That's political suicide." With the last, she gave a smile to her office guest that this conversation was now over.

***

Zhang Wei sat at his cubicle inside the People's Republic of China, reading the same email moments earlier posted on the US Secretary of State's private server. His job, along with a fortress of several thousand professional computer hackers, was to infiltrate classified and unclassified networks used by dignitaries inside the US government. All the hackers were government employees, with rows of side-by-side cubicles stationed inside a warehouse style building big enough to hold a fleet of commercial aircraft.

Earlier in the day, a memo popped up on all the screens from the Ministry of State Security. It contained keywords to look for in whatever order the operator felt most penetrable, specifically Yemen, Reaper and anything associated with the CIA.

Wei utilized an embedded keystroke logger created by a team of Chinese PhDs that started by embedding a one pixel by one pixel image into top politicians' unclassified computer servers. It took him less than fifteen seconds to crack *Facebook*, *LinkedIn* and *Outlook* accounts without the owner knowing—easy prey for a computer illiterate and technically careless politician.

Within thirty minutes, he received multiple messages from congressional representatives and senators that his keystroke logger had become active. It took only a few more keystrokes to get his digital worm to crawl further into their systems. As long as his worm didn't touch a classified network, the breach would not trigger an intercept from the US professional government hackers who also held full-time jobs with *Microsoft*. The same people who wrote Windows and knew when a worm penetrated into a classified operating system.

Wei saw a message pop up coming from the US Secretary of State's Outlook account. He pressed the switch that turned on an orbiting red light above his desk. He now became the priority network hacker for the Chinese government. He typed out a message for everyone to hold back their cyber worm from burrowing any further within a host computer so as to not cause an alert. Wei had just hooked a big fish—he didn't want to lose it before a network breach became detected and the whole system slammed shut.

As he waited, a password popped onto his screen. Everything the Secretary of State typed echoed onto his computer. Within five minutes, he logged into her personal email account using her own password and began downloading every message received and written. Within the downloaded contents, he performed a search of keywords.

Wei's mastery of the English language was limited to computer forensics. When the search came up with *TOP SECRET - Central Intelligence Agency* in the subject header, he held a golden ticket to a promotion. He ran the file through a translation program, converting the English sentences to Chinese. Reading the names

Parker and Yeheem, prompted an immediate call to the Chinese Foreign Minister's office.

With the Chinese thirst for Iranian oil, the two countries had previously developed a strong diplomatic relationship and a collusion to pass any United States information that might be helpful between their respective intelligence agencies. Before General Soleimani, the Iran's Director of the Republican Guard finished *'Ishā'*, the last Islamic prayer for the day, he knew the person who pulled the trigger that killed his favorite bomb builder.

Chapter 5

THE SANCTION

The First Secretary to Pakistan, stationed at the Los Angeles consulate, read the cypher handed to him by his assistant Kallem, an ambassadorial security agent who also had undercover ties to the Iranian government. Since the US and Iran still had a closed relationship going back to the American embassy-hostage takeover that happened in 1981, the two countries had yet to re-establish diplomatic relations. Seyyed Sadegh's position as first secretary was only a front to gain diplomatic access into the United States. His primary duty was to provide intelligence to both the Pakistani and Iranian government, and do any dirty work sanctioned by the ayatollah. The prospect of going to Las Vegas made this mission appealing, where the sexuality of American women mixed with the sultry nightlife of Vegas would appease his appetite. The order received was an execute order—a military pilot needed to be made an example. It was now time to bring this war onto American soil. Sadegh loved America—it allowed him to do things that would have gotten him stoned in his own country. Having diplomatic immunity, the local law enforcement was powerless to stop him, unless they caught him in the act, but he always sterilized so there would be no trace.

He took out a suitcase from the office closet and placed it on his desk to inspect the contents inside. A small box contained a theater makeup kit to age his appearance, to include a beard and goatee to obscure his face. He also removed a silenced pistol, which he placed in a shoulder holster concealed under his arm.

While he prepared for this mission, a large diplomatic pouch soon arrived to his office. Inside was a small hard-plastic Pelican case, with two locks and a strip of tampering tape that only he was authorized to break. Producing a key, he opened the case and found a US military issued 9mm Beretta, along with four boxes of military ball ammunition. With the suitcase in hand, he closed down his office and left the consulate without telling anyone where he was going or how long he would be gone. Only the Ambassador knew his true role, and he was told to turn a blind-eye on any clandestine operation Iran did in this country. It gave him plausible deniability and added another sizeable sum of money to his Swiss bank account.

The three-hour drive along Interstate-15 to Vegas gave Sadegh time to plan this sanction. His directions said it needed to be dramatic with enough publicity exposure to cause an international scandal. He had the latitude to kill anyone necessary, as long as the evidence pointed at his target—and nothing could point back to Iran. This was the reason for the American 9mm—all to frame the pilot with multiple murders. Add a little sex to the story and the media scandal would explode. What bothered Sadegh was the lack of information on his target, which indicated a reclusive subsistence, many unknowns and the smell of CIA involvement. It did provide a name and a forwarding address to a small town in Oklahoma and it showed his target leased a black Nissan 370Z from a Stillwater dealership using the same address—no police arrest, no listing within the Las Vegas utility database, which meant no address as to where this pilot lived. The message did give the location where the pilot flew UAV missions—Creech Air Force base—an obscure military base forty miles north of the city. This would be his first stop, making a good starting point for a visual identification. There could not be that many black Zs on a small military base. Once he found the car, he found his target.

***

From across the highway, Sadegh sat in a rental car checking each vehicle that exited from the Creech, waiting for the known black sports car to arrive. He had already been watching for two days, each time driving a different type vehicle, wearing different clothes and another disguise. The masquerade ensured he didn't draw any inquisitive attention of why he was outside a US military base. Only the clerk at the mini mart gave him a second look, but he made sure this did not become an issue. The clerk was previously from Pakistan and a devout Muslim. A quick phone call gave him all the information he needed. Prior to leaving the store, Sadegh asked, "How is your wife Maleeha, and two daughters Sehr and Alina? If you tell anyone that I exist, their throats will be slit." He did not wait for an answer.

At seven in the evening, a black Z drove onto the base and did not come off until five-fifteen the following morning. The lack of light made it difficult to see the driver, but it was the only black sports car to have entered during his wait. Sadegh started the car's engine, keeping the front headlights off until the car traveled a distance down the highway. Instead of pulling onto the road, the Z crossed the main highway and stopped several stalls away from where he sat. Sadegh raised a small camera above the windowsill and snapped pictures in the direction where the car was parked, while not actually looking in the same direction. A young man wearing a flight suit got out, looked around, and proceeded toward the store. Sadegh glanced over at the pilot and instantly regretted it. The two of them locked eyes and held their stare, then as quickly the pilot moved off to go inside.

The shoplifting height tape along the doorway showed him to be an inch under six feet tall. Sadegh estimated a weight of two hundred pounds. He had a muscular physique under the green flight suit without the stiffness of a weightlifter, more like a predatory cat, arms and legs swinging in a relaxed synchronized motion. Sadegh made a mental note to be cautious with this one— his target had seen his face, making an opportunity to kill him that much more dangerous. This moment might be his best opportunity. He removed the silenced pistol from underneath the newspaper, tucked it into his concealed holster and followed his target inside. A video monitor mounted behind the cashier displayed a split screen of the counter and store aisles. Even with the glasses and fake mustache, Sadegh had already left a video trail over the last two days. Maintaining a poised demeanor, he removed a bag of Doritos from the display and waited for the target to pay and leave. He overheard the clerk talking to the patron in a familiar tone, and when he left, Sadegh proceeded to the counter. "Who was that person who just came in?"

"His name tag says Parker. That's all I know."

"Does he always come in at this time, this early in the morning?"

"This was the first time I've seen him for a couple of weeks. Otherwise, yes."

Once inside his car, Sadegh got onto the highway and tried to catch his quarry. With few cars traveling back to the city, it took him halfway toward the city before he again spotted the sports car. His target initially traveled ten miles-per-hour over the posted speed limit, which made him nervous to follow at the same speed. Sadegh tried to match the pace while watching for a state police cruiser clocking traffic.

The Z passed several cars and when it came to a straight stretch of road, the distance increased. Sadegh's speedometer passed the hundred mark. His international driver's license legally allowed him to operate a vehicle inside the United States, plus having diplomatic credentials prevented him from receiving a ticket, but there would be a report of his existence near a US military base outside of his normal jurisdiction. State Department questions would certainly be asked if stopped. Not wanting to lose the Z, Sadegh placed the pistol on his lap and stepped on the accelerator to keep pace with the car ahead.

Five miles prior to entering the city limits, traffic thickened, impeding the Z's speed and allowing Sadegh close the distance. Passing old town casinos, it took an exit and disappeared onto a side street. He stomped on the pedal and took the same off ramp, catching him stopped at an intersection. When the light turned green, he maintained an obscure distance, until the Z entered a gate that closed before he could follow.

He parked along the street, climbed over the barricade and searched for the car. The complex contained three-story townhouses side-by-side, each having a basement garage with an upper living area. With every American owning a gun and living in a house wired with an alarm system, even if he found where his target lived, there were too many unknowns to sneak inside. His orders said to make this kill flamboyant with a lot of media coverage. With only one central entrance, there was only one-way out of the complex. Within 48-hours, he now had a picture and a general location where his target lived. With a little patience, he would find the right vulnerabilities.

Back on the street, Sadegh moved his car into a position to allow a clear view of the gate. Less than fifteen minutes later, the black Z emerged, took a left and proceeded back onto the highway. He half expected another race out to the base, but instead they headed toward the historic city center they passed earlier. The Z parked in an outlying parking area of the Royal Sands casino and the pilot went inside through a side door. Every person had a weakness, and he was about to find out Parker's.

Sadegh opened the makeup kit, peeled the mustache from his upper lip and replaced it with a grey goatee that he applied to his chin. He dabbed an opaque powder to his face and slid on horn-rimmed glasses that held rose tinted lenses. When he got out of his vehicle, he slipped on a tattered blazer and went in through the same door.

Inside the casino, he hobbled past a jingling slot machine and took a walker he found unattended. This casino held an older vintage appearance with a western motif. The front entrance even had swinging saloon type doors, allowing the stale air inside to escape. Most patrons were elderly, wasting their days inserting coins from a cup into arcade slot machines. Several dealers sat at empty tables shuffling cards, waiting for someone to take a seat. Except for maybe wearing a cowboy hat, his disguise allowed him to blend in with the other patrons. Checking the saloon, he found a mix in age of Eastern European women sitting on stools talking with the bartender. These women had a haggard look, with droopy eyelids covered by makeup that they layered too many times before each trick they pulled, wearing short frilly dresses and tight halter-tops.

Pushing his walker into the middle of the casino, Sadegh finally found Parker at a blackjack table toward the back of the room. He stayed close to the machines, inserting a single coin to play the game, pulling the lever before moving down to the next until at the last machine prior to the table where Parker sat. Taking periodic glances and catching only clipped conversations, it appeared as though the pilot and dealer knew each other.

After a few minutes, Parker placed a single chip in front of him and the dealer tossed two cards across the table. Even as they played, the two continued to talk in a hushed conversation. Parker would ask a question and then the dealer would talk, as if providing advice.

Sadegh used the walker to hobble behind the pilot, but with all the jingling noise from the machines, he couldn't hear what they were saying without drawing any undue attention. No matter, his target had a friend -this dealer- and therefore a weakness.

Sadegh left the area and sat at a table within the saloon. Two girls he'd seen earlier sat at a table with two older men, prompting the bartender to bring over more drinks. A sinister smirk spread across his lips as he developed a plan on how he would bait the pilot into a hotel room. The setup would be perfect and the pilot would take the blame. A sexual masterpiece people in America would love to read about.

Sadegh placed three hundred-dollars on the table, ordered another drink and waited for the right fish to swim into his net. Casinos were like smorgasbords for whatever pleasure a person desired. With the right bait and a little patience, it was only a matter of time before the perfect fish bit the hook. The bartender took notice of the money and went over to the end of the bar where a large Russian sat, and whispered a message. An older woman for her profession, mid-thirties he guessed, came to his table showing interest in him, but he brushed her off saying, "I'm sure you are very experienced, but I'm old and frail and would like a woman who will make me feel young again. Please take no offense." As the woman walked away, he noticed the Russian quickly type out a message onto his phone. Sipping his third drink, a younger girl who looked like she skipped her high school class, came to his table and asked if he wanted company. She expressed a nervous-inexperienced demeanor, which made the anticipation of what he was about to do that much more exciting. He placed two twenties on the table and took her hand.

She began to pull him along. "I have a room upstairs. Let's go there. There's vodka we can drink."

"You're a sweet girl, but I would rather go to my room. I'm staying at the Palazzo ... a little nicer than this place. You look hungry. We can order food—they even serve beluga caviar. You can have whatever you want."

She easily went with him, wrapping her arms around his as he led her out into the parking lot. He opened the passenger door for her to climb in, and then went back to the trunk, popping it open to place his jacket inside. From a satchel, he removed a syringe, keeping it concealed until he climbed into the driver's seat.

Before she realized her fate, he stuck the needle into her neck and pushed the plunger filled with *Rocuronium*, a neuromuscular blocker, using his opposing hand to muffle her scream until the numbing agent took its effect. Within a minute, paralysis set into her muscles while keeping her brain and nerves aware of her impending death. When her body slumped off to the side, he started his car and drove alongside the black Z. He got out and kicked the right side mirror until it finally broke off and put it in his backseat.

He stayed extra vigilant to maintain all the traffic laws while he drove out of the city toward the mountains, turning onto an isolated dirt road ten miles past the city limits. His breath quickened when he slid his hand up her dress, ripping her silk panties off her body. The road led to a rock quarry, where he found an isolated spot to stop. He slowly looped a garrote around her neck, twisting it slightly so she would know what was about to come next. Her eyes widened with terror—she knew. Her mouth tried to speak, but the drug overpowered her facial muscles. In his other hand, he held a military grade 9mm pistol, loaded with United States government standard ball bullets taken from the diplomatic pouch.

Using a knife, he slit the front of her dress, nicking the single bra strap to expose bare skin, pulling her clothes off her body. He ran his hands along the inside of her legs, causing her nerves to quiver while her muscles remained subtle. Her body shivered, an indication she was already metabolizing the drug, but not enough to stop him. He stepped out of the car to remove his own clothes, placing them alongside his jacket, before he opened her door.

When he was done, he pulled the naked body to a ditch, piled her dress and panties on her stomach, and fired a single 9mm bullet into her forehead. Using a stick, he wrote in the ground, "The killing is making me kill. There will soon be another." He removed a can of petrol from the trunk, dousing the entire body, making sure the clothes became soaked with the flammable liquid. He torched a flare and tossed it onto the mound. Removing the black side mirror he'd broken off earlier, he let it fall outside the flame radius near her outstretched hand.

Chapter 6

THE BAIT

Brent handed the Reaper off to the LRE who took the aircraft to a landing. This night, nothing happened. The entire twelve hours were spent watching a Special Forces team sleep underneath flora camouflage waiting for nightfall. While they slept, he flew circles over their location looking for anything suspicious. If something came close, he would have called them on the radio or fired a missile—that would have woken them up. Most of the past week was spent answering questions with a physiologist to ascertain whether he still could follow orders without question. Since the Yemen mission, he made the mistake of telling the doctor about his visions seeing the praying woman. This caused several more pages in his medical file and a handful of late afternoon therapy sessions sitting on a couch.

Brent knew where this was heading - *say too much and lose everything he had worked toward, say too little and they suspect you are lying.* He used manipulation as his ally, using the doctor's body language as indicators and only giving small tidbits of the pain and guilt he felt. Downplaying the effect it had on his life, he played the role of introvert and blamed a crummy childhood on his lack of close friends. Eventually, it was enough to pacify the doc, and he released him back to flying, but not until he sat watching a couple of missions all night... *I guess to see how it is supposed to be done.* His real therapy came from playing blackjack with the dealer at the Royal Sands. This dealer had seen the harshness of life and always provided good wisdom, even though

Brent never told him what he did during the night. He suspected Joe already knew.

The doctor said he had an acute mental PTS disorder—all within parameters for the line of work performed. No one mentioned his DO forcing him to take the shot or who he even killed. The CIA case officer didn't want Brent to fly anymore of their missions—he didn't trust that Brent would take the shot when told. Just as well, he disliked flying those missions anyway, there was a way to do the job - and do it well - without hunting down ghosts who would just haunt him later. His first night back, now morning, he flew lazy circles around a Special Forces team who slept all day ... easy duty.

With his shift over, he got in his car and proceeded off the base. Johnson stared at him as he drove by. Brent finally felt good about himself and this job—today would be a new beginning. Once off the federal perimeter, he hit it—laying a patch of rubber, waving his hand outside the window so Johnson could see. The morning air felt good, cool and brisk. Nothing could ruin this day.

After making a quick stop at his townhouse, he got back into his car and headed into the old downtown section of the city. Brent enjoyed playing cards early in the morning, after a night flying a remotely piloted machine. It gave him an opportunity to relax before attempting sleep during the day. Between four and six in the morning, only diehard players played the tables, which always presented an empty seat with the same dealer. The stability kept him from thinking about those he had killed and his friendship with this dealer connected him back to humanity.

He pushed his chair back from the blackjack table and smiled at the dealer, showing a double down with a pair of Jacks. "It's my lucky morning." He showed a ten and a nine under each card.

The dealer had a seven showing and flipped over a five. The next card gave him a jack. "Good play. I would have done the same thing without seeing my other card. The odds were in your favor. Want to try again?"

Ending the morning on a win and overall stopping while ahead meant this day would be great. His watch indicated eight in the morning—time to leave before the morning crowd became awake enough to play. It had already been a long night with only a few hours of sleep the previous afternoon. Only two poker chips remained in front of him, probably a good time to go home. "Let's play one more." Brent placed a single chip in front of him. As the dealer dealt the next set of cards, Brent looked up to watch a woman walking across the casino floor—young, his age, with simple makeup accentuating her eyes and lips. Her mane of silky black hair laid along her shoulders in soft waves. A one-piece summer dress highlighted a lithe body. A little straw colored clutch tucked underneath her arm matched a pair of short cowgirl boots that rode halfway up tan calves. Shoulders pulled back and slight arch to her back accentuated pert breasts. Her entire ensemble flowed together perfectly of a sophisticated cowgirl on a morning stroll into the city.

"Do you want another card?" Brent heard the dealer ask. When he didn't respond the dealer also took note of the young woman. "Are you playing or gawking?"

"Where did she come from?" He asked, not really looking for an answer. "I've never seen her here before. Who is she?"

She looked over at Brent and her lips broke a smile. When he looked back, he watched her lithe dress sway as she sauntered around a row of slot machines.

The dealer broke Brent's stare, by saying, "Hey, I need you to look at me. Let me give you some friendly advice, she's out of your league. Best you leave that filly alone."

"Come on," Brent said, "she looks like she's looking for someone. We're two wayward souls swimming in the same ocean. Maybe she's lost."

"Don't give me that bullshit. You come early in the morning when most normal people are sleeping and only sit at my table, wearing faded blue jeans with an old flannel shirt. The most you ever bet is a dollar chip. Either you don't have a lot of money or you're looking to escape. You never talk to anybody except me and I'm just a card dealer. I can guarantee, she's not lost... and by the way she looks, she's looking for something. Somebody paid a lot of money for her to walk in here."

"What are you talking about? You're more than that Joe, you're my therapist. You keep me balanced from what I do during the night."

"Then listen to what I have to say. I also moonlight at Caesars before I finish my day working at this dump. I've seen her before with players who can afford the penthouse. She flips either way depending on her client's sexual appetite. My bet is she's looking for her next john... if you know what I mean. This is the first time I've seen her here, so maybe she's slumming for someone like yourself. I can tell you she is not your typical streetwalker. Her clients pay a lot of money in advance, and her pimp is a badass within the Russian mafia—big burly guy who doesn't take kindly to his girl's freelancing. If she is here, she's working. That means she's trouble. My advice is to stay away from her." The dealer tossed another set of cards across the table to continue the game. He looked past Brent and said, "Dammit, don't look. She's coming back this way."

Brent turned and caught the woman coming around a row of slot machines behind him.

She placed her hand on Brent's shoulder, initiating the first touch. "Hopefully I'm not interrupting your private game. I'd like to join you two boys." She took the seat next to Brent and gave a bright smile to the two men. From a *Chloé* clutch, she removed a stack of chips and set them on the table.

Brent breathed in her scent. Up close, she smelled sweet, like blackberries in bloom. With her hands resting on the table, he couldn't help but notice no rings on any finger. "Joe, toss a few cards toward this lady."

"I'm sorry, but this is my last hand," the dealer told the woman. "You will have to find a different table."

"Please don't leave because of me," she said, while her attention alternated between Brent and the dealer. "I had a long night and came here to relax. I saw you two friendly faces ... I can leave if you want. She bit, partly sucked on her lower lip, waiting for either of them to answer. She placed a single chip in front of her. "Let me play one game."

"Joe, shuffle the cards. Let's play one more." Brent caught the dealer shaking his head, mouthing the word -run! He placed a chip on the table and waited to see how the cards would fall. Something about her approach and seductive appeal made him curious. Her story lined up with his, but he also trusted what Joe said. She looked too good and she smelled too fresh for someone who had been up all night. Whatever game she wanted to play was about to begin. The next set of cards the dealer busted, allowing him to get a chip back to the five he started with. "It's been a long night. I also must go. Joe, thanks again for your advice." Brent got up and rested his hand on the back of her chair, making sure she could feel his touch. "You're very beautiful. Thank you for brightening up my day," he murmured in her ear and left without looking back. He heard her say, "Wait, please don't leave," but he continued to weave his way through a row of slot machines until out of sight. He circled through the casino and came back around from a different direction to watch what she did next. If she left the casino, he would follow her outside and ask to see if she would join him for coffee—on his approach ... not her's.

He peered between two slot machines, but both the dealer and the woman were no longer at his table. After searching the casino, he finally found her sitting at a craps table next to an elderly Middle Eastern man—his face obscured by a goatee and dark glasses, wearing a shiny grey silk suit with a matching paisley tie. Except for his age, he looked out of place for this casino. His clothes were too expensive. The smile was gone from her face as she leaned over and whispered into her new companion's ear. Whatever she said caused him to scowl.

He stood and forced her up with him, causing her to flinch. She tried to pull away, but he said something that made her relent. Taking her by the arm, the couple proceeded past the cacophony of jingling slot machines and took a side exit, the same one Brent used to bypass the front security cameras.

For Brent, the entire sequence of events didn't make sense. First, she came onto him and within seconds, she's with another. To top it off, the man she was with appeared familiar. A face he'd seen before, but masked by the facial hair and glasses, nothing popped. It was more the way he looked around, watching the people around him that piqued Brent's concern. His posture and physique did not match the persona of an old man, more like a predator on a hunt.

Outside under the lights of the neon incandescence, he inhaled a deep breath of the dry morning Nevada air, while surveying the massive parking area. The couple mixed with a few patrons leaving the casino, who staggered to their cars after an all-nighter drinking and gambling. Brent watched them walk across the parking lot near where he had parked his car. When they were almost out of view, he tucked his hands into his front jean pockets and followed.

The couple headed toward an area where there were few cars, to a nondescript Ford sedan thirty yards from his Z. The man opened the passenger door for the woman, but she appeared reluctant to get in. She slapped him, trying to get away and almost made it until he reared his fist back and punched her face, dropping her like a ragdoll into the passenger seat. With her now lying backward, he pinned her down while he removed an object from his jacket. Her hand's flung wildly as she tried to keep him from pressing onto her.

Brent had seen enough and sprinted toward them. The man forced his body on top of her, pinning her down where her arms no longer had the strength to push him off. He fumbled with an object he held, trying to get the angle right to jab her with it. Brent closed the distance and grabbed a fistful of the man's collar, yanking him backward off the woman and onto the ground.

The cylinder clattered near a tire. Utilizing the momentum, the man rolled away from Brent onto his knees, ready to spring at his attacker. When he saw Brent, he said calmly, "She said you left." He rose up onto his feet, no longer looking like an old man. "Parker, right?"

The statement alone caught Brent off guard—made him hesitate. Before he could react, the man launched an attack, throwing a straight fist that caught Brent's temple. The impact staggered his senses, dropping Brent to a knee. Before he could shake off the blow, a roundhouse kick to his ribcage knocked him off his feet. This man moved fast, faster than Brent anticipated. He needed time to recover, shake off the first punch, but his attacker kept the pressure on as a boxer senses he has the fight won.

Brent took each blow as best he could by rolling away. A kick to his chest caused his diaphragm to spasm. He tried to inhale, to force air back into his lungs, but each impact systematically shut down his bodily functions. His head spun and he could not get air into his lungs. He tried to force his body to respond, but instead went to a knee to keep from falling over.

The man circled like a cat, looking for an opening. The way he attacked and his stance showed he definitely had training. On the next attack, he threw a looping punch that Brent saw coming. He parried, letting the clenched fist go by to overextend his opponent. With his body coiled, Brent blindly threw a straight right knockout punch to the chin. The impact felt good and solid, wobbling and finally forcing the man off balance.

When the next attack came, Brent ducked under the swing and coiled like a snake, driving forward to catch his attacker's arm. Clutching near the elbow, he peeled back in the opposite direction to hyperextend the joint until it popped. Before it became dislocated, a heel kick caught Brent's groin, causing Brent to release his grip. The two circled each other, the man held his arm—shaking it to relieve the pain, while Brent pushed on his lower extremities, trying not to vomit. He charged, bulldozing Brent off his feet and onto his back. The man knocked Brent's feet to the side to plop onto his chest in a full mount position. Even with one arm useless, he threw several punches to Brent's face, and then grabbed hold of Brent's collar, using the fabric to stop air and blood flow inside his neck.

Brent squirmed underneath the pressure, throwing blind strikes to reduce the grip, but no air entered his lungs. His vision began to turn black while oxygen depleted from his brain. When it felt like he was done, the man suddenly relaxed his hold, allowing Brent to roll out from underneath. Coughing uncontrollably, he tried to force air back into his lungs enough to clear his head from the blackness. Sensing the reprieve, he sprung onto this hands and knees to prepare for another attack.

The man attempted to stand on wobbly legs, trying to reach behind his back—the woman backed away from behind.

Seeing his opponent vulnerable, Brent launched upward, landed and spun, performing a pirouette that swept the man's legs out from underneath him. The attacker's entire body inverted and his head thumped like a watermelon against solid pavement.

Not waiting for a reaction, Brent stomped on the man's knee—crushing cartilage—then kicked him in the ribs hard enough to throw him onto his back. Not understanding what had just happened, he was about to stomp on the face, but noticed the man no longer moved. This fight was over. A rush of silence permeated the parking lot—the combative flow of adrenaline still pulsating through his veins. He took deep breaths trying to clear his head from the chokehold. "What just happened?" He asked aloud. Other than the woman, this time in the morning, the area remained empty. A pool of blood began to spread outward from the man's head with an arm pinned underneath the body at a precarious angle. For a moment, Brent wondered if the man was dead. He knelt down and felt for a pulse, feeling a slow steady beat and a slight rise and fall of the chest, eyes remained open and the pupils focused in on Brent, otherwise the body remained limp.

The woman stood in lethargic shock, clutching a syringe, thumb pressed on the plunger. Her dress, torn around her shoulder, exposed a sheer bra ripped along the cup.

"Are you okay?" He asked. "What's in your hand?"

She looked at it, then let go. The glass cylinder hit the pavement and shattered. "He tried to stick me—dropped it when you grabbed him. I picked the needle up and stabbed him in the back."

Brent ground the glass into the pavement as he went to the woman. Even with her arms wrapped around herself, her body shivered uncontrollably. He stepped close, unsure what to do next, letting her melt into his chest. Her body calmed long enough for him to remove his flannel shirt to place it across her shoulders. Looking at her from arm's length, he asked, "I saw him hit you. Who is he? He somehow knew my name. I don't know him."

"We met late last evening. He wanted me to ...." She turned away, losing her balance before she could finish the statement.

Transferring his hold around her waist, he helped her to remain standing. He closed the front of his shirt to cover her up and then held her close to him. She nuzzled her face into his chest and softly cried. No one took notice of a couple embracing, while the assailant lay unconscious near his feet. It was only a matter of time before the police were sure to investigate—most likely already on their way. They would ask questions that he did not have answers for, and the person on the ground may be someone important, which meant Brent would be the one arrested. A video of him sitting next to the woman at the blackjack table showed collusion. No matter how the situation looked, there would be a record of the incident and a police report. He already had one expanding file and certainly didn't need another. Anything involving breaking the law certainly killed a security clearance. His last mission already had him under a microscope. "If you want the police, I need to go. I can't be involved with this fight and why

I'm here. If you tell them what happened—I'm an unknown who you briefly met. Hopefully by the time the police find me, this whole story will be a non-event."

"The police will not help me either," she mumbled. "This was not supposed to happen this way. You were supposed to like me. A surprise, there's a room at the Palazzo waiting...."

At first, Brent wasn't sure he heard her right, and then quickly put all of what happened together. "Then we need to leave, right now. Can I take you somewhere? Do you have a car?"

"I didn't drive. We rode together, figuring I'd be with—" She looked away. "I'm so sorry to have gotten you involved."

"You should go to a hospital. You're not thinking straight. Do you have any friends you can call?"

Her face filled with fear "Please no. My employer—he's not going to be happy with what happened." She looked hopeless ... scared. "I must go." She pushed herself away, but fell into a nearby car.

"Here, let me help you." He took hold of her arm to keep her steady. "We'll go to my place—I live fifteen minutes from here. You really shouldn't be alone until that contusion on your face subsides. I have ice ... not much else though. It will help reduce the swelling where he hit you. When you're ready to leave, I promise to drive you to wherever you want to go." Before they walked away, he took one last look at the man lying on the ground, still not moving. "We can't leave him to die. Here ... lean against this car, I'll be right back."

He went over and reached into the man's jacket pocket where he found a cell phone in an inside pocket and a pistol tucked into a shoulder holster. Unsure who he was dealing with, he considered searching for a wallet, but the immediacy of their situation prompted him to hurry. They needed to leave before an ambulance or police arrived. Using the found cell phone, he dialed 911 and waited for the dispatcher to answer. Placing his hand across his mouth to muffle his voice, he said, "I need an ambulance. I'm in the parking lot of the Royal Sands Casino near the south side entrance. Please hurry. I fell down and can't get up." He left the connection open, setting the phone on the man's chest.

Back with the woman, he supported her weight by wrapping his arm around her waist. She felt slim and smelled of a slight hint of spring—expensive, not overwhelming. Her legs stumbled as he hurried her along. She kept her head nestled into his chest while they walked the short distance to his car. He buckled her in before he climbed into the driver's seat and started the engine. Once on the road leading away from the parking lot, an ambulance with its red lights flashing sped by them headed in the opposite direction toward the casino.

Neither spoke during the drive back, giving Brent time to think. Police, an assault, an injured beautiful woman in his car—individually he could deal with each element, but mixing it together overloaded his mental reasoning, causing his hands to shake. *Like before, this will also probably change my world.* His thoughts went back to a time in college—a virtual repeat of tonight. This event reopened a wound that had not fully healed—when he made a mental promise that he would not make the same mistake again.

***

Three years ago, after a late night shift bouncing at a local university cowboy bar, Brent was about to climb into his rusted F-150 truck. In the neighboring parking stall, a shiny black Cadillac Escalade rocked back and forth on its tires. He would have let it be, until he heard, "Hold her down." When a female pleaded for them to stop, Brent made the decision to yank the door open.

He'll never forget the girl held down in the backseat, her dress pulled over her head, with two university football players—both had their pants down—one on top while the other pinned her arms back. Brent remembered grabbing hold of the player's legs who was raping the girl and dragged him out of the vehicle—face down—across the pavement. Before the player could get up, Brent kicked him first between the legs and then stomped down on the head. When the police arrived, they found him still unconscious with his pants hanging around his knees, testicles and nose crushed.

The other jumped out of the vehicle and came at Brent. He threw a left that Brent ducked under, but quickly reversed his momentum, throwing a straight right that caught him along his cheek, slicing a diagonal length of skin. Across the player's middle finger, he wore a gold ring with a protruding diamond inlay. He smiled at seeing the gash on Brent's face. "I'm *gonna* fuck you up."

Brent touched his face and when he saw bloody fingers, something snapped inside his consciousness. As he had done a hundred times facing an opponent on a wrestling mat, he forced his body to relax to prepare for the physicality of what was about to come. Like tonight, it was fast and efficient.

The player leaned over into a three-point stance, snorted like a bull and charged.

Brent sidestepped the assault and slammed a straight right fist into the attacker's ear, causing the assailant to stagger off course.

The player rubbed where Brent hit him and said, "You hit like a girl." He took a hard look at Brent. "You have no idea who we are. The person who owns this Escalade owns this town. We're star football players. They won't touch us." He charged again, but this time he brought his hands up to block Brent's next punch.

Brent faked a left hook, swooped down and closed his arms around both knees, lifted the player off his feet while inverting the body, ramming the head into the solid pavement. With the body sprawled onto the ground face first, Brent pounced on top and grabbed hold of the arm that held the ring finger, forcing the arm backward toward the head until the shoulder popped from the socket. While still holding the arm, he busted the finger with the ring, stripping skin until the ring came off and threw it into a nearby field.

Brent later found out the Escalade belonged to the town mayor who also owned the largest car dealership in the state. The police and the school administration never prosecuted the players involved in the sexual assault and Brent never saw the girl again. Rumor had it that she dropped out of school and went back home. The campus gossip asked how two of their best athletes sustained bone fractures and concussions, ending their season and making them ineligible for the NFL draft. Except for the girl, no one saw Brent dismantle the two athletes and no one saw him leave the scene. The dean of the university did not want the adverse publicity and the town mayor ordered his police chief to make it all go away.

Within a week, his wrestling coach called Brent into his office to tell him his scholarship was revoked and now officially off the team. He gave no reason as to why. Brent tried to contact the girl, to see if she would be willing to tell her story. What he found out crushed him into a deep depression. Her father answered the phone to say his daughter had committed suicide a few days after she returned home. She had come home alone and withdrawn. Never said why she left school and then ended her life. Brent felt her death was his fault. What happened to her forced her to be alone—no one helped her deal with the ugliness of the event. The school only cared about their two star football players—to keep what happened quiet. Brent saved this girl, only to lose her a few days later. Her memory he would never forget.

***

During the short drive to his place, Brent glanced at the woman, being coy not to stare. He reached for a pile of fast-food napkins, handing one over. "You might want to take these, there's blood dripping from your nose."

"Thank you," she said, using it to dab her nose. Looking out the window, she said, "I'm sorry. I'm sure I look a mess."

"I must say, you've looked better." Thinking about his failure saving the last girl, he made a pledge to make sure this one stayed alive. Trying to remain positive, he added, "If it wasn't for your swollen nose and the goose-egg over your eye, a hot bath should fix you right up."

She gave a faint smile and went back to looking out the side window. Once he entered the front gates that led inside the condominium complex, he slowed in front of his rented townhouse and pressed a remote on the upper visor opening the garage door. Upon pulling inside, he waited until the door closed to help her out of the car and up the stairs to the main living area.

"Wait here, I'll be right back with some ice." In the kitchen, Brent found a plastic bag and filled it with ice. He washed two tumblers and poured a couple fingers of Elk Rider bourbon. "Did you know the man before tonight? I saw you two together after I left. He didn't look very friendly—you said something that seemed to make him mad." He waited for a reply, but no answer came from the other room.

Carrying the two tumblers and the bag into the living room, Brent found her sitting on the couch, her hands covering her face. He set the glasses down on the nearby coffee table and lightly touched the bag to her eye. "I'm sorry ... It's going to be alright." Unsure what to do next, he asked, "What were you doing with him? Please talk to me. I'm really lost here. I need to know the connection—how he knew my name. Why he wanted me to be with you."

She took a moment to look at him. "He was a customer. A john. He hired me."

"I gathered that. I saw you sitting together. The dealer I was with had seen you before working the Strip casinos. We're friends." He intentionally left out the part about Joe giving him advice to stay away from her. "When you were at the craps table sitting next to him, you said something that caused him to get angry. Afterwards, he literally dragged you out to his car. What happened ... what did you say?"

"I thought you left, weren't interested in me. He actually hired me to be with you. It was to be a surprise ... your birthday present. I assumed you were friends." Tears welled up in her eyes and as quickly, she wiped them away. "He had reserved a room at the Palazzo through my agency that I was supposed to take you to. When I told him you left, he became angry—different."

"I knew something wasn't quite right when he pulled you up by your arm. What he did didn't look right. So I followed you out of the casino." Brent paused for a moment and held her gaze. "I play cards there in the mornings after work. Joe is my therapist and keeps me grounded. He has experienced a lot, so we just talk about life. It's my ritual to decompress when the old people who play here haven't yet woken up. Someone of your caliber doesn't usually frequent this type of casino. When you came in, you looked out of place, more suited to what you'd see at Caesars. And, when you came onto me, I really wasn't sure what was going on. Your approach was too obvious, which put me on guard. I left the table figuring I'd find you again, but on my terms." No sense telling her everything the dealer said.

She thought about what Brent said. "The man you fought told me to wear a summer dress—that you were from Oklahoma and liked the cowgirl type." She got up from the chair. "I think I'm going to be sick. May I use your shower? Since my dress is torn, do you have something I can change into?" She pulled her boots off and walked barefoot down the hallway. His shirt she let fall off her shoulders.

"The bathroom is first door on the right. Towels are underneath the cabinet."

She glanced back at him and gave a weak smile, before stepping into the bathroom.

Brent went into his bedroom, fumbled inside a laundry basket until he found a clean pair of grey sweats along with various other articles of clothing. Before the water turned off, he hung the clothes inside the bathroom—they were not elegant, but at least they were clean. From the kitchen freezer, he filled another bag with ice, and then waited until she came out. Thinking back to what she said, *he knew where I used to live!*

After several minutes, she stepped out wearing his clothes, her hair wrapped in a towel. The arms and legs rolled at the ends. She sat down on the couch, drawing her legs up to her chest. "Thank you for saving me. I don't even know your name. My name is Katya ... Katya Kozachenko. It's Ukrainian. My mother came to America as a mail order bride to some southern hillbilly who liked to hit her. As soon as she could, she got a divorce and moved away. My clients call me Amber. I like that name better." She held her hand out for a proper handshake.

Brent took hold of her outstretched hand. "My name is Brent ... Brent Parker." Her hand felt warm and soft. "What name do you want me to call you?"

"Please call me Amber. You rescued me, which makes you my friend."

Brent felt a heat of passion rise up, quickening his heart. There was a lot about her that he liked, both trying to figure out their placement in this world. Pushing his thoughts aside, he went back to the events of what happened ... it made no sense. "Tell me what you can about this man. I went to college at Oklahoma State, lived in Stillwater, before I moved to Vegas. I need to know how the hell he knew I once lived in Oklahoma."

"I don't know. As I told you before, he said you were friends. The escort service I work for is called Destiny Delights. Our assignments are sent by text message: what time, where and whom we're meeting, and anything unique the client desires. I'm not sure what he did. The way he dressed, my guess is international banking. My pimp gave me explicit instructions on what to wear and how to act. We met in the parking lot—he entered through a side door and I entered by the front. I was even shown a picture of what you looked like and where you'd be sitting. That's how I found you." She stared off into the distance.

Brent gave her moment, before he asked, "Do you remember his name?"

"Nasir something. Most men give a false name when they meet with an escort. Even though we're the upper class of the escort business, our clients are usually well mannered and want to remain secretive." She turned her face away. "I usually find out during our love sessions their real names and what they do. Most have a kinky fetish, but they certainly wouldn't hurt me."

When she looked back, Brent noticed another tear trickle down her cheek. This time he gently brushed it away.

After a moment, she regained her composure. "Other than when I told him you had left, he seemed quite sincere. He said we would go back to the hotel, and then my services would no longer be needed—the upfront fee of three days had already been paid. When he hit me in the car, I must've blacked out. I do remember him holding a syringe trying to stick me. When you pulled him off, he dropped it. It looked like he was about to kill you, so I stuck him instead. I don't know what would have happened if you hadn't shown up."

Brent looked at the bruising on her face. "Keep the ice against your eye. You're going to have a nice shiner tomorrow."

"Thanks, I saw my face in the mirror. It does look bad." She reached over to touch his cheek from where he took a punch—the one that almost knocked him out. "Your face is not much better."

Her warm hand felt good. When she started to trace his scar, he laid his hand against hers to pull it away. "That was from a long time ago," as he remembered the girl in the Escalade. "What did you do before Vegas? How did you get into this line of work? I can't imagine what a night would cost to be with you." The look on her face told him he made a misstep asking the question. What he really wanted to know was, *why did you become an escort, a hooker for rich men?*

"I came to Vegas three months ago with the desire to be a showgirl. It's a difficult business to break into without prior experience or a degree from Juilliard. I am a fabulous dancer." She got up and performed a pirouette, toppling back onto a chair away from him. "I know the question you really want to ask. Men always ask the same question. Why do I fuck men for money? I'm sure whatever you do is probably a lot worse than sex. I have friends and don't need a dealer to be mine. It's just business. Right now I don't have a choice."

"I'm sorry. I didn't mean to pry. It's just that I've just never met anyone as special as you. You're perfect in so many ways. Everyone has a reason for what they do." She was right ... thinking about what he did at night. The woman's body disintegrating from his missile flashed through his memory. He also became quiet and distant.

She scooted forward in the chair. "When I saw you sitting by yourself, I really did want to meet you. You have sadness in your eyes, something we have in common." She held his gaze. "I don't have a personal relationship with anyone. My pimp forbids it. He controls everything within my life. He will kill me if I try to leave ... or worse. It's how he controls his girls."

Still wanting to know more, he asked, "How much did this Nasir pay to seduce me?"

"He actually paid for three nights. It depends on what is prearranged. Our starting rate is five a day."

"Hundred?"

"Thousand—and that's just for dinner and a movie, and a happy ending of course." The last she gave a shy smile. "The rate goes up for anything kinky or a sleepover. In your case, he paid thirty thousand dollars—I get about a third and Vlad takes the rest. Our clients can afford it and the service we provide is more than just fucking. Normally I spend an entire weekend, or sometimes a week or two—depending on what the client desires. I've sat at business dinners discussing billion dollar deals, ridden on private jets to Europe, even slept with senators and two congresswomen who have issues with controlling men and want a submissive female to dominate—all secretive so they don't lose their next election. Their husbands are only a façade to win the conservative vote. They give me gifts like this clutch, not something I'd normally buy for what it costs." She reached inside to remove a business card and handed it to Brent.

Brent held it in his hand, flipping each side over. Gold emboss lined the outside border. On the front, *Destiny Delights* was stamped above a phone number and the back had the name - *Amber.*

"That's my working name. It's all prorated depending on how long you want me."

For Brent, a hundred dollars felt like a lot of money—the cost of all the clothes he had in his closet didn't come close. *Why would someone he didn't know pay her fee to seduce him?* Thinking about everything that happened, *who was this man and what did he want? Is there any way this was connected to the mission that went wrong?* Questions he needed answered.

She attempted to stand up, but had to steady herself by clutching the arm of the couch. "Thank you again for helping me. I need to go, I shouldn't stay here." Stumbling again when she took a step.

"Please stay ... at least until you feel better." He helped her settle back on the chair.

"I'll stay only if you tell me who Brent Parker is? I sense a mysteriousness about you. You saved me, which makes you my knight in shining armor." She got up from the chair to kiss him on the cheek. "I told you my life story, now it's your turn for show and tell. What brought you to Vegas? Why do you only play cards in the morning with the same dealer ... Joe? Your eyes are bloodshot like you've been up all night."

The tension of the night and morning felt like a week ago. "My life also didn't turn out the way I'd planned." He felt uncomfortable talking about himself, and most of what he did he couldn't tell. "I'm in the military. There is a base about an hour north of here. Like you, I work mostly nights. I see things and I do things that people only read about. It's crazy, but that's all I can tell you."

Neither spoke for a moment at the awkwardness of opening a door about themselves. Amber broke the silence. "Let's start at the beginning. Where did you grow up? You said you once lived in Oklahoma. Let me guess ... you like the cheerleader type with a little country girl mixed in. I put this all together for you. I hope that you at least liked it."

He did like it. "You're half right. I went to high school near Seattle living with my mother. I also happened to be good at wrestling with a little fighting mixed in. Oklahoma State offered me a wrestling scholarship to attend their university and I trained with friends who did MMA when I had time. There was a girl I got involved with, but it didn't go so well for either of us, which got me kicked off the team and her life fell apart." He thought about what he did to the two athletes ... what he'd never told anyone.

"I'm sorry." She reached across and again traced the scar along his cheek. "It makes you look like GI Joe. This girl was very lucky to have you. Do you still keep in touch?"

This time he tried not to flinch. It surprised him how close she came to knowing the truth. "I bounced at a local bar full of drunk cowboys to make some money while I went to college. A dude cut my face with one of those gaudy rings. It itches when I'm stressed. Like right now." He forced himself to not rub the burning sensation. "When I fight, time stops—I have to force myself to relax, which enables me to lose myself in the moment. For some reason, time slows down. The man I faced today was quick, faster than I anticipated. I could tell from how he moved, he definitely has done this before, especially the way he acted with you." Brent remembered seeing the gun in the holster. "He's killed people. The cruelty within this world overwhelms me sometimes—can't really describe it." Brent looked away, embarrassed he had divulged an inner secret.

"It's okay—I get it—I also saw it. He deserved what you did to him. He wanted to kill me and you stopped him. You saved my life and for that I'm forever grateful."

Changing the subject, Brent said, "You really shouldn't be alone tonight—you might have a concussion. I've seen the signs before—slight memory loss and unbalanced coordination. You have both. Stay here and I'll take the couch."

"I couldn't do that. I'll take the couch and you sleep in your bed."

Eventually they agreed to lay on opposite sides of his bed with several pillows nestled between them. He watched her sleep while thinking about what had happened. The adrenaline of the fight and the excitement of this girl finally ebbed and he closed his eyes wondering what the night would bring.

When he awoke, she was gone. The shirt and pants she wore were folded on his couch. A written note on top of the clothes read, *Call me sometime. My cell is 310–2258. Love, Amber.* Other than the phone number and her name, he knew nothing about her—where she lived or if she even dated without having to be paid for.

He sat down next to the clothes holding the note, unsure whether to call her or not. There wasn't anything in his security clearance questionnaire forbidding him from dating certain professions. More than anything, he worried about whether she was physically and mentally alright—the ice did help reduce the swelling around her eye, but he heard her vomit in the bathroom while she thought he was asleep. Something about her intrigued him. Looking at the note for the second time, she threw out a lure to see if he would bite. What she didn't realize was that she already had him hooked.

Chapter 7

THE SWITCH

Brent left his place in the early evening, wearing jeans and a black tee shirt, storing a flight suit and boots in the Z's trunk. Before he spent another all-night shift at the base, he wanted to find his friend Joe the dealer to see what he knew. The delusional story of sex didn't make sense. *Why did this Nasir character hire Amber to seduce me? That's a helluva lot of money to spend on someone you don't know.* Above that, Brent felt sure he'd seen him somewhere before. The pistol and the way he fought indicated formal self-defense training—his stance and the arsenal of strikes—plus the gun. Mix all these ingredients together made a very dangerous person. This encounter with Amber wasn't about sex, but about something else—something more sinister. *Who and why?*

He passed the *Welcome to Las Vegas* sign before entering the Strip, pulled into the Caesars parking lot and went inside looking for Joe. The sheer expanse of this casino felt overwhelming—even opulent with all the gold glitz. After forty-five minutes of searching, he finally found his friend tossing cards at a Blackjack table to a young couple. He took an open seat and placed a chip on the table.

Joe flipped him a card. "I see you're upping your taste." He took notice of the black and blue welt under Brent's eye. "What happened to you? Looks like you ran into a brick wall."

Brent ignored the question. "I wanted to thank you for your advice this morning. You were right. She was working and I was supposed to be her john."

Joe paused dealing cards. "Too bad. She looked like she'd be pure fun." He finished the round and waited for each to respond on whether they wanted another. When he got to Brent, he took a solid look at his face. "The police are looking for her. She's involved in an assault investigation. It happened soon after you left. Since she first sat at my table, they asked me if I knew anything—if she said anything. After you left, she was seen with another man ... the same person assaulted in the parking lot. They found him still unconscious in the back parking lot where you like to park. Completely disabled, which they thought was drug induced."

Brent wondered if his face had also been recorded on video. "Did the police ask about me?"

"They asked if you knew the girl. I told them you didn't want whatever she offered and left the table."

"The girl sitting at our table was not a random chance. She wanted me."

"That was obvious."

"Not in the way you're thinking. I'm trying to figure out why. Did the police happen to mention his name?"

"I overheard them say he is a foreign diplomat from the Pakistani government—Sadegh something. If you're curious, you can now find him at the Sunrise Hospital. Busted up pretty bad—my guess is the fucker probably deserved it." He brought his voice down to a whisper. "The police think her pimp did it, but we both know that's not what really happened." This time he looked at the scrapes on Brent's hands, shaking his head. "I warned you she was trouble."

Brent instantly began linking the small clues he had so far... *Pakistani government, knowledge of his hometown, a set-up. Just how far did this rabbit hole go?* "Since you brought up her pimp, what do you know about an escort service called Destiny Delights? The girl was also banged up pretty bad, which will keep her from working for a while. I think the diplomat planned to kill her and I think he wants to kill me."

"Destiny is the Porsche dealer in a mostly used car market. Very exotic and expensive—like I told you before, you can't afford her. Most of the girls who work the casinos are all run by the Russian mob. A brother runs the girls who frequent my other gig at the Sands—his stable is a lower echelon of call girls who have just entered the profession—most can't escape, because they're here illegally or hooked on drugs. Either they are very young or old nannies who can only get the geriatric crowd. The girls you see working the streets are usually outcasts or they're freelancing until a pimp gets their hook into them. I must warn you, these Russians are territorial and they do not like giving free handouts. Mess with their girls without paying and they'll be paying you a visit to collect. If you don't have the money, they'll cut you up into little pieces."

"You need not to worry about me. I can handle myself." Brent got up to leave.

"Once again, take my advice ... leave it and walk away. These Russians have connections everywhere, even within our police force." He paused a moment looking at Brent's steady focus. "If you are going to hit them, hit them hard. It's the only thing they understand." Before Brent left the table, he said, "I hope it works out for you and the girl. Remember, I'm your therapist. I want to hear your confession later."

After leaving the casino, Brent first stopped at a florist to purchase a bouquet of flowers before heading to Sunrise Hospital. Inside the foyer, a young girl wearing a candy striper outfit sat behind the desk near the main lobby. He approached her with the warmest smile he could muster. "I have flowers from the American Embassy for Ambassador Sadegh—the person they brought in this morning from the Pakistani government. Can you help me get these to him?"

She scrolled through her computer before responding. "That would be Seyyed Sadegh. He's still in the ICU, scheduled to be moved to the third floor later this evening. I'm sorry, but it says no visitors are allowed. You can leave them with me and I'll make sure he gets them." Nodding his thanks, Brent walked away.

He contemplated this new information he had gathered during the last two hours. As far as he knew, none of the missions—including those involving the CIA—had anything to do with Pakistan. Except for the Yemen bomb maker, the rest were clean and sterile. Thinking over all the missions he'd flown, he had another flashback of the woman looking up as the Hellfire raced toward her. His scar itched as the scene quickly flashed through his mind.

Walking through the hospital foyer, Brent purchased a newspaper and took it back to his car. On page twelve, he found the headline -*First Secretary Seyyed Sadegh from the Los Angeles Pakistani consulate was attacked at the Royal Sands Casino parking lot. Any person who might have seen this assault, please call the Las Vegas Metro Police.*

***

Sadegh opened his eyes. He had no idea what day it was or how long he had been out. A mask covered his face blowing cool air into his lungs. He could hear people, but every time he opened his eyes, his world spun in a blurry kaleidoscope. His thoughts jumbled together as he tried to figure out how he got here. He tried to focus on the far wall, but the room kept spinning in a slow rotation, making his vision wander. His head and stomach felt as if he'd drunk a dozen martinis on an empty stomach. He tried to push his body up, but pain shot through the narcotic barrier causing him to cry out. Burning vomit erupted from the depths of his stomach, splattering onto his chest and blankets.

A nurse entered his room. "Mister Sadegh, you need to lie back down."

"Where am I?" He coughed, spitting the contents from his mouth.

"You're at the Sunrise Hospital and Medical Center. You've had a very bad accident and you need to lie still and rest." The nurse did her best cleaning his vomit and changing out the soiled blankets. "Now that you're awake, you have a visitor waiting outside your door. I'll let him in, but only for a moment." She left the room, motioning for someone to enter.

A large man came into the room and pulled a chair alongside the bed. "*As-salamu Alaykum* ... Is there anything you need?"

For a moment, Sadegh stared at him. "I ... I know you?"

69

"I am Kallem, your personal assistant." He hesitated. "The doctors said you might have some memory loss. Do you know who you are? What happened?"

Pieces of Sadegh's long-term memory snapped into his conscious, but the last forty-eight hours had become a distant blur. *A First Secretary stationed at the Los Angeles consulate and a clandestine attaché for the Islamic Republic of Iran's Ministry of Intelligence service.* It took a moment before he finally recognized this person standing in front of him. "Kallem, I remember who you are now. Who else knows I'm here?"

"What happened to you?" Kallem asked. "Ambassador Mehar is very worried. He is concerned—an attack against a diplomat on foreign soil is taken very seriously."

"I'm guessing it was a simple mugging, nothing more." He remembered an American pilot and the drive into Vegas, nothing more. "Please tell him I will be alright."

"He has already called—"

"Called who?" Interrupting, not wanting his whereabouts known.

"The American State Department—he wanted to be sure all your needs are met. Your room is now guarded—he's placed twenty-four hour diplomatic security outside your door until you get out of this hospital and it will continue back at your residence. He said your actions within this country have been ... let's say ... prolific enough. He's placed a request for you to be sent back home. The police have requested a formal investigation into your activities. They didn't say why, other than indicating you had an unusual paralytic drug in your system."

"How dare you talk to me this way." Pain shot through his body. He could not recollect the number of women he had sedated. "You do not know anything." Again, he could feel burning fluid bubbling up into his throat.

His visitor placed an emesis pan under his chin, catching what Sadegh spit. "Please forgive my directness—I am here only to serve. Before you left the consulate, you did not tell anyone you were coming here. Did you come to Vegas for personal pleasure or business? You should have told someone where you went."

"I don't have to tell the ambassador anything. I don't work for him. Kallem, shut up and listen. I know who attacked me. You will not discuss what happened with anyone. I came here only for a brief vacation—that is all anyone needs to know. Higher authority directed what I'm doing here! If Mehar wants to know more, tell him to go ask his neighbor. He doesn't tell me when I can and cannot leave."

"You have my loyalty. The police are in the waiting area, they want to ask you questions. I wanted to see you first before you spoke with them."

"Tell them I don't plan to press charges. He drives a black Nissan 370Z off Creech—the military base north of here. Find him for me." Sadegh collapsed his head against his pillow trying to hold back the pain. The target needed to be killed before his inability to finish the sanction order leaked out.

"You are not making any sense. What military base?"

Before Sadegh could answer, he heard a tap on the door and two men in suits entered. They both showed different type badges. "I'm Detective Edwards from Vegas Metro and this is Agent Lewis from the State Department. We'd would like to ask you a few questions," the Metro detective on the right said, who wore a cheap gray suit with a stained tie.

Kallem's massive size blocked the two men from getting close to the bed. "This room is off limits. No guests are allowed. The First Secretary is not taking visitors or answering your questions right now."

"And who might you be?" Agent Lewis asked, allowing the Metro detective to move around to the side of the bed. "A foreign diplomat mugged in a casino parking lot is an embarrassment to both the United States and Pakistan. We're here to make sure we take every precaution."

Detective Edwards removed a set of pictures and held them in front of Sadegh to look at. "Do you know this woman?"

The pictured showed a beautiful woman sitting next to him and then another with his hand holding her arm leading her out of the casino. "I have no idea." Seeing the picture brought pieces of what happened into a fuzzy focus."

"That is you with makeup and a goatee. Why were you trying to disguise your face?"

"It looks like me. I don't remember," Sadegh lied.

He showed another picture of them walking into a parking area. "What is her name? We would like to ask her a few questions."

"As I said, she is someone of no importance. Leave it—leave me—now!"

They showed another picture of the woman sitting next to a young man at a blackjack table. "Do you know who this person is?"

Sadegh closed his eyes to ignore any further questions. Any association with the target only validated the premeditation of the assault. *I should not have used a prostitute as a decoy.* Pictures showed him as a disguised old man, entering and leaving with a woman. Her role was to seduce this target to get them to her hotel room. There should be an extra Palazzo room key in his pant pocket. The plan was to enter the room during their lovemaking—where they would be most vulnerable—and extract any classified information on America's UAV operations. Eventually killing them both while they still lay naked. A perfect setup to frame the pilot for both murders. Excitement surged through his body as he dreamt about her, slowly striping her clothes off.

He overheard Kallem say, "As you can see, the First Secretary is not feeling well. Can this wait? He does not know what he is saying. You must leave now, unless you want me to call the Ambassador. It will then become an embarrassment to your country."

Overhearing Kallem, Sadegh questioned himself whether he spoke or dreamt these thoughts. Flashes of light popped in his eyes as his body began to uncontrollably shake. The nurse returned and told everyone to leave. She inserted a syringe into his intravenous port, feeling a cool sensation enter his vein before darkness closed in.

***

Brent left the hospital and drove out to the base for his nightly shift. Thankfully, this night's mission was uneventful, compared to the stress of CIA pre-sanctioned targets. Once he received control of the Reaper, he flew circles around a point, videoing a trail that went from northern Iraq into Syria. Nothing of significance appeared from sunrise to sunset—only a boy moving sheep, otherwise time crawled by.

At midnight, he took a chance and called Amber. This late at night, he didn't expect her to answer. After the third ring, about to hang up the call, he heard her voice say "hello."

"You left without saying goodbye. I want to see you again." Brent held his breath waiting for her reply.

"I'll come over to your place tomorrow. You can make me dinner."

***

When he saw her, he was taken back. Amber's face looked like a prizefighter who lost. The bruising around her eye puffed to a dark purple. She wore a little more makeup than when he first saw her, trying to conceal the rainbow of colors forming underneath her eye. She wore black stretch pants tucked into a black ankle boots, with a white silk blouse he could almost see through. Black lipstick accented the bruising and dark charcoal shadow highlighted her eyes, giving her an exotic Goth look.

"May I come in?" She said with a slight grin.

"Of course." He took her by the hand and led the way to the upper floor. "I know it's morning, but I've been up all night. Can I get you a glass of wine?" He went into the kitchen and poured two glasses before he heard her reply. Entering the room, he handed her a glass and took a seat across. "After you left, I spent the day finding out who the real Nasir is. His name is Sadegh, a Pakistani diplomat, a first secretary, not an international executive. I'm still not sure why he set us both up. That part doesn't make any sense."

She reached for the glass and took a sip. Her hand softly touched the side of his face. "We look quite the pair. I was hoping you'd call. Don't keep me guessing so long next time."

"I'm glad you answered, even if it was in the middle of the night."

While they talked, her phone began to ring, interrupting their conversation. When she looked at the caller ID, even with all her makeup, the color in her face turned a whitish hue. "I should probably answer this. Please excuse me." She left the room and spoke from the kitchen. Brent overheard her say "I'm not ready yet. My face is still a mess. Please Vlad ...."

Brent could hear a deep male voice cursing on the other end of the connection. He got up and went to where Amber stood.

As Brent approached, she held up her hand for him to not to intervene. When the call ended, she said, "I need to go. Thank you. I had a wonderful time."

"Wait. Why?"

"That was my pimp, he can be very cruel. He somehow found out I was out on a date. He said if I can date, then I can work. I'm sorry, but he scares me when he gets this way."

Brent walked her out to her car. Before she got in, she turned and wrapped her arms around his neck, pulling him closer for a kiss. Her lips felt soft and her mouth tasted fresh.

When she pulled back, she said, "I do want to see you again. Call me anytime. We will need to be more discreet so Vlad doesn't find out." With the last statement, she got in her car and drove away.

Brent watched her taillights until they disappeared around a corner. "I wish I had five thousand dollars," he said to himself.

***

The next morning, after another benign night of flying circles, Brent got in his car and proceeded off the base, crossed the highway and pulled into the mini mart parking lot. The same Pakistani clerk stood behind the counter and two young men wearing military uniforms paced in front of the beer cooler, otherwise, nobody paid Brent any attention as he removed a Gatorade and brought it to the counter. Back on the highway, he passed a car on the side of the road with a man wearing dark sunglasses, sitting in the driver's seat, staring intently at his car as it passed. As soon as he went by, the car pulled out and began to follow, keeping pace with his speed. Whomever it was, Brent decided it needed to end—now!

Entering the city, Brent slowed to allow the car to close the gap and came to a stop at a stoplight. When the light changed to green, he did not move. Drivers pressed on their horns—a few passed, yelling obscenities. The car that followed stayed in place, now encased with cars in front and behind.

When the light turned back to red, Brent got out and walked along the line of cars. With his cellphone, he took a picture of the license plate of a black S-Class Mercedes, and stood off to the side and took a picture of the driver.

The person rolled down his window. "Give me that phone." He had the same dark features and verbal accent as Sadegh.

With the window now down, Brent mocked, "Smile for the camera," and snapped another. "Tell Sadegh if I ever see him again, I'll make sure he never gets up. Next time I find you following me, I'll break you in half."

The man got out of his car. He towered above Brent with a waist twice as thick. He tried to grab Brent's phone, but Brent kept it at arm's length while he continued to snap pictures. It looked like two grown men playing keep-away on a playground. The light turned green and drivers resumed honking their horns. Before anything developed, a siren pierced the air followed by a Metro Police car racing through the intersection toward them. The officer pulled alongside and got out. "Whose black car is blocking the road?"

The Pakistani said, "His"—pointing at Brent. He produced official looking credentials and showed them to the officer. "My name is Kallem. I'm a security specialist from the Pakistani consulate. A member of the diplomatic staff. May I speak with you alone?"

The officer addressed Brent, "Stay right there," and went to the Mercedes with the Pakistani. Several times the man pointed at Brent as he addressed the police officer. Within a minute, the officer came back and the big man climbed back in his car.

"What's wrong with your car?" He pointed at Brent's Z. "Move it out of the way or I'll have it towed."

"This person keeps following me."

"Give me your license and move your car." He took Brent's identification and went back to his patrol car.

Brent moved his car out of the intersection, followed by the patrol car with its lights still flashing. Stopped and out of the way of traffic, a bright spotlight snapped on, shining directly into his rearview mirror. "Get out of your car with your hands above your head," came a command over a loudspeaker.

Looking back, the officer crouched behind his open car door, holding a large caliber pistol pointed at Brent's car. Cars slowed as they passed, gawking at Brent with his hands up, wearing a military green flight suit. *This is not happening.*

"Turn around. Lace your fingers behind your head and walk backward toward me."

Brent complied. Near his trunk, the officer grasped his hands and bent him over, separating his feet. Handcuffs snapped first on his left wrist, and then the cop pulled both arms back, securing his wrists together.

"What's this all about?" Brent asked.

"The person you threatened in the intersection said you are connected in an assault on a diplomat. Your profile matches a suspect in the case. My detective wants to talk with you."

"What's with the gun and handcuffs?"

The officer patted him down.

"Am I being arrested?"

Instead of answering his questions, the officer placed Brent in the back of the patrol car while he searched Brent's Z. He came back holding his vehicle's keys.

Neither spoke during the drive to the police station. He placed Brent in an interrogation room and locked his hands on a ring secured to the table. Mirrored glass ordained an entire wall, a single steel table sat in the middle, and two empty steel chairs were on each side.

Brent waited close to thirty minutes before a man entered wearing cheap grey suit and a stained dress shirt with an open collar. He held a manila folder, placing it on the table. Brent guessed this must be the detective who wanted to talk.

The detective opened the folder, removed a picture, and slid it across for Brent to see.

Brent glanced at the photo and back at the detective. The photo showed him sitting at a blackjack table with Amber sitting next to him.

"Is this you?"

Brent didn't say anything.

"Do you know this girl?"

If they're asking questions—they aren't sure. Brent knew his best course of action was not to say anything.

The detective removed another photo and held it up—a mugshot taken of Amber with a date on a board indicating six months previous. "This is the same girl arrested for prostitution. Was she working you for a trick?"

Brent still didn't answer.

The detective shoved an official photo of an older man wearing a full suit.

Brent recognized the person as Sadegh; smiling, wearing a dark suit and mustache. Seeing him without dark sunglasses and goatee brought back a memory. Brent analyzed the picture longer than he should have.

"So you know this person?"

"I've seen him before. Who is he?"

"A diplomat—a guest in this country. My guess is you had your own interest in this hooker," pointing at the picture of him and Amber sitting together. "I'm guessing you followed them out to his car and found the girl giving him a *knobber*. Made you angry, so you assaulted him."

Brent stared across the table at the detective without breaking eye contact.

The detective removed another picture and held it up for Brent to see. It showed the back of Brent leaving through a side exit.

The detective pointed at Brent in both pictures. "I think that is you?"

Brent took a moment to put the puzzle pieces together. Moreover, he wanted to keep this detective off balance. The official photo jogged his memory of the person he walked by a few days ago. "I saw him at a mini mart buying a bottle of water. The store happens to be outside the military base where I work. When I left, he followed my car."

"What were you doing yesterday?"

"Sleeping. I work nights."

"What exactly is your job at the base? I'm assuming you're in the military, a prissy flyboy, since you're wearing a flight suit."

"It's classified ... by children in action."

A moment of silence developed between the two verbal combatants.

The detective broke the silence and said, "That's it?"

"What I do has national security implications. I do things I'm not allowed to talk about."

The detective pounded his fist on the table. "We found a side mirror that matches your car at another crime scene involving another prostitute. Do you know how it might have gotten there?"

"I have no idea." This all was too much of a coincidence—his mirror found at another crime scene involving a prostitute. He took a wild guess. "Ask the person in the picture. I bet he broke it off and placed it there. If you actually did any investigative work versus eating donuts, you might figure it all out."

"You're a little shit. I could arrest you right now and throw you in with all the rest of the queers we have locked up. They'd have fun with you."

Brent sat back. "And you have a foul mouth. I'm only stating a fact." Looking at the detective, he saw beads of perspiration dripping under his lip. Brent motioned to the large glass mirror that framed an entire wall. "Who is watching behind the mirrored glass that you're nervous about?"

Not waiting to answer, the detective got up and proceeded to leave the room. Before he closed the door, he said, "We arrested your girlfriend last night giving a blowjob in the backseat of a lowrider Chevelle. She left with her pimp about an hour ago—he posted bail. A big bad Russian—goes by the name of Vladislav. He doesn't take kindly to johns who don't pay for his women. Something you might want to think about the next time you sleep with one of his girls without paying." He left the room, laughing as he closed the door. The room again became silent. Only the ventilation fan in the ceiling made a soft sound. Another thirty minutes went by before a different person entered. He removed the handcuffs and set a glass of water on the table. *A typical good guy, bad guy interrogation tactic.*

"I'm the mystery man behind the glass curtain." He set Brent's car keys and cellphone on the table. "I'm Special Agent Lewis with diplomatic security. I want to confirm what you said to the detective." He took the picture of Sadegh and laid it on the table. "You saw this person near the Creech military base?"

"Yes sir."

"That is troubling. What happened at the casino?"

"As I told the detective, I have no idea." Brent had yet to find out Sadegh's true intentions. "When the police pulled me over today, a man with similar features followed me into the city from the base. The patrol officer let him go. I have his picture on my phone." Brent took hold of his phone and scrolled through the picture file, but found all his pictures deleted. "Did you delete my pictures?"

"The Pakistani embassy has filed a complaint of harassment against you. The story they tell is not the same as yours. They said you're harassing them. You threatened one of their security officers at a stoplight today. I'm just trying to get my head around what is really going on."

"Why don't you go ask Sadegh what this is all about?"

"I did. He's still in the hospital—refuses to say anything. We even showed him these pictures—especially the one of you sitting next to the girl. Nothing! What is even more troubling is your previous connection with him. We have video surveillance of a man, very similar to the disguise he wore the morning you two were seen in the casino, kicking off your mirror before climbing into a car with a woman who is now deceased. I find this all very curious. My job is to ensure a foreign diplomat's protection while they're in our country. And to make sure they are abiding by our laws, though they do have diplomatic immunity unless we catch them actively fulfilling an unlawful act—buying secrets from an undercover agent or murder. This person you're involved with is very dangerous. I suggest you stay away from them. Their internal security personnel are not nice people."

"He came searching for me versus the other way around. If they try anything again, I will deal with it in my own way. I'll let you know so that you can pick up the pieces. If I'm not under arrest, I'd like to leave now."

The Special Agent took out a card and handed it to Brent. "Call me when this gets beyond your control. My job here is done. These people have diplomatic immunity—the only thing we can do is have them expelled when they break our laws. You on the other hand fall within the jurisdiction of the Las Vegas prosecutor. Since no charges have been filed and we'd like to keep this quiet, I suggest you keep a low profile." He got up and stood by the door. "By the way, we never told you this diplomat's name, but you already seem to know."

After a moment, the door opened and the agent stepped aside for Brent to leave. "I read about the assault in the newspaper. My guess is he came up against someone tougher than him."

Outside, he hailed a cab for a ride to his car. When he arrived, he found a parking ticket tucked underneath the windshield wiper for illegally parking.

"Just another day in paradise."

Part II

SECOND WEEK

Are U.S. air attacks imminent in Libya?

AP
12:00 AM ET, September 30, 2011

Washington, DC. (AP) – The United Nations Security Council unanimously passed a resolution, authorizing member states to establish and enforce a no-fly zone over Libya and to use "all necessary measures" to prevent attacks on civilians. Gaddafi's forces stationed inside the Benghazi Security Camp have indiscriminately fired into local neighborhoods. Local hospitals report hundreds of women and children killed by this ruthless civil war.

Chapter 8

ANOTHER WAR

A yellow tug pulled a large gray MQ-9 Reaper past the hangar doors, escorted by four airmen who maintained a constant watch to make sure the sixty-six-foot wingspan cleared the outer edges. Its three spindly tripod legs, kept the ungainly duckling from tipping over. The hanger's doors were originally designed for the thirty-three foot wingspan of the F-16 Falcons, purchased by the Egyptian Air Force ten years earlier, forcing them to pull this bird past the outer frame at an angle into the fresh early morning air.

One man plugged an umbilical cord into its side while another spoke into a walkie-talkie as if talking directly to the robotic airplane. "All equipment is clear. Fire her up."

On cue, the Reaper's turbine engine emanated an escalating pitch. The rear propeller began spinning until the blades shimmered in the early morning sunlight. With the RPM stabilized and all internal systems registering normal, the crew severed the connection. Satisfied all clear, he spoke again into the radio. "Good start. Let's do a systems check."

The large camera ball began to rotate up and down, and swivel left and right while all the control surfaces that would control the bird inflight oscillated, similar to a prizefighter loosening his neck before stepping into the ring. Satisfied its internal systems were healthy, he pulled the red streamer pins from underneath each wing. "All ordnance are now live. Your aircraft."

The aircraft moved forward onto the airport's taxiway, finally coming to a stop in front of the runway's hold-short line.

Sitting in a control module two hundred yards away, the pilot controlling the Reaper pressed the radio transmission button on his side stick. "LRE control with Hunter zero-six, holding short, ready for takeoff."

"Hunter zero-six, line up and wait on runway two-two," the tower controller replied.

"Roger, line up and wait," the pilot said. Pushing the left control stick forward sent a digital message to increase the turboprop engine. Watching the upper video display, he moved the left control stick to maneuver the Reaper's nose gear on runway centerline. The next transmission came several seconds later, "Hunter zero-six is cleared for takeoff. On departure, turn right to a heading of two-eight-zero, climb to six thousand feet. Good hunting ... Hunter!"

A keystroke initiated a takeoff command by sending a line-of-sight signal to increase engine RPM to maximum power. Hunter zero-six accelerated down the runway until it had enough airspeed to disengage itself from the ground, climbing toward its first waypoint. The pilot typed out a message over mIRC, an internet relay chat room used within a SECRET classified network, to the controllers at Creech Air Force Base. -*Ready to transfer control. Your aircraft.*

***

Brent monitored the instruments, waiting for the handoff from the Egyptian base LRE pilot. With the satellite link established, he typed a message back that he now controlled Hunter zero-six. His moving-map plot confirmed the Reaper on a northerly heading toward its first waypoint in the Mediterranean Sea halfway between Crete and the Libyan-Egyptian border. The upper display showed the coast of Egypt passing under the Reaper's nose with position, course, altitude and airspeed all within the mission profile.

Watching Hunter cross the Egyptian coastline—going feet-wet flying over the Mediterranean—he typed a new radio frequency, switching the internal radio channels inside the aircraft. Brent pressed the transmit button. "Red Crown control, Hunter zero-six checking in as fragged." He used the term fragged to relay his aircraft had two Hellfire missiles loaded under each wing. The transmission sequence bounced across three satellites and transmitted back down to the Reaper on the other side of the world, all within a fraction of a second. Upon receiving, the Reaper's onboard computers unscrambled the message to an analog signal, broadcasting his voice over the aircraft's UHF radio to any listening radio within its line-of-sight envelope.

Brent's pre-mission brief said a command-and-control Aegis missile cruiser, USS Shiloh, would be floating one hundred miles off the coast of Egypt. This Aegis missile cruiser, known as Red Crown to all combat aircraft who flew within her control area, had a primary responsibility to monitor all aircraft traffic for the George Washington carrier battle group. Since Libya and Egypt had adjoining ocean front property, Shiloh's AN/SPY-1 phased array radar panels tracked anything solid that flew over the ocean's water.

Hearing the Reaper's transmission, the Red Crown controller responded back, "Roger, Hunter, radar contract. Climb and maintain angels plus four. Turn left to a heading of two-seven-zero. You are cleared to proceed on your fragged mission."

For the next twenty-four hours, angels represented a baseline altitude of twenty-two thousand feet. Adding four to the baseline, Brent typed in twenty-six into the system, telling his aircraft how high to climb. Utilizing the right control stick, Brent pitched the nose up to ten degrees and turned the Reaper in a thirty-degree right bank until the heading display approached -270, where he leveled the wings for its initial cruise course. After flying west, crossing over a series of overwater waypoints, Hunter turned south toward the Libyan coast.

An hour later, Brent placed the Reaper into an orbit over pre-designated coordinates that fell within the Benghazi security compound, a fortress Gaddafi still controlled. The camera mounted underneath the nose recorded two *Palmaria* heavy howitzers firing into the surrounding neighborhoods, with subsequent explosions a mile away.

"Son of a bitch," Brent huffed, "he's killing his own people." He typed out a message on mIRC requesting authorization to strike from AFRICOM, Africa Command who controlled all military missions within this sector. A minute later, the reply he received back only said, "Standby."

Thirty minutes later, while still recording the carnage below his Reaper, the camera recorded four five-ton trucks plow through and over people who were rioting outside the front entrance. Soldiers hidden within the fortress walls fired upon the civilians, forcing those still alive to move away before they could open the massive steel gates. Once inside, the trucks stopped in front of a large warehouse type building. Soldiers carried large crates out of a nearby building and began loading them into the back of the trucks.

"This is not good," Brent said to the system operator sitting next to him. "They're moving something valuable to another location. Spin up a missile while I get authorization to shoot." This time he dialed AFRICOM J3 directly.

"We're watching the same activity. You now have a change of mission. The Navy is being notified to prepare for a strike mission. You will be the laser designator for a JDAM strike. Right now you are to wait and watch. We don't want to spook them until the airstrike happens. They should be on station within an hour."

***

Three hundred miles off the Libyan coast, in the middle of the Mediterranean Sea, the super-carrier USS George Washington, designated CV-73, powered through the dark waters. This vessel measured three-and-a-half football fields and weighed a colossal ninety-seven thousand tons. Admiral Grew, the battle group commander, sat atop his perch one hundred feet above the water line. He looked over at the Automatic Identification System display, which showed the location of his eleven US warships, two snooping around underwater and nine sniffing the air above. Each had an array of weapons more formidable than this small country he was about to go to war with. The red phone next to his chair lit up and started ringing, silencing the chatter from the sailors working within his area. When it rang, either the president wanted an immediate action or something bad happened. Sometimes it meant both. "Admiral Grew," he answered.

"Sir, please wait, I have a priority one incoming call from the Secretary of Defense," responded a communication officer, six decks below, before connecting a direct line to the Pentagon.

"Let the game begin," Admiral Grew muttered to himself. The latest intelligence report indicated Gaddafi's forces were killing civilians and the growing insurgency of the Free Libyan Army the United States president had decided to support. *Your enemy's enemy is not necessarily our friend*, he said to himself. *It's the worst of two evils.*

Answering the link, he heard, "Admiral, hope I didn't disturb you." The voice came from the SecDef.

"No sir, we're having another beautiful day on our Mediterranean cruise. People pay good money to ride a boat in the middle of these waters. What can the Navy do for you?"

"I'll get right to the point. The president has authorized immediate military action against Gaddafi's forces. The UN recently passed a resolution that gives us the authority to strike when situations dictate—right now, it dictates. I'm watching footage from one of our Reapers over the Benghazi security camp—the bastard is at it again killing his own civilians! You have the greenlight to launch as soon as possible. The United States has sat on the sidelines long enough watching Gaddafi kill his own people. Strike as soon as you can before the city awakens."

"Usually there's a timeline established before the US military becomes involved in another war. We've allowed other dictators to do the same thing without stepping in. I sense this is not the only issue that's causing this quick action."

"What makes this urgent are these crates they're currently moving out of a building inside the camp. We're certain they contain weapons. If they are able to hide these damn things, or the rebels get their hands on them, who knows what will happen. We want this camp destroyed—anything that remotely resembles a warehouse flattened."

"Yes sir, I'll get this war machine rolling. It won't take us long before we rain down a boatload of JDAMs."

"Thanks admiral. The president has already authorized this execute order. I'll let him know that as of right now, the US has begun military operations inside Libya."

"Good night sir." The admiral hung up the phone and for a moment looked out beyond the two front catapults. His sailors will be leading the charge in America's newest involvement into another war. "Put the battle group at General Quarters." He commanded his staff on the bridge.

Alarms sounded throughout the ship, causing a beehive of activity to develop on the flight deck, as multi-colored shirted sailors prepared for launch. A faint vibration resonated throughout the ship as it plowed through the water to get enough wind over the flight deck to launch aircraft.

Pilots pulled and pushed on pieces of their F/A-18E Super Hornets to make sure all were secure. Under each wing hung a TER, triple ejector rack mounting system, with three five-hundred-pound JDAMs attached, giving each jet three thousand pounds of high explosive destruction. Once the two pilots were satisfied their aircraft was mission ready, they climbed up the side ladder and strapped themselves into their ejection seats. With the orchestrated preparation of aircraft and flight deck, the quietness of the ship ended with an eruption of sound as four General Electric F414-GE-400 turbofan engines fired up, blasting hot exhaust from the tail section of the two Hornets.

Men leaned against the thirty-knot wind, holding their arms out and showing a thumbs-up—indicating their job complete. A yellow shirt -shooter- stood midsection between the two catapults, while clouds of hot steam billowed the inside of his khaki pant legs. He looked up at the pilot, saluted, then made sure he saw acknowledgements from his flight deck personnel. With his right hand pointing at the Hornet's engines, he raised his left hand in the air with his two fingers extended, twirling in a circular motion, signaling to advance the jet's engines to full power—a roar reverberated throughout the massive ship. Then he opened his left hand with all five fingers spread out.

With the "high five" signal, the pilot pushed both throttles into burner, which sent a signal to spray raw jet fuel into the engines' tailpipe—two white-hot flames shot out from the two General Electric engines producing a concussive force of forty-four thousand pounds of thrust. With instruments indicating normal and no red warning lights, the aircraft's anti-collision light flicked on.

The shooter knelt on a knee, touched the deck, and pointed his finger forward toward the bow of the ship. The catapult fired— separating the holdback knuckle—blasting Boomer 504 into the air. The same choreographed hand signals repeated between the shooter and the pilot of Boomer 507, as they both readied the jet and the catapult for the next launch. In less than twenty seconds, the two aircrafts were airborne for their impending mission.

***

Brent acknowledged the check-in with the two Navy Hornets. Time seemed to slow to a crawl as he watched a set of trucks leave the compound, followed by another set driving over dead bodies to get through the front gates. With this new set of trucks, there was an increased level of intensity underneath his aircraft. He held the camera's aim point on a specific building with the most activity; little human ants moved about, going back and forth between the entrance and the trucks carrying larger coffin size crates. "Boomer is five minutes out," came a transmission over the Reaper's radio.

"Laser on," Brent announced over the radio, pressing the laser fire button on the right control stick. Laser energy from the Reaper bounced off the target, directing where the fighter's bombs would seek and explode.

Twelve JDAMs sliced through roofs penetrating various floors. A millisecond later, large explosions disintegrated entire structures. The building Brent had been watching took two direct hits. His screen flashed white before the camera recovered, flashed white again—this time remaining blank for multiple seconds. "Holy shit," Brent looked over at his sensor operator. "Did you see that? That warehouse must've been loaded!"

Once the Reaper's camera recovered, fire ripped through the compound. Periodically, a rocket shot across his screen and bandoliers of bullets flashed from the intense heat. It looked like a fourth of July celebration, except for the incineration of several hundred soldiers.

Brent rolled his seat back from the console. Mixed emotions flooded through his body of what just happened. The Reaper maintained its orbit over the compound, with the camera auto-locked on what remained. A fighter pilot dropped bombs and left the area without knowing the aftermath. The main mission of the Reaper was reconnaissance, which meant he recorded both the cause and effect—the destruction and the aftermath.

Watching from his perch at twenty-six thousand feet, the few Libyan soldiers who survived tried their best to douse the flames, but each time the heat forced them back before something exploded causing another fire. Portions of the fortress walls were now mounds of rubble, blown down when a nearby warehouse exploded. As he continued to watch, two trucks came upon the front gates, their drivers flashing headlights to get the soldiers' attention. White flashes popped from a street corner, prompting the driver to ram his truck past and breaking the gates open.

Once inside, they stopped in front of the only structure to have survived the attack. A nearby building flicked its fire into the air, pushing floating embers to settle on a nearby roof. Soldiers met the truck and began taking crates from the burning building and loaded them onto the trucks. Brent noticed these crates were larger than the other—the size of a human coffin. "What's so important to remove from a burning building?" Brent asked himself.

Chapter 9

INTELLIGENCE IMMEDIATE

Ali stood by the window as successive explosions lit up the interior of the room. Flames shot above the fortress walls illuminating the neighborhood with flashes of light. His men, seven Iranian Quds special operatives, abruptly awoke and reached for their rifles. Even though the jets had dropped their bombs from the stratosphere, the faint sound of turbine engines screeched over the ensuing chaos from the Benghazi compound.

Ali and his team infiltrated the Libyan rebels a week prior. Their mission was to monitor day-to-day operations and teach the FLA rebel forces guerrilla warfare tactics. The Supreme Leader of Iran wanted agents embedded with the rebel insurgency, while continuing diplomatic relations with Gaddafi. For Iran, it did not matter who won this civil war. Her influence permeated both sides of this dispute.

"Ali, what do you see?" his second in command asked, walking over to the window where he stood.

"It appears the Americans have become involved in another war—they attacked the comp—" He turned at the sound of footsteps bounding up the outside stairway. His men fanned out along the walls—chambering a round inside their rifles.

A voice outside the door said, "Ali, open up … hurry."

Ali cracked open the door with the standard greeting, "As-Salam Alaykum"

"Wa alaykumu s-salam," the man replied. "Please come. America has destroyed the Benghazi compound. The soldiers inside are in chaos fighting the fires and the walls of the fortress have crumbled. Several trucks have left the compound—soldiers are no longer guarding the gates and they're open. Allah has shown his blessing by giving us this opportunity."

"I agree—it is time to strike. Assemble your men," Ali commanded. "We will be outside momentarily." He closed and relocked the door, then addressed the men in the room. "We will now see if they have the courage to fight for what they believe in." Along with the rest of the men in the room, Ali put on his assault vest, loaded with eight magazines, and screwed a silencer onto the nose of his Finish automatic rifle. Lastly, he made sure nothing shined, including covering his face with charcoal.

Ali stepped out of the building and racked a round inside his rifle to make sure a bullet was in the chamber. Explosions and sporadic flashes continued to light up the sky from detonations several blocks away, creating a nightmarish war zone. Smoky mist mixed with pungent burning rubber permeated the air. Several dozen rebels congregated in the middle of the street as one tattered group—they wore various pieces of mismatched military uniforms, carrying old rusted Soviet bolt-action rifles. Since the United States had sided with this group, Ali already knew that eventually, just like what happened in Iraq, *they will soon reap the rewards of US affluence—new uniforms and new M-16 automatic rifles.* Little did America know, his country had already set the outcome as to who would be the victor.

Upon seeing Ali and his team, the rebels lined up shoulder to shoulder. During the past week, Ali's men instructed them on patrol techniques, movement to contact and ambush awareness ... and rudimentary basics of military formations. For most, this would be their first live engagement and it would prove their manhood.

The FLA leader who had come to the door proudly stood in front of his men. He saluted as Ali neared. "My men are ready. Would you like to inspect them?"

Without saluting back, Ali walked within inches of the leader and whispered, "Do not ever salute me where the enemy can see. Next time I will slit your throat before you raise your hand." Ali took a step back, taking a position behind and to the right shoulder of the leader, and whispered, "There will be no inspection. If they are not ready now, they will never be. Take charge by commanding your men to separate into three groups."

The leader yelled orders while Ali organized his team. He sent two of his men to each of the three FLA groups, with one team member staying behind as a central command center. Seeing a flash from a green laser by one of his teammates, Ali whispered to his group leaders, "Move."

While they walked, Ali overheard several FLA muttering or praying, nervous whether they were going to live or die this day. A block away, the rebel group spread out and stayed close to buildings. They maneuvered around burned out vehicles, tires still smoldering from the evening's firefights. Finding no resistance, the team approached the fortress, congregating in front of a blown out storefront a hundred meters from the front gates.

Ali motioned for his team leaders to come forward. "Gholam, go around to the east and enter from there. Farid, take your team over to the west. I will take my group and try to enter through the front gates. *Insha'Allah*, we will see each other again inside the compound." Gholam and Farid moved out and huddled up with their respective groups, each looking like a ship's captain preparing for battle.

Looking through a monocular night vision scope, Ali noticed the bombing raid had crumbled entire sections of the fortress walls. He stood, flapping his arms like a bird to get his group to stand, and once they did, he waved them forward. "Move out." His group maneuvered around abandoned vehicles, using them to cloak their progress. A rebel off to his left fired a shot, though no targets had yet shown. He marched over to the culprit and yanked the rifle out of his hands. "You will die fighting with only your hands."

Once again, peering through the scope, Ali saw that the front steel gates remained opened. Off to his right, the roar of truck engines pierced the stillness—it appeared to be coming his direction, toward the gates. Ali motioned for his group to hide within the shadows as the trucks sped past, their headlights sweeping over the top of them before entering the compound. Two Libyan soldiers came out and began pulling the gates closed. Ali took aim and fired two quick silent shots, killing both.

93

"Move—spread out." He pushed the rebels into a line abreast formation to provide maximum firepower and to limit a nervous finger from shooting him in the back. Once the men were ready, he motioned them forward as one. "Stay quiet. Do not fire unless seen. We must get to the gates before anyone realizes they are still open."

This time, they rushed to the gates without a shot fired. Ali peeked inside and saw soldiers loading rectangular wooden crates into the same trucks that moments earlier had barreled past them. Flames from a nearby building touched the same structure where the soldiers worked, propelling them to hurry.

Raising his fist in the air, Ali signaled his rebel group to hold back. He took a fellow teammate with him to the edge of the gate, and then the two bounded forward with their weapons pointing at various potential targets, staying concealed, but the men loading the trucks were too busy to take notice of them. Twenty meters away, he took a knee when two sets of men were seen carrying two crates down the steps toward the back of the truck-bed. When they were close enough for a clear shot, Ali whispered, "I have the first two, take the second." He aimed and made two successive shots—two muffled shots sounded behind his shoulder dropping the four soldiers.

With these soldiers down, Ali sprinted to the back of the first truck and climbed inside the cargo compartment. *What could be so important that they would risk their lives to remove from a burning building?* He flicked on a penlight to read Russian lettering burnt into the wood of six wooden crates, stacked two high. It read "Плечом запуск ракеты Игла-S." Understanding Cyrillic, he ordered his partner, "Find me a tool to pry open a lid."

Ali heard the front cab door open and within a minute he had a tire iron in his hand. Using it as both a hammer and crowbar, he was able to pry off the lid. Recognizing the weapon inside, he knelt and placed his hand over long cylindrical objects bowing his head and reciting a quick prayer. *Placed in the right hands, these weapons will change the course of history.*

"What is it? What do you see?" His teammate at the tailgate asked.

"Allah has shined his blessing upon us. These are Soviet surface-to-air SA-24s shoulder launch missiles, four of them packed in foam. Go inside the building and see if you can find any more. We need to get them loaded and out of this compound before someone else comes looking for them. We must hurry. Do not tell anyone what we have found—these missiles are better utilized in the hands of our government than an unpredictable rebel force."

His agent left and went into the building, leaving the rebels to secure the outside perimeter. Only a few remained, while others searched adjacent buildings. Ali hammered the lid back in place and climbed out of the back of the truck, ready to kill anyone who had ideas of taking his new prize. After the rebels had seen him kill without hesitation, they gave him a wide berth as he waited by the tailgate for his men to return.

When he heard grenades detonating inside the building followed by sporadic gunfire, he pulled his rifle tight against his shoulder and moved up the stairs into the building aiming for potential targets. Searching the rooms on the main floor, he found nothing. Two more shots sounded underneath his feet from a floor below. Off to his right, he found an open door with a stairwell that led down into a basement. He removed a flashbang grenade, pulled the pin and called out in Russian a code word. When he heard an appropriate response back, he put the pin back in the grenade and waited. He stood guard at the door until he saw his teammate drag a long rectangular wooden crate up the stairs. "I heard grenades. What happened?"

"There is a secret underground armory below this building. When I went down the stairs, two Libyan soldiers fired shots. I tossed a couple flash-bangs and fired off a barrage of bullets. There are eighteen similar crates like this one down there. No way are we going to get these out before this building erupts in flames and this stairwell collapses."

Ali went outside and found four rebels who were guarding the perimeter and asked in Russian, "Вы говорите на русском языке?" They shook their heads and shrugged their shoulders. Ali asked again in Arabic, "Can you read Russian?" This time they replied "no," in their native language. "Go inside and help this man carry more crates. Load this truck first." He pointed at the lead truck, "And put the rest in the other."

The urgency of what still needed to be accomplished made Ali uncomfortable. They already had been in the compound too long.

The Americans were known to conduct an after action damage assessment and were certainly watching them clear the building. Once they realize what these crates contain, they had limited time before another attack.

After loading an additional seven crates into the truck, his other two groups converged on where he waited. Each group had a few less rebel soldiers than when they first started—now on their way to meet Allah.

Ali approached his group leader Gholam. "Get the remainder of the crates loaded and meet me at the warehouse rally point. Do not tell the rebels where you are going or what we found. The less they know the better. These missiles have changed our mission. We need to take them and leave as quickly as possible."

"Yes sir. It should not take too long. Allah has shown us his blessing."

"You must hurry. I am certain the Americans are watching. It will take them time to mount an offensive to stop us. Take every precaution driving to the warehouse. *Alla akbar.*" Ali tapped his driver. "We need to leave ... we need to leave right now." He hated to leave without his men, but they all understood the tactical situation changes in war. A successful leader must adapt as new opportunities present themselves and these missiles were now a priority.

***

Twenty-five thousand feet above the compound Brent's Reaper silently watched the first truck drive out the front gates. He adjusted the camera to maximum focal power. "What is so important to remove from a burning building?" The limited ambient light made the picture grainy, preventing him from reading the lettering stamped on the side. "I'm putting this thing in an autonomous orbit. I'll be in the intelligence SCIF if anything else pops up. I'm going to find out what's in those boxes. Call the duty officer to see if there is another pilot available ... if you need anything." Brent removed the mission tape that held all the video footage of the Predator and what happened inside the control module, and sprinted out the door and down the hallway, using his access card to enter the Sensitive Compartmented Information Facility containing top-secret material. The two technicians inside leapt from their chairs as Brent barged into the room. "Take a look at this tape. Terrorists are loading coffin sized crates into trucks." When the technicians didn't move, he went over to a video player and loaded the tape into the slot. "It will be too late if we wait any longer." Brent got up and paced around the room. "You need to move ... do your job ... tell me what's in those crates. They're taking them from a burning building. They've got to be important. Search your database for crates similar in size. You might start with weapons we know about that were delivered to Libya in the last couple of years."

Brent squeezed in among the analysts huddled in front of a television monitor, freeze-framing the monochrome Reaper video to get an accurate measurement on the crate's dimensions. Next to the video monitor, another analyst searched the classified database for anything resembling the crates' dimensions. Within two minutes, they found a match. "Sir, you're not going to like this."

He leaned over the analyst's shoulder to read the caption written at the bottom of the picture: *March 2004 - Libya purchases SA-24 missiles from Russia*. The picture showed Gaddafi standing in front of the crates shaking hands with a Russian general. Each crate had Cyrillic lettering stenciled on the side.

Brent called the communication center. "We have a Pentacle alert! Fire a message up the flagpole that we have a national security crisis. Relay that the FLA now has a modern surface-to-air missile capability. We need to close down the airspace over the country of any commercial aircraft."

***

As Brent re-entered the control module, the phone on his desk was already ringing. The caller identification showed HQ AFRICOM. He answered, "Lieutenant Parker ...."

"This is General Shoemaker. Destroy those trucks carrying the crates immediately! Do whatever you need to do to keep those missiles out of the hands of the FLA."

I'm speaking with the commanding general of AFRICOM! Looking at the current video transmitted from his Reaper, only one truck remained in front the burning warehouse. "Sir, we've lost one of them. It drove away. I have no idea where it went."

"Why didn't you hit it when you had a chance?"

"I ... I was busy trying to figure out what was inside those crates." His breathing felt labored from running down the hallway to get back to his console. "I do not have autonomous fire authority."

"You do now. Those crates mustn't get into the hands of these rebels. Destroy the remaining truck and send another into the building. And then go find that other truck!"

Brent noticed his DO enter the room.

"Yes sir, engaging targets." He terminated the connection before his DO realized whom he was talking to and that he'd left his post without authorization—missing an opportunity to destroy a truck full of missiles. Getting caught back up, Brent directed the sensor operator to prepare the Reaper for an attack profile. "Designate the truck in front of the building as the primary target. If possible keep a view of both the building and the truck." The targeting crosshairs were on top of the cab. "Laser on. Spin up a weapon," Brent said.

"Weapon is active. All systems are showing green," the sensor confirmed.

His DO leaned over his shoulder. "Who gave you authority to shoot?"

"AFRICOM. That was who I was on the phone with when you came in. Confirmation is on the tape." He then realized the last tape was still with the intelligence analysts being reviewed and another tape had not been load. *Another screw up.*

"Then you better shoot before it gets away. Kill the son-bitch."

Time seemed to slow as he pressed buttons to get the missile active. Two men climbed into the second truck and it started moving. "They're on the move."

"You better hit it now," his DO said. "Don't fuck this up Parker."

Brent stayed focused—his scar began to burn. He flipped up the red protector over the master armament switch. "Three, two, one, rifle." He pressed the weapon release button on the control stick. A white streak flashed across the camera's video screen. Four thousand miles away from his location, the missile honed in on the laser energy bouncing off the truck's cab. Two seconds later the missile's smoke plume dissipated and the truck came back into view.

The missile slammed into the truck's passenger compartment and a microsecond later, exploded into a huge fireball. The intense heat from the explosion traveled back to the crates, causing multiple secondary explosions. The fireball and resulting shockwave vaporized the truck and everything within a circumference of one hundred feet.

"Designate the building as the next target," Brent commanded. With the targeting reticle now positioned on the building's roof, he fired another Hellfire.

A high-pressure shockwave blasted through the interior, blowing out walls and igniting everything in its path. The exterior walls held against the initial shockwave, but when the super-heated air torched the remaining high-explosive munitions, a massive fireball erupted through the roof. Once the heat signature subsided, the thermal camera caught dozens of body parts burning across the ground.

***

Ali's driver turned left onto *Shari' Ahmed Rafiq al-Mahdawi* Road, a major highway that led out of the city. At the first roundabout, he took the next exit onto the First Ring Road and a left onto *Inhemed al Megharief* Street, which gave them a direct path east—away from the city.

They crossed the intersection of the Fifth Ring Road, the final arterial around the outskirts of the city, when a flash lit up the morning sky and then two seconds later they heard the sonic boom. "It seems the Americans have realized the significance of our crates," Ali said to his driver. He bowed his head and gave a quick prayer to the men he once knew, who he guessed were now dead.

When his Quds team first arrived at Benghazi, they canvassed every portion of the city looking for possible rally points and safe houses, developing contingency plans for various situations. They found an abandoned warehouse across from the Benghazi national stadium. Originally built for professional soccer games, the local militia used it for public executions. For obvious reasons, this stadium and the surrounding area remained deserted.

The driver stopped in front of a warehouse that had a rollup style door. Ali jumped out with a tire iron, smashing the hanging lock before pulling the door open. As soon as the truck's back bumper cleared, he let it fall back down. With the truck now hidden, Ali turned to his driver. "I am going into the city to contact Quds leadership. It should not take more than two hours. If I am not back by nightfall, assume the worst." He slipped out of the warehouse and walked another hundred meters to the main road. Several cars drove by, before a large panel van approached. Ali stepped out into the road, waving his arms, flagging the driver in the hopes of him stopping.

The van slowed and pulled alongside. Stenciled on the side panel displayed *Saluq Distributors*. Ali recognized the name Saluq to be a town forty kilometers south of Benghazi.

The driver leaned across the cab and rolled down the passenger window. "*Wa 'Alaykum As-Salaam*. Where do you need to go my friend?" the driver asked. "I am heading to the port. You are welcome to ride with me."

"Thank you. Where I need to go is only two blocks away."

"Climb in. We will ride together."

Before opening the door, Ali pulled out his PSS Silent pistol from underneath his tunic. "Allah forgive me," he said, leveling the pistol and pulling the trigger—twice—a double tap. The pistol made very little noise as each SP-4 hollow-point bullet blew a pencil-sized hole into the man's head spraying a red mist out the window onto the pavement. Ali climbed into the van and pulled the body over and behind the front seats. He found an old plastic garbage bag, emptied it and slid it over the man's head, sealing the leaking contents by wrapping tape around the neck. He frisked the body then searched the interior until he found a cell phone in the glove compartment.

Ali climbed into the driver's seat. The interior smelled of rotten vegetables with several empty plastic containers. He ground the transmission into gear and drove back onto the highway toward the Port of Benghazi where there would be a concentration of people and panel vans. At the final roundabout, he turned southeast along the edge of the sea, before stopping underneath an underpass—out of site from overhead cameras he knew were searching for him. Tapping numbers on the driver's cell phone, he dialed a local number tied to a computer modem linked to a digital switching station. After several rings, the connection opened, which prompted him to dial an international number that would be answered in Egypt. He thanked Allah for the technology that allowed the phone to initiate a VoIP connection to a computer inside Iran. When he heard a chime, he pressed the number -1- to initiate an encryption process. From Egypt to Iran, Ali's transmission became random gibberish until deciphered.

Within the Quds communication center, a specialist answered with a metallic voice, "Go ahead with your report."

"I have a change of mission," Ali said, wanting to keep the conversation as sterile as possible. Even with all the encryption that took place for this call, Ali knew the weak link in this conversation was the dead Saluq driver's cell phone transmission that had not yet hit the encryption process.

"Please state the reason for the change."

Keep it short before the Americans have time to pinpoint the source of this conversation. "I am in possession of ten crates of SA-24 missiles. Only two of my men are alive. I need a logistics plan to get the missiles out of the country. Now!"

"Wait one," he heard back. Something of this magnitude would fire straight up to the commander of Quds within the IRGC, Major General Qasem Soleimani, ending with approval by Supreme Leader Khamenei. These missiles would have direct implications against the American and Russian governments, and any fallout could lead to further economic sanctions.

While he waited, a pedestrian came alongside his window and tried to start a conversation. Ali remained engaged and jovial, until the person appeared to look inside the van. Ali pulled out his pistol and aimed it at the visitor's head. "Leave!" Sweat glistened off his forehead with each minute while the cell phone connection remained open. An American NSA satellite could take less than a minute to triangulate on his location, though their bureaucracy to register what he said and take action took significantly longer.

After waiting over five minutes, an eternity when it came to triangulation, the phone became alive again. "Your priority is to get the package out of the country. We will initiate the logistics and notify you within twenty-four hours of the plan." With the transmission severed, Ali opened the back of the cell phone and removed the battery, killing any GPS tracking feature. He threw the phone out the passenger window and the battery out his side window. If someone were to eavesdrop on the conversation, the unique SIM identification was certain to now have a high-priority flag attached to it.

***

A NSA satellite, programmed to monitor the cellular spectrum within Libya, instantly keyed in on the phrase starting with "SA-24." The Cray Supercomputer located in the basement of NSA headquarters at Fort Meade, Maryland, ran an advanced data mining analysis, which matched certain words, phrases, voice recognition and languages.

Cross-referencing the Persian language with the words SA-24 and the subsequent encryption across several cellular towers caused a code-1 National Emergency alert to flash throughout the NSA Operations Center. Utilizing the latest voice recognition and language translation software, the entire conversation was deciphered from its original language into English.

"INTELLIGENCE IMMEDIATE" flashed across the NSA duty officer's computer screen. He opened the file and listened to the translated conversation. This cellular connection had a unique caller identification and an embedded destination number, both displayed on the right side of his screen. Software triangulated the various cell towers, locating each phone within a three-meter radius of their actual location. Within seconds, pin dot locations on a graphical map popped up alongside each number.

***

The Secretary of Defense rubbed his temples as he reread the intelligence alert that came over the classified network ten minutes ago.

His headache pounded from sitting all day in front of Democratic congressional committee on appropriations about the last defense budget cutbacks. *Didn't they know the US is at war with terrorists?* Between the Pentacle alert and this latest message from the NSA, the likelihood of getting these missiles back before a shoot-down of a commercial airliner appeared slim at best. "SA-24s in the hands of terrorist—what a fucking disaster," he said to the empty room. Previous intelligence briefings showed the FLA working with Iranian and Russian agents. The second government he wasn't worried about ... "Hell, they sold these damn things to Gaddafi in the first place."

As for the Iranians, they already demonstrated a propensity to destabilize world peace. He hit his intercom button. "Doris, please schedule an appointment with POTUS. It's urgent I speak with the president as soon as possible."

***

As nightfall approached in Libya, Brent descended the Reaper to get a closer view. The forward camera zoomed in on the mass of people approaching the fortress. Once inside, they dragged chairs and tables into the courtyard, loaded onto flatbed trucks and hauled whatever they could take into the city. Anything unsalvageable became kindling and thrown into a blazing mound into the middle of the compound. None of Gaddafi's soldiers were present to stop them.

The same CIA person with the beard, wearing the same ugly Bermuda shirt came into the control module. "Your mission just became a national emergency," he said. "I'm now the mission commander for this Reaper. Until this is over, you are to do what I say."

"By whose authority?" Brent asked. "I've already been at the controls for the past twelve hours." He noted the digital time and thought about his date with Amber this morning. They were to have breakfast together when he got home. But, he hadn't heard from her since meeting with the detective. He said she was back in the clutches of her pimp, Vlad. Now that CIA became involved, this box remained in lockdown until complete—no phone calls, not even a bathroom break.

"Your military flight time rules no longer apply. Under CIA control, we have no rules. We need to look at the last location where a cell phone call came from. I doubt anything is still there, but we need to try. We have a team on the ground already questioning the FLA leadership. Time is of the essence to find these things. "

The spook gave Brent a coordinate location where a cell phone call had come from—the person who they thought drove away in the first truck. "If you see this truck, kill it this time."

"With what? I only had two missiles and they're both already gone."

"Then you'll ram it with this aircraft if you have to. It's expendable."

Brent maneuvered the aircraft over the designated point only to find a mass of people and multiple panel trucks traversing underneath the overpass. "There is no way to know if any have the missiles inside." From the call location fanning outward, he maneuvered the camera in concentric circles until the Reaper's fuel indication finally reached BINGO. "It's time to get this aircraft back on the ground." He gave up the search and turned the aircraft on a heading that would take it back out to sea. As the aircraft neared its approach corridor, he transferred control of Hunter to the LRE terminal controller who would take charge to land the aircraft.

Once the satellite link became severed, Brent took a moment to reflect on what he had done. The vast enormity of military personnel never saw combat: Soldiers never fire their rifle at another human, pilots never shoot a missile at an aircraft, and a ship's captain never sends a torpedo after a submarine. In one day, he had fired his targeting laser for Navy fighters to bomb, killing over a hundred men. He personally targeted another dozen, adding to the total. All in a night's work. *Time to find some reality in this crazy world.*

Outside, he took several deep breaths of cool morning air. After what he'd seen and done the past sixteen hours, it felt surreal to be back in the middle of America. He marveled at the sun's position forty-five degrees above the horizon. Rarely did he see this after getting off a shift—usually the sky was still dark. At the thought of what waited for him, a smile spread across his lips. Amber and him - two wayward souls, each needing something the other could provide. While sitting in the parking lot, he tried calling her cellphone, but it went to voicemail instead.

On the way back toward the city, a sedan pulled out of the mini mart parking lot and began trailing behind. Few cars were on this stretch of road during the late morning. He slowed to see what would happen. The car did the same to keep pace. Brent accelerated, but it sped up to a point where it again paced his speed. He passed an exit sign that indicated a crossing road a quarter mile away. At the last moment, he swerved onto the exit and punched the accelerator, keeping the pedal floored and eventually losing sight.

An hour later, Brent drove the Z into his garage, expecting to see Amber's car parked out front. When he tried calling her again, he noticed she had left a text message. It said, "I made lunch." It listed an address at the bottom of the page.

He quickly showered and replaced a sweaty flight suit with clean jeans. Upon arriving at her place, he noticed her apartment sat on the third floor of a three story broad V-type structure with a central entrance located between the apexes of two adjoining wings. Guests used an intercom system that held the residence names associated with an apartment number. He buzzed her number and waited for response, but none came.

Walking around to the back, where the residents parked their cars, he found Amber's car—the hood still felt warm. Along the backside of the building, near a side entrance, a woman placed an empty UPS box into a dumpster. Brent waited for her to leave to remove the box, and took it back to the front entrance. With the box in his hands, he pushed several buttons until someone finally answered.

"I have a UPS package for Katya Kozachenko. She lives in apartment three-twelve, but she's not answering. Could you let me in and so I can leave this by her door."

The door lock clicked, allowing him to enter. He took the stairs to the third floor and went down the hall until he found her apartment. He knocked twice and waited. When the door opened, he expected to see Amber, but instead a large Russian—shaved head with tattoos running down his neck—framed the entrance. "What do you want?"

"I have a package for Katya."

"Give it to me and I'll make sure she gets it." The Russian placed both hands against the door jam, blocking Brent from seeing inside. With a belly hanging over Adidas' stretch pants and a barrel size chest, he gave the persona of a hard hitter.

Brent recognized the thick Russian accent from Amber's previous conversations. "She needs to sign for it. Is she available?" Brent took a step back from the door to allow for better reaction time if the Russian decided to take a swing.

"You don't look like a UPS delivery man. They wear a brown uniform. You must be her new boyfriend who doesn't pay."

He heard Amber say from inside the apartment, "Vlad, leave him alone. I'll do what you want. Please!"

Vlad looked back into the room. "If she says anything again, do what you want to keep her quiet, but don't damage the face. I need her back to work."

Brent charged, throwing his right shoulder into a blubbery midsection, catching the pimp off guard by forcing his way into the room. Another Russian stood behind Amber, his hands pinning her shoulders back into a chair. He was pulling her head back by her hair to place his mouth onto her face. He would eventually need to defeat Vlad to win this battle, but the other looked just as formidable. Seeing Amber wince in pain, Brent slammed his fist into her assailant's left ear, dropping him like a rag doll. A bone snapped from the impact. Before he could turn to face her pimp, Vlad pushed him backward over a couch. When he came back up to fight, Vlad swung a truncheon that clipped the side of his head.

Brent tried to get up, but his legs felt rubbery and faltered his balance. Another impact hit him in the shoulder. Pain shot through his body with each blow. A boot kicked his side turning him onto his back.

Vlad stood over him. "You owe me forty thousand for fucking her." He swung again, cracking him alongside his skull.

***

Brent awoke smelling something rotten. His entire body ached from the beating. He blinked his eyes, but nothing came into focus—a tomb encased in darkness. For a split moment, he wondered if he was dead. When his hand touched a slimy metal wall, the reality of his situation became apparent. He rolled onto his stomach and tried to stand, slipping and falling against the side. The welts where he took the blows screamed at him. Using his hands to support his balance against the metal sides, he stood, ramming his head against a heavy lid. It popped open enough to let in a seam of light. Curling his fingers over the lip, he pushed it open enough to allow fresh air to enter. With his body now standing upright, he forced the lid completely open.

The dumpster faced outward toward a parking lot along the backside of the apartment building. Brent climbed out and fell onto the pavement, landing on his side. Pain shot through his right hand, now swollen and bruised. He remembered the solid punch to the Russian kissing Amber, either he broke a metacarpal or the Russian's skull—not yet sure which. A setting sun along the western mountain range told him he'd been out most of the day, with only a couple hours to spare before he needed to be back to the base for another night of flying. He still had his wallet, but looking through it, he found all the money gone. His driver's license remained inside, showing him to be an Oklahoma resident with a previous address listed to an old apartment. Checking his pocket, he found his car key was also missing. He staggered into the parking lot where he previously parked his black Z, now containing a white KIA sedan. A cell phone rang inside his pocket indicating Amber's number.

Before he said anything, the Russian answered. "I see you finally woke up from your nap. Good—"

"Where's Amber ... where's my car?"

"You used my merchandise without paying. Now she has damages. If you wreck a rental, you're expected to pay for repairs. My business is no different. I want my money—forty grand. I'll keep your black Z as collateral. Nice car, fast!"

Brent clenched his jaw, trying to hold back his anger. He had seen these Russians before at the casino, muscling into the prostitution circuit. "Bring Amber, so I know she's alright, otherwise no deal—no money."

"Call her number when you have the money. You have two hours, or your car is gone and I'll fuck Amber with a baseball bat—I'll send you a video. Call the police and they both will disappear." With the last sentence, the connection ended.

He went back to the front entrance and attempted to get back inside. This time it proved more difficult. The box strategy didn't work—nobody would open the door for an evening delivery. When he tried slipping inside behind a couple, they took one look at him and threatened to call the police. His reflection in the glass told him why. Dried blood dotted his face with bruising welts along his cheeks.

Brent caught an Uber back to his place to clean up, change into darker clothes and to grab an extra set of keys to the Z. He needed to find a car—the bigger the better. He hated the idea of stealing an owner's car, but Amber's life hung on the success of his next plan. Best-case scenario would be for the stolen car to go missing for an hour without any damages. Worst-case their insurance would cover the loss.

He figured the airport seemed to be the best place to steal a vehicle. People would leave their car running at the arrival area to go inside to find guests, presenting possible opportunities. He caught another Uber to McCarran International Airport and asked to be dropped off on the departure level. Every minute, the roar of a jet echoed off the terminal, while burnt jet fuel permeated the air. He paced the sidewalk looking for an opportunity, but nothing presented itself. Moreover, two police officers walked along the lanes, prompting travelers to keep the flow of traffic moving. Checking the time, he had less than an hour before the deadline. He proceeded off the airport complex and stood in front of a Master Park long-term parking lot to see if this might present an opportunity. This business catered to valet parking, where a traveler left their car underneath a shelter, leaving keys still in the ignition.

After fifteen minutes watching how the system worked, a pattern soon developed. Patrons left their cars underneath a shelter, before they climbed onto a shuttle that soon departed for the airport. Virtually the reverse process developed for those picking up their vehicles. A thirty-second period existed when attendants left the area to drive cars to and from a remote area, leaving the drop off area unattended with several ready to be taken.

Brent waited for a large SUV vehicle type to arrive—the bigger the better. After ten minutes, an attendant brought a black Suburban into the pickup staging area, rolled down the windows, and then went for another vehicle. The darkness and the sound of jet engines hid his approach. As he crossed the street, his breathing quickened at the anticipation of stealing a car—another new experience to add to a burgeoning criminal record.

Stealing the vehicle was actually easier than he anticipated. With the engine already running, he simply drove off the property as if he owned it. The airport sat two blocks from the Vegas strip and a fifteen-minute drive to the downtown section. As long as he kept to the speed limit, not highlighting himself, he gave no reason for the local police to take notice.

While he drove, he called Amber's number. "I have your money. Meet me in the eastern parking lot of the Royal Sands casino. Remember ... bring Amber or the deal is off." This time he disconnected the call before anything else could be said.

He parked in the darkest area he could find that gave an unimpeded direct shot to the meeting area. Whatever happened, the Russian will know he messed with the wrong person.

***

He first saw his Z enter the parking lot, followed by a dark colored BMW 700 series sedan. The cars settled into a parking stall and the drivers doused the headlights. Brent waited until at least one person got out of a car before he put his plan into action.

The person driving his Z made the first move. He got out holding a large caliber revolver with a long tubular cylinder protruding from the barrel.

Brent used the extra key-fob to remotely lock the Z's doors. What they did next would determine his move.

The man with the silenced revolver must have heard the car's chirp and went back to check the door. When he found it locked, he hollered at the person in the BMW.

Brent watched Vlad get out and look around, before proceeding over to his partner. He started the big V-8 engine, waiting a couple seconds before flooring the accelerator. The black vehicle with headlights extinguished racing toward them caused both Russians to pause like deer in the middle of the road. Vlad tried to make a play back to his car, but Brent veered for the intercept. The steel bumper caught the BMW's open door, snapping it off. As he sped by, he saw Amber sitting in the passenger seat. He spun the vehicle around, revved the engine and came back at the two men who stood between the two vehicles.

The man who drove his Z aimed the revolver and began firing shots. Bullets perforated the windshield, whizzing into the interior, shattering the rear glass.

Brent clicked on the high beams and drove straight at him. The Suburban's bumper hit the man's midsection, launching the body over the hood and off to the side. He slammed on the brakes and spun the vehicle around, this time coming to a stop.

Vlad limped toward his car—his hand holding a pant leg to help move a bad knee. The other man lay dormant several feet away.

Brent drove next to the BMW to block Vlad's approach and called out for Amber to get out. When she didn't move, he called her name, which made her look up. Her eyes remained half-open and she kept mumbling something while drool dripped along the corner of her mouth. Brent hopped out of the car and raced over. He took her by the arm to help her out. "What did they do to you?"

She managed to lift up her arm and point at the crook near the elbow, mimicking the insertion of a syringe needle.

"He drugged you?"

She nodded her head. Even in the faint light, he could see another contusion blossoming along her cheek and a recent split lip. It matched the receding raccoon eyes from when Sadegh hit her.

"He did this?" He asked, lightly touching her bruises.

She again nodded. He searched the area and found Vlad limping across the parking lot. Brent sprinted after him and bulldozed him to the ground. He grabbed Vlad by the hair so he could look into his eyes. "Take my girl, mess with me again, I'll kill you." Gauging where Amber's contusions were, Brent punched him once in the cheek and again above the lip, knocking out a front tooth and splitting the lip. "Now we're even—paid in full. She no longer works for you." He hit him one more time to make sure he didn't get up.

Brent had to carry her to his car, placing into the passenger seat. During the drive to his place, he glanced at her several times wondering what they did to her. Most of her wounds were superficial, but he was more worried about the sexual deviancy she must have endured. At his place, he carried her up the stairs and laid her onto his bed where he sat until it was time for him to go. "I will be back in the morning. Don't go anywhere. You are safe here. Nobody knows where I live." He pulled the blankets up around her neck and softly kissed her forehead.

Looking back at her before walking out of the bedroom, she lay nestled around his pillows sound asleep.

Chapter 10

EXTRACTION

Ali drove the van to the dead drop site. Getting out, he went over to a flat rock and removed a small plastic envelope hidden in the dirt underneath. Back in the van, he used an alphabet key and an innocuous pocket dictionary to decipher the note, revealing a logistics plan on how to move the missiles. A coded message at the bottom gave him concern. He deciphered it a second time to make sure he had it correct. It said, "A SF -6H," which meant an American Special Forces quick reaction team had been in the city for the past six hours. The noose around the city had already begun to tighten.

The note provided a time and place to meet with a Taureg, a nomadic tribe of the Sahara. Having no political loyalty, they played both sides of the fence depending on who paid the most. Upon arrival back at the warehouse, the crates were loaded into the back of the same Saluq distributor's van, and in less than ten minutes, they once again drove past the infamous stadium. Seeing no vehicles on this portion of the highway worried Ali—they were able to traverse the roadway unabated, but a single vehicle raised suspicion to someone watching from above.

At the first intersection, they turned left onto *Inhemed al Megharief* Street, a major thoroughfare heading east away from the city. Fifteen kilometers later, they turned right into a cement-manufacturing complex and proceeded to the back area where four *Jinga* trucks were parked. As his panel van approached, tribesmen holding automatic rifles came out from between their trucks' bumpers. Seeing Ali's approaching van, they aimed their rifles.

"Go slow and keep your hands on the steering wheel," Ali said.

An old man with a flowing white beard stepped past these men. When he saw Ali wave, he barked orders to his men to lower their weapons.

"Take it slow, these people are very suspicious. Wait in the van until I signal you." Ali got out leaving his rifle behind.

The elder spread his arms. "Greetings, my friend." His hands were as weathered as his face. When he smiled, the few teeth remaining were coal black. A light blue cloth wrapped around his forehead hung down along his front.

"Thank you for your assistance." Ali bowed, placing his hand across his heart. "As agreed, I have half of your money now and half will be paid at the destination."

"It is always a pleasure to help the Iranian intelligence service."

"Your pleasure is mine. I trust there have been no changes since our agreement?"

"Whatever you have done has caused many to be concerned ... many people are looking for a man who stole crates from Gaddafi's compound. By this time tomorrow, this city will be completely sealed. We need to leave as soon as your cargo is transferred." He waved his hand to Ali's driver, commanding, "Drive between the two trucks," and then gave orders to his men in a dialect that Ali didn't understand. "My men will help move your shipment to our trucks so we can leave. Our first stop will be the city of *Sabhā*. Tonight, we will be guests of my brother so we may be rested to leave at first light for our voyage into the desert."

Ali suppressed his irritation. He wanted out of this country, as far away from the hot center point. "Should we not get as far away while the roads are still open?"

"The best time to move is during broad daylight, when the roads are jammed with traffic. This is our usual schedule. It is wise to travel as expected. If Libyan soldiers search the trucks, they know to not look closely at what we have unless they want their throats cut, and their children's. My brother will take us south, across the *aṣ-ṣaḥrā' al-kubrā* to your final destination. This will be a three-day journey over very inhospitable conditions. Once we enter the desert, no one will bother us."

Both men turned to watch the Tuaregs drape canvas across his van and over the back tailgate of another truck.

"If the American's eyes are watching from the sky, they will not be able to see what is hidden. We will leave the canvas over your van. By the time it is found, we will have disappeared into the desert along with the man who once drove it."

Ali stood between the trucks to monitor the transfer. He noticed the Taureg men were delicate with the merchandise as they loaded each crate. His government must have paid a considerable sum of monies to ensure the success of his new mission. After the crates were loaded into two separate trucks, they placed various bags and rolled fabric around the cargo until it appeared to be a jamboree of household goods. The laden trucks resembled other nomadic caravans traveling the busy roads. With everything strapped down, the men climbed into their respective vehicles. Ali and his driver each climbed into separate trucks that carried his precious cargo. A billow of black exhaust puffed from the engine stacks as the caravan pulled onto the main highway, heading south toward the country of Niger where few peering eyes or roadblocks existed.

***

Ali awoke when he felt the truck come to a stop. Before opening his eyes, he gripped the silent pistol inside his shirt when he felt a hand touch his arm.

The driver held out a GPS for Ali to look at, illuminating the number display. "We have arrived at the spot you requested."

Ali looked outside—the night was pitch black. The driver had turned off the headlights, with only a faint glow from the digital readout. "Where are we?"

"Welcome to Niger. We came off the main road about an hour ago. I would have woken you earlier, but you were sound asleep."

"This is where our journey ends. We will unload my cargo and you can leave. Thank you."

"Nothing is out here. We are in the middle of the desert."

"Ma'a Assalaamah." Ali took hold of his rifle and climbed out the truck. In the darkness, household items hiding the crates were

strewn next to the trucks. The crates were individually stacked on the ground, then what was taken off reloaded. In a matter of minutes, Ali and his teammate watched the trucks disappear from view. Ali removed a thermal imager from his vest and scanned across the horizon. A fox roamed in search of food, otherwise the stillness of the night closed in on them. Not seeing anything that would cause concern, Ali activated a beacon and waited.

A half hour later, he heard the distant sonic thump of an approaching helicopter. Snapping the inner glass vial inside an IR *chemlight*, he tied one end to a long string and began to twirl it over his head. Soon a dark shadow descended upon them, causing sand to sting their skin.

Ali stood off to the side of the Russian Hip helicopter's sliding door, while men loaded the crates into the interior. "I will only be taking four crates into Syria. The remainder will stay on board."

The crew chief walked around the exterior of the aircraft and climbed into the back with the cargo. In preparation for the launch, the two pilots began flipping switches, sending the helicopter's interior to a closet blackness. Ali flicked on a miniature red LED light mounted on a *Petzl* lamp strapped around his head to look at the faces of three new Quds operatives for his next mission. He wondered if they would live longer than the last set.

The high-pitched whine of the twin turbines rotating broke Ali's solitude. The aircraft lifted off, tilted forward and accelerated across the rolling terrain at twenty meters. Nothing existed on the ground along their route. What worried the pilots were American AWAC planes that monitored anything that flew. Tonight, a window of opportunity existed between the spacing of the off-going and on-coming aircraft. For the next forty-five minutes, no radar coverage existed.

Ali monitored his Garmin GPS tracker, another present from the Americans. No sense looking outside—the open door only revealed a black void. The helicopter crossed an imaginary line signifying the borders between the two countries, banking back and forth, as it followed the terrain contours until they reached their destination.

Crammed into an oscillating interior caused him to feel helpless. At any second, the pilots wearing night vision gear could make a mistake and crash into a hill. Russian mechanics maintained all the aircraft's systems, and it still creaked and dripped hydraulic fluid. To add to his discomfort, his new men removed paper bags, similar to what passengers find on a commercial aircraft to vomit.

After a four-hour flight, the Hip went into a hover, hesitated, then settled to the ground. Ali and his men pulled out the crates within thirty seconds, allowing the helicopter to ascend back into the black void. Three additional Quds agents, who drove the vehicles to the location, helped load the crates into the back of a truck and soon this caravan proceeded south to *al-Hasakah*, a small Syrian city in the northwestern province. His mission was to meet with a former Iraqi general, relieved of command by the Americans when Saddam fell from power, now head of ISIS Special Forces brigade, the new Caliphate Army that will soon retake Iraq and Syria.

Chapter 11

THE RAPE

Brent found Amber's recovery to be slow and withdrawn. After a few days, the swelling around her eyes had reduced, replaced by a spectrum of purple. When he came home in the mornings, she would prepare breakfast, but only pushed her food around her plate. Normal conversation felt stifled, like the first time they met. It was as if the flame of her candle had been snuffed out. When he awoke one night from sleeping, he found her sitting in a chair in the living room, legs curled underneath with her face buried into a pillow. He went to her to rest his hands upon her shoulder. "It's okay," but the moment his hand touched her, she flinched. He kept the personal contact. "It's okay," he said again. Eventually she nuzzled her face into his chest and began to sob. When he knew all her tears were gone, he asked, "Let me take you to see a doctor?"

She leaned over and kissed the tip of his nose. "They will want to run tests. They'll know I've been raped by the bruising and tears inside me. The doctors will want to run an exam and the police will be called. They'll know I'm a hooker." She emphasized the last statement with disgust. "I can't handle being judged."

"You have legal rights along with everyone else. There are counselors who specialize in helping women get through this. I'm certainly not an expert. I can fix what's on the outside, but you need to see a professional for what they did to you." Brent was beyond worried - he had never realized the meaning of helpless until now. With Amber to focus on, he had been able to push aside the usual feelings of guilt from the missions he flew. For once, he had physical access to help someone who was hurting, but he could do nothing to touch the amount of pain trapped inside her.

"You don't understand. It will start a chain reaction. They will link us to both Vlad and Sadegh. Right now, they know nothing about you. As soon as the police get involved, they will tell Vlad and he will hunt you down and kill you. He has connections everywhere—including the police department. One of our clients is a senior detective with the Metro police department. His name is Edwards. He's a disgusting man."

Brent thought back to his brief visit at the downtown police station. The card with the agent's name sat atop his nightstand. "There is something I need to tell you. The police picked me up several days ago. One of Sadegh's goons followed me from the base into the city. Being an American, I thought I had more rights than a foreign diplomat. Instead, they took me in and I met with a Special Agent for diplomatic relations. He was actually cool, but the person investigating the assault—it was this detective you mentioned. He tried to link me with Sadegh. They showed pictures of you walking out with him and the two of us sitting together at the Blackjack table. Thankfully, my driver's license still has an old address. They think I live on the base where I work. As far as I know, no one, except military personnel knows where I live. I sublease this place from another flyer who's at the Pentagon. Doing what I do, I try to stay off the grid."

"Vlad will find you. He is not easily threatened. Both of our lives are in danger until he is dead." The last word she almost spit. "His links within the Russian mafia span every major city. I'm sure he is searching for me right now. He will want me back, spreading my legs for million dollar clients. Until this all happened, I was his top girl. Clients paid thousands to sleep with me."

"Then why did he do this to you?" He lightly touched the bruising on her face. Her internal injuries caused him the most concern.

"He used me to set an example for the other girls. We do as we are told, or else." She bit her bottom lip, holding back tears.

Brent felt her stiffen and shiver. He sensed her reliving a memory. He held her close until the memory passed. "Do you want to tell me what happened?"

She hesitated. "Please don't judge me for what I'm about to say. Vlad owns a big brick building on the outskirts of the city. His office is on the second floor with a row of plush sex rooms he uses to throw parties for his friends. The lower level is where he makes his pornographic films. We call it the torture chamber. The room next door is the library. If a girl is disobeying, he'll make a video of her being raped by a big giant and have us watch it—his enforcers do the training while Vlad holds the camera. The man who tried to kiss me, who you knocked out, is one of them."

Brent thought back to his conversation after pulling himself from the dumpster. Vlad had threatened to film Amber.

"They drugged me so I wouldn't fight back and Vlad allowed him to do whatever he wanted." She went into detail describing how they assaulted her body. At times, she paused to catch her breath, eventually getting through what happened.

As she told her story, Brent could feel his anger increasing. It took all he could to sit and listen. He knew getting her story out became her therapy, but it also felt like a spike rammed through his inside. The anger spinning up inside actually scared him. He'd felt anger before, but nothing could touch this. His need to protect Amber was the most intense emotion he had felt about another person in a long time. Too long to remember.

"If I do not come back to work, he will sell this film to one of the internet porn sites. He threatens to send a copy to our parents. My mother does not know what I do."

Her demeanor seemed to change for the better after their talk, but Brent already made a decision on what he needed to do. Toward evening, he gave an excuse of needing to be at the base early and left his townhouse wearing black jeans and a matching tee shirt, packing a flight suit for later. He backed the Z out of the garage and took side roads to the warehouse district of the city.

He replayed the story Amber had told about her ordeal. Everything about it was beyond comprehension. He had seen the bruising on her body when she showered. They effectively had snuffed out her flame. What Vlad did to these girls needed to be stopped.

Finding the warehouse, he parked his Z a block away on a side street and walked back to toward the building. The front entrance had a metal door with a close-circuit camera tucked up in the corner eve watching the entryway and all the lower windows held bars across the front to prevent access. He went around to the alley and found a steel door to a back entrance.

Noticing no cars parked around the building, Brent knocked on this door and waited to see if anyone would answer. An upper window had a rod iron fire escape with a pull down ladder, but it was well above his jumping distance. Taking several large garbage cans, he stacked them making a pyramid, and climbed high enough to make a leap for the lower ladder rung. His hands caught hold of the cold metal, allowing him to pull himself onto the steel grate bolted outside a sliding window.

Peering through the glass, the room appeared to be empty. It had a large king size bed next to the window and various bean bag type cushions situated on the floor, along with a sink and mirror for the patron to clean up afterwards. The door into the room was closed, keeping his entry silent.

Brent used his elbow and broke the window around the latch, reached inside to pull open the window.

At the door, he opened it enough to listen for any activity. A hallway ran through the middle with seven doors, three on each side, lining the corridor. Brent went down the hallway and peered inside the rooms—each having a similar layout. The last door located across from a stairwell had a glass panel that allowed him to see an office interior. He tried turning the doorknob, but it didn't move. Peering through the glass, a large oak desk sat in the middle with vertical filing cabinets positioned on either side of a picture frame window that overlooked the front entrance.

Brent went down the stairs to the lower level, finding a similar layout of doorways. One room was definitely the filming studio where they shot porn movies. A four-post queen size bed sat stationed against a far wall. Each post held leather straps to restrain whoever laid on the bed. A lighting system, similar to what a grip would use on a movie set, stood on stands at each corner of the room. A camera hung on tracks atop the ceiling and another sat atop a tripod at the foot of the bed. Brent left this room and went to the one next door. Inside there was a large desk with two large monitors on top, and underneath a computer server cabinet.

Along the far wall, an array of bookshelves held DVD cases. A female's name and date were written along the edge of each case.

He removed a disc from inside, broke it and repeated the process until he found one with Amber's name—this one he tucked into his pocket. When he destroyed the last disc, he focused on the computer. He first searched the room for a utensil to remove the back screws, and once inside he pried apart the hard drive, yanking it free from the attached cables. With it removed, he placed it on the floor and crushed it with his heel until it became a flattened metal pancake.

"Hey, what are you doing?" An accented Russian voice bellowed from behind him. Brent turned and saw a big Russian standing in the doorway—he still had a large contusion from where Brent hit him in Amber's apartment—the same bastard who raped her. He looked around the room at the destruction and glared at Brent. "You are going to pay for this." He flexed powerful arms the size of Brent's leg.

"How's your head?" Brent asked, noticing the purple welt near the ear.

The realization of recognizing Brent dawned on his face. "You're Amber's boyfriend. You hit like a girl." He rubbed the side of his shaven head.

"I get that a lot." Brent maneuvered around the room to keep the Russian from grabbing hold. The man had over sixty pounds on him and could easily throw him around the room if he got his hands on him.

"I'm going to kill you," the Russian said, as he lunged to place Brent into a bear hug.

Each time he was able to slip under the grasp. Brent fainted with a right punch—this brought the Russians hands up—leaving an opening to thrust a kick in-between the legs.

The Russian moved faster than Brent anticipated, causing his foot to glance off center. Brent twisted, utilizing his momentum and threw a left hook that clipped the jawline. It felt solid, but the Russian remained standing.

With most of Brent's weight now on his front foot, the bear charged, hitting him in the chest, knocking him off balance into the desk.

The Russian forced his body on top, pinning Brent against the table. "I'm going to fuck you like I fucked your little girlfriend. She whimpered just like you're going to." Holding Brent off balance with his forearm, he slammed punches into his side and several across his face.

Brent tried his best to fight back. Being pinned backward gave little leverage. A rib snapped from the impact. With the palms of his hands, he boxed his attacker's ears, causing a pause to the beating. This relinquished the pressing hold, allowing Brent to twist from underneath the weight, drop to the floor to regain his center, and grab hold of a leg. Driving his shoulder into the knee, he forced it to the side, causing the joint to buckle. With most of the weight now on the supporting leg, Brent picked the other ankle and drove forward in a wrestler's single-leg takedown, sprawling them both across the floor.

The Russian fell over like a toppled tree. Unfamiliar with the ground game, he rolled onto his stomach in an attempt to stand up.

Brent swung his forearm around the thick neck, locked it with his other around the back of the head and squeezed. The Russian squirmed across the floor, and then rolled onto his back in an attempt to dislodge Brent's hold. This allowed Brent to wrap his legs around the body to stretch it out, forcing more pressure around the neck. Each time the Russian moved, Brent squeezed, cinching his hold tighter.

The Russian clawed at his arm, trying to pry his hands between Brent's arms. He got on his knees and fell backwards, crushing Brent against the floor. Arms began flinging as oxygenated blood depleted from the brain. Each time he struggled, his movement became slower. Foamy spittle fell from the Russian's mouth as he tried to breath, but neither air nor blood passed through the neck.

Brent's arms burned from the constant pressure. Slowly the Russian's strength leaked from his body. When the Russian stopped moving, Brent held his grip another couple of minutes to make sure he would never get up.

Brent slithered from underneath the hefty bulk and crawled across the room away from the dead body, each time he moved he pressed a hand against his ribs to keep the burning fire abated. His breathing became spasmodic during each wave. Propping his back against the door, he surveyed the area. It looked like a tornado had landed in the middle of the room. The two monitors that were once on the table now had spidery cracks across the screens. Broken DVD cases lay scattered across the floor.

Brent took note of the time—he had already been in this building too long. Making sure he left nothing behind, he left the building through the back entrance. If he hurried, he would barely make his check in for the evening mission. When he sat in the seat of his car, he felt the DVD case still tucked in his pants. When he got home, it would be a present to Amber, so she could start a new life.

Part III

Third Week

Where have all the missiles gone?
AP
12:00 AM ET, October 22, 2011

Washington, DC. (AP) – Alarms are clanging within the intelligence community. U.S. officials and security experts are concerned about thousands of heat-seeking surface to air missiles once held by Gaddafi's military. Before the civil war began, Libya had 20,000-man portable surface-to-air missiles. Each missile, four- to six-feet in length and Russian-made, weighs as little as 55 pounds. They lock onto the heat from aircraft engines and are deadly at a range of more than two miles. With sections of the country now controlled by the Free Libyan Army, who has control of these missiles and where did they all go?

Chapter 12

ODA TEAM

Forward Operating Base Geronimo
The village of Faysh Khabur, Iraq - two miles
from the Syrian border

Captain Jeremy Zender, the team leader, stood in front of a large map taped on the wall. Zender, 32, had a frame to be a football tight end, tall and muscular. The stench of body odor from the men in front of him and a metallic smell of blood that dotted the floor added a unique aroma to the room. Adding to the flavor, smoke of burning goat dung drifted in through an open nearby window. Cracks zigzagged down each wall from the perforation of multiple bullet holes during a previous firefight. With it raining outside, the two buckets stationed within the room produced a steady -kerplunk- as droplets fell from the ceiling.

This room had a few stories. While he waited for his men to quiet down, his thoughts drifted to the young boy who had taken a gunshot to the neck causing an arterial nick—he bled out in ninety seconds while his 18D medic frantically tried to clamp it shut. The humidity still kept the blood splatters from completely drying out.

The team sergeant and operations NCO, Sergeant First Class Jose Perez, stood off to the side. Perez, 38, was built like an offensive lineman, thick and powerful, with a dark complexion, full black beard and a black Afghan *Pakol* hat pulled down to hide a shaved head. Wearing a sleeveless shirt, his *Norteño* gang tattoos scrawled down both arms. When wearing an ISIS black uniform, he easily passed as a Taliban from neighboring Afghanistan. He volunteered for the Army right out of high school to hone his shooting skills with the anticipation of going back to the hood, tried out and made it through Special Forces selection— gang life became a distant past, these men in the room were his new brothers. He glared around the room to make sure everybody listened and were ready for the night insertion mission. The one person who appeared to be sleeping he left alone. "Captain Zender, the team is ready."

It was time to get focused on their next mission. Zender stood behind a makeshift podium made from a stack of ammunition boxes. "Tonight's mission will be a night helicopter insertion into the middle of bad-guy country. We are to find and hopefully kill a top ISIS commander, his name is General al-Obeidi." He held up a picture of an Iraqi general shaking Saddam Hussein's hand. "He was once one of Saddam's top lieutenants before we came in and banished all the generals. He's now turned his skills to commanding ISIS." Along the wall behind him was an array of landscape photographs taken from a high altitude reconnaissance aircraft. A piece of tape connected the photos in a series, providing a detailed depiction of their operating area. He tapped a precise spot. "This will be our infill point and we'll hike along the Turkish border before dropping down into Syria. A UAV has been watching the route over the past forty-eight hours seeing only a young boy herding sheep. We need to be on the lookout for him."

Of the eleven men, four rested on wooden pallets that hadn't broken apart from their latest C-130 delivery, five sat on foldup lawn chairs purchased from Walmart before they left the states, and another sat alone on the floor in the far corner of the room with his eyes closed—meditating.

Zender's men were members of Special Forces ODA, Operational Detachment 562, team Alfa. Their uniform ensemble consisted of a black tunic over faded Russian military cargo pants. Several wore a black-and-white checked tribal scarf known as the *keffiyeh* around their necks obtained from a nearby village as a gift for fixing the central fresh-water well pump. Except for their solid American-made Danner boots and an automatic rifle that was always within close grasp, everything else was foreign made and obtained from the local region. From a distance, they wanted their appearance to blend in as another foreign Islamic fighter who came to kill Americans. Except these men were professional killers—trained to hunt and kill the very men they attempted to impersonate.

"Sir, we've received confirmation back," reported Technical Sergeant Samuel "Pepper" Jackson, an Air Force JTAC - Joint Terminal Attack Controller - "that a Reaper will have eyes on us most of the way. There will be a window when we'll have no overhead coverage." He looked at a sheet of paper. "Our Reaper's call sign will be Hunter zero-six."

"Will it have any ordinance loaded?" Zender asked, knowing that whatever it carried would be limited.

"It's scheduled to have four Hellfire missiles. I've also requested some XCAS to be on standby—a pair of Navy F/A-18s Hornets in case this mission gets ugly. With my ROVER's datalink connection between the Hornets and Reaper, we will have a bird's eye view of our position along our route and after we settle at our hide site."

While they were talking, someone outside the door began knocking. Zender stopped and motioned for Perez to see who had the guts to interrupt his isolation briefing.

Perez unlocked and cracked the door open, keeping his right hand resting on the hilt of a 9mm pistol.

A sheet of paper appeared through the opening, which Perez took and handed to Zender.

Zender read the message several times, making sure he understood its exact meaning. His responsibility rested on their mission's success and his team's lives. "It says our mission is a Go. Everybody will be suited up and ready on the flight line by twenty-one hundred hours, liftoff is at twenty-two. I expect the helicopter ride to our infill point to take just over two hours. Once on the ground, we have six hours to reach our observation point before sunrise. This leaves sixty minutes to handle anything unexpected ... not a whole lot of time." Moving his pointer across pictures that showed a mountain ridgeline, he said, "From this swayback, we'll follow an old silk trail straight to our objective village. This spot here," he again tapped the wall, "is where we'll establish an OP and wait for this General al-Obeidi to arrive. The sooner Tilley can put a bullet in his head, the sooner we can get back home. Are there any questions?" He made eye contact with every man in the room. "Perfect ... Perez, over to you."

Perez stepped into the middle of the room. "Nobody must know we are here. This is a black op. Shoot only when necessary if seen. Keep all weapons silenced. Tilley, you'll be point and I'll navigate right behind you." He made eye contact with each man in the room, each gave a thumb's up acknowledgement except one. "Hey Tilley, give me a signal that you've heard me."

Sergeant "Tilley" Tilleman sat alone in the corner. Every element of his body remained motionless. At times he would sit for hours without moving, making his teammates wonder if he was even alive. Admired and feared by those who didn't know him, as the team's sniper, he had the most kills of the entire group combined. When and if the time came, his teammates had made a blood agreement with him... to make sure none of these men were ever captured alive. Tilley looked up and gave a head nod, and went back to his solace in silence.

Perez continued. "We've got a great trail to follow. J2 has reported no activity in this sector at night, but lots of activity during the day. This means we need to be off the trail by zero-four hundred and established in our hide-site before the rise of daylight. Keep your eyes open for any potential IEDs. Let's not assume anything. Pack extra water and ammo in case this mission goes haywire and we need to extend our stay a couple of days. Our first rally point will be our infill point where the helicopter drops us off. If you have any questions or concerns, express them now." He waited three seconds and hearing none, he continued. "Boss, you have any last comments?"

Zender looked around the room. "The general guidance for this mission is to degrade the ISIS network. The specified task of this mission is to kill a new commander who has taken power within this sector. Our secondary mission is to film any al-Qaeda or ISIS leaders who show their face. We've already completed several of these types of missions, but this one has the potential to get ugly early. al-Obeidi is known to be especially brutal. He has a network of informants and a history of chopping heads off. We are going to sneak in, kill this fucker, and sneak out before anyone realizes what happened. Everybody get some rest before we head out tonight—I need you alert and on top of your game. As Perez said, plan to take extra ammo, grenades and water, in case we encounter a sizeable force. Unless there is anything else, I'll see you guys at twenty-one hundred."

***

At 2130, a cold wind blew across the flight line from the west. The high overcast spread a midnight black canvas across the heavens. The men hunkered over from the weight of an eighty-pound rucksack strapped to their backs and a bulging assault vest that held a combat load of ammo, water and food to last a week. Ten of the men carried the 5.56 Colt M4 rifle with a quick attachable silencer, and two had the heavier 7.62 Mk 17 SCAR, Special Operations Combat Assault Rifle. Together, they moved as one mass toward the awaiting helicopter.

A maintenance crew chief finished the preflight inspection on the MH-60L Direct Action Penetrator helicopter, a modified Black Hawk for special operation missions. An electrical cart hummed alongside, powering internal systems, causing the cockpit instruments to glow a faint green. Both side doors were open and a red glow from an overhead light illuminated the back crew compartment.

Zender stood by the helicopter's door and counted each person who passed. Perez brought up the rear and gave a thumb's up indicating he was the last. Zender climbed in and gave the crew chief a pat. "Everybody is on board."

The turbine engines fired up and within five minutes, the helicopter lifted off. As the aircraft ascended above twenty feet, all external lights switched off, making it a void of space in a pitch-black night. Total flight time to destination would be an hour and twenty minutes, with a couple of false insertion stops along the way prolonging the ride.

At 0115, the helicopter went into a hover over the only flat area the pilots could find, halfway up a mountainside, two hundred meters from their infill point. Zender jumped out the right side, ran to a spot outside of the rotor wash and dove into tall grass. Looking back, he saw his last man exit before disappearing into darkness. With everyone fanned out in a perimeter defense, the helicopter arose back into the blackness leaving only a sonic thump in its wake. He raised his head above the swaying grass, flipped down the night vision monocle and scanned the area, watching—waiting to see if anyone took notice of a team of Americans in their backyard. With the clattering helicopter gone, he removed his earplugs and inserted an earbud with a lip microphone connected to a small Motorola encrypted radio.

Mist enveloped his face as he exhaled into the frosty night air. His teeth chattered either from the cold ground sapping his core temperature or from the adrenaline of a night insertion. Flexing his leg muscles helped his uneasiness. He swung his rifle in the direction where several dogs were heard barking. They too soon quieted down, allowing the stillness of the night to descend upon the team.

Zender pressed his radio transmit button once, followed by three quick bursts—the signal to move out.

Looking through his monocle, changing one side of his field of view to monochromatic daylight, his men rose from their prone position as ghosts arise from a grave, keeping audible sound and sudden movement to a minimum. After counting eleven glowing specks, Zender pressed himself upward, trying not to stumble while balancing the additional weight he carried, and moved into his expected position in the middle of his men.

He could see the ghost of Tilley take point with Perez five meters back. The two men waited along the trail's edge for everyone else to fall in. Tilley fired a quick laser flash outward along the trail, indicating they were ready. Perez carried a SCAR, with a suppressed 9mm accessible in a holster strapped across his chest and Tilley held a lighter weight suppressed MP4 9mm rifle; his sniper rifle he kept tightly wrapped and secured along the side of his rucksack.

Through his night-vision monocle, Zender saw the flick of light. "Let's move," he transmitted.

In orchestrated unison, the men moved as one. Off in the distance another dog barked, but soon faded away. Only nocturnal insects and the occasional scurrying animal broke the solitude of the night.

***

Brent checked in at the front counter, grabbed a cola and proceeded down the hall to the briefing room. From behind him he heard, "You're late." When he looked to see who made the comment, he recognized his DO coming toward him.

"What happened to you?" While looking at his face.

Brent tried to not show any discomfort, though his ribs felt on fire. "I fell against a desk. I'm alright."

"You look like hell! Go get briefed and go to Box 1. We are currently monitoring an SF team in Syria. If you can't handle it, let me know and I'll find someone else." As Brent proceeded to leave, he heard, "Hit the restroom before you start and wash the blood off your face. Looks like that desk got the better end of the fight."

Inside the restroom, he looked at himself in the mirror. A cut along his cheek still oozed blood highlighted by the first stages of purple swelling. He squeezed the skin together, using tape to keep it closed. From a side medicine cabinet, he took several packets of painkillers and chewed the pills inside, washing the sour taste away with the cola.

After getting the information he needed to fly the mission, he stepped into Box 1. He let his eyes adjust to the darkness before proceeding to pilot's chair.

The other pilot got up for Brent to take the seat. In the darkness, he didn't notice Brent's face. "We've been following a SF team all day, their night. They have about two hours left before daybreak. So far, it's been a nonevent. See you in about twelve hours."

Brent kept the Reaper in a slow orbit. If the team needed him, they would call over the Reaper's radio, otherwise, this mission required radio silence. The only sound came from the hum of the air-conditioning system within the room. The thermal image showed a group of twelve men snaking their way along a trail, the head and tail switching back and forth while they marched along the face of a mountain.

At 0430 hours in Syria, from thirty thousand feet, Brent could see the first glow of morning beginning to illuminate the sky. He also found a herd of goats in the middle of their trail. Flipping the camera over to thermal imaging, he searched the surrounding area, finding a single heat source lying prone between two large boulders.

***

Pepper finished his radio transmission while standing next to Zender. "Hunter just reported a lone figure between two boulders just ahead up on the hill. It appears to be lying down—not moving—more than likely asleep. My guess is it's a sheepherder. If we move through the goats, they are going to make noise. Then we'll have a problem if that person wakes up."

Zender held his suppressed rifle out in front of him, pointing the IR beam like a flashlight. The early morning sky provided a hint of ambient light for his monocular to amplify. He worked his way across several boulders, keeping the goats to his right. Stepping around a large boulder, Zender kicked something soft. Whatever his boot met gave a low grunt.

It appeared human—short and starting to move. A boy cried out speaking a dialect that Zender didn't understand.

Zender pounced, slamming his body onto the prone figure, scrambling around until he found a head and slapping his gloved hand over the boy's mouth. Whispering in Arabic, he said, " نه چلیہرم ... Do not move or say anything, everything will be all right." He turned the body over and secured both wrists with zip ties. With the body trussed up, he rolled it over and shined a flashlight onto the face.

A frightened face stared wildly up into his red flashlight beam. He tried to squirm from Zender's hold

Zender pressed his internal radio button. "Shepherd secured. I'm at ...," providing a GPS reading on his location. He worked his way back to the trail carrying the boy under his arm as if he was a hundred pound sack of cement. "Look what I found. What shall do we do with him?"

Perez knelt down to look in the young boy's face. "Nobody is to know we are here. Right now, he has no idea who we are. I doubt he understands English. We can't take him with us or slit his throat. A third option is to leave two men behind to babysit. They can also guard our rear in case we need a quick extraction or someone decides to sneak in behind us."

"I don't like the thought of thinning our team, but I agree. Pick two to stay." Gauging the amount of light coming over the horizon caused him concern. "Time is burning. We need to go."

***

Dawn began to shine on the village at the same time the team finished laying out camouflage netting to conceal their position and shield them from the day's sun. They divided into groups of two, spreading out in a half circle. Each pair pulled netting over the top of them and poked their rifles out through holes.

The soldier Brent guessed was the JTAC, shined an IR laser into the sky, catching his attention. The radio announced, "Our mission timeline shortened up considerably. As you pointed out, we're babysitting a young boy. We'll watch the objective for one day and schedule an early pick-up the next evening. What's your playtime and just confirming what you have to play with?"

"My playtime is at six hours with four Mavericks loaded. Standby while I take a look several klicks from your location." Fanning outward in a circular motion, Brent scanned the area around the team's location looking for anything that might cause them trouble. Seeing nothing, he moved the camera along the road away from the village. Twenty miles out, three vehicles entered the edge of his video screen. The middle vehicle, a sport utility type, was sandwiched between two trucks. The convoy moved fast, throwing a trail of dust behind them as they worked their way along a dry riverbed. "You have a convoy approaching in twenty minutes." Brent maneuvered the Reaper overhead to get a better sight vantage, zooming in for a closer view. Four men sat in the back of the first truck holding rifles, and another pointed a long tubular RPG over the cab. In the back of the last truck, several men held onto a tarp that covered large rectangular boxes. He banked the aircraft further to the south to see if he could count the number of occupants inside, but from his vantage point and altitude, no way of knowing.

Brent pressed the radio transmit button. "You have three vehicles approaching from your right. Men riding in back have automatic rifles. In the trailing truck, there's something underneath a tarp—I'm estimating eleven men coming into town. ETA now is in fifteen minutes."

***

Pepper crawled over to Zender. "Hunter is reporting three vehicles approaching—two trucks and a SUV, coming up the ravine from the south."

Zender's earbuds again crackled with three clicks followed by one click. "It sounds like Tilley sees something. I'm going to check what he wants."

He crawled over to where Tilley lay. When he arrived, Tilley leaned away from his spotting scope to allow Zender to look. Down in the village, a group of men - at least twenty - were congregating in a courtyard. "This is not looking good. Several dozen ISIS soldiers just came out of nearby houses. They have AK-47 automatic rifles and they're wearing loaded assault vests. These are not your local villagers!"

Over the buzzing flies, the sound of car engines escalated in pitch. Zender swung the scope over where the sound came from. Seeing an approaching dust cloud, he said, "Here come the vehicles Pepper reported." He slid back so Tilley could continue his observation. "Take as many pictures as you can of anyone who looks important. One of them should be our HVT." He paused before he said, "I do not like this—it's too obvious, too quiet. The way they're standing out in the open carefree, there's something I'm not seeing."

"Whatever it is, we're about to find out. I think our general just came out of a house," Tilley whispered. "He's wearing an IOTV—probably killed an American soldier for it. My bullet should penetrate it, but to be on the safe side I'll aim for a head shot."

"Is there any other activity in the village?"

"Just the same group standing around. There could be more—no way of knowing."

The convoy of vehicles drove into the village—the first truck rolled a few yards past, allowing the SUV to pull alongside the greeting party. Men in the front and rear vehicles jumped out of their trucks and fanned out in a defensive perimeter, all wearing traditional ISIS black clothing. Three men, one from each truck, got out wearing camouflage pants with an assault vest over dark colored shirts. Their persona fit the profile of Black Water mercenaries, but from a different country and company. Instead of carrying AK-47s that the regular ISIS soldier used, they held more modern assault rifles.

"What do we have here? These guys are not our usual ISIS players," Zender whispered. "It looks like one of them has a FN assault rifle—nice. Hold your shot until we know more about what we're dealing with. Let's get a photo confirmation from J2 on who we're seeing before this place becomes a gunfight at the O.K. Corral." With the camera attached to the satellite radio, an intelligence analyst back at headquarters would soon compare the pictures to known terrorist operatives.

"Let me know as soon as you hear from J2 on who these guys are. I'm going to head back to let the team know it's game time."

Back at his makeshift command post, Zender found Pepper peering through the SOFLAM laser scope. Pepper said, "I have sent the target coordinates to the Reaper. We're now waiting on final clearance to strike."

Not liking what he was seeing, Zender continued to watch the village. "Something's amiss. It's too obvious. I'm not sure what— maybe the lack of security. They're standing out in the open without a care in the world. Way too obvious."

Pepper looked up from his scope. "What do you want to do?"

"Make a call to get those hornets overhead." He felt a raindrop splatter atop his hat. Looking up, a dark overcast covered the landscape. "I'd like to wait to smoke this target until those fighters are here. As soon as we make ourselves known, we'll have jammed a stick into a hornet's nest. I have a feeling it will cause a swarm ... a lot more than we anticipated."

Pepper switched his radio to broadcast on the aviation frequency. "Playboy Two-Five with an immediate," he whispered into the radio.

Chapter 13

CHANGE OF MISSION

Stepping out of the vehicle, Ali took a deep breath of fresh air. The man who sat next to him during the previous three hours smelled as if he had slept with his goats. Combined with a lack of ventilation, the interior stunk of a latrine mixed with a male goat in season—sourly pungent. He thought about placing a bullet in this foul smelling piece of humanity and dump the body for the vermin to eat, but he needed this elder alive long enough to facilitate this meeting. While waiting for the introductions to be made, Ali watched the new ISIS general standing pompously in the courtyard while talking animatedly with his soldiers, the same general who fought the Americans at Ramadi in Iraq before Saddam Hussein died, then disappeared to reemerge as a formidable ISIS commander. Given all the spies lurking everywhere, this general only met with people he had known for some time—hence why Ali needed to put up with his smelly riding companion.

Seeing the number of ISIS soldiers carrying automatic weapons, his elder companion began to fidget. He leaned over to say, "I have fulfilled my end of our agreement. Call the bank and have the money transferred that you owe me."

Ali tried his best to hold back from crushing the man's esophagus to stifle any further blather. Without looking, he said, "You will be paid after you introduce me to General al-Obeidi." He glared at his companion. "Your will receive *no more and no less*, and nothing if this meeting does not go well." He hefted his FN rifle from the interior and slung it over his shoulder, ready to fire if this meeting went down wrong. Already, he didn't like how exposed they were with only a handful of men providing security.

When the general's soldiers saw Ali remove his rifle from the vehicle, they aimed their weapons at him and at his three other Quds agents. The general waited in the courtyard to see how Ali would respond. Ali took the initiative by giving no indication of his situation, held his weapon, and proceeded to where the general stood.

Relieved to be finally out of the vehicle, he allowed the elder to make the appropriate introductions. He began by saying, "*As-salamu Alaykum*, General al-Obeidi. May I introduce you to an agent of the Iranian government, he goes by the name of Ali."

Ali stood off to the side, watching for any change in demeanor. Only two of his lieutenants monitored the introductions, their fingers resting on rifle triggers. Out of respect for their leader, the remainder of men faced away, watching for any threats. Ali took a step forward and bowed.

General al-Obeidi wore the standard all-black uniform with three gold stars adorning his lapel. Protecting his chest, he also wore an Improved Outer Tactical Vest, Ali guessed were compliments of a deceased U.S. Army soldier. Strapped to his leg, a matching tactical holster held a Beretta 9mm semi-automatic pistol. The dossier indicated him to be both cautious and reclusive, two behaviors mandatory in this obscure mountainous region. Iranian intelligence had internal networks with the Taliban and al-Qaeda, and recently infiltrated the Iraqi National Intelligence Service. With the growing formidable strength of ISIS and the atrocities already committed, Ali knew to be cautious. This former Iraqi general was known to flay the skin off people he did not like.

"It is an honor to meet you," Ali said, bowing and placing his hand over his heart. The two men locked eyes.

al-Obeidi nodded a response to the greeting. "What interest does Iran have to our part of the world?"

"I have come to congratulate you on your new leadership position. My country is very interested in what happens with our neighbors. We are here to help and support whatever you require—unlike the infidel Americans and the Russians who take what they want."

"Don't patronize me. There's a strategic reason why you are here. Is it because we are growing in strength and now a recognized force to your Islamic law?"

"It's simple. Your enemy is our enemy. *Nothing more, nothing less.*"

"What makes you think you can help us? The Americans ran away from my country, leaving us to take all the weapons we need. Now they hide behind their jets versus facing us to fight. All you have to offer is old Soviet rifles ...," spitting onto the ground. "Give me a weapon to kill their aircraft. Then they will either leave or send real men to fight."

"In the back of the truck, I have brought you a gift from Allah, the very weapon you seek." Ali looked around and gestured at their openness. "Before we begin, might it be prudent to go inside. You never know who may be watching, especially the Americans." He glanced at the few men providing security before looking up into the mountains. "Your security is less than I had hoped, for a general of your status and reputation."

al-Obeidi frowned. "Your statement is bold for an Iranian. So little you do not understand. I control everything and have spies everywhere. The men you see are only a fraction at my disposal. They arrived in intervals over the past week, not to attract any suspicion to our meeting. If someone is watching, my men are unseen and if an enemy is watching, I will be told."

"I commend you on your wisdom and foresight," Ali said, though their face-to-face greeting confirmed his dislike for this man's arrogance. Being exposed outside made him uncomfortable. Representing the country of Iran, his clothes were not of local origin, causing him to stand out from the ISIS soldiers. He had survived over the years by blending into his surroundings and the local populace.

al-Obeidi took control. "Since I sense you are still uncomfortable, we shall go inside. I am curious as to your gift. You are probably thirsty after your long journey."

Ali again took a long look at the surrounding mountainside. Something felt out of balance. The same sensation right before the Americans attacked in Yemen and later in Libya. His ears sensed a slight vibration in the air, making him wonder if a UAV was watching. Prior to entering the house, he signaled over his three men. "Bring in only one crate. I do not trust al-Obeidi. Something is not as it seems about this place. Be ready to move out at a moment's notice."

***

Brent held the Reaper in a circular orbit to the northwest of the village, descending to sixteen thousand feet to stay below the developing overcast. At this lower altitude, the turbine engine consumed more fuel and the sound it made produced a faint sonic vibration. He zoomed to medium optical power, displaying a five hundred meter radius around the center point of the target. The internal laser bounced energy off the roof, ready to launch a Hellfire missile. The only thing remaining was to press the launch button.

Two of the men wearing casual clothes, who arrived in the convoy, climbed into the back of the third truck. They untied straps and pulled a tarp off, revealing four oblong wooden crates.

He zoomed in and tapped the joystick over, focusing the reticle onto the truck bed. "I don't believe it!" Brent said into the quiet room, recognizing the size and shape of three familiar crates. He picked up the phone pressing speed dial.

"CENTCOM J2 section," Brent heard over the phone.

"This is Lieutenant Parker from Creech, controlling Hunter zero-six over Syria. You might want to look at the video feed from a Reaper overhead a Special Forces operation in the northeast sector. I have eyes on the missing SA-24s taken from Libya."

"I'm not sure I know what you're talking about. Even if I did, what you said is highly classified—"

"Listen, I'm the one who reported them missing in the first place." He couldn't believe the incompetence of some people. "Tell the president, tell someone we found them!"

Chapter 14

HORNET'S NEST

Following custom, the villagers removed their shoes inside the door. The general kept his boots on, so Ali did the same—if they came under attack, he wanted to be able to move quickly. Walking into an open room, he did not like the idea of being packed inside a clay wall structure—an easy and concentrated target. Ali followed the general through the interior, past a small fireplace that belched smoke into a ceiling chimney, and went down a hallway to a small bedroom. In the middle of the room, a rug had been pulled back, revealing an open hatch in the floor.

"As I said, not all as it seems. I am also certain we were being watched. They saw us go into a house and not leave. When they strike, I will know where they are. Fresh American meat is very tasty."

Ali followed the general down a wooden ladder and walked underground for another fifty meters before climbing up a similar ladder. The labored breathing and stench from his companion made this tunnel feel claustrophobic. Back above ground, the new house was cold with no internal heat, giving no indication people were inside.

While he observed the layout, the house-host scurried about. "Please ... please make yourself comfortable and have a seat. I have hot tea prepared to warm you."

The men in the room waited until al-Obeidi sat. Ali waited a moment longer before he sought his placement. He trusted no one, except for his Quds agent standing by the door across the room. As customary, his riding companion sat next to the general. Ali sat across the rug, his back against a wall.

al-Obeidi clapped his hands together to get everybody's attention. "Now that we are away from any prying eyes, what brings an Iranian agent to see me?"

"I brought you a gift ... a weapon that will defeat al-Assad and initiate total Islamic theocracy," Ali said.

"There is nothing your country has that I want ... unless you're bringing me one of your nuclear weapons. I already have automatic rifles, money and power, without your government meddling in our affairs."

Ali kept his anger in check. If he said anything sarcastic, he might lose his head. "The American people are weak. They will only send aircraft and supply weapons. Once you show the world how formidable ISIS really is, only then will they send soldiers. That is when you will have your caliphate. I bring a missile that can shoot down these aircraft. Blind the eyes of a snake, it can no longer see to strike. Without American airpower, as the Russians discovered in Afghanistan, their army will be isolated and alone. You will be able to strike at will. Kill all of them. This weapon will make you a legend within the Islamic world, more famous than Awad bin Laden, who only brought down four planes against America—you have a chance to bring down many."

"I am intrigued. Show me now what you have brought. Then I will decide if you live or die today."

"My men are outside—they should be in any moment."

While they waited, a young boy brought in an aromatic steaming pot of jasmine-spiced tea. The boy placed the teapot in the middle of the rug on a short table and poured the amber liquid into each cup.

Ali's men soon came into the room carrying each end of a wooden crate. The sides had Cyrillic lettering stamped on the outside. al-Obeidi must have comprehended the contents inside the crate, for a slight smile spread across his lips. "Open the box—show me what is inside."

Ali pried open the lid and lifted a two-meter tubular weapon. "This is a 9K338 Ingla-S anti-aircraft missile—a SA-24 known to the outside world. It is a substantial improvement over the American-made Stinger that defeated the Russians. It has a longer range, more sensitive seeker, improved resistance to countermeasures and a heavier warhead."

Emulating a child who had received an enormous birthday present, al-Obeidi wiped his mouth and clapped his hands together.

Ali gave a brief demonstration on how the weapon worked. "Be warned, you do not want to arm the missile until ready to fire. Once the battery is energized, dependent on the age and how it was stored, the missile operator will have between two and ten minutes to fire. After the battery expires, the operator will have a worthless souvenir in his hands."

The men in the room intently watched Ali place the tube back into its coffin as if it was a religious artifact once held by Allah. al-Obeidi broke the silence by again clapping his hands together. A big smile spread across his face. "This missile will change how we fight this war—it will change the future of the world. How many of these do you have, how many did you bring?"

"I brought four crates. Each holds four missiles—sixteen total. I have more, but I need your assurance that you will keep them within your control."

"Ah, again you question what you do not know. Not to worry, you have brought me a powerful gift. It is ironic," he chuckled, "the Americans were in a cold war with the Soviets when they invaded Afghanistan. American agents supplied their missiles, defeating the Soviets. Iranians are now in a cold war with the Americans. It's ironic that you now give us Soviet missiles to defeat the Americans. One day, someone else will come to help us dispose of the Iranians." al-Obeidi laughed at his own absurdity. "History has a tendency to repeat itself."

A cell phone rang in the pocket of a man standing behind al-Obeidi. He answered the call, listened for about thirty seconds and hung up. With the phone call completed, he leaned toward the general's ear and whispered a message.

al-Obeidi stood and again clapped his hands together. "Gentlemen, I have been informed the Americans have found out about our meeting." He stared into Ali's eyes. "As you can see, I have spies everywhere. We have found their soldiers who are watching." As he spoke, rifle shots sounded and several radios came to life. "It appears the Americans are sending two jet fighters. It is time we gave this new weapon of yours a real life test. With Allah's blessing, we will shoot down their aircraft."

Ali tried to listen, but between the staccato of bullets and the sporadic language dialect, he had difficulty understanding what was said over the radios.

He overheard al-Obeidi say, "Five of my men have been shot by an unseen enemy."

"A sniper is making those kills," Ali announced to anybody who cared to listen. "We need to leave ... now!" Ali ushered his men through the house, dragging the crate behind them, finding a backdoor that concealed them between dwellings.

Outside, he looked into the sky, and saw a glint of light and heard a distinct sound.

***

Zender heard muffled shots from where Tilley lay. He also could see over fifty combat ready ISIS soldiers swarming out of houses. "Oh no, it's started." Three more shots sounded from Tilley's direction. His radio crackled, "Boss, we have enemy approaching." It was Tilley.

"I heard shots fired," Zender replied. "How many?"

"Five Tangos were getting inside my comfort zone. The rest are lying low, reevaluating. Several are poking their heads up, standby..." Two more soft reports sounded. "Body count is now at seven in front of me and another half-dozen in the village. So far, they're not sure where the shots are coming from."

Pepper looked up at Zender. "If we are going to kill number five, we better do it now and get the hell out of here."

While Pepper spoke, Zender's satellite phone began ringing. He listened for several minutes. "Affirmative—out."

"What did they want?" Pepper asked.

"HQ has confirmed what's in those crates. They also got a NSA intercept on a cellphone call. We are watching the wrong house, they must've moved underground to another location fifty meters away. We've been ordered to destroy them—no exception. We're on our own. It's our Reaper and us until those fighters get here. Destroy those damn crates so we can get out of here."

Pepper again keyed the radio. "Hunter, you are cleared hot on the house and destroy the truck. Now!"

***

"Cleared hot on the house and truck." Brent repeated back. Human targets scurried throughout the village. To make matters worse, an additional twenty were gathering at the trailhead that led straight toward the Special Forces team. "I have the target and friendlies both in sight. I should have weapon release within sixty seconds." The Reaper currently had its nose pointed away from the house, along with the missile seeker's ability to see the energy. He needed to fly outbound for thirty seconds to get enough wings level time for a clear shot.

"We also have multiple active areas. On my mark, I will fire a two-second laser burst to confirm exact location of your target. PRF code is one-five-six-six. Laser line is one-two-one degrees."

"Ready." Brent typed in the laser's Pulse Repetition Frequency, a sequence of energy emitted from the JTAC's SOFLAM that the Hellfire will seek.

"Ten seconds ..." after ten seconds passed, the JTAC reported, "laser on."

"I have the spot." Brent confirmed the Reaper camera had picked up the pulsating laser energy against the first target. "I have the laser spot. Weapon impact in twenty seconds."

A missile traveling at nine hundred fifty miles an hour slammed into the top of the house. The AGM-114 Hellfire II, designed to penetrate and kill armored fighting vehicles, punched through the thin roof and penetrated the floor by several feet. A millisecond later, twenty pounds of high explosives sent fragmentation and incendiary shrapnel, along with rocks and dirt, ricocheting off nearby walls into an empty room.

***

A fireball shot out through the roof twenty-meters from where he stood, sending a flame up toward the heavens. If anyone remained in the room, after seeing what happened to the Chef, Ali knew they were now an indiscernible mass of charred flesh.

A second explosion sounded in front of the original house, followed by a larger secondary explosion, confirming the UAV had targeted the other crates. Visibility went to zero as dust billowed between the houses, obscuring the chaos of war. Ali motioned to his men to pick up one end of the crate to drag it away from the engagement area toward the far side of the village where there appeared to be an opening for a clear shot. His team used the swirling dust and alleyway between houses to stay concealed, while giving way to a mass of soldiers running towards the chaos. Passing a nearby garage, a rumble from a small tank smashed through a closed door, entered the roadway and began firing its cannon into the opposing hillside.

***

A massive heat signature blossomed from Brent's video camera. A Russian armored BMP emerged from a cloud of dust on the far side of the village. Brent recognized the recoilless rifle mounted on a rotating turret next to the open hatch. Spits of fire the size of softballs flew towards the team's location. The first volley hit fifteen meters in front of their sniper, erupting the hillside into miniature exploding volcanoes.

Not waiting for authorization, once the targeting reticle rested on top of the vehicle, he squeezed the trigger.

It took the missile twenty-three long seconds to travel the distance from the Reaper to the BMP before it smashed midsection. The Hellfire pierced through the vehicle's top like butter. Hot molten metal sprayed throughout the interior shooting a flaming geyser back out the hole. The entire vehicle raised up off its wheels ten feet before crashing back to earth.

Brent heard over the air-to-air frequency the Navy F-18E fighters checking in with the Air Force Boeing 707 AWAKs who controlled the airspace. The waypoint where they announced crossing showed them at 230 miles away—30 minutes of flight time traveling near the speed of sound.

"Get out of there before the fighter's show up, otherwise you'll be fragged." Brent relayed over the radio.

The men on the ground must have sensed the cavalry coming. Over the SatCom radio came, "This is an immediate request for close air support. Target is personnel in the open. Friendlies are danger close."

"The cavalry is coming. A flight of two Navy Hornets have an ETA in thirty minutes."

"We don't have thirty minutes. Our situation has become too hot for us to control these Hornets when they arrive. We're on the move. You will have to play air FAC. Use your last Hellfire to mark for the fighters."

"I have you covered. Good luck," Brent said.

An afternoon overcast enclosed the mountaintops. Small cumulonimbus clouds ascended the steep cliffs, creating pockets of rain showers making visual confirmation difficult. One by one, the team materialized from their hidden observation points. The sniper slid out from underneath his blanket of netting and shrubbery. Within half a minute, they formed up in their standard patrol positions and began to move. The sniper took the lead with the JTAC near a soldier who appeared to be giving orders. The two front men alternated shooting targets as the rest of the team moved close behind as one pulsating centipede.

Several men staggered and fell down, only to be helped up by another. They fought their way halfway up the mountainside along the same previous route they walked before, this time being driven by a group of fifty ISIS soldiers, while another group attempted to circle around in front—like a herd of cattle being led to slaughter. They now were fighting two battlefronts with them pinned in the middle, halting further progress. Smoke trails from RPGs zipped across the ground—showering the team in razor-sharp fragments.

Brent heard two Hornets checking. "Playboy two-five, this is Boomer-ten, flight of two F/A-18s. We each have two GBU-54 laser seeking JDAMS and five hundred rounds of twenty mike-mike. Our playtime is ten minutes. Clouds appear to be obscuring the target area. We'll try to get underneath this overcast for a visual of the target, but we'll be dropping above the overcast."

Brent said, "The enemy is too close for a five-hundred-pounder dropping on GPS coordinates alone."

The JTAC on the ground came on the radio. His breathing labored. "We're dead unless something breaks free." Loud percussive bangs from rifles and nearby explosions pierced through the transmission. "Fire a Hellfire fifty meters due north to mark our location." A pause ensued with automatic gunfire. "Boomer, your target is five hundred meters northeast from the missile impact point. Estimate fifty-plus personnel. Danger close authorization is Juliet Zulu. Hit it with a JDAM."

Chapter 15

DANGER CLOSE

Brent shifted around in his seat. The back of his flight suit was now soaked as he watched the life and death action unfold on the other side of the world. *This is a crazy nightmare.* Another streak flashed across the video screen—showering his team with smoke and rubble. The Reaper now descended to a lower altitude, causing its fuel burn to increase, with only a half hour remaining before the Reaper would need to BINGO back to land. One missile hung underneath the wing to direct the Hornet pilots onto targets close to the team's location.

Brent pressed on the transmit button. "Hunter is orbiting over the top of Playboy at angels minus five. I see them, but not for long—this overcast is making things difficult. I suggest you work your way south toward the valley and shimmy under the overcast. When you're inbound, I'll mark the target area with my last Hellfire."

"We're underneath you skimming the ground. I'll give you a one-minute call followed by a fifteen-second call prior to commencing our run," replied the Hornet lead.

Zooming the camera lens completely out, Brent searched for holes in the clouds for the best vantage to see the team. He turned the Reaper south, let the clock tick off one minute, and turned back toward the team's location.

"Boomer-ten is one minute," he heard over the radio.

Brent watched the clock countdown seconds. After forty-five seconds, the Reaper's laser sent flickering energy at a group of

ISIS. Brent pressed the weapon release button, which sent an electrical charge into the Hellfire's motor. A smoke trail flashed across the outer area of the screen towards the center point of the camera.

***

Lieutenant "Shaky" Shook punched the keyboard on his multifunctional display with his right hand, flying the F/A-18E of Boomer-ten 200 feet above the ground while still flying combat formation a hundred feet aft of his lead. Traveling at 480 knots, 550 miles an hour, underneath a cloud layer and between two canyon walls didn't allow time for sightseeing. The right MFD provided a moving map of the outside terrain. In the center of the display, a circle popped up, indicating the Hellfire's impact point as seen from his lead. He heard his lead report, "Playboy two-five, I've hooked the missile's impact point. Confirm point of impact, where do you want the first bomb?"

The JTAC on the ground responded, "Make the missile impact point the bull's-eye. Put your bombs one hundred meters northeast from bull's-eye. I'll put a laser spot where I want it to impact. Laser line is zero-four-zero degrees," the JTAC reported.

"I'll call one minute out from delivery," came his leads reply over the radio.

Now that they had established the target location, the two pilots pitched their jets up into the vertical to get away from the raising terrain and any small arms fire. Above the overcast, the day brightened with a few mountaintops poking above the cloud layer. Shaky did his best to keep his jet in proper tactical formation, but with all the maneuvering his lead was doing, it made it difficult to ready the MFD for a bomb release.

Shaky hooked the point and toggled over a half kilometer northwest of the impact point. He pressed a button on the edge of the MFD, which designated this as a new target and fed the coordinates into the JDAM's GPS guidance package.

"One minute out," Shaky heard. He advanced the throttles, tapping burner, which sprayed raw jet fuel into the engine hot sections. His lead's bomb came off the jet, then the nose pitched up. Shaky tried to mimic the same move, punching his bomb off before it was within parameters. He felt a kick in his seat when raw jet fuel sprayed into the engine's hot section, igniting the afterburners. The nose of the fighter pitched straight up into the vertical heavens—the jet gave a quick shudder as the weapon punched off the wing.

***

Zender would have liked to have the first bomb hit closer, but dropping bombs on GPS coordinates alone in a danger close fight—one digit off and the situation became detrimental. From his vantage point, the first hit one hundred meters farther down the valley than he wanted. The shockwave knocked the enemy down, but didn't kill them. It did cause the intensity of firing to diminish. Zender yelled, "The shootings stopped—let's move out. Pepper, you go first. If you need to set up your laser for the next run, we'll cover you while you take care of business."

Pepper unplugged the umbilical cord from the SOFLAM laser to the battery pack. He picked up the laser with the attached tripod and started running up the hill, carrying his rifle in his right hand and the laser assembly in his left.

Zender figured they had a couple of minutes before the second fighter sent the next bomb. Off to his left a JDAM penetrated the clouds, its relative motion did not move—a black spot that grew bigger as it closed in. "Get down!" he yelled.

Two hundred and fifty pounds of high-explosive Tritonal detonated, sending zinging metal shards whizzing past his body. A shockwave of a heated pressure knocked him off his feet.

***

Zender wasn't sure how long he had been lying on the ground. His entire body hurt from the inside out. Trying to breathe, only dark phlegm came out his mouth. He pulled up his scarf to cover his mouth, which helped ease the burning inside his lungs. All he wanted to do was lay still, but he needed to move to survive. He forced his knees underneath him, pressing up on his hands and knees—even this took considerable effort. Once he got to his feet, his coughing became spasmodic. "Is everybody alright?"

One man had taken a metal fragment in his left shoulder— blood dripped out noses and ears. Those who were not wearing noise-canceling headsets clasped their ears in pain.

Zender crawled over to Pepper. "Pepper, what the hell happened?"

"I don't know," Pepper yelled back, lying a few feet from Zender. He pressed the transmit button. "Abort! Abort! Abort! You hit our last position. That last one almost killed us!"

Each man slowly stood, coughing dust from their lungs—bloody spots blossomed from uniforms. They shook the dirt out of their rifles, removed magazines, trying to work the action back and forth to clear any obstruction.

Zender assessed each man, making sure they still mentally and physically could fight. Each man's face blended into the dirt that swirled the air. "Get up, we cannot stay here."

Once the smoke cleared, he looked down at the village and spotted five pickup trucks with heavy machine guns mounted in the back and as many Land Rovers filled with men. Their path would soon intersect where they needed to go near the apex of the mountain.

Zender began pulling each man up to his feet. "We need to keep moving." Every muscle in his body hurt.

Tilley and Perez again took point. Zender's determination seemed to pull the team along.

The trail snaked its way up the mountainside with large crevasses and boulders limiting their sight distance. On the straight path, they made good time. When the two point men came to a corner, it became a choke point.

Perez suddenly stopped and froze in place, as a pointer would on scent. Zender held his fist up, halting the team. Perez took a couple steps, stopped, and sighted down his rifle. Zender brought his rifle up and aimed at the same rock edge—not yet sure what Perez saw. All senses on full alert, his heartbeat pounding in his ears.

Perez looked over back at Zender, pointed at his nose and pointed his finger forward. He inched forward a few steps while unclipping a grenade from his vest. Zender's eyes continued to focus down the length of his barrel. He heard Perez whisper, "*As-Salam Alaykum.*"

A black turban atop a bearded head poked out from behind a large rock—he hesitated when he saw Perez wearing his tribal hat—long enough for Zender to squeeze his trigger, sending a

5.56 bullet into the man's forehead. At the same time, Perez pulled the pin from the grenade and threw it over the rock. The two crouched down as each mentally counted off seconds.

When the grenade exploded, Perez bolted around the boulder with his rifle up and ready, squeezing off rounds as he moved.

Zender closed the distance behind, yelling, "On line," prompting all rifles to point at the ambush site and attack. When he came around the boulder, eight ISIS lay dead and two were hobbling down the mountainside. He sighted on the center mass of the furthest, waiting between heartbeats before he squeezed off two rounds. The man tumbled down the hillside. He tried to shoot the other, but his first shot missed. Before he could get off another round, his target disappeared into a ravine.

Zender caught up with Perez. "If you hadn't stopped, it would have been us lying on the ground versus them. How did you know?"

"They smell bad ... they stink. Thank God for the wind—it pushed their stench right under my nose."

"Now I know why you wear that stupid hat. When he hesitated, gave me time to put a hole in his head."

"I keep telling you this hat is my lucky charm." Perez peered up the trail and back at the ambush site. "Something's not quite right. There weren't enough of them to take—" Perez's arms flung forward, while his back smashed into the ground. "I'm hit," he yelled, digging fingernails into his chest.

Zender flipped the selector on his rifle to full automatic, firing in the general direction where the sniper bullet had come from. Twenty bullets blasted out of his barrel in a matter of seconds. He took hold of Perez's assault vest collar to drag him out of the kill zone. Another bullet snapped past his head

Getting behind cover, Zender pulled open Perez's vest and felt for an entry wound. His hand found a divot right in the middle of Perez's hard ceramic bulletproof plate. Zender looked into the face of his friend. "Perez, talk to me. Are you alright?"

Perez ran his hand over the spot where the bullet hit. "I think it shocked my heart, knocked me off my feet. I can tell by the shit-storm we're in that I'm still alive." He proceeded to sit up, saying, "Thanks for pulling me out. I owe you one."

Zender ejected the magazine from his rifle and inserted another. "Grab my hand, I'll help you to your feet." Halfway through the lift, he let go. "Perez!" He groaned, before he fell backward. His shoulder went numb, causing him to drop his rifle. His vision began to darken.

He heard someone yell, "Medic!" A face leaned over, telling him, "Stay with me." An acrid smell burned his nostrils, forcing him back to reality. Pain cascaded into Zender's senses as the shock of being hit took over. He managed to say, "Ah shit," before his head fell back against the ground.

***

Brent watched one man go down and then another. The leader had yet to get up. He searched out in front of them, crisscrossing the camera back and forth until he picked up a small heat signature. As he focused in on the spot, a flash emerged confirming the sniper had fired another shot. Brent pressed the radio microphone. "Boomer-ten, are you still with us?"

"Not for long. We're about on fumes," came the reply over the radio.

"Do you have enough for one more pass?"

"With the overcast, I'm not sure we'll be able to come down and play," the fighter pilot responded.

"The team is pinned down. I can lase the target if you have time for a strafe run. Fire everything you have."

"You name it—we're there."

"The trail they're on intersects with a road. Enemy vehicles have cut them off and they have a sniper that's got them pinned down. Hose the area down with your cannon."

"In your estimate, how high is the overcast from the valley floor?"

"The mountain tops are in the clouds. Down in the valley, you have about three thousand feet of clearance. Your target is about five hundred feet underneath the overcast. If you start shooting your cannon a couple of miles out, you'll have plenty of clearance to climb."

"We're on our way. I'll radio when inbound."

Chapter 16

MISSILES IN THE AIR

Ali could still hear the fighters circling above the overcast. He sensed something was about to happen, otherwise they would have left by now. Pointing up into the sky, he said, "They are planning another strike. With this overcast, they will need to get underneath for their next attack. Get the missiles ready. Right now we cannot see them, but they will soon show their face—a perfect target."

He and his men carried the crate to an area above the village with a clear view across the valley. Once there, they pried open the top and laid four missile systems along the ground. On each handgrip, his men flipped up a switch energizing the internal battery to initiate the cooling sequence for the missile's seeker head. He called out the last step in the sequence—removing the front and rear tube covers.

The men looked up when they heard the fighter's engines race overhead to a lower flat plain south of their location. "The jets are coming. Be ready," Ali said. Knowing fighters flew in pairs, he directed the man standing next to him to shoot at the trailing aircraft and for the other two to shoot at the lead. "With four missiles in the air, we will hit something. Allah will guide us."

Off in the distance they watched two tiny specks emerge underneath the clouds. The jets engines were silent, which told Ali the fighters were traveling close to the speed of sound.

"Ready ... aim," Ali commanded.

All four men picked up their launch tube. Each man rested a tube on his shoulder, tracking the fighters with the optical sights.

"Wait until they go by us. The missile will seek out and destroy the hot engines."

The fighters appeared together flying in close formation, which made aiming easy—Allah would decide which one needed to die. The twin -V- tails flew past with the emblem -US Navy- painted along the fuselage. "Fire!"

Each man focused on the jets' twin engines. The three men next to Ali pulled the trigger at his command. Ali waited another second before he pulled his own trigger. Within two seconds, four missiles raced out of their launch tubes at fifteen hundred miles an hour, ready to deliver five and a half pounds of directed blast fragmentation energy.

***

Shaky looked through his HUD, focusing in on the sight picture. He maneuvered his jet's nose, overlaying his cannon reticle on top of the energy pulse and squeezed the trigger on the control stick. His entire aircraft vibrated as 20mm rounds at a rate of one hundred per second spit from his cannon.

"Missile warning!" permeated the speaker system in his helmet—red missile warning lights flashed on the aircraft's dash; the aircraft's internal self-preservation computer took over engaging its self-defense systems. White-hot flares and thin metal strips of chaff popped from twin buckets underneath his lead's fuselage. Next, his lead pitched his jet in front of his own to fight the inbound missiles, forcing him to pull the throttles to idle to miss from colliding.

Afraid of losing sight, he lit both burners and pulled the control stick hard over and straight back into his lap. Looking back between the 'V' tails, a single exhaust plume raced toward him. "Where did that come from?" It detonated behind his tailpipe, drawn off by the countermeasures.

"Missile Warning!" continued to blare in his helmet. Still inverted, a fourth missile raced toward his tailpipe, seeking the hot afterburner exhaust as a moth seeks a light in darkness. Five milliseconds later, it detonated. Metal particles shredded the tail section, severing hydraulic lines and electrical connections, ripping through the right engine's high-pressure compressor. Within a fraction of a second the engine—spinning at ten thousand revolutions per minute—became unstable and disintegrated, blowing fan blades out the right side of the fuselage and shredding the aircraft's V tail. With one engine at full power and the other no longer existent, the aircraft snapped over.

Inside the cockpit, multiple audio warnings blared inside Shaky's helmet—red and yellow warning lights flashed in front of his face. As if in slow motion, the entire fuselage began a slow dance as the tail and nose swapped ends. Shaky let go of the stick and pulled up on the ejection loop between his legs. The SJU-5/6 Martin-Baker ejection seat punched through the acrylic canopy rocketing Shaky out of the tumbling Hornet. At six-hundred miles an hour, his body hit a solid wall of air producing instant unconsciousness.

***

Brent watched in disbelief as the Hornet became a fireball. "I see a chute. Keep the camera on the pilot," he said to the sensor operator. They watched the slow descent of the limp pilot until he hit the ground. "I've got to do something," not sure who to call or who might be watching his video feed—if anyone. He keyed the microphone, broadcasting out from the Reaper's radio. "Mayday—Mayday—Mayday, Boomer-ten's wingman is down. An F-18 Hornet was just shot down!"

A controller on board the AWACs responded back, "Goliath has received your Mayday. Repeat, you are down?"

"No, a Navy Hornet is down. Coordinates as follows ...."

"I have reported your coordinates to the combat rescue center. Did you see a chute?"

"Yes! I also saw him hit the ground. He's near the enemy. Send a rescue helicopter quick."

"Copy, we are coordinating with CRC. Repeat reason for the crash."

"ISIS has surface to air missiles. They fired four SA-24s SAMs," Brent yelled back into his microphone.

***

Admiral Grew recognized the number that displayed across his STU phone—it belonged to his longtime friend General Shoemaker from a hardened command center within a US military installation at Al Udid, UAE. "The Seahawks are going to trounce Denver in this year's preseason opener," the admiral announced when he answered the phone. "My bet is Seattle goes all the way to the Super Bowl." Twenty-six years ago, General Shoemaker played middle linebacker for West Point and was known to wear a Bronco jersey to work whenever Denver had a game.

"Grew, sorry, but this isn't a social call. I'd love to talk football with you, but I have some bad news. One of your Boomers was shot down over Syria fifteen minutes ago. I just got a call from the AOC."

"How did that even happen? We've jammed all their radar systems."

"I was told they used those missing SA-24s. The ones taken from Libya."

"Did they say whether my pilot is still alive?"

"A chute was reported seen—no way of telling whether he's alive. I spoke with Washington right before I called you to let them know what happened. The president wants to keep a lid on this shoot down. Any military involvement in Syria is still classified—hell, even losing those damn missiles is a national emergency that the public doesn't need to know about."

"I understand. But he's our pilot and we have an obligation to get him back."

"I do have a SF team in the area. They've been ordered to ensure ISIS does not get their hands on your boy. CIA has also gotten involved and they're pushing for an execute order—an elimination. If ISIS gets their hands on your boy and under torture tells what happened, the implications will be devastating. After what they do to him, your pilot will wish he is dead."

For a moment, silence permeated the connection—both men knew the implications of the last statement.

Shoemaker said, "I'll do everything on my end to try to get your boy back. We have one man down, let's not risk a hundred soldiers until we know more, or at least until the weather clears and we can bring your fighters in from outside of the SA-24 envelope. Your pilot is going to be on his own for a while, if he is still even alive after his ejection."

"Yes sir, the Navy is standing by. He's going to need a lot more than luck if we are going to bring him home. Navy out!" Admiral Grew hung up the phone. "Son of a bitch," he blurted out. The sailors working within the conning bridge stopped what they were doing. The admiral looked out the side window onto the flight deck below. *God, please help him. He's going to need it*, he prayed. Addressing the sailors on his perch, "Get two Hornets loaded and standing by on alert five. That means right now people! Make it happen!"

Chapter 17

EXECUTE ORDER

The 18 Delta medic knelt beside Zender examining the entry and exit wounds. He stuffed both with a wad of *QuikClot* to stop the internal bleeding, securing the area with a large piece of tape. Zender clenched his teeth as he tried to find a mental happy place before the pain took over. The medic asked, "How are you feeling boss?"

Zender wiped the moisture from his eyes. "I've never felt better." Even with the cold temperatures outside, drops of sweat dripped off his forehead.

"Can you deal with the pain?"

"Are you done sticking your dirty fingers inside my body? It stings like hell. How bad is it?"

"You're going to live. The bullet passed through without hitting anything important, minus your sense of humor. It went clean through your trapezius muscle—a nice little hole about the size of my little finger—a little messy out your back shoulder. A couple of stitches and a good dose of antibiotics, you'll be good as new. Let's get you up so we can get out of here."

Zender got to his feet and looked at the chaos around him, unsure what to do next. Half his team had taken hits and now a smoldering aircraft lay scattered across the valley. At least the enemy sniper no longer had them pinned down, shot up from the fighter's 20mm. He grabbed the SATCOM microphone to report to HQ, trying his best to compose himself. "ODA 562 has an immediate SITREP." He waited several seconds. "Answer, dammit!"

"Go ahead," came the nonchalant reply.

"We have a Navy Hornet down. The pilot ejected."

"We were told through Air channels. Your Reaper overhead relayed the message. Can you get to him?"

"Not sure. His chute landed between my team and the enemy. The fighting is quiet at the moment, but we are not doing so well either. I'm close to critical on ammunition and half my team is wounded."

"Stand by." The radio went silent.

While Zender waited, his mind ran through various scenarios, whether to keep pressing forward to their pickup point or attempt a rescue. Their odds of surviving either played against them. He made a promise to himself long ago to never leave a man behind. "Perez, get the team ready for a rescue. Plan to take only essentials."

His men spread out in a defensive perimeter, taking shots they knew would kill, conserving as much ammo as possible. The crash stalled any further aggression from either side for the time being. While he waited for the call back, he peered through his scope at the enemy. His shoulder felt hot like an open ulceration pulsating with battery acid. Every time he moved his arm, blood trickled down his back.

After waiting over ten minutes, an eternity in a firefight, his radio came alive with a new set of orders. "Your team has been chopped to OGA. They are in charge on this one. Standby for an execute order."

He listened in disbelief, with a brief reply of "Roger," and waited. Already he did not like what he heard. Chopped over to OGA meant CIA involvement, which usually meant they wanted someone executed—killed. He already had an idea of who their target might be, but was reluctant to actually be told to do it.

A different voice sounded over the radio. "Your orders are to execute the pilot. He is not ... repeat not ... to be captured alive. Preferably, not taken at all—either rescue or destroy the body. Confirm acknowledgement."

Zender waited a moment before he said, "Confirm." He hung up the handset, saying to his group, "This sucks!"

"What'd they say?" Perez asked, noticing a growing concern crossing his leader's face.

"We're to ensure this American pilot is not captured."

"What the hell does that mean?"

"It means we've been given an execute order. Our orders are to execute this pilot—kill him—unless we can figure out a way to rescue him," Zender said. He got up and searched the surroundings for solitude.

After a moment, Perez followed to where his leader stood. "I didn't sign up to kill Americans. Is this even a legal order?"

"Me neither. They said this is now a national security directive, which has CIA stink all over it. It's a grey order that smells rotten!"

"Who would give an order to kill a fellow American?"

"It's either from the director or the SecDef. It insulates those at the top with deniability. We'll be signing our life away no matter how this turns out."

"You already know what we need to do," Perez said. "I'll get the team ready. You go tell Tilley what he needs to do."

Zender searched the faces of his men. "If ISIS captures our pilot, you know they'll torture him and videotape it for prime time news. I know we're short on ammo, but dammit—a fellow soldier needs us right now. The alternative is putting a bullet into his head, which I'm not ready to do yet—I'd rather die trying."

His eleven men all nodded their heads in agreement, accepting this new mission. Perez performed a quick inspection of each man. "This is going to be a run and shoot operation—the lighter and more agile we are increases our odds of survival. Only take what can kill. Nothing more."

The team began removing non-essential items from their rucksacks and made sure they had a fully loaded weapon. If it could kill, they kept it—everything else fell in the dirt.

Zender went over to Tilley and placed a hand on his shoulder. "I'm sorry Tilley."

"Sir, I know what needs to be done. I'm going to tell you straight up, I don't like it one bit."

"Shoot anyone who comes close. Any raghead shows his head, put a bullet through it." He hesitated a moment before his next statement. "The odds aren't in our favor and we may not make it out there. If we don't succeed—I'll be forced to give you the execute order. Make sure we all die honorably."

Watching his sniper prepare for the ultimate challenge, Zender felt sorry for him and knowing the weight Tilley now carried. They had an agreement with him: *nobody is to be taken alive.* It's why the men left him alone with his quirkiness.

Zender looked at his men. "Boys, let's go rescue us a pilot."

Chapter 18

TAKE THE SHOT

Tilley crawled behind one large rock, waited a couple of seconds, before moving to another. Branches and flora stuck out from his body, making his progress slow and sporadic. He looked more like a moving vegetation alien than an actual man. Years of living on a farm had helped him to refine his ability to blend into the flora. His goal was to emulate the landscape—to become one with nature—undetected and unseen. When the time came to pull the trigger, he would make every shot count—hit where he aimed. His mission was simple—to kill anything that came close and not let his teammates become captured ... alive. Once he settled in, it took patience, waiting for exact time and place to make a perfect shot. When he hunted coyotes on his parent's farm, he learned an animal had a tendency to momentarily stop and look around when it sensed a threat. Humans he found were no different.

He crawled to a location where he had a clear view of the pilot—his chute still billowing in the breeze. Seeing the body not moving concerned him. With vapors coming off the jet when the pilot ejected, he had to have ejected near the speed of sound—like being thrown into a brick wall. On the opposite side of the valley, a cluster of ISIS had gathered and several were pointing toward the tri-colored parachute. Taking a shot that far would only highlight his position. Analyzing the atmospherics, the drizzling rain and a southerly breeze added an additional complexity to a bullet's flight variables to cause a mortal wound. He would have to wait until they came upon the pilot. Even this distance to the pilot was at the edge of his accuracy envelope—any closer and he would lose site of the target—any farther, he could not guarantee a clean kill. As the temperature dropped, he could feel it pulling strength from his core. He draped camouflage netting over his body and down the length of his rifle barrel, maneuvered his scope so he could see through a hole. The only piece of his weapon system showing was the protrusion of a foot-long silencer that extended off the barrel.

He scanned his riflescope over his target area. Hands trembled slightly, causing a slight vibration in his scope making a shot inaccurate. He blamed the cold for the shivering as he tried to make peace with himself, calm the adrenaline that pulsated through his body. "They are not to be captured alive," he told himself, as he watched his teammates prepare for a suicidal rescue a half mile away. He placed eleven bullets next to his rifle, one for each member of the team—these he would save. For himself, he removed a grenade, pulled the pin and placed it under his stomach, making sure the spring flipper stayed in place. If the enemy found him while he lay in this vulnerable position, for his final act all he had to do was roll over.

***

The rescue involved a three-pronged coordination, with the essence of timing mixed in. Off in the distance from where he came, he could see Zender and the team snaking their way off the hillside, inching closer to the pilot's location. Above them, Pepper … the JTAC set up his SOFLAM laser, where he had a better vantage to coordinate a Close Air Support mission when the Air Force fighters finally showed up. If they arrived in time to suppress any advance from ISIS.

Off in the distance, Tilley saw a force of over fifty men clad in black. He did a quick inventory of available bullets. Reaching into his vest confirmed what he already knew. He could sit up on this hillside for days if needed, but he had one big problem—he had already expended eight magazines with three remaining—sixty bullets total. To cover his team and execute his order, he would have to make sure every bullet hit its target.

He flipped down the Harris swivel bipod to steady his rifle; a custom built M110 SR-25 SASS sniper rifle with a floating barrel. Snugging up against the rifle's stock, he and the rifle became one killing unit.

He first focused in on the billowing parachute, and then brought the crosshairs down onto the pilot's prone body. He saw movement off to the pilot's left. Moving the scope over an inch, he focused in on two ISIS soldiers closing in on the pilot. They were close to the finish line and his team hadn't even started. He took a measurement to the target. Right now, the ragheads were beyond a successful shot. A situation similar to shooting coyotes—it involved patience and timing.

Further off in the distance, an unmistakable thump sounded from a 60mm mortar—a plume of smoke billowed outward on the opposing mountainside where the enemy had set up. He swung the scope over to the rescue team and saw them spread flat against the ground; they must've also heard the unmistakable thump and inbound whistle of a mortar shell. The round impacted several hundred meters to the team's left. The thump of another mortar and its impact landed fifty meters to their right—a good bracket before initiating a fire-for-effect artillery mission.

Tilley moved his rifle back over to the pilot. The two soldiers he had seen earlier were now twenty meters from the stricken pilot. He placed the crosshairs on the closest man and gauged the distance at twelve hundred meters. Both were still moving as they climbed over rocks. With the bullet's time of flight at one-and-a-half seconds—his targets could move considerably. When they stopped to watch the mortar shower, Tilley took a shallow breath, releasing it as he steadied the crosshairs on the nearest man's chest. His heartbeat bounced the aim point around the target. Between beats, his scope steadied back onto the man's chest. He applied a miniscule amount of pressure to the already pressed trigger—the hammer released, sending the bullet on its way before his next heartbeat.

His target moved before the bullet arrived. Tilley guessed it flew past by an inch before disintegrating into a rock ten meters behind the target.

"Damnit," Tilley muttered. With the silenced barrel and the distance between the man and the bullet impact point, his target appeared unaware he came within inches of having his head blown off. *At least I still have the element of surprise,* Tilley thought. He watched through his crosshairs as the two continued their progress toward the pilot as if they were two lions stalking their prey. "Patience," he said, waiting for the next open shot opportunity. They continued to move up and down, over and around rocks, nearing the pilot's location.

***

Shaky awoke between two large boulders. He tried to move his right arm. A bolt of pain shot through his shoulder to the end of his spine. He screamed, muffled by his oxygen mask still clasped across his face. He managed to unclip the mask and pull off his helmet. He tried his best to hold back his despair as he tried to think through, *What happened?* He remembered pulling the ejection handle with his left hand, still holding the stick with his right—a swish of sound, and then a blast across his body into the air traveling at seven hundred miles an hour.

His fingers dug into the hard soil—it felt real, hard. Rolling off to his left side, pain again seared his senses, ribs crackled each time he breathed. Pressing on his side, the fire inside caused him to cry out. His hands and legs shook. Dampness spread down from his groin—the realization he urinated himself made him cry out, "I'm going to die." His hands and legs continued to shake. "God help me!" He tried to get a hold of himself, but quickly lost this battle and tried to curl into a ball.

Rocking back and forth, he happened to notice his parachute draped over a rock, fluttering in the wind. "Nothing like marking your location," he told himself. With his good arm, he reached up to unclip the parachute connection from his integrated torso harness snugly strapped around his body. He contemplated whether to pull the chute down or leave it in place. His fingers already felt numb from the cold and his entire body shock. At eight thousand feet of elevation, the temperature had to be close to freezing. He began to shiver uncontrollably, grinding teeth until one broke. After several conflicting moments, he belted out "Ah shit," and reached for the shroud lines, but the pain in his shoulders prevented him from a sustainable grip. The best he could do was to wrap the cords around his body and roll until the chute ripped free. With the nylon now clustered in a pile, he slithered underneath, trying his best to conceal the orange panel within the green and brown. The added layers helped ward off the cold breeze, but he still shivered.

Reaching inside his vest, he removed the 9mm pistol, aiming at various imaginary targets. Hefting the cold steel gave him a little more confidence. "I can do this," he kept telling himself.

When he heard voices of a foreign language, he froze. "They're coming after me!" Shaky slithered across the ground to get away, shoulder and ribs throbbing with every movement.

After crawling no more than twenty feet, he heard something behind him. He rolled onto his back and was startled to see two men wearing black headdresses jumping off a rock where his chute had been draped. They both raised their rifles.

Time stopped—his heart thumped in his chest, a rodent scurried off in the distance, a small black bird flew overhead—while waiting for the inevitable bullet.

The man on the right began yelling as the two crept forward, their barrels never wavering.

Too scared to be captured, Shaky placed the barrel next to his head and pulled the trigger. The hammer fell on an empty chamber, producing an audible click—when he took the gun out, he forgot to rack a round. With the torn ligaments in his shoulders, he did not have the strength to pull the slide back.

The man on the right lurched forward, covering the distance of several meters in a matter of seconds. When close enough, he pulled his foot back sending a kick to Shaky's head.

Shaky felt his head snap back, jaw pop, then something drove into his midsection, causing him to curl up into a ball. Ribs snapped and air drained out of his lungs. Darkness closed in—he no longer felt the impacts, only peaceful oblivion.

***

Tilley placed his crosshairs on the man kicking the pilot. His target moved too much. *Patience*, he told himself. If he waited any longer, the pilot would soon be dead. He steadied the crosshairs as best he could over the moving figure, taking a mental average between oscillations. He squeezed the trigger until the rifle bucked

The man must've felt the bullet's shock wave zip past within an inch of his ear. Like a coyote, he stopped and looked up. Tilley released another bullet.

The 7.62 bullet entered the upper left side of the man's head, penetrating the skull an inch above his right eye socket. Overpressure created inside the cranial cavity, liquefied brain tissue. The downward traverse of the bullet exited out the back, spraying blood from both eye sockets and out the entry and exit holes. The head exploded, splattering blood and brains as it were an erupting melon. The headless body dropped straight down on top of the pilot's body.

Within two heartbeats, Tilley sent another bullet into the other black-clad soldier who stood bewildered upon seeing what just happened to his dead partner.

With the rush of concentration over, he again heard exploding mortars echo off the mountainside. The flying debris kept his teammates pinned down, while the ISIS soldiers marched forward in front of the explosions. "Oh God, this is not happening." He thought about getting up from his hidden position to go help the pilot, but if he did this, then his teammates would be left alone without his support. His job was to shoot—to kill from afar. The number of bullets he had remaining did not match the number of targets to shoot. This posed a huge problem with the eleven bullets lying next to his rifle.

***

Zender pressed his body into dirt, trying to get below the zinging shards of shrapnel that whipped above him. He had cuts everywhere. 60mm mortars continued to rain down upon his men stifling any further progress. With all the dust in the air and the pressure waves from the blasts, his lungs burned as if he was about to suffocate. Breathing became labored, his body jerked with every impact. "God, make it stop." Within a minute it did, replaced by bullets zinging through the air over his prone body.

"Here they come," Zender yelled over the radio. Seventy meters off to his side, he saw a man firing an AK-47. Zender sighted his rifle and pulled the trigger. The hammer fell forward to a resonating click, his arm too numb to reload a fresh magazine quick enough. Instead, he dropped his rifle and pulled his 9mm out of his tactical holster, firing inaccurate rounds that missed.

The bearded man took aim.

Zender waited for the searing heat. Taking his last breath, he watched the enemy's chest explode without a bullet report. *Tilley, I owe you!*

Zender pressed the transmit button for his lip-mic, "Pepper, we're critical on bullets. Where's that air support?"

"Fifteen minutes out," came the reply.

"We don't have fifteen minutes," Zender yelled back. "We're down to our pistols. They're closing in fast—they have us pinned down. We'll be throwing rocks soon."

The radio crackled, "You've two groups converging toward your right and left—they've got you pinched in."

"I see them," Zender said. He aimed his pistol at the closest man, thirty meters away and dropped him. "We're out of options. Get out—" a bullet slammed into his ceramic chest plate. "Shit!" He got up on his knees, fumbling for his pistol—searching for where the shot came from. "Have grenades ready!" he yelled, before another bullet careened off his helmet.

Zender felt proud of his team. Each second he heard another click of an empty rifle. It came down to the basic principle of mathematics—more enemy to shoot than bullets. His team needed to move to survive. If they stayed in place, they would die. "Pull pins," Zender yelled. "Throw what you have—keep one." Zender placed his radio microphone up to his lips. "Tilley, execute the pilot—prepare for alpha order." *Hopefully Tilley kept back eleven bullets*, he thought.

***

Tilley became a killing machine, dropping targets that came near his friends. He took a breath, sighted and squeezed, adjusted his aim to repeat the process. Only three bullets remained in the magazine to shoot, minus the eleven he had set aside. Hearing Zender's order, he acknowledged receipt with two microphone clicks. He sighted through his scope, resting his crosshairs on the unconscious pilot. Peering through his scope, his vision blurred.

He tried to steady the rifle on the pilot's head—while forcing his heartbeat to slow. Settling into the zone took longer than normal. This shot needed to be his best. He wanted to ... needed to make sure the pilot didn't suffer. He flexed the large muscles in his legs in an attempt to burn the adrenalin out of his body. Meditating—finding his focus—his body relaxed, as it had done a thousand times before.

***

The Reaper's thermal camera pierced through the cloud layer. Brent watched the confrontation unfold between the two opposing forces. From where he sat, it felt like a scene from Call of Duty, except his team was losing. The ISIS soldiers were in a wedge that spanned twenty meters. The men in the front row wore battle armor, and the three sets of men behind wore only the thin black cloth. The triangle marched forward as one formidable mass. The SF team tried to retreat up the hillside, but their progress became stalled by the enemy's barrage of bullets. "They're going to die!" he blurted out.

The fuel indication had already depleted past what the aircraft needed to BINGO back to a runway. If he left now, only fumes would be sucked from the tank upon touchdown. Each minute he waited, another twenty pounds of fuel flowed into the engine reducing his options. He had one last card to play to offset this engagement back in his team's favor.

Brent programmed the JTACs location as waypoint one, and then moved the camera over to the front of the enemy's position, designating this location as waypoint two. He released the Reaper from its orbit and manually flew the aircraft to the first waypoint. Brent pressed the button to transmit over the UHF frequency. "Tell your teammates to get their heads down."

"I thought you were out of missiles," came the reply from the JTAC.

"I am."

***

The sniper settled into his zone—ready to take the fatal shot. His target had now become impersonal, like so many before. He timed the beating of his heart, took a shallow breath and started a slow squeeze on the trigger, when he heard, "Tilley, hold your shot." Tilley froze—his trigger a hair from releasing. He eased the pressure off while moving his aim off the body.

Tilley looked up from his riflescope, hearing a scream from the Reaper's turbine engine pierce through the clouds. Seconds later the aircraft popped underneath the cloud layer, nose pointed at the ground, heading straight toward his teammates. If it didn't pull up soon, it would be too late. "It's going to crash," Tilley shouted. He raised up onto his hands and knees to watch—giving away his position. Whatever happened now didn't matter. Either they all died or they all lived.

The Reaper flew over the top of the team by a mere fifty feet. The turboprop engine spun at its full nine hundred shaft horsepower, pushing the aircraft past three hundred miles per hour. The Reaper had become a guided missile with high explosive jet fuel inside. It banked over like a jet fighter and flew down the face of the mountain on a straight course for the ISIS front lines. The nose did not waiver. Hitting the ground, an eruption of flying metal and ignited jet fuel cascaded over the top of them. Those who were far enough to survive the initial flash of heat had oxygen sucked from their lungs. Molten aluminum shrapnel impaled anything above ground. Upon impact, the course of the battle changed.

Tilley swung his riflescope toward his teammates. None of them moved. He waited, internally counting off seconds, scanning across the burning battlefield for anything that appeared alive. Slowly, one by one, his team started to move, pushing first to their hands and knees, and then to their feet. Several tried to stand and then fell. He could see Zender rallying his men forward to exploit whatever was left of the enemy. Those who could walk formed up into a wedge toward the pilot's location. They picked up the enemy's AK-47 rifles—those still capable of firing they used against their previous owners. Not many showed signs of life. A few tried to run and several tried to fight. Tilley used the remaining eleven bullets to kill those who still had a will to fight.

As the team worked their way toward the pilot, the "burp" from a 30mm A-10 GAU-8/A Avenger seven-barrel Gatling gun resonated throughout the valley. The Air Force finally arrived to push this battle to his team's side.

***

Ali watched from the opposing mountainside as the Special Forces team closed in on the pilot. Nothing he could do to prevent it. When he heard the unmistakable burp from the A-10's gun, it was time to leave. Looking upon the carnage below his location made him sad—such a waste. The Americans once again won a battle, in a land that they do not understand. Force against force only caused hatred. *Nothing more, nothing less.*

Guessing a new set of American soldiers would soon descend upon the village, he decided it best to proceed along the road that led to the apex. There was nothing more he could do here—the tide of this battle had changed. Once again, he felt like a desert gerbil with an eagle circling overhead. From a front pouch, he removed a map and traced his finger along a trail that would lead him north into Turkey—about a three-day walk. His assault vest held enough water and food to last two days, then he would have to forage off the land until he found civilized humanity.

Just over a kilometer away, he saw something move along the hillside. Looking through binoculars, he saw what appeared to be a man dressed in a shaggy dog costume. Ali worked his way higher up the hillside, closing in from behind. If he couldn't have an alive pilot, a Special Forces team member was almost as good. Neither moved very fast as they both traversed their route trying to remain unseen. It appeared the sniper was headed toward his fellow teammates, while Ali closed in from behind. With the sniper's rifle now slung over his shoulder, he used both hands to help him move between rocks, which gave Ali enough time to aim his rifle.

Ali tried to gauge an intercept point and work his way toward that direction. Tired and dehydrated, he needed to slow the sniper down before he got too far away.

Ali slid a scope onto the rail of the FN rifle, took instant wind and temperature calculations that might affect the bullets trajectory, and appropriately placed the crosshairs over the sniper's left exposed shoulder. The rifle's muzzle suppressor hid the flash as the bullet raced from his position. Seeing the sniper drop, confirmed it to be a clean hit.

Ali traversed his way to the last known position and found nothing. A blood splatter on the ground confirmed his shot. Following blood droplets, he found the sniper leaning against a rock, one hand covering the entry wound and the other holding a grenade. Even from this distance, Ali saw that the pin had already been pulled.

The sniper made no effort to move. His face remained expressionless.

Ali sat on the ground outside the blast radius. To warriors facing each other, waiting for the other to move.

Speaking in perfect Persian, the sniper asked, "Nice rifle, where did you get it?" The left side of his shoulder was soaked in blood.

Ali gave the answer in English. "Your CIA left it behind as they seem to do with every country they fight in."

"Hmmm. You're right." He began to cough, spitting a glob of blood onto the ground. "I probably should get going. Your bullet tore up my shoulder and as you can see, I'm not doing so well." He coughed again.

Ali needed to make a decision. With the hand still holding the grenade, the element of capturing the sniper as a hostage was no longer an option. Watching him hold it made him appreciate life ... and the honor of death. He found no purpose in killing this man. "There is no point in taking your life. No cause, no effect to change this outcome." Ali got up and proceeded up the mountain, stopping when he guessed to be 100 meters from the sniper. He took a moment to unclip a smoke grenade from his vest. With the wind blowing from the south and a throw downhill, the smoke would help mask his escape and take notice of their fellow wounded teammate. He pulled the pin and hefted it as hard as he could in the direction where the sniper lay. When he heard the canister pop, he increased his pace as red smoke filled the valley below him.

Nearing the apex, he looked back. A helicopter hovered over the sniper, soldiers sliding down ropes. "Time to disappear from this godforsaken country." A days hike and he would reach a silk road—two more days, he would be enjoying a cappuccino in an

Islamabad café. His thoughts turned to the carnage he had seen—holding the little girl in his arms who was innocent in this war—and the men he had killed for his government—who said it was for the Caliphate. He started to have doubts on where this war would lead.

As he walked along the trail, his satellite phone in his backpack started ringing. Ali stopped to answer it, recognizing the caller identification. "*As-Salam Alaykum,* your highness." He listened to his new orders. "Yes sir. I should be able to arrive in America in a week—this is my specialty. It will be a privilege to take care of this matter for the honor of Iran. Consider it done."

Chapter 19

AFTERMATH

Brent slid his chair back from the Reaper console. Looking over at his sensor operator, he said, "I'm really sorry to have gotten you involved. This is all my doing—my decision. Get ready, shit is going to hit the fan."

"Sir, we're in this together—I would've made the same decision."

"That's if they're even alive—it will be awhile before we find out. When I tell my DO that I flew an airplane into the ground, he's going to throw a shit-fit. I doubt any general is going to agree with what I did. Thanks for your support anyway." Brent lifted himself out of his seat. His flight suit soaked with perspiration. He went to the door, stopping before he opened the interlock. "Give the LRE a call and let them know their Reaper is not coming back. I'm going to let command know we now have one less aircraft in our inventory."

He proceeded out of the control room, turned right, and headed toward the duty desk at the front of the building. "Is the duty officer around?" Brent asked the person behind the counter.

"No sir. Is there anything I can do?"

"Do you have the operations officer's phone number? I crashed a Reaper. I should give him a call. You should find the duty officer and let him know."

Brent dreaded making the call to his DO. He managed his pilots with an aggressive top-down approach, always threatening of putting them in purgatory if they deviated from standard operating procedures. The last time, when he blew up the apartment building, almost cost him his career. This time he had a feeling—purgatory will be far worse.

He stared at the duty phone, not wanting to make the call. The thought of walking out of the building and not looking back, crossed his mind.

"Are you alright?" The person at the counter asked.

"I'll be better after I make this call." Brent dialed the DO's phone and waited for the inevitable answer.

After the sixth ring, he heard a groggy voice answer. "What?"

"This is Parker. Sorry to wake you, but I thought you should know I flew a Reaper into the ground."

"What the hell ... Parker! Did you accidently crash it or did you purposely destroy it?"

"A Special Forces team was in trouble. They needed help—"

"Don't tell me you deliberately destroyed a flyable airplane!" the DO yelled into the phone. "Officers are graded on not CRASHING AIRPLANES!"

"But the circum—"

"I don't give a flying-fuck what your reasons were. People go to jail for destroying government property and a sixty-million dollar airplane will certainly send you away for a while. You're officially off flight status and restricted to base quarters until a full investigation has concluded. After I'm done with you, I doubt you'll ever see the inside of a cockpit or officer's mess again."

"But, let me explain—"

"Get your ass over to medical for a post-accident evaluation. When you're done, go to the BOQ. You're confined to this base until further notice!" With the last, his DO slammed the phone down.

***

At the medical clinic, the lab technician stood next to him in the bathroom stall to watch him urinate in a bottle. When he finished, another technician escorted him into a side room and stuck a needle in his arm for a blood sample. After providing bodily fluids, he waited in an examining room for several hours before a doctor arrived. Snapping off his gloves, the doctor asked various psychological questions to see if he had any post-traumatic stress. Brent kept telling him he actually felt good about what happened. The doctor kept emphasizing that he purposely crashed an airplane, seen men die ... unusual in a day's event.

Leaving the clinic, he stared out his windshield. *What's wrong with them?* "This is so fucked up," he yelled out, slamming his palms against the steering wheel. He didn't care anymore about his career. He felt convicted and already sentenced. Whatever they wanted to throw at him, he did what needed to be done.

Brent drove out of the hospital parking lot, unsure where to go first. He drove past a patrol car parked along the road, near the hospital exit. Johnson sat in the driver's seat watching him drive past. He tried to control his temper, so as not give an excuse to be stopped, making sure he stayed five miles under the speed limit.

Since all he had to wear was a set of bloody jeans and shirt wadded up in his trunk, and this sweaty flight suit he had on, he wanted something fresh to wear. Going to the pimp's office seemed like a week ago, versus the previous evening. How quickly his life became a disaster. Then he remembered Amber's DVD under his seat. This gave him a glimmer of light. With his current predicament, telling her would have to wait.

Not knowing how long he'd be staying courtesy of the US government, he stopped at the mini-mart to pick up necessary toiletry items, a pair of gym shorts, a t-shirt and running shoes. At the liquor display, he found a bottle of his favorite Elk Rider whiskey and set it on the counter for the cashier to ring up. With all items paid, he got back into his Z and drove over to the bachelor officer quarters.

His room was plain and functional. The floor had wall-to-wall beige one-foot square tiles accented with cinderblock walls painted a sandy hue. A wooden desk sat next to the door with a rusted metal chair pushed tight against it and a single twin bed was the central focal point along the opposite wall with a dirt brown wool blanket used as a bedspread. Home sweet home—though it already looked like a jail cell. He extracted himself from the sweat stained green jumper, swapping his flight suit with the new shorts and t-shirt, and left his room for a run.

He no doubt trashed his military career. The question was, *How long before the big wheels of the military machine started moving.* Whatever they decided, he had had enough—tired of the bullshit—tired of killing people.

He ran at a full sprint along the perimeter road paralleling the flight line where Predators and Reapers stood on their spindly legs. Brent knew he would always feel the connection with these planes. As he ran, the cool morning air felt good against his body, and the exertion stripped the anxiety he felt.

On the far end of the base along the perimeter fence, he passed a patrol car. Seeing someone running this early along the flight line must have prompted the driver to flip on the overhead blue flashing lights and spin the car around until it came alongside. He recognized Johnson before the flashlight shined into Brent's eyes. "What are you doing out here?"

Brent shielded his eyes from the bright light and leaned over towards the window. "I'm just out for some fresh air."

"You shouldn't be out running at this time without a high-visibility belt on. You know the rules. If I stop you again, I won't be so nice. You owe me." Johnson soon drove away, leaving Brent alone.

"I owe you nothing." Brent waited for the car to distance itself before he set off again—not toward his BOQ room, but he'd get there eventually. He backtracked along the road to investigate an animal hole under the fence to see if it was large enough for him to crawl under. The hole looked to be large enough for a coyote—with a little digging and he could slide underneath to freedom.

Once back at his room he turned on the shower to full hot. Steamy jets washed the tension out of his muscles and the sweat off his body. He let the water run until it turned cold, stood there a few minutes longer—trying to let what happened wash down the drain. Walking across the small room naked, he pulled the cork out of the whiskey bottle and poured himself three fingers, savoring the warm liquid as he thought about his situation over the past couple of weeks. A foreign intelligence agency tried to seduce him, the police suspected him of a crime, a Russian pimp wanted to peel his skin off while a drugged prostitute lay in his bed—now this... the unknown of whether he saved those men. When the plane crashed, he lost all radio contact with them. He said a quick prayer, starting with ... *Please God, save these American soldiers.*

***

Brent woke up to banging on his door. The alarm clock next to the bed read 1000. Brent rolled out of bed, knocking over the whiskey bottle from the bedside nightstand, and grabbed his boxer shorts. "I don't need anything." The knocking continued. He opened the door to find a not-too-happy female officer—she had the collar devices showing her to be a rank of major and a silver badge patch sewn into her front blouse pocket. Framed on either side of her stood two base policemen. One of them was Johnson, who snickered upon seeing Brent, the other he hadn't seen before.

"Can I help you?" Brent asked.

"Are you Lieutenant Parker?" the major asked, wearing a tailored uniform that accentuated long legs and slim arms. *She is definitely a marathon runner.* Her brown hair rolled in a bun and stuffed underneath a matching patrol cap, slim lips that were not smiling—all business indicating this was not a social call.

"Yes ma'am. What can I do for you?" He read her name on her starched uniform, "Major Lannon?" Both officers had a nightstick in their hands.

"I'm Major Lannon from OSI, office of special investigation." She flipped open her credentials for Brent to see. "May we come in?"

"Are you asking to be polite or do I have a choice?"

"We can either do this here or we can do this down at the brig. Either way it's your choice."

"Come on in and make yourself at home," Brent said, leading the entourage back into his room.

Brent made sure he kept his movements subtle, nothing sudden to give anybody a reason to start swinging sticks. With Johnson's smirk on his face, he appeared to be itching for a reason. Both police officers took up a position several steps behind the major, letting her take the lead. Everybody watched Brent put on his flight suit and lace up his boots. Once dressed, he sat on the bed. Major Lannon sat at his desk and her two friends stood guarding the only exit out of the room "What can I do for you?" Brent asked. *Keep calm, only answer what's asked.*

"Before we start, I need to inform you of your rights. I have been assigned as the investigating officer and these two are here as witnesses. I've been appointed by General McDougal to conduct an investigation into the purposeful destruction of government property."

"He's a ways up the leadership flagpole. Not the person who I thought drove this train." Brent said. "Looks like my little accident escalated to the top."

"From what I've read, and given the reaction from leadership, it doesn't appear your -little- situation was an -accident. The evidence against you is clear. We have already interviewed your sensor operator who provided a sworn statement indicating there was nothing wrong with the Reaper prior to the crash. All evidence so far shows you flew a perfectly good airplane into the ground without authorization."

"If I may interject, have you ever heard of someone being given authorization to crash an airplane?"

"Please don't interrupt me unless you have a serious question to ask." Lannon took a moment to collect her thoughts. "Ultimately, lives were lost because of what you did."

"Whose lives are we talking about?" Worried he had killed the wrong side. "Did they all survive?"

"Did who survive?"

"—the American SF team and the pilot ...."

"I'm not at liberty to discuss—"

"Come on major. I did what I did to keep them alive."

"You don't know do you?"

"No!"

"Yes, they all survived, but that's not the issue here."

Brent sat back, relieved—his actions offset this shit storm of trouble. Whatever they did to him, it no longer mattered—he had saved these Americans.

"—Lieutenant, did you hear what I said?" The major asked.

"Sorry, you've no idea what I've done." For once in the past twenty-four hours tension released from his soul and a slight smile spread across his lips.

She held up her hand. "Before you say anything more, I need to read you your rights. Under the provisions of Article thirty-one of the UCMJ, you have the right to remain silent. Any statements you make, oral or written, may be used as evidence against you in a trial by court-martial or in a judicial or administrative proceeding. You have the right to consult a lawyer and to have a lawyer present during this interview or any subsequent interviews. You have the right to military legal counsel free of charge. In addition to military counsel, you are entitled to civilian counsel of your own choosing, at your own expense. Do you understand your rights?"

"Yes ma'am, I understand my rights."

"Do you want a lawyer?"

"It depends on how and what the military has in store for me. Right now, I do not think I need a lawyer to continue our conversation. Since you have witnesses for your meetings, for the record I will require a lawyer for any future meetings."

"Are you willing to answer my questions?"

"It depends on what you ask."

"Tell me what happened during your flight yesterday. Did anyone give you authorization to crash your Reaper?"

"Major, you appear to be very thorough. I'm sure you've already sequestered the flight data recorder and interviewed anybody pertinent prior to meeting with me. I would surmise you already know the answers to your questions and answering them only verifies that either I'm lying or telling the truth. What happened was recorded in high-definition detail—this includes the entire video link, radio transmission and all conversations within the Reaper control module. I'm sure by now the tape is secure in a vault somewhere. I highly doubt there's anything else I can add."

"Just for the record, did you receive authorization to fly," the major opened up a tablet to read some notes, "Hunter zero-six into the ground?"

"No ma'am, nobody gave me authorization to fly the aircraft into the ground."

"Did you try to notify anybody before you took it upon yourself to crash the aircraft?

"I told the team on the ground to get their heads down. There wasn't enough time." He stopped saying anymore. Not liking where this series of questions was going, Brent decided to derail the line of questioning by asking a one of his own. "Am I under arrest?"

"Right now you are restricted to base. Once formal charges are filed, you'll have the opportunity to wear my steel bracelets," Lannon said.

"If I may inquire, what are the formal charges?"

"It's still early to tell and I'm not at liberty to say. When something like this comes up, the depth of charges are dependent on whether the news media gets wind of it. If there is a large justified body count—and through your dereliction it is determined you directly contributed to this body count—you will appear in front of a court-martial board. Right now, you're restricted to base. If leadership decides to charge you with murder, you'll be staying in one of our finer facilities with bars and no windows."

"I would presume by -leadership- you mean General McDougal?"

"General McDougal ordered this investigation and he's the convening officer, but your little incident goes up several more levels. Once my investigation is complete, a formal arrest warrant will be presented."

"How long can I expect to be restricted to this base? Or has my punishment already been decided before your investigation is even complete?"

"You're an active duty military officer. This means twenty-four hours a day, seven days a week, your superiors can place any type of restriction they deem necessary on what you can and cannot do. Since your accident has criminal implications, you are restricted to this base until the court-martial."

He dropped his head into his hands.

"I also need to inform you everything about this case is classified. I'm told CIA may be involved, pushing what happened to the SecDef level. You are not to discuss what happened with anybody outside or inside of the military who does not have a need to know. You're already under investigation for the destruction of a multimillion-dollar aircraft, let's not tack on more charges with a security violation. Do I make myself clear?

"Yes, crystal clear."

"Are there any other questions I can answer?"

"I have one question. Have you watched the camera video or listened to the audio?"

"No. The entire flight data recorder had been sequestered before I was notified to conduct an investigation. I'm told what happened is beyond my need know, which is the reason why I'm confirming your answers."

"How high does this classification go?"

"It's at a code word level. Way beyond mine."

"That explains what's going on here."

"I'm not sure I understand your comment."

"If you'd been able to watch the mission video, you would have a different opinion about what happened. This dealt with saving the lives of Americans. It's not your typical black-and-white case. Don't judge me too quickly, until you know all the facts."

The major left his room followed by the two police officers. Brent dropped in line behind the OSI entourage. Two cop cars blocked his Z from moving—their roof lights flashing. People gathered along the sidewalk to watch the show. Major Lannon climbed into a nondescript government sedan and drove away, leaving Brent to wait for the vehicle barricade to move. With his path now clear, Brent started his car and drove over to the base JAG's office. He needed to find a lawyer.

***

The Secretary of Defense looked out his office window down upon the Potomac River. Five stories up, he had a commanding view of the boats along the waterway and the commercial aircraft landing at Ronald Reagan International airport. Usually, there were generals in his office wanting to discuss the latest piece of equipment their service needed. After reading the after action report from General Shoemaker, he told Doris, his gatekeeper outside his office, that he did not want to be interrupted—he needed time alone.

All the soldiers survived, which was a good thing—even the Navy pilot. When he got the call from the CIA Director on what needed to be done to keep the situation contained, the country had a national security crisis that needed a blanket thrown over it. Chances were this Navy pilot was already dead from his high-speed ejection and as for the SF team ... they were all expendable. Their deaths would provide additional arguments for further military involvement against a growing ISIS insurgency. Besides, an escalation in hostilities forced additional funding from congress. This being an election year, the American people would coalesce to a common goal—defeating ISIS—ultimately increasing the popularity of an incumbent president. The problem was ... with everyone surviving, people have a tendency to talk when it comes to a bad decision.

Other than the CIA, the only person within the DOD who had a full picture of everything was General Shoemaker. A former snake eater, hopefully Shoemaker understood why he made this decision.

He opened the oversized door leading out of his office and stood in front of his gatekeeper's desk. SecDefs came and went with each president, but Doris had survived five administrations. "How long has General Shoemaker been a two-star?" He asked.

"Three years." She had a photographic memory when it came to the top tier generals.

The SecDef paced around the office foyer, his hand massaging his chin.

She must have read his thoughts when she added, "I've heard General Stewart is looking to retire for health reasons. This would open a vacancy for promotion." How she knew the gossip that flowed through the five-sided wind tunnel amazed every SecDef. That's why each one kept her as their gatekeeper.

"Thank you, Doris. You once again just solved a dilemma. As soon as you receive General Stewart's retirement request, draft an authorization for promotion for the president to sign. Also, send a message to General Shoemaker that I want to see him ASAP." For the first time this morning, the tension of the morning lifted. People had a tendency to become appreciative when he tossed a good deal their way.

"He is already on his way to see you. I didn't want to disturb you with his message. He sounded very matter of fact when he called. Said you would know the reason for the meeting. Is there anything else I can do?"

Shoemaker escalated his timeline. With all that happened, their meeting would not be a social call. Everybody else involved were buttoned up. The SF team should be in isolation debriefing the mission or heavily sedated in a hospital. The F/A-18 lead pilot had safely landed aboard George Washington—confined to quarters in the middle of the Mediterranean ocean. This left the Reaper pilot, Lieutenant Parker. He told General McDougal to keep him on base until they could figure out what to do with him—throw the book at him to keep him contained. The quicker the door closed to this mess, the less likely what happened would be leaked. "Before General Shoemaker arrives, I need to see the president. Please have his promotion authorization ready before I leave." Walking back into his office, he overheard Doris already speaking with the president's gatekeeper.

***

Brent entered the JAG's office; a converted doublewide trailer parked on the far side of the flight line. A plump receptionist greeted him, who seemed forewarned to his arrival. She escorted him into a conference room, originally designed as a bedroom with a rectangular oak table centered in the middle and four metal chairs—two situated on either side. A single pane window adorned the far side of the room.

"Can I get you anything?" Before Brent could answer, she said, "Captain Davis will be with you shortly." She stepped out of the room, closing the door behind her.

Brent took one of the chairs facing the door. Ten slow minutes ticked by before an Army captain entered the conference room. "I'm Chad Davis. I'll be overseeing your case. Please have a seat."

The Army captain was lanky and stood a good foot above Brent. When they shook, his hand wrapped around Brent's. Wearing dark green slacks and a short sleeve light green shirt, he had the metal insignia of a JAG corps leaf pinned to his collar. "I'm not your legal counsel. My job is to play referee between the prosecuting leadership and the defense counsel, and to help expedite the process. I know you have questions as to what's going to happen next. I'll try to answer a few. Let me start by saying, unlike what you told the major who greeted you in your underwear, anything you tell me is not admissible—like it never happened. My first word of advice to you is next time make sure you have a lawyer present before you see her again. Definitely don't admit to anything."

"I told her the same thing," though he admitted to a few things he should not have said. Brent sat facing forward, his hands folded on the table. "Why an Army JAG lawyer when this is an Air Force disaster?" He clenched his mouth shut and waited.

"I'm actually a reservist doing my two week stint and happened to be in the area when they called me for this assignment. While you were waiting, I briefly spoke with the prosecution to get an idea what this all involves. First, let me tell you what to expect. The military is going to charge you with conduct unbecoming of an officer, dereliction of duty and the destruction of government property. They've also thrown in the possibility of murder charges, but this was during a combat operation that nobody is supposed to know about. I'm sure we did not have authorization from President al-Assad to conduct military operations within his country. Rest assured the US is not going to send you to Syria to stand trial for murder. The charges of dereliction of duty and the destruction of government property are the two you need to be worried about first."

"What happens if they find me guilty?"

"The first charge will land you out of the military with an administrative discharge. The second and third charges— dereliction of duty and the destruction of government property— could send you to a military prison if found guilty. Since the property destroyed is worth sixty million dollars, the options on the table against you can vary between jail time in a military prison, demotion to the lowest rank possible, forfeiture of all pay, an other-than-honorable discharge from the military or any combination of these punishments. Or they will make you pay for what you destroyed."

"What if I hadn't crashed the airplane? Americans would have died—a whole SF team and a navy pilot."

"I'm not here to judge—I'm only here to inform you on what is being charged against you. Your counsel representatives will need to have a Top Secret SCI security clearance before you tell them anything. No one in this office has this extensive of a background check and the time required acquiring one goes beyond the time limits of this case. General McDougal has indicated a desire to expedite closure by either pleading guilty to the charges or by an expedited judicial decision. Off the record, fuck him. Do you understand all I have said so far?"

Brent sat across the table with unfocused eyes. They would've all been dead if he hadn't acted, or wishing they were. *Punished for doing the right thing. Go figure.*

"Lieutenant Parker, do you understand what I said?"

Brent focused his attention back onto the conversation. "You know this is all bullshit! Everything you said, I already know. My guess is McDougal never had to make an operational decision where seconds determine life and death. It seems all he cares about are his little damn planes. Moreover, nobody in the JAG corps wants to touch this case—it's already a loser. I hope you have a short list of JAGs who can actually help me."

Captain Davis removed a sheet of paper from a folder and slid it over to Brent. "This is the contact information for a retired Army officer who is a civilian lawyer. Actually, he's a sitting superior court judge, though I know he never actually practiced law during his tour in the Army."

"Why would I want him, some Army officer who never actually practiced military law? Any idea what his fees are, not considering his qualifications to represent me?"

Captain Davis rested his hands on the table and took a deep breath. "If I were in your shoes, this is the person I would want in my corner. He retired out of the Army a year ago from the reserves, which means his security clearance is still active. He retired as a colonel, which means he knows his way around the military."

"But, he has no experience with the military legal system as a JAG officer, other than he's the only lawyer available with the level of security to represent me. Why him? There must be a JAG somewhere in the military system who has the necessary security clearance."

"I know enough of the circumstances of what happened. Specifically, I heard your actions saved the lives of a Special Forces team and a Navy pilot, which makes this case a Joint military operation. This lawyer was also a former Special Forces officer who knows quite a bit about the judicial system—more than most JAGs. I know this judge would take a keen interest in a controversial action that saved his fellow brothers. I'm not green behind the ears. I'll be honest with you—I smell a conspiracy. Somebody wants your whole situation brushed under the rug, along with you, as quickly as possible. Usually I have weeks to prepare for a case, not days. If I was being prosecuted for a controversial operation against an enemy, I'd want somebody who's been on the tip of the spear with no support other than a courageous Reaper pilot who made the right decision."

Brent realized this Army captain knew more than it appeared. He softened his approach. "What is the best way to get in touch with this colonel?"

"I've already set up a secure teleconference. I don't know the colonel's schedule or if he is even willing to help. That will be up to him."

"Are you saying there's a possibility he won't take my case? What then?"

"Let's take one step at a time. They can't do anything with you until you have legal representation."

"But I need to get off this base." His thoughts drifted to Amber, who he left in his bed.

"I asked Colonel Phillips to at least listen to what you have to say before he says no. Since he's a civilian, I don't know what he'll charge to represent you, if anything. But since no other JAG is available, I've already started a request to have the military cover your legal expenses, whoever you decide to hire."

"Thank you. It's been a tough couple of days."

"From what I've gleaned from your case, you've every right to be mad as hell. Between you and me, this case is bullshit."

For the second time, Brent smiled. He wasn't completely alone in the situation. And he was damn certain the SF team and pilot were at least grateful for the sacrifice Brent made. This glimmer of support gave him a boost of confidence.

"He'll be at Fairchild Air Force base outside of Spokane, Washington where he'll have access to a STU phone at five o'clock this evening. I told him that you would be giving him a call. You can use this phone on the table," pointing to a black phone attached to a conference speaker—this is a non-recorded line. Stay as long as you like." The young lawyer stood and left the room.

While he waited, he thought it best to give Amber a call, unsure when he would have another opportunity. Dialing her number on the table phone, he paused for a moment when he heard her soft voice answer. "I'm sorry, but I won't be coming home for a while."

"What happened? Are you alright?" he heard her ask.

"I've gotten into some trouble. I can't say what happened. There is so much I want to tell, but I can't right now. I hope ... I need you understand, there is no place I'd rather be than with you. Right now that is not possible."

"Brent, you're scaring me."

He could feel his throat starting to constrict. "Stay positive. We will be together soon. I miss you." He forced himself to sever the connection.

***

"Hello, Colonel Phillips. Captain Davis told me to give you a call."

"Please call me Vince. I might have served in the Army, but to clarify I was Special Forces, which means we didn't abide by the pomp and fluff that permeates a regular stiff-shirt soldier. I'm now retired, which means I hung up my military rank a year ago. I'm not sure how much time I can spend on your case with my bench schedule. All I know is Chad called and said you needed my help. By the way, how is Chad these days? Whatever you do, don't play basketball against him."

"Thanks ... thank you for taking your time to talk with me. How do you know Chad?"

"He clerked for me while attending law school at Gonzaga University. He also played hoops for the Zags, which makes him a decent basketball player. As a sitting judge, we often have law students as part of their educational experience. Chad attended my alma mater and had an interest to serve in the Army. We had a lot in common—so I hired him. He's smart and ambitious. I know you might be a little pissed off at the military right now, but not everybody is against you. He's on your side."

"Yes sir. I figured that out toward the end of our conversation. He speaks highly of you. I'm in a tight spot—the military has hung me out to dry and I have nobody in my corner. I really do need your help."

"I'm not sure I can. Chad did mention your case is about destroying government property, which is a serious offensive. It's been a long time since I had to argue a case in front of the bench.

My advice is to hire a good a criminal defense attorney—I listen to lawyers pontificate about illegal traffic stops and or the equitability of a divorce. I know a few attorneys who have experience battling against the military establishment. They're more familiar with military law than some old judge. I'd be willing to give them a call to see if they're interested in taking your case. If I find out anything, I'll send Chad the information. I wish you the best of luck."

"Wait—don't hang up. Chad only knows a fraction of what really happened. If this were a simple I-fucked-up case, we wouldn't need to talk on a secure phone line. There's a lot more information and there may even be more that I don't know. The bottom line is I saved an entire Special Forces team. Time had run out for them. I needed to make an immediate decision. You know, you've been there. Chad said you'd help me if you really knew what happened."

"The SF community is a closed society of professionals, though we've been known to help those who've helped us. As you are aware, our work falls under a classified umbrella, which keeps our missions hidden from the scrutiny of the public. We do things the higher echelon of our esteemed government orders us to do that the general public may not agree with—on the fringe between right and wrong. Sounds like your situation fell smack under one of those umbrellas. Start at the beginning and run me through all the details of what happened. Don't leave anything out. Whom you like and dislike, whom you can trust and who is out to get you. Then give me a day or two to think over what happened. If I can help I'll take this case, otherwise you will need a good criminal defense lawyer."

Hearing the last part, Brent became conflicted about what to tell. His friends boiled down to a casino dealer and a prostitute—not much to brag about. He did not trust cops and he disliked his DO. And there were two people who wanted to see him dead. For the time being, he decided to keep his story limited to the last twelve hours. "I found some missiles ...."

Part IV

Fourth Week

Chapter 20

FIRST SECRETARY

One week later

The route to the United States from the mountains of Syria had taken Ali a week. Crossing the border into Turkey took the longest, first finding an Iranian safe house and then getting an official passport listing him as a British citizen. The flight from Turkey to Vancouver, British Columbia, going through Canadian customs validated his passport authenticity.

He stayed in Vancouver long enough to obtain another passport, severing his weeklong existence. The passport's previous owner, a professor at University of British Columbia, had an extra $100,000 in his bank account and was told to disappear for two weeks on a sailing voyage through the Canadian Gulf Islands. Using hair bleach and dye, he greyed his black hair along his temples with matching streaks along his beard. To finish the transformation, a foundation powder with an eyeliner pencil gave his skin an aged look.

Within the Vancouver airport terminal, a U.S. Customs agent took a cursory look at the photo, scanned the NEXUS card into the system and said, "Good luck." Looking beyond Ali, he called, "Next," motioning for another passenger to step up to his kiosk.

Ali sat in seat 2B on a WestJet Boeing 737, across the aisle from two elderly women who he overheard talking incessantly about their slot machine strategy. Three hours later, the 737 made a smooth touchdown at Las Vegas McCarran International Airport, with the flight attendant announcing "Welcome to Las Vegas. You can pick up your baggage from carousel two."

When the airline captain turned the seatbelt sign off, Ali stood to remove his soft-sided bag from the overhead compartment. He also removed overnight satchels for the two elderly women who chatted incessantly during the entire flight. His grayed-out hair hung to his shoulders—a full beard covered most of his face. Clear spectacles hung from his nose and his posture drooped around a padded stomach. Even with his disguise, his shoulders were broad, with powerful arms hidden inside a loose fitting dark brown blazer. His appearance matched that of a sixty-one year old physics professor. With all the traveling he had done over the past month, he felt every bit the age—knees ached and stiff neck.

***

Pakistani First Secretary Seyyed Sadegh awoke. He could hardly recall the first week in the hospital. All he knew was a political deluge befell the State Department—a foreign diplomat mugged in a casino parking lot became an embarrassment to both the United States and Pakistan. To release a buildup of cranial pressure from his head hitting the asphalt, the doctors drilled four holes in his occipital lobe. His convulsions and the swirling room finally stopped once the swelling in his brain subsided. Right now, his mind felt like a bowl of mush with all the pain medications surging through his brain. At first, he didn't recognize his own leg bound from ankle to hip in a gauze wrap, elevated with a pulley system. Even his arm had a large mesh-fabric stretched to his shoulder. He imagined he looked like a wrapped up mummy from some old Hollywood movie.

A warm hand touched the side of his face. A nurse sat at his bedside, and when he looked upon her, she got up and left the room. She looked a lot like the prostitute he hired to seduce the pilot, prompting him to call out, "Amber, don't go." Her slender arms and long legs made his body quiver. "She's mine," he cried out. Excitement surged through his body as he dreamt of what he wanted to do to her.

A doctor with a cover over his face stepped into his room, followed by the nurse he'd seen previously. "Mister Sadegh, I see you are awake."

With all the tubes protruding from various orifices, he gave a nod.

"Your operation was very successful. Once your vitals are stable, we'll be taking you upstairs to the post-surgical ward for your recovery. You now have a synthetic patella. You will be walking around with a cane for a while, but you should have full mobility with physical therapy. There will be brief spasms as your muscles adapt, otherwise you should be good as new. Do you have any questions?"

Sadegh shook his head indicating no. He didn't know why he even had surgery.

"I'll let you rest and will check on you later."

After the doctor left, a new set of people came into his room, checking to make sure all his vitals were normal, adding another bag of fluid to his IV drip. After several hours of poking and prodding, an orderly finally wheeled him out of the room, onto an elevator and into another. Kallem, sitting in a chair alongside the bed, stood when they rolled him in. Once they had the transfer complete, the nurses left, leaving him alone with his assistant.

"Sir, you have a visitor," Kallem said. "Should I show him in? He flew in this afternoon specifically to see you."

Sadegh forced a smile as his guest entered the room, waiting behind Kallem. He knew he had met this person somewhere before, but right now he couldn't remember where.

The guest took a chair and pulled it next to the bed. "*As-Salamu Alaykum*, my friend."

"I have seen your face before. Tell me your name and why are you here? Who told you to come?" Sadegh replied.

The man raised his hand for him to stop. "I am known as Ali. I am only here to make sure your situation is dealt with properly. I would have been here sooner—"

From the physique and demeanor of this guest, Sadegh placed him as a Quds agent. *If he was here, then he was sent to deal with any loose ends.* "I don't care about your excuse. Find who did this to me. I demand revenge."

"I will do what is required. *No more, no less—*"

"You will do as I say."

Ali placed his hand firmly on Sadegh's shoulder—even with the narcotic barrier, it felt like a vice. "All in good time ... all in good time." The pressure came off, before he said, "I noticed you had an ambassadorial guard sitting by your door. Your future involvement in this matter may pose a problem while you are in this hospital."

"You do your part and Kallem, my assistant, will do what I tell him—he will assist you."

"This is not necessary—I tend to work alone," Ali countered. "I will do what is necessary. When I am done, I'll disappear like a ghost." Ali got up from his chair and looked out the window. "To expedite what you desire, do you have any idea who attacked you? Was someone with you?"

"I was alone—" Sadegh thought better and recanted his story. "Find a female escort. Her name is Amber, works for a service called Destiny Delights. Find her—she lured me outside—that's all I know, all you need to know. You must find her before the police do. Kill her when you find her. Now go—leave me! If you don't have the stomach for it, I will kill her when I get out of this place."

***

Ali drove across the city, looking for a pay phone. The shell of booths stood on street corners, with only a wire bundle hanging out of tubes. Like the rest of the world, America became a casualty of technology.

Driving into a low-income residential area, he found a booth with a working phone on the outside wall of a 7-Eleven gas station. He would have preferred more privacy, but after driving around the block, he found no cameras monitoring the building's exterior.

He drove his rental car into the store's parking lot, staying away from the gas pump area and parked alongside the booth. He pulled on tight-fitting gloves, inserting the required number of coins into the slot before dialing the phone number given to him. Ali heard several rings in the handset before someone answered.

"Destiny Delights, my name is Vlad. How may we be of service?"

"Hopefully you can help me," answered Ali. "I am a British journalist writing an article about the mega casinos in your city. This is my first visit to Las Vegas. I am in need of someone who can spend several days showing me the attractions of this city. A friend of mine said if I was ever in Las Vegas, I should call you and specifically request a woman called Amber. I am told she works for your service. May I ask if she is available for several days?"

"Certainly, she works for our agency. We also have other women available who would meet your needs."

"My desire is to only meet with Amber. A colleague highly recommended her."

"I'm not sure she will be available at this short of notice. If you'd tell me your preferences, I can assure you we've someone available who will match your requirements."

"I am willing to triple your fee, but only with her—nobody else."

"I appreciate your generosity. Please give me a moment to check her schedule."

"I will be at this number for twenty minutes," he said and ended the call

***

Amber stepped out of the shower. Most of her clothes were now at Brent's place, except for the essential things a woman needs to be seen in public. Unsure when Brent would be back, she did not want to scare him into thinking she had moved in. From what she knew about Brent, he was independent—the thought of a live-in girlfriend needed discretion. She staggered the time each day as to when she would go to her apartment, just in case her pimp had one of his goons watching, to change into a clean set of clothes and apply her necessary makeup.

Looking at herself in the bathroom mirror, most of the bruising on her face now had a slight green hue—replaced by the purple. The bruising around her pelvic area still hurt—something felt torn inside and the continual spotting made her concerned. She needed to see a doctor, but was afraid the type of questions that would be asked. Her memory of Brent rescuing her from Vlad was still vague from whatever drug he had injected into her. He wanted to get her hooked, so that she'd need him versus the other way around. Coming back to her face, she began dabbing on a concealer until her skin appeared normal. While she applied her makeup, her phone started vibrating on the countertop. The caller identification showed it came from her pimp, Vlad. Instead of answering it, she let it go to voicemail. She didn't want anything to do with him. What they did to her still made her shake.

Before, it was about the money. Now that Brent was confined to the base, she didn't know what to do. She wanted out of the business, but the money always drew her back. With Brent's interception into her life, it was as if they both yearned for a personal connection. She put on her mask of makeup only for her customers, and when off, it was none of Vlad's business who she slept with.

Since the attack, she had stayed hidden in Brent's townhouse, venturing out for some coffee and a few groceries. Twice she went to her apartment for a few extra clothes, trying not to be too obtrusive. Always in and out before anyone noticed.

She stared at her phone, building courage to listen to the message. She made herself a coffee and threw on a bathrobe, before she finally worked up the courage to listen to what he wanted. The first part of the message he apologized for what happened. He needed her and tried to relay that she needed him. The second part was the usual Vlad—greedy. A customer specifically requested her for a gig tonight—and he would pay double to be with her.

Knowing how he operated, he would keep calling, keep pursuing her until she told him no and moved to another state.

She gathered up her courage and called him back.

He picked up. "Amber, I'm sorry about what happened. I need you. I have a new customer who has personally requested you— he wants nobody else. He's a journalist writing a story about our Vegas nightlife and wants you to show him the city. He sounds foreign, maybe English. He said you came highly recommended by a mutual friend and he's willing to pay extra."

"Vlad, I'm not available. I'm out. Gone!"

"It's time for you to get back to work."

"You let him rape me while filming the whole thing. How could you? I trusted you. You are supposed to protect us."

"If it makes you any happier ... Yuri is dead. Someone killed him. And your DVD is missing. I'm guessing this new boyfriend of yours did it. You know I will eventually find him and kill him. He cannot hide forever. I don't want you to get in the way. Come back to work and I'll leave him alone. That's the deal. If not, I'll peel off every inch of his skin. You know what I'm capable of doing."

"I don't know what you're talking about. He's gone...." She remembered Brent leaving early to go to work wearing jeans and a black tee shirt. Since then, he hasn't come home.

"If he's gone, come back. I need you."

"I quit. I'm out. I don't trust you anymore. You hurt me."

"Seriously, you're being melodramatic. Sex is part of this business. You of all people should know that."

"You don't understand. You drugged me and made me do things—"

"So you got knocked around a little—it happens. Your sensuality makes men lose themselves, which is why our clients pay a higher amount. Men desire a beautiful woman."

"You're not listening to me—."

"Put your big girl panties on—touch up with a little more makeup. I need you for tonight."

"Fuck off Vlad." Amber disconnected the call. Vlad called several more times, leaving pleading messages—the last one he threatened to kill her.

***

Ali stood guard by the payphone. Several people had approached, but upon seeing Ali's demeanor, nobody ventured close. Finally, the phone rang. "Hello?" Ali answered.

"This is Vlad from Destiny Delights. Amber will be available to meet with you tonight. Since your request is such short notice, she had to cancel with another client. I hope you understand, she has requested a thousand dollar bump on top of the agreed fee. An advance payment is required to secure this arrangement."

"Have Amber meet me at the *Carnevino* steakhouse at nine o'clock this evening. Tell her there will be a reservation for two and we will later attend a social hosted by the Associated Press. I want her for three days—all at our agreed upon price. Please have her wear black and carry a white rose—the evening social is formal."

"If you decide additional days are needed, I'm a phone call away. Is there anything else you require? I can arrange a suite at the *Bellagio*. Perhaps two women?"

The thought of doing a deal with this man disgusted Ali. His trafficking of women as if they were a toy to be sold pushed him to make another promise. "My hotel accommodation is already arranged, thank you. Make sure she knows to arrive promptly at nine—no earlier, no later. Please remind her about the rose. I will look for a beautiful woman precisely at nine o'clock carrying this precious flower."

***

At 2053, Ali already staged a stolen delivery van across from the restaurant. A car drove past and parked in an open slot a half block from the restaurant. A woman got out carrying a white rose. Her physical features matched Amber's description Sadegh had given: long slim legs, dark hair, and a form fitting black evening dress made to accentuate round hips. Ali felt a passion rise in his chest, not sexual, but as a father would feel towards a beautiful daughter. She looked fresh and innocent, as all women should be revered, not an object for perversion.

She walked along the sidewalk, took a glance at her watch and paused in front of a store window to check herself in the reflection—brushing a strand of hair away from her face, reapplying a fresh touch of lipstick. With three minutes before the appointed time, she turned.

Ali had the van's engine running at idle. Kallem sat in a door alcove two doors down from the restaurant, slumped over with a sweatshirt hood pulled over his head, his face concealed. An empty bottle of wine rested next to him. Sadegh's personal assistant looked like any other homeless person trying to sleep away his drunkenness.

"She is moving toward you," Ali reported on his radio. "I am moving alongside." Wearing delivery coveralls, his appearance didn't cause an alarm.

She disregarded Ali and took a step in the direction of the restaurant.

"Excuse me ma'am, do you have any spare change?" the homeless man asked.

Somewhat startled, she turned to look at him. Ali placed a rag soaked with *Sevoflurane* across her mouth and nose. She struggled, inhaling a deep breath of the sweet-smelling inhalational anesthetic. Her knees buckled—the white rose fell from her hand onto the sidewalk.

Ali caught her before she collapsed and loaded the limp body into the van, climbing in with her before closing the side door— while Kallem hustled into the driver's seat as if nothing had happened. As Kallem drove, Ali zip tied the girl's feet and hands, blindfolded her eyes and placed tape across her mouth.

They drove the van out of the city onto a dirt road toward the mountains. When the road ended, they stopped. Ali held her head, breaking open ammonia smelling salts and placed it under her nose.

She flinched away from the acrid smell—disoriented and frightened. The interior lights within the van were kept off to add to her confusion. Ali snapped on a penlight and shined it in her eyes. "I am not going to harm you. I only want to ask a few questions. If you scream or yell, I will hurt you. If you answer my questions truthfully, I will let you go. Do you understand?"

The girl nodded.

"I am going to remove the tape from your mouth. I will leave the blindfold across your eyes." Ali reached over and eased the tape from her lips.

"What is your name?"

"... Amber."

Ali noticed the brief hesitation. "What is the name of the agency you work for?"

"Destiny Delights."

"Who is your manager?"

"Manager? I guess that would be Vlad. He's my pimp."

"I'm sorry, tell me your name again?"

"Ah ... Amber."

Again, Ali noticed the slight hesitation in her voice. "Do you remember a client several weeks ago at the Royal Sands Casino?"

"I don't know what you're talking about. I ... was out of town visiting friends in Los Angeles."

"This man was assaulted in the casino parking lot?"

"I didn't see anybody assaulted. We don't frequent the Royal Sands; it's not a place we'd meet a client. The Sands is a low-end casino located in old town—has a western cowboy feel. You can call my employer if you don't believe me. He schedules all our clients."

Interesting, thought Ali, *why was Sadegh at this type of casino?* Ali reached into the woman's purse and removed her driver's license. "Your name on this license does not say Amber."

"We do not give out our real names to clients. It keeps us protected from prowlers."

The face in the picture matched the girl lying in front of him except for the hair—short cropped and auburn in the picture versus a longer dark brown, almost black hair color. He grabbed a fistful and pulled out a length of hair extensions, causing her to cry out. "I am going to ask you again and I want you to answer me truthfully. I now know who you really are and where you live. You do not want me to hurt you, do you?"

The girl shook her head, "Please, no."

"Tell me your real name. Be truthful this time."

The girl began to cry. "I am sorry. My name is Lexi, not Amber. Please don't hurt me."

"As long as you keep telling me the truth, I will let you go. I am a man of honor. Did Vlad tell you to be Amber tonight?"

"Yes," whimpering and shaking her head as she answered.

"You were ill-advised Lexi. Is Amber her real name or is it also a name used for clients?"

"Her name is Katya ... Katya Kozachenko. Vlad told me to make myself look like her."

"Do you know where she is, where I can find her?"

"I don't know. I've never gone to her place—we communicate on Facebook and text each other about various clients, but we don't socialize unless there is a request for two girls. Vlad knows where she lives. He calls our cell phones for assignments."

"Where might I find your manager Vlad?"

"A warehouse type building at 3700 Las Vegas Boulevard. His office is on the second floor. He owns the entire building, uses the bottom to film his girls."

The thought of pornography made Ali's skin crawl. "You have been very helpful. I am going to cut your ties so you can walk away. Leave your blindfold on until we are gone. The main road is several miles along this dirt road—you can see the lights of Vegas." Ali cut the zip ties around the girl's wrist and her ankles, and opened the sliding door for her to leave. "Now get out and walk straight ahead—do not look back."

Not being able to see, Lexi stumbled getting out of the van. With high-heels, she took small delicate steps along the uneven gravel.

Kallem got out and walked around to the front. Initially Ali thought he was going to help her. Instead, Kallem raised a 9mm pistol, aiming at the girl's back.

"No!" Ali yelled.

Too late—Kallem pulled the trigger twice.

Ali leapt out of the van like a tiger pouncing on its prey.

Kallem must've heard Ali coming, for he turned—startled to see Ali so close. "Wait—"

Ali drove his fist into the surprised face, snapping the head back and knocking Sadegh's assistant to the ground. "What did you shoot her for?" Ali yelled. "I gave her my word. I should kill you right here." He kicked Kallem's side, causing him to curl up. Ali picked up the fallen pistol and pointed it at the man's head. "The Koran teaches we do not kill the innocent—women or children. Her death does not support a higher purpose."

"Please no ..."

Ali fired, snapping a bullet next to his head, sending dirt into the man's face.

"Sadegh wanted her dead."

"This girl was not Amber you idiot. Do not assume every infidel must die. This is not a war of attrition." Ali jammed the barrel into Kallem's mouth, pushing until he screamed. "Kill another woman—and I will put a bullet in your foul head." He backed off the pressure, picked up the dropped gun and went over to where Lexi lay.

He found her still alive, barely, trying to crawl away—digging her fingers into the dirt—her legs dragging behind her. Blood gurgled from her mouth.

Ali had seen enough death to know she had a severed spine. The gurgling indicated a perforated lung, drowning on her own blood. Ali recited a prayer, raised the 9mm pistol, and shot her in the back of her head. He looked over at Kallem, now sitting up on the ground. "Get up or you will be joining her. Drag her body off the road where nobody will find it."

Kallem limped over to the girl while holding his side. He picked up a leg and pulled the body to a trough, then rolled it in. Ali sat in the driver's seat, watching to see if Kallem gave the girl any dignity even in death. Ali got out of vehicle and went over to where the girl lay to close her legs together and fold arms across her chest. With the body properly situated, he went back to the vehicle and started the engine, while Kallem sat quietly in the passenger seat.

During the short drive back into the city, nothing further was said. Ali drove to an abandoned car lot, where they had left their rental car prior to stealing the van. He got out of the van and went over to the car, opened the trunk and pulled out a five-gallon gasoline can filled with fuel. He poured gasoline throughout the van's interior, splashing most of it in the rear compartment where the girl had been. He poured a trail of fuel across the pavement, tossing the empty fuel-can back toward the van. Pulling out a pack of matches from his pocket, he lit the entire pack and threw the flame onto the fuel stream, which raced towards the van's interior.

Both men returned to the rental car. Ali removed the girl's cell phone from his pocket and placed a call to Destiny Delights.

"Lexi, why are you calling? Is there a problem with this journalist?" Ali heard Vlad say, but he hung up severing the connection. "He is still in his office. Drive to thirty-seven hundred Las Vegas Boulevard. We are going to pay this Vlad a visit."

***

Ali drove past a nondescript two-story brick building. A single light showed through the window on the upper floor. This portion of the city had been abandoned for several years—buildings had either plywood across windows or there were bars to keep intruders out. The street remained empty of cars and the single streetlight on the corner had the lamp shot out. In the alley, a new

BMW was parked—the driver's door was wrecked with wide strips of tape holding it closed. Ali stopped the vehicle at a corner and got out. "Drive to the front of the building and wait. If he comes out, stop him—do not kill him—understand. I want to ask him a few questions first. Then I will kill him."

Once Kallem's vehicle left the alley, Ali waited in the darkness, watching to see if his presence alerted anyone. The back door was inside an alcove stoop, with two cement stairs to get in. Within seconds, Ali picked the lock on the door and entered the building. He paused in the foyer and listened. The building smelled stale—lifeless. An exit sign above the door and another across the foyer cast a glow into the interior. Off to his left, he noticed a faint outline of a stairwell with a light above that cast a dim glow into the corridor.

Ali proceeded up the stairs to the second floor. He flicked the hall light off, casting the hallway into a red glow from the overhead EXIT sign. Lying flat along the last few stairs, he pointed his gun into the interior—and waited. Ali learned long ago, *humans are curious animals who lack patience.*

Ali could hear Vlad's feet clunking toward the office entrance.

A large Russian appeared in the door alcove—he held a Smith & Wesson 357 magnum revolver. He entered the hallway, sweeping the barrel back and forth like a flashlight until he got to the same light switch. He aimed at the top of the stairs. "I see you—"

Placing a bullet in the big man's knee at a distance of ten meters took timing. Placing a second bullet into the opposite leg before he could pull the trigger took speed and precision. Both knees buckled beneath his immense weight, slamming him into the floor. He screamed with agony, as he fell over like a fallen tree.

Ali bounded off the stairs toward his target, removing the pistol from the Russian's hand. "You must be Vlad." Ali said, standing over the man while aiming the barrel at the head.

The man cursed in Russian, yelling and screaming profanities.

Ali waited. "Shh ... боль утихнет ... the pain will subside." He knelt down and continued in Russian, "I have a few questions I need you to answer."

Switching back to English, Vlad yelled, "Who are you?"

Ali followed with the transition. "I seek information."

"Fuck you asshole."

Ali stepped on the big man's left knee, which crunched under the weight of his foot, causing Vlad to scream. "I do not think your neighbors care who screams within this building." Ali waited until the Russian regained control of himself. "If you use profanity again, I will step on your other knee."

"No, no, please ...."

"I want to know where I can find Amber."

"I don't know who you are talking about."

"Why did you swap the girl Lexi with Amber this evening?"

"You ... you're the person who called earlier. She wouldn't take the trick. I put Lexi in her place."

"Then you must know where she lives?"

"I don't have her address—just a number. Her information is on my desk—on a Rolodex card."

Ali went into the office and came back with a card. The card had the name -Amber written on it, with a phone number. "Is this the card ... the only card?" On the back had a written name -Katya Kozachenko.

"Yes ... yes. That's all I have."

"No address? You have to know her address."

"Seriously, I peddle hookers to clients. I pay in cash. If vice raids this building, my girls are safe."

"Do you have any information on where she might be? Is she staying with a friend?"

"She has a new boyfriend. Doesn't want to do tricks anymore. The bitch needed time to recover—she had a bad encounter with a client. Hasn't been the same since. My knees are on fire—please help me."

"Do you have any information on this man she had the encounter with?"

"What man?"

"The one she met at the Royal Sands casino."

"His name and credit card information are on file. We schedule everything over the phone without seeing the clients. Only the girls meet with clients."

Ali already knew the credit card to be untraceable. All the money remaining depleted. At least Sadegh was smart enough not to have used his real name when soliciting a prostitute.

Vlad moaned in pain. His eyes focused on Ali. "Since you're asking about Amber, what did you do with Lexi?"

"Lexi is no longer in this world. You may now go and see her." Ali raised his pistol and fired a single bullet into the Russian's brain.

***

Thirty minutes past midnight, two Jeeps threw up a dust cloud as they raced to the end of a dirt road. Large off-road LED light bars illuminated the desert floor in front of them, brightening the landscape—hard rock music pounded base notes from oversized speakers strapped to roll bars. At the end of the road, the vehicles skidded around, the front bumpers facing opposite directions. Empty beer cans fell out onto the ground as the occupants climbed from the vehicles. Each vehicle contained two couples as they began their own party in the middle of the desert.

From the back of a Jeep, the drivers removed several bundles of wooden logs and stacked them in a nearby pile. With the help of a splash of fuel, a bonfire soon blazed, casting shadows across the young faces. A girl wearing a light colored dress sat on the ground with her boyfriend, watching the flames flicker into the evening air. He leaned over to kiss her, pressing her back against the flat earth. "The ground feels damp," she said. "Go see if there's a blanket in the Jeep and bring back a couple of beers while you're there."

As she waited, a jet descended over the mountains on approach into McCarran International. They all got up to watch, as the lights from the jet fanned out across the sky. "What's that on your dress?" One of the girls asked the other. "It's all over you're back." When they stood in front of the Jeep's lights, they found her dress stained in red. "What is it?" The girl asked. She looked at her hands and forearms, both coated in sticky blood with small gravel rocks holding it to her skin as if a binding glue. She screamed—frantically trying to brush it all off.

A boy moved a Jeep to allow the lights to illuminate the area, showing a fresh set of tire tracks. He first maneuvered the Jeep's lights to where the girl sat and found a large circle of blood soaked into the dirt—it looked like an animal dragged a body away from the road. He followed the trail with an entourage walking close behind the bumper. Cresting a raise, he stopped and got out with a flashlight. "Oh my god, get over here quick," the boy yelled. "There's a woman's body."

***

Brent had returned from his morning run. What he heard from the television in his BOQ room caught his attention. The newscaster said something about twin murders. When she said, "prostitution" and "murder," he stopped and turned up the volume.

"A female victim with an arrest history of prostitution was found just outside the city limits brutally murdered. Authorities went to question the owner of Destiny Delights. They also found him murdered sometime during the night. Destiny Delights is an exclusive escort service that caters to the elite and has Russian mafia ties to every major city. This scandal is similar to the New York Emperor Club VIP scandal, which had connections with the mayor's office. A press conference is scheduled for ten o'clock this morning."

Brent recognized the name Destiny Delights as Amber's employer. He called her right away to see if she had seen the news.

After several rings, she answered, "Brent, I miss you. How are you doing?"

"I'm fine. I miss you, too."

"When do you think the military will let you come home?"

"I'm not sure—it's complicated and classified. I can't talk about it—these things have a tendency to take a while. Listen, have you seen the news this morning? Something's happened with your previous employer. It's all over the Channel-Seven news. They said a prostitute and the owner of Destiny Delights were both murdered last night."

"Oh my God. Did they say who?"

"The newscaster didn't give any names—she said the names are being withheld. She did say there would be a press conference at ten this morning with more information." There was only silence coming from the phone. "I'm sorry ... I thought you'd want to know."

"Brent, something's going on. Vlad, he is the owner of Destiny Delights. He called me yesterday, adamant I entertain a journalist who requested me."

"What are you talking about?" Brent huffed.

"Vlad said the client was referred by a friend. I haven't ever been with a journalist. I told him I wouldn't do it—to find someone else..." Amber's voice trailed off. Brent could almost hear her shaking on the other side of the phone.

"Slow down. You think the murders are related—you could have been the girl murdered?" Brent's blood ran cold. The thought of some maniac coming after her, killing her... he felt his scar begin to itch. Vlad, hell yeah, he deserved it, but not Amber or this other girl.

"Yes! Knowing Vlad, I'm sure he assigned someone who looked like me. Now Vlad is dead and so is this girl. Brent, I'm scared. Something's not right. After what happened, someone is looking for me." Her voice faded off.

"You're not making any sense. There's no reason for him to want to kill you. You haven't done anything to deserve this."

"What should I do? I can't be involved with the police. I have an arrest record. They know what I do. I'm scared Brent. You need to come home."

"I will get off this damn base. Don't go out anywhere. Did you tell anybody at Destiny where you're staying?" Brent's heart picked up its pace.

"No, I haven't told anyone."

"Amber, I need you to stay calm. You'll be safe at my place at least for now. I'll try to get you a pass onto the base, or I'll get off and come to you. I ... I love you." The words tumbled out before Brent could even think about them. His heart surged at the thought of anything happening to Amber. He made a promise to himself that he would keep her safe ... no matter what.

"I love you too. Please hurry."

Brent hung up the phone, surprised he said those last three words. It slipped out—he'd never been able to say those words before. This was different: he missed her and she missed him. He went back over what he already knew and what she had told him—it didn't make any sense.

He needed someone to talk to, but who would give him advice about his relationship with a prostitute and involvement with a killer? He thought about confessing to a priest—*a hell of a confession.*

***

Sadegh hobbled around his hospital room. His right arm hung over a crutch to help support his weight—his entire left arm immobilized in a sling. "What do you mean you cannot find the girl?" Sadegh yelled. "In America you can find out anything by doing a quick search on the internet. I don't care how you do it—find her—find who did this to me!"

Ali closed the hospital room door, before this lunatic drew attention. "The nurses outside can hear you. What you are saying might even be recorded—"

"I don't care who's listening. You now have her real name ... Katya. Use your resources. Somebody has information on her. Find this girl and you'll find my attacker. I personally want to be there to slit them both!"

For a moment, Ali wondered if Sadegh had lost his mind. In a calm voice Ali asked, "Why do you think the two even knew each other? She is a prostitute." He already knew Sadegh had a history of hiring this type of woman. His persistence in wanting her dead made him think there was more to this story. Just the close proximity to this man made him feel unclean. "How were you even involved with her?" How he answered would either confirm or deepen the lie.

Sadegh turned away and peered out the window. "I saw them leave together. Find her and you will find him. Then you can leave. Now get out," he cursed. "Leave me!"

Ali stood in the room, questioning Sadegh's sanity. What was said he knew to be another lie. "I am here only to clean up what has already happened. I will find them both and bring them to you. If you want them dead, you can do it yourself. Next time you hear from me, I will have them hidden away so you can do what you want with them." He needed to get Sadegh out of the hospital and away from any guards. Then he would be done with this mission.

"Kallem told me about your reluctance to kill the prostitute. I gave him strict orders to leave no trail."

"There was no reason." Ali held firm. When he was a young boy, he despised the SAVAT, the secret police who came to his house to take his father. With no one to guard his family, they repeatedly came back to rape his mother and sisters, losing their virginity before they could even marry and bear children. He could still hear their cries to stop. Shaking his head at the memory, Sadegh was this same kind of man. In the process of their own despicable evil, they created an efficient assassin, and he had found each one. He did not make them suffer—the less time they lived with humanity, the better—*no more no less.* "If they live in this city, I will soon know where."

A nurse must have heard the commotion in the room. She barged through the door. "Sir, you need to leave now. Mister Sadegh, I have a sedative to help you rest."

Ali heard Sadegh yell more profanity at the nurse before he proceeded out of the room, past the guard and down the corridor. Time to get this mission finished.

He drove his rental car back to the same pay phone he found earlier. He would have to be careful what he said during this next phone call. The NSA were known to actively monitor their own people's conversation—especially international connections to a Muslim organization. The payphone was most likely off the grid of a public phone system. He inserted the required coins and dialed a number to a computer maintained by an Iranian US citizen. Hearing two chimes confirmed the network connected. Ali punched in a number sequence, which forwarded his call through a series of encrypted servers over the internet network, ending at the QUDs command center in Iran. On the third ring, his call was answered.

"Hello." A technician answered from the other side of the world.

"This is alpha-three-six-two-five-delta."

"Stand by for confirmation." After several seconds had elapsed, he asked, "What is the reason for your call?"

"I need an address of a female who goes by the name of Katya Kozachenko. Her residence is somewhere in the city of Las Vegas, Nevada. My guess is she lives in an apartment complex. Search the city's public utility databases first—she has to have an account for electricity and water," Ali requested. "She also might have an arrest record for prostitution."

"It will take a moment to hack into the city's database."

Ali could hear clicking in the background.

"I'm in. I have one name listed living in the metropolitan area. I'll cross reference now with Nevada motor vehicle for a driver license picture and any convictions."

"When you have both, email me her address and photo."

Ali hung up the phone, got in his car and thought about what Sadegh had divulged and what he now knew. Moving forward, Ali powered up his iPhone. He already had an email message from an anonymous sender. The message came with two attachments: a woman's picture and address. After uploading the files, a photo showed a picture of a woman who looked similar to the prostitute he had killed the previous evening—the two could have been sisters.

He logged on to an anonymous Facebook account used to track a person's location. It was always amazing the amount of people addicted to social media—anybody could find out anything on anyone: pictures, where they worked, even where they lived. Ali tapped *Find Friends*, typed in the name *Katya Kozachenko* and typed *Las Vegas* in the *Search* space, and immediately had a match. He flipped through her recent photos, saving them onto his iPad. A selfie showed Katya with a man her age. He had a military appearance with a close-cropped haircut and muscular physique. The picture showed their intimacy by the way they smiled and touched each other. The caption said, *Hi mom, I'm doing well in Las Vegas. Meet my new friend.* She added to her profile, *In a new relationship with Brent.*

With the girl's photos saved, he opened the Photos application icon on his iPhone's home screen. He tapped *Places* at the bottom, initiating multiple red pins to appear on a map. He opened -Maps- and typed in the address the Quds analyst had given him. Both locations overlaid each other and ... a cluster of red pins popped up at another location. *I bet this is where her boyfriend lives.*

Chapter 21

A CONSPIRACY

Vince Phillips had presided over numerous cases during his twenty years as a Superior Court judge for the State of Washington, but he hadn't seen a cloak of secrecy of this magnitude before. *Most cases are black-and-white, open-and-shut.* When the evidence was stacked against the defendant, the defendant usually pleaded out to a lesser charge and the case became settled.

He finished reading the investigative report on the allegations against Lieutenant Brent Parker. He looked at Parker's official military picture from his personnel file, which also contained an outlined history before entering the military. Brent went to college on an athletic scholarship, NCAA ranked and an Olympic prospect, but for some unknown reason it all ended mid-season. *A national contender, Olympic material—interesting, I'll have to ask him what happened, why he quit?* He reread the written version of the audio tape recording of the mission and his admittance to the investigative officer.

He understood the prosecuting counsel's' acclamations. What baffled Vince was why. He requested a copy of the camera footage, though he didn't expect they'd actually give it to him due to the classified nature of the content. The rules of evidence requiring a full disclosure to the defense didn't apply in a military court. All the court cases he heard over the years—*there was always a motive in premeditated action. The question of -why- must be in the video, which is the reason they won't let me have it.*

He sent a request to have the members of the Special Forces team subpoenaed, though he already knew what the answer would be - *Denied due to the mission critical operations of the team.* He requested the testimony of the Navy pilot and received the following back - *Lieutenant John Shook is still in serious condition. At this time, he has no recollection of what happened to his aircraft or the circumstances leading up to his rescue. No further inquiry is necessary or required.*

Vince knew the Special Forces community to be an exclusive club. The community did allow outside individuals access—those who show the determination to be a contributor to their team and had the necessary skills to augment their force: Air Force JTACs, Pararescue and Combat Controllers, and Navy SEALs. No matter who they were, the SF community stayed very loyal to those who pulled them out of a mess and Brent's situation qualified. Vince knew if he could talk to this team directly, they would be interested in helping Parker—who had become an honorary member of their code. Reading between the lines confirmed, *Parker saved those soldiers. I need to find the SF team and hear their story.*

From the Reaper's audio transcripts, he had the SF team's JTAC call sign—Playboy two-five. After a phone call to a team leader he knew, who had recently returned from the same theater, Vince connected the Playboy to a specific ODA team. Phillips went into his bedroom and opened a cedar chest that contained all his military memorabilia from his active duty days. Pulling aside the tiger-stripe BDU from his tours in Vietnam, he found a green notebook. Flipping through the pages, he searched for a secret email address monitored by the Green Beret community—*I hope it still works*—it hadn't been used in a long time.

Vince emailed out a very specific, though simplistic message: *ODA562/318405, HUNTER 031111 needs help.* The digits *318405* stood for the SF member who originated the message, with *3184* representing the Special Forces class number of the thirty-first class of the year 1984, and *05* representing the fifth graduate within the class. Finally, *HUNTER 031111* stood for the narrative of the message. Vince hoped whoever monitored the SF message traffic would route his email on to the appropriate team leadership. The team leader reading the message would understand and make the connection: a UAV pilot involved with their operation on the 3rd day of November 2011 needed their help. *If the ground action had been as ugly as he speculated, the members of this team would remember this date for the rest of their lives.*

***

Several days later

Standing near the front entrance to the café, the judge heard the roar of two Harley-Davidson motorcycles permeating the open country well before the bikers approached the second exit off Interstate-90, which looped around toward the eastern community of Ellensburg, Washington. They brought their Harleys to a stop at the cloverleaf intersection—the café to their left had a dozen semi-tractor trailers parked in front. Vince found this café prepared the best steak and eggs before driving over Snoqualmie Pass or across the flat plains of the I-90 corridor. He went inside as the two men glided their motorcycles around the large sixteen-wheel trucks and rolled to a stop in front of the restaurant. Each pulled off their helmets, revealing shaggy dark hair and a full beard.

Vince found an empty booth and ordered a cup of coffee, keeping an eye on the two bikers as they approached the restaurant. Their black leather jackets complemented the persona of any hard-hitting motorcycle gang: weathered and scruffy. Several clans resided in nearby Yakima valley—*and two, just now, walked into the restaurant. Bikers and truckers ... great mix of testosterone.* He also recognized they each had a distinctive bulge up underneath their armpit, hidden inside their leather—the telltale sign they were packing heat. Vince slid a Glock from a side holster and laid it on his lap, placing a napkin over the weapon to keep it concealed.

The big Mexican entered the restaurant first and looked around the room in one sweeping arc, blocking the doorway from anybody entering or leaving the establishment—never making eye contact with any one person, but noticing everybody. The other man stood outside, facing away from the entrance, watching the parking lot for anything unusual. The Mexican gave a hand signal and he stepped aside to allow his partner access into the restaurant. He whispered something when his companion passed, and sat at an empty booth near the entrance.

The other approached Vince. "Colonel Phillips, I'm Captain Jeremy Zender. May I sit?"

Vince got up and reached out to shake hands. He noticed Zender lean and wince when they shook. "Jeremy, please call me Vince. Have a seat—thank you for meeting with me."

Zender pulled up a chair and sat across the table. "It's an honor to meet you sir. After what you told me about this drone pilot, coming to see you is the least we can do. If he hadn't done what he did, I would not be here talking with you. Sir, what can I do to make this right?"

"For starters let me buy you and your friend a cup of coffee, and something to eat. This place is known for their biscuits and gravy." Vince referenced the big Mexican sitting by himself near the door. "Not much has changed in the SF world. Is your friend over there your team sergeant?"

"Yes sir. He's Sergeant First Class Jose Perez. My senior NCO— the best operator I know at sniffing out trouble. He can sense trouble before it ever begins—I'm not sure how he does it. He recognized you right off—something about your character, body language and the gun you're holding on your lap."

Vince chuckled. "He is aware. I wasn't quite sure who you were when you walked in," removing the pistol and holstering it. He didn't give away that he knew they were also carrying weapons.

"Perez never lets me out of his sight—it's why he's sitting by himself watching to see who comes in and who takes notice of our meeting. We've been together a long time." Zender studied the silverware on the table. "We've gone through a lot of together. Our last Op was the closest we've come to not coming back."

Vince understood the vacant look on the man's face. He had seen the thousand-yard stare many times from people who'd seen death up close—too close. "If I may, let me tell you what I know so far about this UAV pilot, whose name is Lieutenant Brent Parker. Someone is pulling strings hard on this investigation. I believe they want to stuff him into a black hole to keep a lid sealed on a bad decision. The charges against him are valid, but things happen in combat that makes breaking rules justified."

"Please fill me in on what's going on."

"I'd be happy to share the details, but there are a few holes I hope you can fill in for me. As we know in the SF world—we work in a lot gray with no real right answer. This war on terrorism is a muddled mess—we send warriors who have to look their enemy in the face before they die. This lieutenant did the right thing. He had the guts to save good men. Truthfully, I don't understand why they are going after him."

"Sir, I think I know why."

Both men held each other's attention.

"What happened out there?" Vince asked.

"I'm thinking we should go outside for some fresh air." Zender stood up from the table and proceeded to the door. As he approached Perez, he saw Zender give a momentary hand signal, then walked out the door and stood by his bike.

Vince laid a twenty on the table and walked past the big Mexican, who gave him no recognition. He followed Zender out to where two tractor-trucks were parked with diesel engines running, which produced a low rumbling noise.

Perez followed close behind and climbed onto his motorcycle. He lifted a cigarette out of his leather jacket and stuck it in his mouth, lighting it with a Zippo. He gave the impression he'd done this a thousand times, watching for anybody suspicious who might disturb the meeting between his friend and the retired Special Forces colonel.

Zender stopped and waited until Vince caught up. "What I'm about to tell you is highly classified. I doubt anybody followed us or is listening to our conversation, but I've survived this long by never assuming anything." Zender took a moment before he proceeded with this next statement.

Vince let Zender have his moment. Hopefully what came next would shine some light onto what actually happened.

"We were on a mission to monitor a village. We had prior intelligence a top leader within ISIS, a former Iraqi general by the name al-Obeidi, had scheduled a meeting. Before the meeting started, a three-vehicle caravan entered the picture. We're still trying to figure out who all the players were in the meeting. The trail vehicle had crates stacked in the back."

Vince interjected, "From what I read, Parker recognized the crates. HQ confirmed they contained SA-24 antiaircraft missiles."

"Yes sir. We were later told the missiles were smuggled out of Libya about a month ago."

"Crazy world. Parker told me the same thing when I spoke with him over the STU. He was the UAV pilot who exposed the theft in the first place." Vince took a moment to think. "Now I'm starting to understand why the military is trying to pressure my client. I bet the CIA is scrambling to find those missiles before this war escalates or an airliner is shot down. No wonder they have Parker locked away on a base—they're maintaining damage control, trying to contain what happen. I bet I know what happened next—"

Zender nodded and squinted, as if to say, "Go on."

"—Navy fighters were called in to attack the village and they shot down one of them. Is this how it all played out?"

"You're essentially correct—the fighter part comes later. Our orders changed from a quick assassin to blowing up the house and destroying the truck with the crates. We hadn't done anything yet, but somebody must've tipped them off. We sure poked a hole in a hornet's nest. The enemy swarmed out of every house in the village. This is where our pilot comes into the picture."

"Parker?"

"Yes sir. He shot two Hellfire missiles. We thought we'd destroyed all the hand-helds that might expose the Navy jets. Parker kept the Reaper overhead during our egress out of the area—he provided us intelligence reports on the enemy's location. We were a force of twelve against a force of at least eighty."

"Those are not odds I'd ever desire."

"Me neither, but we didn't have a choice. I kept having a bad feeling, but didn't figure it out until it became too late. We were barely holding our own when I gave the command to move out. Then a flight of two Hornets checked in to support us. We used the last Hellfire to designate a target for the Hornets to drop on. The lead aircraft dropped short, but the wingman almost killed us. I suspect he placed the bomb a hundred eighty degrees out, dropping it instead on our heads—that one numbed us a bit. Aside from the confusion, we were able to continue toward the mountain pass. By this time half of my men were wounded."

Vince noticed Zender roll his shoulder. "How bad were you hit?" Vince asked.

"We all had to stay in the fight if we were to survive."

Vince wanted to know more, but he could tell Zender needed a moment as he relived his story. He waited ....

"ISIS drove multiple vehicles along an old Silk Road, blocking our ability to get out of the valley. We requested the Hornets to make a high-speed gun run underneath the overcast ceiling. This is when they shot down the wingman."

"With all the self-protection systems on the new Super Hornet, I'm surprised a missile could knock down one of our fighters."

"They actually fired four missiles. Dash two threw his engines into burner and the last missile went right for it. It's a wonder the pilot even survived. Supersonic vapes were coming off his jet when the missile blew up his tailpipe."

"Why didn't you call for a QRF rescue team?"

"We didn't have the weather to bring in additional fighters and HQ didn't want to risk any Air Cav helicopters being shot down. Besides, CIA became involved. They gave me an execute order to terminate the pilot if we weren't able to rescue him."

"Son of a bitch. I've done a few nasty things for God and country, but killing one of our own," Vince shook his head. "This explains the military's reaction."

"Yes sir. The odds of success were not in our favor, but we had to try. We'd been providing SITREPs to headquarters on our status—our JSOTF leadership knew our situation. I did what I had to do—I deployed my sniper, knowing this was a suicide mission." He took another silent moment as he looked up into the sky. "We were to kill the pilot if we didn't succeed. Either we all live or we all die—it's our motto." He stopped his story, kicking at an imaginary rock on the hard pavement.

Listening to the story, Vince could picture how this all played out. Making the ultimate decision whether to live or die.

"Things didn't go our way. They had us pinned down. I was, well ... we all were down to shooting pistols against AK-47 rifles. Several of my men had pulled their last grenade pin versus being taken alive. I gave the order to my sniper to execute the pilot and to initiate plan Alpha—to make sure none of us were captured alive."

During his tour in Vietnam, Vince removed team's bodies who had initiated this order—no SF soldier ever spent a day at the Hanoi Hilton. "Do you know if anybody else outside of your group heard you give the execute order?"

"Our internal radios are encrypted. There's no way the Reaper pilot heard my order. He must've realized what we were up against and recognized the shit-storm we were in." Zender stared off, eventually coming back to his story. "Your young Lieutenant told us to get our heads down. We were already hiding behind anything we could find. Parker crashed his UAV into an advancing ISIS wedge, allowing my men to rally forward and take out those still alive." He paused. "My sniper later told me he had an ounce of pressure remaining before his hammer would've released—our JTACs yelled over our internal radio for him to hold fire." He stopped his story, as if deciding how much to say next. "The military thinks we're heroes for saving the pilot. Most people don't know I gave the order to kill him."

"Who else knows about what happened?"

"After the mission, Perez and I were in isolation for several days, being debriefed by the JTF general, an admiral and a couple of CIA spooks. They still don't know I gave an execute order."

"Do you know who gave you the order to kill the pilot?"

"When the missiles were found, the CIA took over the operation. I don't know who gave the order—I would imagine a decision of this magnitude comes straight from the top—my guess is it came from the SecDef. Either they had a national security shit storm or a dead Navy pilot—they chose a dead Navy pilot and a team of SF soldiers. I'm sure if either one is leaked to the press, they'd have a heyday with the information."

"My guess we'll never know who sanctioned the execute order. Do you remember the name of the JTF general?"

"I've worked under this general on several operations. His name is Shoemaker. First time I met the admiral. He seemed appreciative that we rescued his pilot. He said if I ever needed anything to give him a call."

"I know Shoemaker. He and I went through the SF qualification course together. I hope that you're right and he meant it. We can't allow this lieutenant to be taken down for saving lives."

"Please let me know when the hearing is going to take place. I would assume I'm invited to the party."

"Absolutely. Keep our meeting quiet. I'll enter your names with the clerk at the last minute so they don't have time to deny my request. The military has expedited a court-martial hearing sometime within the next couple of weeks, maybe earlier—they haven't said when. It is indisputable Parker crashed the aircraft. The hearing is restricted, but I think it would be helpful if you could be there—I'll make sure you are on the access list."

The two men again shook hands.

"Let me know if there is anything else you need." Zender said.

"I appreciate you coming to tell me what happened—you shed a bright light on this whole mess. Now I know who and what I'm dealing with. Initially I thought this case involved a hotshot pilot who decided to crash a multimillion-dollar flying machine. We both know there are much bigger ramifications."

"You're very welcome. Parker needs someone like yourself in his corner. We should head back. Thank you for representing him, and I look forward to meeting the man who saved my life and the lives of my brothers."

Zender went back to his bike and swirled his finger in the air, indicating, *let's go*. Both men fired up the engines and proceeded back toward the Interstate on-ramp.

Vince watched them ride away. He felt sorry for Zender, still fighting with his mental demons. It seemed only a short time ago when he fought on the pointy end of the operational front lines. As a sitting superior court judge, he had a unique opportunity to be back in the game. Just like on a SF mission, this case had multiple dynamics with a lot of grey mixed in. No disputing the evidence, the military had an ironclad case.

***

Zender motioned for Perez to pull his Harley off the road before they got onto the on-ramp.

Perez came alongside. "What's up?" shouting over their engines.

"They're going after the Reaper pilot." Zender shouted back. "Trying to put him away in a black hole."

"What the hell for? That's ridiculous!"

"They're going to hold a hearing against him within the next couple of weeks. I'm going to ride down to Vegas—maybe hang out for a while, see a show or two. I owe it to our pilot to be at the hearing."

"Now?"

"Sure, why not. I'll be on medical leave for at least another month. If anybody needs me, they can reach me on my cell."

"I've always wanted to see the nightlife of Las Vegas. There's a new Cirque du Soleil act with naked women swishing around a large wine glass. Now that's something I need to see." Perez revved his Harley and throttled onto I-90 eastbound—leading the way south toward Nevada.

Before Zender could say anything, he watched his friend take off down the road. *I guess he's going with me.*

Chapter 22

THE SECDEF

The Secretary of Defense paced around his office located on the fifth floor on the E-outer ring of the Pentagon, at times taking a glance at the panoramic view of the Potomac River. He looked at the two generals sitting on the couch in his office—one wore an Army Service Uniform with a ribbon rack that went to his collar and the other happened to be in a green flight suit. These two men were members of the top leadership for the Army and Air Force.

"We need to somehow contain this," the SecDef said. "I hate to even think of what our men and women in uniform would think of our government's decision to sanction an execute order against our own warriors—and if the general public finds out, the media and the opposing congress will have a field day. Hell, the American people do not even know who ISIS is yet. They soon will, unless we can put a lid on this mess. The Reaper video feed showed four crates brought into the village—three we know were destroyed and the others were fired at our aircraft. I have the CIA turning over every rock and cashing in owed chips to find the remainder of those missiles before it leaks out."

"Sir, I have placed a cloak of classified security over the entire operation," Lieutenant General Gary McDougal said, who wore a flight suit for this meeting. "Anyone who even mentions what happened will be locked up and reprimanded for divulging classified information. Right now, I have the Reaper pilot restricted to base, facing a multitude of charges, to include destroying one of my multimillion-dollar aircraft. By the time I'm done with him, he'll be busting rocks at Leavenworth." He sat back against the couch with a pompous smirk on his face.

"Gary, I do not think this is a good idea," the SecDef reprimanded. "You created adversity and speculation. I don't know what history books you've read, but history has proven when you back someone into a corner with no options, they tend to fight back even harder. The people we hire into special operations and to fly our airplanes tend to be very loyal and stubborn. Traits we look for in a fighter pilot and a snake eater—someone who does not, will not, give up in a fight. What makes you believe this pilot," the SecDef looked down at a piece of paper to recall the name, "Lieutenant Brent Parker is going to be any different?" Agitated, he paced about the office.

"Sir, if I may give my input," interjected Major General John Shoemaker—a Special Forces tab and a Ranger tab stitched on his left shoulder. "I ordered the SF team involved to return from Afghanistan. Half of these men are in the hospital and the other half are in some local drinking establishment trying to forget what happened. They came as close as you can get to having a forward operating base named after them. Before our meeting, I spoke with Admiral Grew—his pilot is still in critical care, but alive and if I may add, in our care. He had considerable internal hemorrhaging from the ISIS bastard who kicked the shit out of him. Thankfully, one of my best snipers sent this asshole to Graceland. We all know what they would've done if they got their hands on him—I shudder to think." He hammered his hands together to make a final point. "My SF soldiers are professionals. They understand the rules on what must not be discussed that concerns national security. I might also add … these men are very loyal. No matter how we try to contain this, they will always help those who helped them. If you back them into a corner, I guarantee they will come out with a knife between their teeth and fight to the death. I disagree with the course of action my colleague is taking. Hell, if it weren't for what he did, I would still be writing letters to their wives and attending another day at Arlington Cemetery. I've already spent way too many days across the river giving a solemn speech to parents about a son who was on a secret mission the public doesn't know about. I tell them it was training, but they know I'm lying."

"General Shoemaker, don't be so melodramatic," General McDougal interjected. "The military has lost a lot of good men in this war, including the Air Force."

"My sincere gratitude goes out to those JTACs and ALOs who died supporting my troops on the ground. But when was the last time you attended a burial of one of your pilots killed in combat?" General Shoemaker asked, bringing emphasis to the flight suit his colleague wore to a high-level meeting, despite not having flown an aircraft in over a decade.

"Generals, stop your bickering," the SecDef scolded. "I don't care how you do it—keep this contained." He focused his attention on General McDougal. "Threaten this kid all you want, but make sure you give him an out, leave a glimmer of hope."

"Sir, we need to make an example out of this young man. I cannot have my pilots go off on their own with a total disregard for standard operating procedures. He made the decision by himself—he will take the punishment by himself."

Shoemaker's temper flared. "If he'd asked permission, what would've been the response? My guess is no! Parker made a split-second decision and a correct decision. It doesn't matter whether he failed to follow some stringent Air Force policy—dammit. He made the right decision."

Undeterred, McDougal pitched back into the argument. "I'm not about to allow one of my pilots to take it upon himself to go off willy-nilly and fly an airplane into the ground every time your soldiers find themselves in trouble."

Shoemaker's face reddened. "Willy-nilly, protect our nation! Are you kidding me? Your pilots need to be able to make quick, responsive decisions. Have you ever had a missile lock onto your airplane?"

"No."

"I thought not. How about a bullet snapping past your head."

"Of course not."

"I didn't think so. I have and it's not a pleasant feeling. When it happens and when you're about to be overrun, you pray the cavalry will come to your rescue. The price of one of your airplanes is well worth the life of one my soldiers. In this case, the cost of a single unmanned vehicle saved thirteen American soldiers. Thirteen men for sixty million dollars, I'd say that's a bargain. Hell, we spend millions on a single Tomahawk missile. Have you counted how many missiles the Navy fired in the opening days of Libya against some thousand-dollar Toyota truck? Hundreds!"

The SecDef went and stood between the two generals to play referee against a fistfight. "I might enjoy listening to the rivalry between the Army and the Air Force, but my patience is wearing thin," the SecDef said. "This war has cost us all, and we've lost too many lives. General McDougal, what you've done has exacerbated the situation—now everybody thinks we are trying to hide something, which is true, but don't make it so goddamn obvious." He walked over and stood in the center of the room, placed his hands on his hips and glared across the room to make a point. "But let me make this very clear and what I'm about to say stays in this office. I'm agreeing with General Shoemaker on this. This Lieutenant made the right decision in the heat of the battle and we need this chapter closed. The decision that was made was mine and mine alone. Now we must make sure it is never told by anyone. Do I make myself clear?" The SecDef locked eyes with both generals. "Do either of you have anything further to say?"

Both generals responded together, "No sir."

"Good. General McDougal, you're excused. General Shoemaker, please stay a moment."

The two generals stood and everybody shook hands, but not as cordially as when they first entered the office. General McDougal proceeded to the door, stopped and turned around—waiting. "Is there anything else for me?"

"Thanks for coming by. That will be all."

"Ah, yes sir." He shook his head and proceeded out of the SecDef's office, closing the door behind him.

The SecDef waited a brief moment. "John, I am thankful your men are alive. I spoke with Admiral Grew this morning on the status of his pilot. They doubt he'll ever fly again. Most of what happened to him, he doesn't remember. He doesn't know and will never know he came within inches of having his life ended, sanctioned by his own government. The president is also very aware of what transpired and so am I. I'm sorry about what happened to your men, but a decision had to be made quickly to put a blanket over this mess. We are coming around to an election year and the last thing we need is for the news media to get wind of this story—they would have a field day if they got hold of what we almost did. We'd lose the support of our veterans and those still in uniform. Mothers expect us to take care of their boys. We need to keep the events of what happened contained."

"Yes sir. I understand, though I do not agree with the CIA taking over. This is my AOR, my men. Don't ever sacrifice my men again. Do I make myself clear? Now that I said my piece, what do you want me to do?"

"I know you and Admiral Grew have a great back channel relationship. I'm sure the admiral is very appreciative of having his pilot back alive. Parker's military career is over with General McDougal still around. I also think it's in the best interest to keep him in the military. I appreciate his tenacity and courage. He's the pilot who recognized these missiles during the Benghazi fiasco. What do you think of the idea of having Admiral Grew transfer Parker into his Navy?"

"I doubt General McDougal will agree with any transfer. I'd take him—I'd make a Special Forces officer out of him."

"I don't care if he agrees with me or not, which is the reason I asked him to leave. I don't plan to give a forewarning, and once he finds out, it will be too late. Besides, his career is almost over, but I'm probably divulging too much information. In the meantime, with an inter-service transfer into the Navy, we can keep control of our new Lieutenant Parker. Otherwise, if he becomes a civilian, who knows what he might share with people who do not have a need to know."

"I'll call Admiral Grew as soon as this meeting is over. I also know this Parker's legal counsel. His name is Vince Phillips—we went through Special Forces training together—he went on to law school after a SF tour to Vietnam. I'll give my old friend a call."

Both men pondered a moment—the past, present and future.

Shoemaker broke the silence. "Is there anything else sir?"

"There is one other item. During my conversation with the president, he appreciates your leadership as the JTF commander. We would both want to congratulate you on a job well done."

"Thank you."

"I have submitted you for another star and the president has already signed the recommendation. Your promotion is certain to pass the Senate. This all means I'm going to lose you as one of my best combatant commanders."

"I'm not sure I understand."

"We all know General Stewart hasn't been feeling well. He has cancer and will be retiring soon. The president has nominated you as his next Vice Chairman to the Joint Chief of Staff. With your acceptance, I'll make the official announcement this afternoon. John, let me be the first to congratulate you on your promotion and new job."

"Please let the president know I appreciate his confidence."

"Because of the delicacy of this situation, I think it would be best if we keep any further discussions contained."

"It's been awhile since I've visited Nellis Air Force Base. I heard they received a squadron of F-22 fighters—very capable airplane as long as it doesn't replace any A-10s. As the president's new Vice Chairman, I think I'll take a short vacation to Las Vegas and drive up to Creech to see how those UAV boys are doing. They don't seem to get enough recognition."

The SecDef picked up a piece of paper off his desk. "This says they also have the highest suicide rate within the military." He shook his head. "The things they must see."

"My men go into isolation after a mission for a thorough debrief. Gives them a chance to talk through what went right and what went wrong, and if they have any issues they're dealing with. A doctor is always available to help them through whatever is ailing them. Our UAV pilots go home to their family and try to lead a normal life. Tough way to live."

Shoemaker got up to leave and proceeded to the door. "Sir, thank you for meeting with me and letting me vent."

The SecDef shook his hand, but did not release the grip. "Perfectly justified. Don't ever threaten me or question my decision again. I'm appointed and backed by the president. You're not." He opened the door for him to leave.

Chapter 23

FIND THE GIRL

The address on the outside of the building matched the location on Ali's GPS. He would have no problem gaining access into the apartment and picking the girl's door should be simple— getting into the building took some digging. The Quds internet hacker found an elderly woman living on social security who lived in the same apartment building. She had no driver's license and lived alone. Husband died five years ago after forty-three years of marriage.

He stood at the front entrance, noting the lack of security cameras. One of the names posted on the side directory matched the name circled on his paper. He pressed the button to apartment twelve, which housed an eighty-three-year-old widow.

"Hello," Ali heard the old woman's voice from the door speaker.

"Yes, I am from the cable company," he said, into the wall intercom. "I'm here to repair your cable service. Would you be so kind to let me in the building?" Ali heard the door locking mechanism click and pushed it open. He picked up his bag and proceeded inside.

An elderly woman in apartment-12 peeked her head outside her door. "Thank you for coming so quickly. Please, please come in. My television has been out since this morning," waving for him to come inside. "I called the cable company right away. They told me it would take a day or two for them to get someone here."

"I was scheduled to service another unit in this building and saw your call requesting immediate assistance. My mother could not live without her television and I am sure a nice lady like yourself feels the same way."

"I've been in a tizzy all morning. It keeps me company. I'd be lonely without it, you know."

"This will not take long. I will have your television working in no time."

"It's over there in the corner," pointing inside her apartment.

An old American-made console sat in the corner of her apartment. Plastic flowers adorned the top. A picture hung on the wall of a young girl holding hands with a young man in a military uniform. She had no life other than watching her television. It would be days before someone checked on her. Nobody would miss her.

Ali knelt behind the television, wiggling the cable connection on the back.

"I noticed your accent. Where are you from?"

"Pakistan. I've been in America for ten years."

"I've always wanted to travel. My husband served in the Korean War. He passed away five years ago."

"I am sorry," though he already knew.

She came over to where Ali knelt. "I don't know what happened. It worked perfectly last night. When I turned it on this morning, I didn't have a picture. I missed Good Morning America. She's so cute and he is really handsome." She tried to fix her hair. "I still have some coffee made. Would you like a cup? It will only take a moment to heat it up."

"No thank you."

"Do you know what the problem is?" She continued to hover near him.

"You need a new connecter. I will need to go out to my van and get it. It should only take a moment. I will have everything back to normal in a few minutes." He noticed her fretting. "No need to worry, this service call is free—no charge for a nice lady like yourself. But, do not tell anyone—I would get in trouble with my employer if they knew I fixed this without billing. It will be our own little secret," holding his finger to his lips.

"Thank you. You're such a dear. I won't tell a soul. Are you sure you wouldn't like some coffee?"

"Let me go get the part first. So I do not have to bother you, what is the code to get back in? When I return, I will have that cup of coffee."

Ali excused himself and went outside to the back of the building, over to the cable box that served all the residents—the lock on the box hung off to the side. Ali opened the cover, reached inside, and reconnected the cable to apartment twelve. He closed and relocked the box, wiping the surface with a cloth.

As he re-entered the apartment, the smell of freshly brewed coffee wafted into the living room from the kitchen. A slight hint of hairspray permeated the air. Using the remote, he turned on the television and flipped through the channels until CNN appeared. He contemplated turning up the volume, but thought otherwise. Instead, he sat on her couch. "Coffee smells delicious."

"I'll bring you a cup. Made it fresh—should be good and hot."

She was only a lonely old woman, so he sat with her for a moment discussing the weather. She changed the channel and soon became engrossed in the show.

The coffee was definitely hot and burnt bitter. He sat down the cup and stood. "I need to excuse myself to repair another nice lady's television. Thank you for the coffee." From the doorway, he reached inside his tool-bag, cocked the hammer back on his pistol, and looked back at the woman.

She looked up at Ali and gave him a smile, and went back to her show.

He stood a moment longer watching her. She never looked back. Her death would not change any outcome. "Remember our secret," he whispered, before stepping into the hallway and closing the door behind him. Killing her had no purpose—since he fixed her television without having to pay, she was now content with her reclusive life. He doubted she would speak to anyone about having her cable fixed for free. Moreover, if she did, his appearance portrayed something he wasn't wearing a cable technician's uniform. He left her apartment, took the stairs to the third floor, and then entered the hallway to Katya's apartment. Utilizing a lock pic, he inserted the stiff metal into the keyhole, finding the tumblers. As he worked on turning the lock, a man came out of the apartment from across the hall. The two looked at each other.

"Can I help you with something?" the man asked.

Seeing the small weasel features of the man, Ali made a quick guess on what name Katya used. "A Miss Amber called the cable company to repair her service. I was about to knock on her door. Do you know whether she is in?"

"I haven't seen her for several days. She usually works late—gets off in the morning." Looking at his watch, "I would expect her back anytime."

"Thank you." Ali turned and knocked on the door. He heard no response from inside. He watched the man head down the hallway to the stairs, look back once and step into the stairwell.

Ali waited, glancing up and down the hallway. With nobody around, he went to work, picking the lock open in less than ten seconds. He stepped inside, closing and re-locking the door behind him. With his senses on full alert, he did not smell any recent heavy perfume nor did he sense any presence within the apartment.

The furnishings were standard for someone who lived a transient life in a large city—the furniture came from a rental store: sterile, cold and impersonal. Nothing lay on the kitchen countertop. Opening the refrigerator, he found an outdated carton of soymilk and a loaf of stale bread. In the bedroom, her bed held brightly colored fluffy pillows, neatly arranged at the headboard. This room showed a personal touch. He picked up a pillow and sniffed the women's scent—it smelled sweet with a hint of an expensive perfume. The closet held a sparse amount of clothes, all made of high quality material. In the bathroom, he found hair products, body soaps and lotions. Both the sink faucet and shower drain held droplets of water. A large basket filled with an arsenal of makeup and perfumes sat on the counter. "No American woman leaves behind this much makeup. She will be back," he said to the empty room.

He went back to the living room and sat in a chair. Inside the tool bag he removed a snub-nosed Taurus .32 Ultra-Lite Magnum revolver. Its barrel extended with a four-inch suppressor, which reduced the report to an audible pop and helped stabilize the recoil. With the pistol now on his lap, he sat back, closed his eyes and waited.

***

Amber pulled into her designated parking stall, got out and removed two plastic clothes bins from the trunk. One contained cleaning supplies and the other remained empty for her left behind clothes. She stacked one on top of another and carried the bins to the side entrance door, which led into the main foyer of the building. Hanging from her shoulder bag, she used her apartment magnetic keycard to get inside. When the door lock clicked, she kicked it open and entered a foyer.

In the central corridor, she opened her mailbox, tossing envelopes into the empty bin. Not wanting to lug the containers up a flight of stairs, she waited to take the elevator. Once it reopened for the third floor, she hummed a song until she got to her apartment door. Setting the bins down next to her door, she searched in her bag for her apartment key.

"Hey Amber, haven't seen you in a while."

Amber turned around to see her neighbor standing in his doorway.

"Oh, hello John."

"Where've you been? I haven't seen you for a couple of days. Is everything all right?" He leaned against the doorframe and looked her up and down, with a slimy grin on his face.

"Everything's great. I've been out of town. Actually, I'm moving—I have a new job. I came back to clean out my apartment and give notice to the building manager so I can get my deposit back." Amber's skin crawled as he checked her over again.

"You're leaving. We haven't had dinner together yet. How about tonight?"

"I'm sorry, but I have a boyfriend." Amber turned back to her door, relieved to have a valid excuse for once.

"I get it, maybe next time. Hey, did you get your cable fixed?"

She stopped from turning the key any further. "What are you talking about?"

"I saw a cable repairman standing in front of your door this morning. He asked if you were home."

"Really, what did he want?" Her heart began to pound in her chest. She was being hunted like the others.

"He said you called to have it fixed. I could've fixed it for you. I'm pretty good with electronics," John said, grinning.

"Did you see where he went?" Amber's voice was wavering.

"Ah, no. He asked if I'd seen you, which I hadn't. I didn't think anything of it, so I went down to the foyer to pick up my mail. I'm not sure where he went. Probably left. I didn't see a Comcast van outside."

"Did you actually see him leave?"

"He didn't go out through the front door by the mail boxes. He might've used a side exit or he's at someone else's apartment. Why? You didn't call to have your cable repaired?"

"Someone is looking for me. Would you mind staying here while I go inside?" she asked, knowing he would.

"Better yet, how about I go inside and look around for you. I'll also check out your cable to make sure it's working. Save you the trouble of another service call."

Amber stepped aside as he came across the hallway, unlocked and opened her door. He took one-step inside then stopped.

"What the hell are you doing in here?" She heard John say.

***

When he heard the key inserted into the door lock, Ali expected to see the woman enter. Instead, it was the same man he had seen previously, who came out of the door from across the hall. He brought the pistol up into view and pointed the barrel at the man's torso. Across the hall, he noticed the opposite door still open. "I would like for you to back up into your apartment."

"Please, don't shoot." He backed into the hall with his hands up.

Ali waited until the neighbor stepped inside his apartment, before pulling the trigger. The revolver bucked in his hand—the silencer kept the report down to an audible cough.

A small hole perforated the man's sternum—bone and cartilage caused the bullet to ricochet off to the left, missing the heart by a fraction of an inch, before piercing the left lung. The exit wound out the back splattered blood across the beige carpet.

When Ali fired, he heard something hit the floor from outside the doorway, followed by running footsteps. He leapt out of the chair and into the hallway—a girl with black hair ran toward the stairwell. Ali raised his pistol and took aim ... *Sadegh wanted the girl alive for his own pleasure—he needed the girl alive for Sadegh.*

He pulled the trigger with the hope of a bullet impacting near her head would cause her stop. She flinched when the bullet smacked the wall, but instead of stopping, she disappeared through the stairway door.

Ali closed the girl's door and did the same with her dead neighbor's across the hall, checking for any blood splatters on the hallway carpet, before he casually walked to the same stairwell.

***

Amber brushed off the shards of cement that speckled her face from the bullet fragments. She yanked open the bottom stairwell door, ran across the foyer and out through the front entrance. She yelled to try to draw attention to herself, but the only people she saw were a couple walking their dog across the street a half block away. Initially she proceeded to run their way. When the killer came through the same stairwell doorway, she wasn't sure what he would do if the couple decided to help. Feeling helpless and not wanting to involve anyone else, she changed direction.

She darted out of view and ran down the sidewalk. Behind her, the assassin came out the front doors and looked toward Amber. The people walking their dog stopped and began yelling. "We're calling the police!" Another cough came from the man's pistol. A dust cloud formed in the concrete near the dog, making it run in the opposite direction. The couple stopped mid-scream and ran after the dog to get away.

Amber ran to the end of the building, used her keycard to unlatch the side door lock, and entered back into the building. Once through, she pulled the door closed—the sensors re-established contact with the doorframe and the bolt relocked.

Just as Amber turned down the hallway, the killer tried to open the locked door, but it held firm against his pull. She ran down the hallway toward the back exit into the resident parking lot, slid into her car, pressed the -Start- button and floored the accelerator.

***

Ali pulled on the door for a second time. To open, it required a keycard. By the time he got inside, she would have either called the police or hidden somewhere. The situation involved too many unknowns. He proceeded to his parked car, reexamining what went wrong—upset with himself for letting the girl get away. Killing the man across the hallway had been justifiable; he witnessed him at the girl's apartment door and posed a threat. He doubted the old woman would remember him, and no reason why anyone would ask her. She had her television, thanks to a nice cable repairman, which brought a slight smile to his face.

After climbing into his rental, a generic grey four-door sedan, he pulled off the brown hair wig, mustache and glasses, placing his disguise into a plastic trash bag. He started the car and pulled onto the road. Ali reviewed the second address he had taken from the girl's Facebook photo and proceeded to drive toward that location.

***

Thoughts poured through Amber's head. *He knew where I lived—oh my God, he killed John!* This killer wanted her. She tried Brent's cell, but he didn't answer. "Brent, call me. I'm in trouble." With nowhere else to go, she drove to Brent's townhouse—she made the decision to pack what little she had and disappear.

With the heavy mid-afternoon traffic, she took several side streets to shorten the commute. A benefit of being an escort in Vegas, she knew all the shortcuts—bypassing the midday rush-hour traffic.

The drive across town gave her time to think. *How did he find me?* Because of her profession, Vlad always paid in cash—never a paystub and no bank transaction involvement. With one arrest and a year of probation, she kept an obscure life—her apartment remained her sanctuary, away from pulling tricks in five-star hotels. Maybe he found her through her cellphone's GPS tracking feature. She was about to turn it off when it began to ring, startling her. Recognizing the caller, she shakily answered. "Brent, something bad has happened inside my apartment."

"Amber, calm down ... what are you talking about?"

"He shot my neighbor. I saw it happen ... I saw the blood." Her voice cracked as she pictured John falling to the ground.

"Slow down. You saw someone killed?"

"Yes. I went back to my apartment to move out. A cable man was seen at my door. I didn't call the cable company—I haven't been home. My neighbor across the hall went inside my apartment. Now he's dead!"

"Who's dead?"

"The man in my apartment shot my neighbor, John. I was in the hallway when it happened ... I saw him die. Why would someone kill my boss and Lexi—now he is after me?" She paced in a circle while she relayed the events.

"Amber, calm down. Did you see the person actually in your apartment?"

"Not initially—I heard the shot and ran. He chased after me outside. I was able to get back into the building with my keycard and the door locked before he could get back in. His features and accent were similar to Sadegh."

"Okay, let me think about this. Does anyone else know where you live?"

"No! I haven't told anyone. I've tried to stay hidden."

"Do you rent or sublet your apartment?"

"I rent. And the police know where I live from when I got arrested. Obviously, Vlad knows where I live."

"My guess he either found out from Vlad before he killed him or he was able to hack into the utilities where your name is registered. I sublet my townhouse from an individual. He pays all the utilities and I only have to send him a check—keeps me off the grid. I doubt he knows where I live." There was a pause before what came next. "Did you tell anyone about staying at my place?"

"No. I haven't told anyone. There isn't anybody I would want to tell."

"What about those pictures you took of us?"

"I posted a few on my Facebook page. I wanted to show my mother that I'm living a normal life and I actually have a boyfriend who cares about me. It's important to me that she knows. She doesn't know what I use to do."

"Oh shit!"

"What?" she squeaked.

"Apple has an integrated geotagging feature on their iPhone camera; it saves the location information for each photo taken. He probably hacked into some government database. With your Facebook account, he could match the two locations. Let me make a few phone calls and I'll call you back. Don't go anywhere."

"When will you be able to leave the base?"

"I've been told my hearing is scheduled for this week. Hopefully the government will decide what they're going to do with me."

"Do with you ... I don't understand. Could they keep you on base longer?"

"I don't know—it's complicated. I'll tell you more when I see you. Right now, you need to call the police—tell them what happened."

"I can't," her voice barely above a whisper

"What do you mean you can't? You neighbor is dead!" Brent barked.

"Brent, you don't understand. I've been arrested before and broken my parole—working. They'll arrest me again and hand me over to Vlad's brother—he runs a few girls out of the Royal Sands casino you like to play at. I'm sure he took over his brother's business. He's much meaner ... he will kill me. I don't know what to do!" She tried her best to hold off the tears.

"Okay, I get it. Stay in a public place where there are lots of people or in your car—stay hidden."

"I will. Call me back soon. I love you...."

He paused for a moment. "Love you, too. I'm going to take care of you, Amber. You have to believe me."

"I do." Amber ended the call—frightened and worried about Brent. Something bad had happened. The severity of her situation hit her. A man lay dead in the apartment across the hall and the same killer wanted her dead. She needed Brent, before her life completely spiraled out of control.

She didn't quite understand what Brent said about the photos in her Facebook account. This didn't make any sense. If Brent couldn't come to her rescue, she would need to run. There were only a few remaining items at Brent's place, she'd be in and out in a few minutes.

At the next off ramp, she took the exit and turned left onto the street that led to Brent's place. If he didn't come up with a plan, her's would be to disappear.

On a side street next to a secondary entrance, she parked her car. She got out and pulled her hoodie sweatshirt over her head. A six-foot cyclone fence surrounded the entire complex, with several access gates on each of the four sides. She went to a side gate and pressed in a code. Taking a glance down the street— nobody appeared to be watching. She sprinted across the parking lot and went around the building to Brent's backdoor. Once inside, she listened for any sound. "Hello, anybody here?" She took the flight of stairs to the second floor main living area.

At the top of the stairs, nothing seemed out of place—nobody inside waiting. She hurried through the rooms, placing any items she would need in a bag. She opened the nightstand and removed Brent's pistol, holding it up in front of her, visualizing what it would be like to pull the trigger. It felt heavy. She placed it in her shoulder bag and left.

Once outside, she checked the driveway again. The sun had already set along the western horizon, but the streetlights had yet to come on. A lone man with his back to her was walking away in the middle of the driveway and two young boys were playing in the gutter. Not seeing anyone looking at her, she ran toward the pedestrian gate and opened it a crack. The street looked normal— two cars drove past, several cars that she had seen before were still parked along the road, and another set further down along the block outside the townhouse complex—those she wasn't sure about. Trying to be casual, she walked across the road, saying hello to a young couple. Back on the sidewalk, she took off at a trot toward her car. Her cell phone began to ring. "Hey," trying to catch her breath, "I've been waiting for you to call. I have what I need for us to start a new life together."

"Where are you?" he asked. "You sound funny."

"I'm outside on your street."

"Get in your car and drive straight to the base. Do not stop. If you think someone is following you, keep driving. Call the police if you need to. When you get near the base, call me. I'm about to go to the security office to get you a pass." Brent picked up his pace when he realized what she'd done.

"I'm walking out to my car right now. I'll hurry. Love you."

"Be careful."

Amber pulled the hood of her sweatshirt over her head. As she proceeded along the sidewalk, several cars passed by, but the drivers took no notice. Reaching her car, she felt a little more secure knowing Brent would take care of her—their lives would be better together.

***

Ali sat in his car outside the front entrance to the townhouse. He thought about going in, but his inner patience told him to wait. The only way in and the only way out came through these gates. He got out and stretched, while keeping a lookout for the girl. A car a block away pulled out and drove past him. Kneeling down to tie his shoe, he watched the girl drive past. With his disguise removed, she quickly glanced his way then took no notice of him.

Back in his car, he lost sight of her car when she turned down a side street. He made a gamble and turned down the next street. Her car spit out onto a street two blocks ahead and took an on-ramp onto the highway that led north away from the city. He guessed she was going to where her boyfriend worked.

For the time being, he needed both of them alive so he could lure Sadegh away. What he did with women disgusted him. This city disgusted him. Soon he would be done with this Sin City—aptly named.

Chapter 24

THE CHASE

Brent drove his car over to the security office stationed a hundred feet back from the front gate. He knocked on the door and went inside. Johnson sat behind a desk, reading a newspaper. He looked up to see who came in, and then went back to reading. Brent stepped up to the counter. "How do I go about getting my girlfriend access onto the base? Is there a form to fill out?"

"Nothing—"

The son-of-a-bitch didn't even look up. "What do you mean nothing?" Brent could feel his muscles starting to tense.

Johnson looked up from the book he had been reading. "You've been restricted to base, your security clearance is revoked. You've lost all base privileges—she's not getting on and you're not getting off."

"But—" Brent rubbed the scar along his face that begun to itch.

"You need to calm yourself down. Turn around and leave right now," pointing to the entrance he had come through, "or I'll arrest you ... again. This time I'll throw your sorry ass into the brig." He stood up and placed his hand on top of his holstered pistol.

"What are you going to do ... shoot me?" Brent stood a moment longer, hands on his hips, daring Johnson to make a move. He turned and left the building, and got back in his car. "What now?" *Escaping will be easier than trying to sneak her on.*

Back at his room, he replaced his flight suit and boots with running shorts and sneakers. The hole he found underneath the perimeter fence during his runs looked like his only avenue to freedom—though getting back on might be another issue. Once he had Amber safe he would turn himself into the front gate guards and ask his leadership for forgiveness.

Before stepping outside his BOQ, he decided to divulge his plan to the one person he could trust and showed an interest in helping him. If he didn't come back, at least this person knew his situation. There was a law about the sanctity of attorney and client protocol, though he wasn't entirely sure this applied to military personnel. He jogged over to the JAGs office, knocked on the door and went inside.

The same frumpy receptionist warmly greeted him. "I'm sorry. All the lawyers are gone for the day."

"I want to talk to my civilian counsel without anybody listening. Can I borrow the phone in the conference room?"

"Go ahead. It's empty."

Making sure the door remained closed, he dialed a number pulled from his pocket. When the phone answered, he said, "Colonel Phillips this is Brent ... Brent Parker?"

"It's good to hear from you. I meant to give you a call. Your judicial hearing is scheduled for tomorrow morning. I requested a postponement but just found out it was denied. I expected this. It's all about producing a paper trail for an appeal, if this all goes badly. Not to lose hope, I have a secret weapon that I think will convince them otherwise. I'll be flying into Las Vegas on the first flight in the morning."

"Colonel Phillips, I may not be at the hearing tomorrow."

"What do you mean you may not be at the hearing? You have to be there—"

"A girl needs my help and the situation has gotten out of control. It's a matter of life and death. I plan to escape from this base," Brent explained, hoping Phillips would understand.

"I thought you were restricted from leaving?"

"My girlfriend is in danger and I'm all she has. It's something I started and now I have to finish it."

"Brent, you're not making any sense. They'll arrest you the moment you try to drive off. These charges against you are serious. Don't give them an excuse to throw you in jail—permanently." Colonel Phillip's voice had a hard edge to it.

"I don't plan on driving out. Hopefully I'll be back in time for court. If not, I wanted to let you know I appreciate all you've done. I can't explain everything right now."

"She must be a very special girl."

"She worked as a hooker on the Vegas Strip. We met a month ago at a casino. It's a long story."

He heard Vince chuckle over the phone. "I got to admit, I like your style. You seem to know how to get into predicaments."

"Thanks, but seriously, there are some really bad people after her. Her real name is Katya, and someone tried to kill her today. I think he's the same person who killed the people associated with her former employer. And I'm involved—something I haven't told you." Brent wondered if Phillips could help Amber get out of her situation.

"Let's first deal with your immediate issue with the military, and then we can focus in on whatever else you've gotten involved in. Now listen, as your attorney and someone who has a stake in getting you out of this mess—you must—and you will be at this hearing tomorrow. I'll be presenting witnesses who will verify and justify what happened. If you're not there, you're guilty until proven innocent. I can guarantee you will go to jail if you're not present at the appointed hour. They want to send you away and throw away the key. Please don't give them an excuse."

"Colonel, I don't have time to explain. I beat up a foreign agent in a casino parking lot and now he's looking for revenge. It's all very complicated."

"Brent, wait for me to get there. I'll be landing in Vegas in the morning. Once I get on base, we'll get this all figured out one-step at a time. If this girl is in trouble, she needs to call the police."

"I'm sorry—I need to go. I'm going to prison no matter what you or I do." Brent hung up the phone. He ruffled up the blankets on his bed to make it look like he had slept in it. He turned off the lights in his room and stepped outside, closing the door behind him. He took off at a jog toward the perimeter road.

***

Vince pulled the telephone away from his ear, bewildered at the developing circumstances involving this pro bono client. He dialed Zender's number.

"Hello, colonel, what can I do for you?"

"Are you guys in Vegas yet?"

"Yes sir. We're playing the tables as we speak."

"Our lieutenant is about to go AWOL. He's going to sneak off the base to meet up with his girlfriend."

"Oh shit! What's he doing that for? Isn't his hearing scheduled for some time this week?"

"Yes it is—tomorrow morning at nine. I will be there and he needs to be there. They both have somehow gotten into some sort of trouble—he said it's internationally related, but it doesn't make sense. Find him and handcuff him to a bedpost. He'll be on foot, so I doubt he's standing outside the front gate—more likely at a gas station or store somewhere nearby waiting for this girlfriend to pick him up. Intercept Parker and don't let him loose. He needs to be at his hearing tomorrow, no matter what. I'll send you his official picture so you know who you're looking for and an address to where he lives."

"We're on our way."

"I'll be available by phone until I get on the plane in the morning. Call me anytime. I'll let you know when I arrive in Vegas."

***

Brent had set a pattern of running along the perimeter fence. Several other people ran the perimeter road during the day and a few even ran it at night. The police had seen him doing both.

The gravel road displayed numerous tracks, both tire, human and animal footprints. It took him thirty minutes to arrive to a spot on the far side of the base. Here, the soft dirt along the road's edge remained undisturbed, except for an occasional animal that left its mark. He leapt over the berm, making sure not to leave a footprint while he searched the fence line—trying to remember the exact location of the hole. With the sun below the horizon, the lack of light made it difficult to find. It took another ten minutes to locate the spot, hidden by a mesh of tumbleweeds. Taking one, he used it to brush away his trail, and after he slid under the fence, jammed the ball of weed back into the hole to conceal his exit. Just being outside the cyclone fence felt good—finally free. Off in the distance to his left, the lights of the mini mart glowed, giving a sense of direction on where he needed to go. He took off at a jog across the desert floor, tripping over several bushes and rocks as he tried to navigate his way toward the highway. Half way across the desert, his phone started vibrating—displaying "Amber." Brent pressed the green answer button, "Where are you?"

"I'm almost to the front entrance. Were you able to get me a pass to get onto the base?"

"I'm off the base now. I'll need you to pick me up."

"At the front gate?"

"There's a mini-mart across the road from the front entrance. Wait for me there. I should be there in about twenty minutes. I'll see you soon."

His jog across the desert to the mini-mart took longer than he anticipated. When the evening sun descended below the mountains, shadows hid rodent holes, causing him to catch his foot and fall. These obstacles forced him to slow to a walk, taking up more time than he estimated. He finally came out of the desert and stood at the edge of the road, waiting for a break in the traffic while picking thistles out of his hands, and brushing gravel and blood off his knees. The mini mart was still a hundred yards away. He recognized Amber's car parked in the front of the store, then her car lights came on and left the parking lot.

"Amber, wait," he yelled. He took off at a sprint. He made it to the side of the road directly across from the store as she drove past, heading south back toward the city. Another car's headlights cast a glow inside of her car, illuminating a person in the car's rear seat.

Brent dialed her cell phone number, but she didn't answer. He ran across the main road and into the mini-mart parking lot. Catching his breath, he went inside.

"Can I help you find something?" the clerk asked, who stood behind the cashier counter.

"I'm supposed to meet my girlfriend here, but she just drove off two minutes ago. Did she happen to come inside—was anyone with her?"

"She came in to purchase a few items and went back outside to her car. A man got into her car and they drove off. Is there anything else I can help you with?"

"No ... thanks." Bewildered, Brent went outside. Several people came and went inside the store while he stood in the parking. *What now?* He went back inside and asked, "I need to get into the city. When is the next bus that comes by here?"

"It leaves every thirty minutes, on the hour and half hour. Next one should be stopping in ten minutes."

This far from Vegas, very few business establishments survived. Only this mini mart had enough clientele from the military base selling gas and beer. He knew of a rental car agency a half-mile outside the city that rented dented wrecks. While he waited at the bus stop, he used the *Find Friends* application on his iPhone to track where Amber was going. His map showed a dot moving along the highway, about to enter the city limits. While watching where it would stop, his phone began to ring—it showed Amber. "Where are you? Why did you leave?" He answered.

Initially there was only silence on the other end. An accented voice spoke, "Is this Amber's boyfriend?"

"Who is this?" Brent felt every ounce of his body as if on fire.

"Everything will be explained when you come to where Amber is. Right now, Mister Parker, she needs you to remain calm. If you call the police or call for help, I will kill her. Do you understand?" The person spoke slowly, matter of fact.

"What do you want?" Trying to keep his voice steady, Brent balled up his fist and began to pound it against his own leg in frustration.

"I have an acquaintance who would like to talk with you. If you meet with this person and all goes well, I will not harm you or your girlfriend. I give you my word."

"I will hunt you down and kill you if anything happens to her." Brent meant every word.

"Right now, you need to get in your car and go to your apartment. I will call again with directions that are more specific. If you call the police, you will receive a recording of her dying. I hope that we understand each other." The phone call disconnected.

Brent redialed Amber's number, but the call went straight to her voicemail. With her phone now off, there was no way to track the dot until someone turned it back on. When the bus came, he climbed aboard and found an empty window seat so he could watch the world pass by. The bus made two more stops before Brent got off and walked over to a car rental agency. In less than thirty minutes, he signed the papers, driving a fifteen-year-old mustard green Ford Taurus. It stunk of stale beer, but it started on the first try. He floored the pedal, the engine chugged a few times, before taking side roads back toward his place.

***

Zender throttled down his Harley motorcycle, bringing his bike to a stop in front of the mini-mart. Across the highway was the steel fence of Creech's main entrance. Perez went inside the store while Zender looked around the parking lot and maintained guard outside. After circling the building, he found Perez behind the counter watching a video monitor. Ten minutes later, Perez finally came out.

Zender stood behind a car parked in front of the store. "What were you doing in there? Did you find out anything?"

"We missed the two of them by fifteen minutes. The cashier said a girl came in and a few minutes later Parker entered wearing running shorts. He asked about the girl, but she had already driven off. Our cashier also said he saw someone get in the backseat of the girl's car before she left. I asked the cashier if he'd seen either person before or if he called the police. He didn't want to get involved with the police and appeared apprehensive about getting involved with the dude who got in with the girl."

Zender walked around a car that was cool to the touch. "Apprehensive, what do you mean? He recognized the guy who got into the girl's car?"

"Well, sort of. Two things of interest came up. The cashier is Pakistani. I asked him about the man he'd seen. He said the man was Iranian and looked like someone you wouldn't want to mess with—solid and focused. There is a security monitor behind the cashier showing the parking lot. So I asked if I could take a look at the video."

"He let you see the store's security camera footage? That takes a court order—I'm surprised he let you see it. What did you say to him?" Zender knew Perez well enough to know how this all went down.

"He was not cooperative at first, until I showed him my gang tats and a peek at the *pistolaro* in my shoulder holster. That got his attention." Perez gave a big smile.

"So, he said the guy was Iranian. Hmmm, why would an Iranian come all the way out here to snatch this girl? There are way easier opportunities in the city."

"I'm not sure, but boss, there is one other thing. After seeing the dude on the video footage, I know I've seen this Iranian somewhere before. I'm not sure where." He took out his iPhone, which held a grainy picture of a man getting out of a car. "Here is what he looks like. I took a picture of the store's security video. It gives us something to go on."

Zender studied the black and white picture. The man had long dark hair with a full beard, powerfully built shoulders. "He does look familiar. Forward the photo up to J2 intelligence to see if there's a match to any of our recent mission pictures."

"One other thing … the clerk said the Iranian drove up in the car you're standing behind."

Zender pointed at the license plate. "This is a rental car. Vince said Parker's girlfriend had an encounter with someone foreign before she drove out to the base to meet up with him. He also said the girl used to be a hooker—this might be one of those sex slave things." Zender waited for a couple go into the store before continuing. "The Iranian must have followed her here and saw the opportunity to kidnap her."

Both men climbed back onto their motorcycles. "Let's go see if we can catch our pilot," Zender said. "If I was wearing running shorts, I'd want to change clothes into something sturdier before I got into a fight. I suggest we head to his place first and if he's not there, we wait and see what turns up. Hopefully we'll get a lead on where to go next."

***

Brent drove his new rental car back to his townhouse. What Amber's kidnapper said disturbed him. It felt like a setup—an ambush. *They know where I live. They want me alive.* At least until he met with - the acquaintance. *Who could this be?* He shuddered at the one connection that came to mind.

When he finally arrived at his townhouse, the time approached midnight. Brent scanned his keycard to open the gate, and drove through until he found an empty visitor-parking stall. Walking toward his building, he stayed hidden in the shadows. The only sound came from neighbors having a noisy party in another section of the complex.

Checking his front door, he found it locked. Sneaking around to the back, he went in through the backdoor and entered the lower foyer. Off to his right a stairwell led up to the living area—no sound—nothing above. Across the foyer, a door led to the garage. He opened this door, flipping on the light to search for his Louisville Slugger P72 bat. Hefting the solid hickory, he climbed stairs. Halfway up, he stopped—he heard movement in the room above. He continued up the stairs to a point where he could peer into the room.

A faint swoosh sped through the air. He ducked at the last second—something hard clipped the top of his head, stunning and knocking him to a knee. Brent swung his bat at knee level and felt it vibrate, making solid contact of a homerun. A man cried out and a dark shadow fell across the floor.

Brent launched into the living area, searching for the intruder.

A Middle Eastern-looking man held the side of his leg while sitting on the floor. He tried to scurry into the kitchen upon seeing Brent raise from the stairwell.

Brent's fury exploded. His scar burned. He advanced, bringing the bat back for another swing.

The man rolled over onto his side to reach behind his back.

Brent threw the bat, slamming it into the man's chest, stopping any further movement, before it clattered across the room. He charged forward, jumped into the air, and drove his heels into the man's lower diaphragm—slamming his knees down onto the intruder's shoulders—air grunted out as ribs snapped. When the man's head came off the floor, Brent thrust a forearm across the nose bridge, snapping cartilage. His intruder mumbled gibberish. Brent grabbed a hold of the collar and yanked the face closer. "What did you say? Who are you ... why are you here?"

The man spit blood into Brent's face. An inch long gash across the nose revealed white bone.

Brent wiped away the spittle. He pressed his thumb into an eye socket until it popped.

The intruder tried to scream, but Brent clamped a hand to keep the mouth shut. "Where is Amber?" Brent eased off on the pressure to allow him to speak.

"You have no idea who you are dealing with. You're going to die."

He tried to spit again, but Brent pressed his forearm across the neck until he felt the larynx crush, causing eyes to snap wide open, mouth gaping like a fish out of water. When oxygen no longer fed the brain, the remaining pupil became fixated within its socket. "Welcome to paradise—asshole." Brent turned him onto his side and found a gun in a concealed holster. Searching pockets, he removed a wallet, car key-fob and a cell phone. The ID in the wallet showed the name *Kallem Karimi*, and below it said *Diplomatic Security for the Country of Pakistan*. Scrolling through the phone's history, an incoming call came in five minutes after his call from Amber's kidnapper—the caller ID showed it came from *First Secretary Sadegh*. Thinking he could use the phone later, he jammed it in his pocket.

In his bedroom, Brent changed into jeans, a black t-shirt, and pulled on boots. He found a pair of thin leather gloves and put them on. Checking the top dresser drawer, he looked for his handgun, but wasn't in the usual spot. Amber could have hidden it or taken it. He searched her side of the bed, the closet and pulled open dresser drawers—throwing clothes onto the floor—still no gun.

Back in the living room, he reached under the dead body to remove the holster holding a pistol and transferred it onto his waistband. He also took hold of the intruder's key-fob and went outside, standing in the middle of the residence parking lot while pressing the unlock button—searching the parking lot for a flashing headlights or a car horn. When he did not see or hear anything, he went outside the complex and pressed the button again—a car parked across the street beeped and its front headlights flashed. Brent walked over to the car and climbed into the driver's seat, and drove it back to his townhouse. Surveying the area, the only sound still came from a nearby party, otherwise the parking area remained empty. He opened his garage door, backed the car into the garage and went upstairs where the dead man lay. He lifted the body in a firefighter's carry and hauled it back down the stairs, and into the front passenger seat, securing it upright by draping the seatbelt across the chest and latching it into place. The man's head fell off to the side, clunking against the window, giving the appearance of being asleep.

Brent dialed Amber's phone number, but the call again went straight to her voice mail. He drove out of the garage, unsure where to go next until they called again. When their guard didn't check in, they would get worried and call either this phone or Brent's—it didn't matter which one. Eventually they would answer Amber's phone, and when they did, he would know where they were.

Driving out the front gate, he passed two bikers sitting on large motorcycles, parked across from the entrance. They both glared at him as he drove past.

***

Zender and Perez watched the car leave the complex. The lampposts on each side of the gate briefly lit the interior as it went by. Zender held up his phone that showed the official picture Vince had sent. "That is Parker leaving."

"Did you see the person sitting in the passenger seat?"

"What the hell's going on?"

"Hell if I know—only one way to find out."

The two soldiers started up their Harleys and roared off behind the car.

***

In his rearview mirror, Brent saw the two bikers start up their bikes and fall in behind him. He took the first left down a deserted street. When the two motorcycles followed, he turned right on the next available street. They did the same, closing in behind while flashing their lights. "What the hell do these guys want?" Brent said to his dead passenger. "I'm not in the mood for anymore bullshit." After he killed the man, the rage inside his head subsided, but with these two bikers trailing him, he struggled to keep it at bay.

One of the motorcycle riders tried to come up alongside. Brent stomped on the accelerator and swerved into his path, which seemed to dissuade any further attempts. They hung back off his bumper and continued to trail behind, not giving up their pursuit. Brent drove out of the city into a more deserted industrial section, passing a dark side street with no streetlights. A plan developed on how best to lose them.

Making another turn at an intersection, he punched the accelerator and whipped the steering wheel left onto a side street, keeping the pedal floored until he turned left again—tires screeching on every turn. He raced back to the darkest street he'd past moments earlier, turned down it and slammed on the brakes.

***

When Parker didn't stop when he pulled alongside, Zender realized he didn't know who they were. Their appearance had its benefits in some situations, but not tonight. Parker's car bolted down the road like a bullet, made several quick turns, before disappearing at the next corner. Harley Davidson made motorcycles for cruising the open road, but he had to slow his big hog to a crawl to navigate each turn. After two abrupt turns, Zender lost contact on the next stretch of road. He slowed his bike, looking down each street. Three streets over, he found the car parked off to the side, front and taillights still bright. This stretch of road was deserted, no illumination, with abandoned buildings lining each side.

Zender stopped his bike next to the driver's side, but found Brent no longer in the driver's seat. Looking across the interior, someone appeared asleep, resting his head against the opposite window.

Perez got off his bike, went around to the passenger side, and tapped on the window, but the man didn't move. Seeing a bloody face with a popped eye socket, Perez opened the passenger door. The occupant fell off to the side, restrained by the seatbelt. "Hey Zender. something's not right here. This guy doesn't look so good."

Zender watched Perez feel for a pulse and frisk the body while he stood between two buildings and listened for any movement.

"You're not going to believe this. He's dead."

Zender came back to the car to see for himself. "You're kidding."

"I've seen enough dead guys to know when dead is dead."

"See if he has any identification."

Perez checked pockets, and found a wallet and a leather identification badge holder. "You're again not going to believe this either. It says—" holding up a flip-open identification used by FBI and other gun carrying agents, "he's internal security for the country of Pakistan. Take a look," tossing the ID over to Zender.

Zender snapped on a penlight, seeing the various official stamps and the man's photo. "What the hell has Parker gotten himself into? Can you see how he died?"

Perez lifted up the man's head. Taking a small penlight, he shined it on the face and over the rest of the body. "He's been destroyed. His throat, nose and knee are crushed, and left eyeball is popped. Somebody did a job on him."

Zender glanced up and down the street. This stretch of road was both dark and deserted. "There's enough evidence here to put Parker away for a long time. We need to make it look like his car was stolen by this raghead." Zender got off his bike and looked inside the car. "The key is still in the ignition. I've got an idea ...." Zender opened the driver's door. "Unbuckle his seatbelt and help me pull him over."

Zender propped the body up behind the steering wheel and started the car.

"Can I ask what you're thinking?"

"He stole Parker's car and lost control of it. That's what the police are going to find." Zender rolled down the driver's window and pulled the dead man's arms through the steering wheel, stabilizing it from turning. "Find me a stick about two feet long."

Perez closed the passenger door and trotted down the road to a wooden fence, busted off a picket, and handed it to Zender.

Zender reached into the car, put the car's transmission in neutral and pressed the dead man's foot against the accelerator—the engine raced. He closed the car's door until it clicked shut.

With the engine running at full power, he inserted the stick through the window and knocked the lever into drive.

The car's transmission clunked into gear, the tires squealed and the backend fishtailed before rocketing down the road. The car accelerated for several blocks as an unguided missile launching from a liftoff pad. With nothing in the car's way, it accelerated past one hundred miles per hour before colliding in a violent head-on collision with a parked truck past the opposing intersection. The body blew through the car's airbag, smashing headfirst through the windshield like a missile. Both arms dislocated at the shoulder and one tore clean off the body before it shot through the air for another hundred feet.

Zender fired up his motorcycle engine and turned his bike around. "We need to leave before anyone comes to investigate." He took off in the opposite direction, with Perez close behind.

Three blocks away he found a vacant parking lot, where he maneuvered into and came to a stop. "I'm going to call Colonel Phillips, let him know what we've found. He said to call if we found anything strange, and this sure as hell qualifies!" Zender scrolled through his contact list until he found Colonel Phillips's phone number.

The connection answered, "If you are calling me at this time of night, it's probably not good news. What did Parker do this time?"

"Good morning, colonel. Sorry to wake you, but you said to call anytime. We almost had him, but he threw us a curveball. We lost him when he abandoned his car on a dark industrial street ... with a dead Pakistani security agent in the passenger seat—tore him up pretty bad. We found the man's identification in his wallet. My guess is Parker found him in his place and did the damage."

Zender heard Vince say, "Parker indicated his situation involved a foreign diplomat. I didn't believe him initially, but now I guess I do."

"When he saw us, he took off, not realizing we're on his side. Colonel, can you give him a call and let him know who we are and we're here in Vegas on his behalf? You might mention what we look like."

"As soon as I hang up, I'll call him. For his sake, I hope he answers."

"There's one more thing I need to tell you. We also think some Iranian kidnapped his girlfriend. Let me tell you what we know so far ...."

***

Brent ran until he came to an all-night café. As he approached the building, his phone started vibrating. He pulled it out and checked the caller identification—it came from Amber. While his phone continued to ring, he opened the *Find My Friends*. With Amber's iPhone now turned on, its location displayed on his iPhone's internal map. The address he recognized as the warehouse of her former employer.

Brent called a cab. Once it arrived, he had the cabbie drive him to a location several blocks from Destiny Delights. Sitting in the back of the cab, he thought about his next move. *No matter what, it's ending tonight.* His hands trembled from the adrenaline of what he had done and the unknown of walking into a gauntlet. The gun gave him some courage with unwavering determination to rescue Amber—nothing else mattered. While the driver drove into the city, he checked the gun taken from the agent and found one bullet in the chamber and fourteen in the magazine. His phone again began to vibrate, and seeing who it was, prompted him to answer.

"Hello, colonel. It's a little early for a call." Brent noted the time as 2:13 in the morning.

"I need you to listen to what I have to say. Two leaders of the Special Forces team you saved in Syria are in Vegas for your hearing."

"Colonel, I need to fix a problem I've gotten myself into before I can face what the military has in store for me. I'm not coming back to the base until I get this resolved."

"Stop fucking around! Listen to me. I know you are in deep trouble with the Pakistani government. The Special Forces team leader and his NCO rode their motorcycles to Vegas to help you. His name is Jeremy Zender and his NCO is Jose Perez. They're on their Harleys and they both still look rough and unshaven from their time fighting ISIS."

257

"Oh shit. I saw them outside my complex. They tried to follow me. I thought they were members of a motorcycle gang out looking for trouble."

"Son, I know what happened. They found a dead man in your car."

"There's more to this story than you know. I don't have time to explain. They have Amber and I know where they are."

"Give me the address. I'll send the guys as a backup."

"Colonel, I don't want anyone else involved. This is my mess. I'll call you when it's over. It's ending tonight."

Chapter 25

DESTINY DELIGHTS

The cab driver dropped Brent off several blocks from Destiny Delights. From across the street, he walked past the front of the building, where he noticed a man standing in the shadows of the entrance. There were no cars parked in front of the building, which told him they must have entered through the back alley entrance.

Hunched over, Brent continued down to the end of the block and into a dark alley. He kept in the shadows, slinking along the exterior wall while holding the pistol out in front. A single low wattage lightbulb shined above a back door entrance, illuminating a full-size American-made sedan and Amber's car. A slight scent of cigarette smoke permeated the air, telling him someone was waiting in the alley.

Staying in the shadows, he continued to sidestep forward until he found the source of the smell. His foot brushed against an empty bottle, making a slight clink. Before it could roll into the alleyway, Brent picked it up and he held it like a club, waiting and listening for any motion near the door. When none came, he placed the gun back in its holster, and transferred the bottle to his throwing hand—his success of rescuing Amber alive depended upon a surprise entry.

Twenty feet from the entrance, Brent finally saw the soft ember from the tip of a cigarette moving, glowing bright each time the man brought it to his lips to inhale. He needed to draw the person away from the door and into the open. His heart rate accelerated with each step he took. He tried to relax his muscles—dropping his stance lower to keep his outline smaller, taking slow deep breaths to harness the adrenaline surging through his veins. As a former collegiate wrestler, he relished the sensation before stepping onto the mat at center stage, controlling and harnessing the energy until the moment of engagement.

Brent closed within ten feet of the door when the phone in his pocket began to vibrate. Not waiting to see if the guard sensed someone, he tossed the bottle toward the far end of the alley. The heavy wine bottle arced over the door light before it descended back to earth, shattering on impact, with the sound of crashing glass echoing off the walls.

The man standing guard jumped out of the shadows, looking toward the direction of the sound. He towered above Brent by several inches, with thick legs and a protruding belly that fell between the openings of a single-breasted dark jacket.

Brent pushed off with both legs and closed the distance.

The guard must have sensed Brent's approach, for he quickly turned and upon seeing Brent, swung a loopy fist.

Brent ducked under the wild swing and drove his fist under the ribcage below the armpit—ribs snapped and he heard the guard grunt.

The man stumbled backward and shook off the initial attack. He smiled at Brent, and then charged with the fierceness of a bull against a matador.

Brent was able to sidestep, but not quickly enough—the darkness concealed a left fist that slammed against his eye, knocking him off his feet, blurring his vision. Brent scrambled back under wobbling knees. Blood dripped into his eye from a cut along the eyebrow.

His attacker stepped toward Brent, punching his fist into the opposing palm. Brent could see the glint of large rings lining the knuckles. "You run, I shoot you. Stand up and fight."

Brent pushed himself onto his feet. He stepped away from the alley wall, closing the distance with the guard. On the next attack, Brent stepped aside, parried the lazy swing and threw everything he had into the same rib area.

This time the guard doubled over, retreating while holding his side.

The two parried in a circle waiting for the other to attack, giving Brent time to clear his head. *Fighting is all about anticipating the action after first contact—how the body will react.* He beckoned for the bull to come to him.

The guard snorted and charged, swinging a loopy haymaker at Brent's head.

At the last moment, Brent ducked under the massive fist, overextending the attacker's body, which threw the guard off balance. He tried to follow up with a right hook, but Brent had already moved inside the power radius, using both forearms to block the approaching right bicep—stopping the attack—and sent a piercing elbow into the ear followed by a straight palm that shot like a rocket up under the chin, rocking the guard backward onto his heels. Brent followed with a roundhouse kick to the inside knee to open up the man's legs and an opposite kick crushed the left testicle. Solid contact on both and the giant began to topple.

When the guard bent over from the intense pain, the head dropped where Brent needed it to be. He spun, unleashing an elbow strike against the center point of the face, splattering bone and cartilage into the guard's eyes, dropping him backward against the ground flat onto his back. Each time he excelled, blood bubbled out of the nose without any other body part moving.

Brent searched the body and found a pistol held in a side holster—he tucked it into the back of his pants underneath his shirt, making sure the gun taken from the intruder still held secure in the holster.

He remembered his cell phone that vibrated before his attacked. The call came from Amber's phone, but no message. There was also a text message from an unknown number, which read, "Playboy to Hunter, ETA to your location in 25 mins." *How did the SF figure out my location?* Acknowledging their message, Brent sent a reply, "Bad guy in front. B careful. Thx. Hunter."

Brent opened the rear entrance door and peered inside. The hallway led through the building to the front entrance, with a stairwell along the side leading to the upper floor. Slipping inside and locking the door behind him, he went across the hallway to the front entrance door and peeked through the security glass, making sure the other guard still stood within the alcove. Brent turned the deadbolt, locking the door, securing the building from an unanticipated entrance.

As he stepped away from the door, his phone again vibrated, announcing another incoming call from Amber's phone. This time he answered, but didn't say anything. A scream from both the phone's speaker and the floor above made his skin crawl. Adrenaline surged through his veins—he tried his best to control it, to harness the energy, but it overpowered his soul. He disconnected the call, but the screaming above continued.

Brent drew the semi-automatic pistol from his pocket and ran to the stairs. From the floor above, he could hear Amber pleading for someone to stop. Halfway up the stairs, silence permeated the building as her cries became muffled.

At the second floor, broken crime-scene tape hung from each side of the landing casement and a large chalk mark outlined a silhouette on the floor in front of him. Brent stepped into the foyer, listening. He knew Amber was behind one of the doors, but with who and how many he didn't know. He cocked the hammer back, ready to shoot the first person he saw. *It's ending tonight.*

Not knowing which door to try first, he removed the intruder's cell phone and pressed the call button, redialing the last number called—Sadegh. Though dark inside, a phone rang from behind the glass office door directly in front of him. A man answered, speaking in a foreign language. Brent closed the connection and stood in front of the door—he could hear someone talking and he heard Amber whimper. Brent twisted the door handle, redialing the same number and entered.

Brent pointed his pistol, ready to shoot. He felt along the edge of the doorframe until he found the light switch, flipping it up. A desk lamp, lying along the floor, brightened the room. What he saw caused him to hesitate.

Amber lay on her back stretched across the top of a large office desk. Her shirt ripped from her body with only a black bra keeping her covered. Hands and legs bound to the four corners. A trickle of blood dripped from her nose as she tilted her head towards Brent. Sadegh pressed a tip of a knife to her throat, his other hand holding a phone.

Brent kept his aim as he proceeded into the room. "What have you done to her? I should have killed you the first time we met."

A frown spread across Sadegh's face. "Where is Kallem? He was supposed to have brought you here."

"I killed him. Now you are also going to die."

Sadegh pushed on the knife tip, causing Amber to flex her head back. "Glad you could finally join us. You can put your gun down."

Brent felt the cold barrel of a pistol press against the back of his neck—he hadn't heard the man sneak up behind him.

The person behind him spoke. "Do not turn around. Do not move. Raise the pistol up over your shoulder." He recognized the voice and inflection—the person who kidnapped Amber.

Brent released the pressure off the trigger and raised the pistol over his shoulder. It was quickly grabbed out of his hand.

"Step into the room, but do not turn around." The person said from behind.

Sadegh released the knife pressure from Amber's neck, and instead used it to slice the seam along her pants. She cried out, startled and afraid. "When Kallem failed to check in with us, I wondered if you would find your way here. I thought he might have killed you since you failed to answer our calls. You will pay for what you did." His hand moved along her body, stopping at a breast. "I was about to have some fun with her before you walked in." He squeezed, causing her to wince with pain. "She is a beautiful woman. It is a shame you will not be alive long enough to join us in some fun."

Brent saw fear and revulsion spread across Amber's face. She tried to move her head away from this filth touching her, but her bound arms and feet kept her from moving.

"Why are you doing this?" Brent asked.

Holding her head firm, Sadegh kissed her mouth. Looking back at Brent, he said, "I think you know why. You're here to complete the loop. The police will want to know why a military man like yourself has a sick fetish to kill prostitutes. I think your mental health professionals call it Post-Traumatic Stress Syndrome, caused by this war on terrorism. You seem to enjoy killing innocent women and children, and afterwards go home to lead a demented life—all in the same day. You are the terrorist, not us."

"I don't know what you're talking about—"

"Oh, I think you do. Why do you think your lovely girlfriend and I were at the casino? You think your encounter with her was a coincidence. I hired this whore to entice you. She is a hooker who fucks men for money, nothing more. You think she loves you, but she doesn't. I used her as a lure and you bit the bait. And she used you."

Brent looked over at Amber, who shook her head no, her eyes pleading with him. "As for what I've done, that's between you and me. Let her go." He knew part of what Sadegh said was true—the same mental struggle he dealt with every day to justify pressing the release button. As for Amber, he already knew her side of the story. He knew Sadegh had the people associated with her killed while he searched for him.

"You brought this war to our lands, now we bring it to yours. Your police will think you killed her." He laughed. "My friend Ali, the person who has a gun pointed at your head, killed a fellow prostitute with a nine millimeter Beretta, the same pistol you can find on any military base. I also killed one with the same weapon. The police will find you dead from your own apparent suicide, a note detailing what you've done, with your own gun I might add. You have not realized it yet, but you are a very sick person, Mr. Parker."

He watched Sadegh pick up a semiautomatic handgun from the desk. He recognized it as the one he kept in his bedside dresser.

"Amber told me this is your pistol. It is ironic your whore girlfriend will die from your own gun." Sadegh set the gun down next to Amber. He ran his hand up the inside her leg. "You will first watch me snuff her life out." Spittle fell from his mouth as he said the last word.

The filth started yanking her panties down. Brent would rather die trying to rescue her than watch what this monster was about to do. He flexed his muscles to move—

"Sadegh, stop," commanded Ali. "It is time for us to leave this place."

Sadegh looked up and glared. "She is mine to take. Go take him to another room until I'm done with her."

"You are not going to kill any more and I am not going to let you violate this woman. Your actions are not what the Koran teaches." Ali's voice was firm and steady.

"Who do you think you are? You do not give me orders. You are here because I commanded you. You of all people should know your place. You have killed many and now you are questioning me." Sadegh turned his head, looking through Brent with a fire in his eyes.

"This is where you are wrong. I do follow orders, and yes, I do kill people. I kill for my country—I kill for Allah. *No more, no less.* Unlike you, I do not take pleasure in it. Whereas you kill for fun … your sickness with women disgusts me."

"Then I order you to shoot him—now. He's the pilot responsible for killing the Chef in Yemen. I heard you were there—another failure of your incompetence." When nothing happened, Sadegh grabbed the pistol and pointed it at Brent.

"You have been misinformed on the reason why I am here," Ali said. "I came here upon the request of the Ayatollah. He called me on a mountain in Syria. My orders are to bring you back to Iran by any means necessary, not because of your silly request. You seem to have forgotten what I do. I kill people who show incompetence—who are no longer worthy of living. You are an abomination to humanity. You are so blinded—I brought these two here to lure you as bait, without your guards knowing your impending demise. The enticement overwhelmed you. You can either come with me or die here. It is your choice."

The implications registered across Sadegh's widening eyes. His glare focused in on the man behind Brent.

The voice behind him said, "We have known about your involvement with prostitutes for some time. Discarding their very lives as some would dispose of trash. You have become an embarrassment to the Muslim faith—a liability to our cause."

Sadegh's pistol moved off Brent. Suddenly, the sonic wave of a bullet fired snapped past his head. The sound reverberated through Brent's head, splitting into the air. He looked up to see a red dot forming on Sadegh's forehead—brains and blood splattered the back wall, his lifeless body crumbled over like a deflated blow-up doll.

Brent waited for the emptiness of death to take him next.

"Back up out of the room one step at a time. Do not turn around," Ali commanded.

Brent backed out of the room into the hallway. At any moment, he expected the assassin to put a bullet in his head.

"Turn right and walk to the first door on your right."

Brent did as told.

"The door is unlocked. Open it and go inside."

Brent felt the presence of the assassin behind him. "What about Katya?"

"As you witnessed, Sadegh will no longer require her services."

"But, why ... why did you kill your friend?" Brent was in complete shock. This was not what he envisioned happening.

"Sadegh became misled by his power ... and I have no friends. You were the bait to get him to come here. *Nothing more, nothing less.*"

"I don't understand," Brent said incredulously.

"With twenty-four hour diplomatic security, a guard always watched him. I knew he would leave the sanctity of his hospital room when he found out I had both you and your ... your girlfriend. He ordered his guards to watch the entrances, so he could do what he wanted without anyone knowing. I'm sure he planned to kill me either before or after. This is how the world turns."

"How did you know I would be here?"

"Kallem was to apprehend you and bring you here. My guess is he is no longer with us since you have his phone. You did me a favor in killing him, saved me the trouble. When you no longer answered your girlfriend's calls, I guessed correctly."

Brent heard Ali chuckle as he tossed Amber's iPhone in front of him.

"It is amazing the amount of information a person can find from one of these things. Would you not agree?" The accented voice rang out.

"But why ... why did you kill him?"

"Your authorities would have eventually linked his murders to him. Our diplomats should not be associated with this sinful city or with women of the evening. So he made his own destiny," responded Ali dully.

Brent noticed the assassin's voice distancing into the hallway. "Are you going to kill us?"

"As I told you earlier ... when you met with an acquaintance, I would not harm you or the girl. I am a man of my word. What played out went as planned—no more, no less. I was sent to stop Sadegh from further embarrassment between our two countries. Sadegh was sent to stop you. Your flying drones have caused me many problems, Mister Parker.

Don't you know it.

"I am a man of my word, which means today is your lucky day—tomorrow, only Allah knows. Please turn around and face me."

Brent turned around and looked at Ali. Even with a silenced pistol pointed at his face, he recognized him from the Syria mission—the man who got out of the vehicle to meet with the ISIS commander. "I am a United States military pilot. We try to do the honorable thing." Brent's voice took on a cool demeanor.

"There were women and children in that building. I held a lifeless baby, its body burned to the point I could not tell if it was a boy or girl. My guess is you knew families lived inside, but you launched your missile anyway."

The carnage from the aftermath to kill the bomb maker flashed through his memory. "That was you who drove up in a Toyota truck right before the explosion." Brent suddenly realized how often their paths had crossed. "You knew about the bomb maker ... that's why you followed his runner—who indiscriminately killed innocent women and children, and you facilitated it all. We are both honorable soldiers in this crazy war. At times, we must do unpleasant things our government leaders order us to do. *No more, no less.*"

Ali stared at him—no expression on his face—just cold dark eyes piercing into his soul. A slight smile spread across his face. "Those are words well spoken. It seems we now understand each other."

Deep-throated motorcycles sounded in front of the building. Shouting began outside then a gun fired, followed by abrupt silence.

Ali turned to look down the hall. When he looked back, Brent had the hidden gun once tucked in his back, now pointed.

Ali's expression remained stoic, pistol aim never wavering. "Two guns, I should have known. I think your western movies call this a Mexican standoff. We can either shoot each other or we can go our separate ways. I am ready to die. Are you?" Seconds counted off .... "I will choose for us." He lowered his pistol, turned and walked back down the hall into the room with Amber and the dead First Secretary.

Brent hurried behind, unsure of Amber's safety. He watched Ali pick Sadegh up like a roll of carpet and carry him out of the room.

Ali spoke once more. "Both of our countries do not need this embarrassment. Tonight, this part of history ends. Pakistan will be embarrassed enough when your intelligence realizes they are harboring the top terrorist in the world. Next time you fly your machine, look in Abbottabad. There you will find the person who initiated your country's war against Islam. Maybe then we can end this war." Ali turned on his heels and walked away.

Brent watched him carry Sadegh out the door and down the stairs—stunned at what he witnessed and what Ali said. He went over to Amber, still tied on top of the desk. As he approached, Amber looked over. He untied her, picked her up, and held her tightly. Looking into her beautiful blue eyes, he asked, "Please tell me you're alright?"

"Yes." Tears fell down her cheeks. She was shaking in his arms.

Helping her from the desk he asked, "Can you stand?"

"I think so. How did you know where to find me?"

"They kept calling using your cell phone. Each call pinpointed your location. I realized they took you back to your former employer's building to link all the killings. I'm so sorry to have gotten you involved. They came after me, not you." Brent said tenderly.

They both turned toward the office door when they saw two men in biker leathers enter the office. Both held pistols that they aimed in their direction.

Amber let out a shrill scream.

"They're good guys—here to help me."

The leaner biker of the two said, "Lieutenant Parker, wait here. Do not move. We're going to clear the rest of the rooms." Both hurried out of the office, followed by the sound of doors being kicked open. After a minute, they came back to the office. The same person came up to Brent. "I'm Captain Jeremy Zender. What happened here?"

A big Mexican stood watch within the door alcove. "We would have gotten in sooner if we knew where you were going."

"How did you find me? I didn't tell Vince where I was going," Brent said.

"We called in a few chips with a connection we know at JSOC. Through a NSA channel, he was able to triangulate on your cellphone signal."

Brent told them about the man in the alley and the two cars parked in back.

Zender addressed the big Mexican, "Perez, go check the back alley."

Several minutes later, Perez came back into the room still holding his pistol. "I didn't find anyone, even the person I shot— only a smeared blood trail that goes from the front entrance hallway to the back. The only car I found had these keys in the ignition."

Amber recognized the keys. "Those are mine," and took them from Perez.

Zender went to the window. "It's almost morning. I don't know if anybody else uses this building. If we stay any longer, we'll be telling our story to the police. Lieutenant Parker, we need to move fast. You have a court date this morning and you will be there. That's an order from Colonel Phillips."

Brent reached for the key in Amber's hand. "We'll take your car back to my place. I'll change into a clean uniform and return my rental car—I had to leave my Z on base."

Zender stopped and shook his head .... "What? Whose car were you driving when we first saw you? We found a dead Pakistani agent in the front passenger seat."

"I drove his car. I thought it best to dispose of the body in his own car ... as far away from my place as possible until you two showed up and spooked me to expedite my plan." Brent hesitated a moment. "What did you do when you found out he was dead— call the police?"

"Let's just say he's not having an open casket funeral. I doubt the police will come looking for you—at least for killing him." The smallest hint of a smile crept across Zender's face.

Perez coughed. "Boss, I don't want to interrupt this party, but we need to go."

Zender and Perez made a quick sweep around the office one last time for any evidence. Brent and Amber went out the back door, and Zender and Perez went out the front. Brent helped

Amber into the car and drove to where the two riders were waiting.

During the drive, one bike stayed in front and the other behind. Brent chuckled. "It looks like we have our own personal motorcycle escort. They're not letting me out of their sight."

Amber looked over at him, resting her hand on his. "Who are these guys and why are they here? Please tell me everything that is going on."

"I made a critical decision during a mission, saving those two men along with their entire team ... and a Navy pilot. When I step into the courtroom today, there is a strong possibility I will be going to prison. Knowing you are now safe, I am ready."

Chapter 26

THE ACCUSERS

Brent took Amber back to his place, cleaned up the best he could and changed into his service dress uniform. "I'll call you as soon as I know something." He gave her a long kiss, hugging her tightly.

Zender sat on his motorcycle waiting, then took a glance at this watch. "Brent, we need to go."

The three left, with Brent in the rental and the two bikers following behind. They arrived at the rental agency a few minutes before 0800. Brent came out of the office and went over to where Zender waited on his Harley.

"Climb on the back, I'll give you a ride to the gate."

"A bus should be by any minute. I don't know what the military police are going to do when they see me outside of the gate—I have a feeling it will get ugly. It's best we're not associated ... for your sake."

"Don't worry about us, we can handle ourselves. We'll follow the bus and your entrance in case the situation gets out of hand. I assured Colonel Philips we would have you in the courtroom by oh nine-hundred."

Brent stepped off the bus in front of the mini-mart, crossed the Nevada State Highway and proceeded along the sidewalk toward the front base entrance. The morning's rush hour traffic at the security gate slowed prior to entering. As Brent approached, he noticed Johnson standing next to the guard shack with his stupid beret pulled across his brow at a forty-five degree angle.

Between cars, Brent watched Johnson waive cars through, waiting for the inevitable eye contact as he proceeded toward the gate. When Johnson finally saw Brent, he stepped in front of a bumper to stop traffic.

Brent, wearing his dress blue uniform with bars on his shoulders—pinned to his chest were a set of pilot wings above a single row of ribbons, kept walking. *It's game time.*

"What the hell are you doing outside this gate? You're restricted from leaving." His hand reached for his 9mm service weapon. People stopped what they were doing to watch the spectacle.

"Obviously, I'm now returning."

"You're under arrest. Get down on the ground now!"

"For what, I haven't done anything. I'm here for my court appearance. It starts in fifteen minutes." Brent proceeded toward the pedestrian entrance holding his ID. With his hands up in a surrender position, he showed the card to Johnson.

Instead of pulling his pistol out, Johnson removed a yellow handgun Taser, and pointed it at Brent. "I said stop!"

Brent felt something sting his side. When the volts hit his muscles, he fell to the ground in convulsive spasms.

"Get cuffs on him," he yelled, prompting another guard to come out of the shack toward Brent.

Both of Brent's arms were pulled behind his back to allow cuffs to be snapped onto his wrists. The two policemen lifted him up from the ground and took Brent to a hood of nearby patrol car, slamming his face into the metal. Legs were kicked out as they began to frisk him. Finding no weapons, he stood Brent upright and shoved him in the back of the patrol car. The cut along his face reopened, dripping blood onto his uniform shirt.

***

Zender watched the whole takedown. No one passed through the gate while they proceeded to arrest their pilot. With Parker now sitting in the patrol car, cars once again began to move up to the gate entrance. Zender and Perez inched their Harleys forward in the conga-line until they were alongside the guard shack.

Johnson resumed his post and glared at the two bikers. As they approached, he motioned for them to stop. "Did you two take a wrong turn? This is a military base for military personnel. You two made a wrong turn a long time ago."

Perez looked the police officer up and down. "You'd better take a close look at the blue sticker on the front forks and address this man as sir. Make another stupid comment and I'll personally stuff your attitude where the sun doesn't shine."

Zender smirked from his friend's remark.

Johnson took a step back from the motorcycles. "Do you have any military identification?" His hand resting on his pistol.

Zender removed his military ID from his pocket, displaying his card.

Johnson snatched it out of Zender's hand, studied it, trying to match the official military picture to the man sitting on the motorcycle in leather, sporting long hair and a shaggy beard. "Please remove your sunglasses and helmet."

"Is there a problem?" Zender asked. "Any identification I have will be the same. We are both in Army Special Forces with authorization to have relaxed grooming standards. We came here with the man you tossed in the back of your patrol car. All of us are scheduled to be at a hearing," looking at his watch, "ten minutes ago. Can you call someone with authority who knows what's going on?"

"You're entering a military base. It's the base commander's policy—all motorcycle riders must wear a high reflective vest before being allowed to enter. If you don't have the required equipment, I'm not letting you on. You can turn around or move aside. I'll contact headquarters to verify your identification."

Zender and Perez killed their engines and pushed their Harleys alongside the fence. Both men sat on the grass next to their bikes and waited.

After ten minutes, a government sedan pulled up to the main gate and a female major walked over to the two soldiers. Both men stood. "Which of you is Captain Zender?" She looked from one to the other.

Zender raised his hand like a first grader in class. "That would be me major." The nametape on her uniform said Lannon.

Acknowledging Zender, she looked at Perez. "And you must be Sergeant Perez."

"Sergeant First Class Perez."

"Excuse me?"

"My rank is sergeant first class. It's an Army rank, ma'am."

"What? Ah, yes." She dismissed Perez's correction to address Zender. "We've been expecting you two and Lieutenant Parker." She glanced over toward the patrol car. "I see he's all trussed up and you two have dressed appropriately. Lieutenant Parker's attorney said we should expect two Army soldiers—he didn't mention you might look a little rough. The hearing started fifteen minutes ago—everybody is waiting." She looked at both men and shook her head. "If you'll follow me, I'll give you a ride over to the base courtroom."

The two men followed the major through the gate to the patrol car where Brent sat. Lannon directed, "One of you can ride in the back with Lieutenant Parker and the other can ride in the front."

Perez climbed into the back seat and Zender sat in the front. She flipped on the overhead blue lights and briefly hit the siren to stop traffic and to get Johnson's attention. "Your presence will be required at the Wing's courtroom in twenty minutes. Please be prompt." She drove off without waiting for an acknowledgement.

Nobody spoke a word during the short ride, eventually stopping in front of the Wing headquarters building. When the major got out of the car, Zender and Perez also got out. She helped Brent out of the backseat and escorted him toward the building.

"Do you think the lieutenant needs to be restrained? I don't think he's going anywhere," Zender asked.

Without acknowledging the question, she led Brent through the building's front door and directed them toward a row of chairs next to double doors of a large conference room. "Please wait here. I'll let the senior officers know you have arrived." She knocked twice on the conference room door and entered, closing it behind her.

The three men sat in the empty hallway. A sign on the door said, *Classified Hearing in Progress: Do Not Enter.*

Brent sat stoically, arms bound behind his back. Attired in his uniform, the stitching along the upper shoulder ripped open, blood dripped from his nose and cut, his face swollen and purple from where the bat and the giant's fist hit him. Zender and Perez still wore their leather motorcycles jackets, with leather chaps covering faded blue jeans, hands resting on their laps, smiling and saying hello to people who took notice of them. Several staff personnel stared at the two bikers and a bloody lieutenant in full uniform, in handcuffs, outside a classified courtroom.

The door opened and the female major took Brent by the arm. "They are ready for you. Please follow me."

After being up all night, they all looked more haggard than usual. Brent felt like he was about to walk into a gauntlet, with no turning back. The two soldiers squared their shoulders as they prepared for battle.

Brent recognized the wing commander at a podium behind a large conference table. Sitting to the commander's right was his squadron commanding officer, and next came the asshole DO. His CO's face appeared expressionless—his DO stared at him the whole way into the room. Brent held eye contact until he won the staring game. A lone table sat in the middle of room. A distinguished-looking man in a full business suit sat alone with an empty chair next to him.

The wing commander spoke first. "Lieutenant Parker, glad you could join us. Please have a seat next to your counsel, Colonel Phillips or do I call you judge?" He looked at the clothes of the other two with disgust. "Captain Zender and Sergeant First Class Perez, thank you for being here. I'm Colonel Drake, the wing commander of the Four Thirty-Second Wing." Not waiting for them to find a place to sit, he continued, "I am surprised you're not attending this formal hearing in uniform, but you must have found out about your subpoena to be here the same time I did." He glared at Parker's counsel. "Thank you anyway for being here. You can take a seat in the back of the room."

Zender nodded his head toward the men at the front of the room. He acknowledged Colonel Phillips in the business suit and gave a hand signal. Perez looked like he wanted to kill somebody.

Vince stood as Brent approached to shake hands, instead he turned to show them restrained.

Vince addressed the men on the podium. "Do you think handcuffs are necessary?"

"Mr. Phillips," Drake spoke from behind the long table. "Your client knowingly disobeyed a direct order by leaving the base. Then he has the audacity to show twenty minutes late. He obviously has no respect for the seriousness of this proceeding. He does now."

"Sir, he also returned to the base on his own accord. May I ask on what pretense was Lieutenant Parker confined to base?" Vince shuffled through various papers on the desk in front of him. "I do not see any conviction or are you prejudging my client before due process of a trial by his peers. Did you even present any pretrial release conditions?"

Silence permeated the room.

"I thought not. So far you have violated the constitutional rights of a defendant—something we will have to take into consideration later."

"I gave an order to Major Lannon, a CID officer, to inform Lieutenant Parker to remain on base until this hearing has concluded—my verbal order should be sufficient."

"Colonel, I could argue otherwise since our constitutional rights apply to every citizen of the United States—even you do not have the authority to breach this. Even if my client disobeyed an undocumented order, he is now here for this hearing. It does not justify a reason for him to be in shackles. I would also like to know why his face is bleeding."

"Your client not only disobeyed a direct order, Major Lannon informed me Parker would not stop when told to do so. He seems to have a total disregard for authority. I would rather not have another spectacle happen in my courtroom."

Vince leaned over toward Brent, speaking in a whisper, "Did you assault a security guard?"

"No sir. He shot me with his Taser before I entered the base." He looked back at Zender and Perez. "Our two friends in the back of the room witnessed the whole thing."

While they spoke, a knock sounded at the door. Lannon opened it, allowing Johnson to enter the room. He stood in the aisle, uncertain what to do next.

Drake knocked his gavel against the oak table, getting everyone's attention. "Officer Johnson, your timing is impeccable. We were just discussing the arrest of Lieutenant Parker. Could you please enlighten us as to what happened?"

Johnson stepped forward and stood at attention. "Good morning sir." He glanced around the room, holding his gaze on Brent before facing back to the front bench. "I was present with Major Lannon when we notified Lieutenant Parker of his impending arrest and your restriction. Our security checks of his

BOQ room last evening confirmed he had not left. At oh-eight forty this morning, I was surprised to see Parker entering the base on his own volition. Recognizing him, I ordered him to stop, but he refused."

Vince stood. "Colonel, I have a question for the officer." He set his gaze on Johnson. "Was Lieutenant Parker inside or outside of the gate when you asked him to stop?"

"Sir, he had not yet entered the gate."

"Did he show any signs he might be a threat to you or to himself?"

"No sir. He walked straight toward the gate. Hands were in full view with his ID in one of them."

"Thank you, Officer Johnson. Colonel, I'm not sure of the security protocol you're imposing, but Lieutenant Parker was neither on the base nor displaying a threat. I do not see any reason or jurisdiction for the actions by your security guard. It is apparent he had not yet stepped onto federal property where a base security guard has the right or legal authority to detain a commissioned officer." Vince sat back down in his seat. Before Drake could say anything further, Vince stood up, interrupting what came next. "Did you *tase* my client?"

"Parker would not obey my commands to get on the ground. He wouldn't stop."

"We already covered your lack of jurisdiction authority or cause since he did not display a threat. Did he threaten you or give the impression he was going to be a menace to society?" Without waiting for a reply, Vince answered his own question. "Oh that's right, you said he had his hands already in the air holding his ID. I suggest you find a good lawyer after this meeting. I wonder who sets the policy for this base."

Drake banged his gavel on top of the table. Red in the face, he said, "I've heard enough. The police have my authority to use non-lethal force without question. I'm not about to sit here and listen to your further questioning of a respected officer of the law. Major Lannon, please escort Johnson out of this room. Now!"

Everybody waited in silence as the two left the room. Several minutes later, Lannon reentered and returned to her seat.

Vince remained standing, hands flat on the table, fuming. Once the courtroom was back in session, he directed his comments to the men facing him. "Colonel, I'm trying to understand what is going on here. From all indications, my client has done nothing wrong, yet he sits here as if this inquisition is resting on a capital punishment conviction. Hands bound in shackles. Look at his shirt," pointing at the fresh blood. "It appears to me that my client has been the victim of an assault. What type of operation are you running here?"

"Mr. Phillips, be careful what your implying and who you're talking to."

"My apologies, but the last time I looked, my collar devices looked a lot like yours," Vince retorted. "But for this hearing, I'm a registered attorney authorized by someone a lot higher than you to represent Lieutenant Parker. Which means I can argue what is appropriate within the jurisdiction of the JAG manual. If you feel otherwise, then I move for dismissal on the grounds of violating the sixth amendment rights of the defendant—part of the United States Bill of Rights, applied to all criminal prosecutions, including this kangaroo court. If you so desire, I can take you back into chambers for a quick lesson into judicial law." He sat back down and whispered to Parker, "What a pompous ass."

"They all are," Brent whispered back.

"Mister Phillips, let's not lose sight of Parker leaving the base against my direct order."

"I'm not going to get into semantics with your order. If I recall, you gave an order for Lieutenant Parker not to leave the base, which granted, it appears he ignored. If I apply military logic, you did not give an order against him returning to base. In fact, you gave an order for him to be available for this hearing. Personally, I think he has done a remarkable job to be here and on time if it wasn't for your goons." Vince sat back down with a smirk on his face.

The three men at the front of the room conferred amongst themselves. Finally, Drake spoke. "Major Lannon, would you please remove the handcuffs from Parker's wrists."

She came over and removed the handcuffs. Once everyone sat, Drake rapped his gavel on the table. "Gentlemen, this is a formal investigative hearing to a court martial, conducted in accordance with the Manual of the Judge Advocate General. I will make a report of my findings to the Commander of Twelfth Air Force, who will act on them as he sees fit. One of his options, I would like to point out, is to convene a general court-martial. The preponderance of evidence shows Lieutenant Parker willfully and knowingly destroyed a multimillion-dollar aircraft, is negligent of his duty as a Reaper pilot and has violated a direct order. Lieutenant Parker, please stand."

Both Brent and Vince stood.

"Lieutenant Parker, before we proceed with the evidence against you, how do you plead?"

Vince coughed to interrupt the proceeding. "Colonel, I would like to speak for my client."

"Yes, Mr. Phillips, please proceed."

"Lieutenant Parker pleads guilty to the charges of purposeful destruction of government property. Anything else can and will be argued in a court of law."

For a moment, stunned silence permeated the room.

Brent looked alarmingly over at Vince, who in turn reached over and rested his hand on Brent's arm. He leaned over and whispered, "Trust me."

Vince looked back at the officers. "Lieutenant Parker pleads guilty under one condition."

"Mr. Phillips, your client is not in a position to place conditions on known facts. We have a statement from Parker stating he willfully destroyed a valuable piece of government property."

"Colonel Drake, you see the two men seated in the back of this room? Captain Jeremy Zender and Sergeant First Class Jose Perez, and the rest of their team would be dead if it were not for the actions of Lieutenant Parker. I want you to take a hard look at these men. Is one of your replaceable flying machines more valuable than their lives?"

Silence fell across the room. Zender smiled at everybody, whereas Perez appeared to want to put a bullet through the pompous wing commander's head.

Vince continued, "The actions of my client saved the life of a Navy pilot by the name of Lieutenant John Shook. During testimony to build this case, I will ask how the shoot down even happened and our government's decision to cover it up." Vince chuckled to build upon the absurdity, "When you fail to answer my question truthfully, I will ask to have you confined for withholding testimony. I'll slowly work my way up the leadership ladder until someone provides an answer. If nobody spells out what happened, this case will be dismissed and your career will be tarnished forever."

"Mr. Phillips, I do not like your tone. Do not threaten me."

"I have only just begun. We all know there is more going on here than a destroyed *replaceable* aircraft. Now I can either subpoena these men sitting in the back of the room to provide official affidavits on what happened during their mission or you can drop all charges against my client. The shenanigans you have employed against my client have been solicitous and egregious." He stood, pointing a finger at Drake. "I promise this trial will be epic and it will be a media nightmare for the military, and this being an election year, will have a profound impact on the approval ratings of our esteemed leadership, the president included, and a professional nightmare for you personally. Imagine, a commanding officer abusing his authority by directing the assault of a subordinate officer by an enlisted man or leadership authorizing an execute order."

Drake glared at Vince. "I have no idea what you're talking about. And, I did NOT direct anyone to assault Parker! Your client resisted being ... detained. The results of what happened were caused by his own actions." His face became beet red as he wiped perspiration from his forehead.

The conference room temperature felt like it climbed ten degrees as Brent waited for the next move. Silence fell across the room. Vince had fired off arguments like a prizefighter jabbing the head, followed by an uppercut to the body that took the air out of his lungs. Vince scribbled notes on a legal pad, then began tapping his pen. Brent glanced over to see what he wrote. *Here comes the knockout punch.*

Vince spoke in a calm voice, his theatrics over. "I will prove otherwise how a person, walking freely in a non-threatening manner onto your base or this courtroom, warrants the type of behavior your men have displayed over the past month. In all my years sitting on the bench, the common person usually receives treatment that is more humane. It is evident your leadership has a top down approach, and I will prove your security guards' actions are a direct reflection of your management. Heads will roll back up the leadership ladder until some general has heard enough bullshit and orders a cleanup of your mess. There's a strong case for tort judicial negligence. I must say, I'm actually looking forward to representing this case in a formal court, where I will ask General McDougal and the Secretary of Defense, under oath, what happened to you-all's collusion to harass my client. I'm sure nobody wants to hear about how a Navy pilot was ordered to be shot and the expendability of these men in the room, all saved by the heroism of this man here."

Drake banged his gavel, breaking the handle and sending the head on a ballistic arc across the room. "That is enough! Who told you this?"

"I guessed and you just confirmed. Thank you."

With the hushed silence, the three officers huddled together, whispering among themselves. Everyone waited. Drake looked up to fix a glare at Vince. Other than the unintelligible whispered conversations, the room remained silent.

After several minutes, Drake broke up the huddle. "Lieutenant Parker, I will notify General McDougal of my recommendation. For better or for worse, we cannot have our pilots destroy aircraft whenever they feel like it. Someone will notify you of General McDougal's decision. In the meantime, I'm releasing you to your counsel. Is there anything else you'd like to say on your behalf before we adjourn?"

Brent thought a moment. Now was not a good time to bring up his involvement in a foreign diplomat's death, killing a foreign agent, and beating up another, and oh, his romantic involvement with a Las Vegas hooker. "No sir," was all he could think of to say.

"If there is nothing else, then you're dismissed. Mister Phillips, I believe you are no longer required and I would invite you to leave my base as soon as you can!" The stump of his gavel slammed against the table.

Chapter 27

BLACKJACK

Amber, Vince, Zender and Perez sat in various chairs around Brent's sparse living room. "I'll sure be glad when this is all over," Brent said from the kitchen while pouring his Elk Rider bourbon into tumblers. He brought the drinks to where everyone sat. "Vince, I wasn't sure what side you were on when you told them I was guilty. For a moment, I saw myself looking through a set of bars for the rest of my life."

Vince took a sip before answering. "If they tried to push the situation any further, there was a good chance what happened would eventually be leaked. They were in a catch-22 scenario."

"I'm not sure I understand."

"A decision was made by a senior government official to keep you detained. They needed time to figure out how to contain the mess they created. You discovered a crisis they wanted—still want—resolved. An Air Force general had an axe to grind against you for crashing one of his precious airplanes. What you did helped the national security of this country, not hinder it."

Zender interrupted by asking, "You keep saying *they*. Who are you referring to?"

"Let's say within the top levels of the Defense Department," Vince answered. "Someone wanted to keep the missing missiles quiet, and they didn't want the execute order to murder a Navy pilot disclosed. They needed a way to keep you quiet, so they locked you onto a base. When you snuck off, that worried them. They tried to back you into a corner, instead you backed them into a corner. Bottom line is they want this all to remain quiet. They're going to offer you a deal—I'm just not sure what it will be."

Brent looked down at his hands. "I'm not sure what I want or if I even want to go back to a Reaper box. It's so impersonal, killing one moment—trying to lead a normal life the next—all in a day's work. I killed someone last night with my bare hands, and several others died for what I did." He thought about Ali. "The assassin they sent was the same person who gave the missiles to ISIS. He carried a unique looking rifle—I zoomed on him as close as I could with my camera so I could see his face."

Perez snapped his fingers. "I knew I recognized him from somewhere."

Zender looked at his friend questionably. "What are you talking about?"

"The mini mart security camera—he's the same person we saw get out of the vehicle to meet with the Iraqi general. Everybody else carried AKs or old vintage rifles, and he carried a FN FAL rifle. Tilley called it out. During the seventies and eighties, special operations squads and CIA operators were known to carry this weapon. Several were stolen from our embassy during the Iran hostage crisis."

Brent realized how close he came to death. He took Amber's hand and held it tightly. "I saw him taking the missiles—killed a whole company of Libyan soldiers—and he gave them to ISIS. The same dude killed Sadegh." Locking eyes, they shared a moment of relief and heartache at what could have been.

"Whose brains are smeared all over the office?" Zender asked.

"Yes." Brent realized their destinies had crossed four times.

Brent's cell phone rang, breaking his bewilderment. Everyone stopped and waited.

"Hello?" Brent answered. "I'll be there at oh nine hundred."

Amber, watching Brent asked, "Who called?"

"Colonel Drake. They'll be discharging me in the morning—he added *the sooner the better*. I'm to report to Personnel to out process." Brent paused. "It's been a long day. I want to thank you for everything. Especially you, colonel, thank you!"

"I'm a little surprised at the decision," Vince said. "But I think this is for the best."

Zender stood up and reached out his hand. "On behalf of myself and my men, I would like to thank you for what you did. You took a risk and saved our lives. You also saved us from taking the shot—a decision I'm not sure I could have lived with."

Once everyone left, he relaxed enough to look around the interior of his place. He found she had added a personal touch with a few decorations not there earlier. Amber stood from her chair and said, "I've wanted to give you a present for all you've done, but we keep getting interrupted. Wait here, I'll be right back." She went down the hallway and closed the bedroom door. While she was in the bedroom, Brent went down the stairs to his Z and removed the DVD from underneath the seat. He took it back upstairs and waited for her to come out.

Amber sauntered down the hallway wearing a cheerleader skirt and a sweater with a big "O" stitched across her chest. Cowgirl boots extended midway up her slender calves and a crushed straw hat propped on top of her silky black hair woven into pigtails. A twig of straw stuck out from between her teeth. "Are you waiting for me cowboy?" She gave a bashful smile and kicked at an imaginary rock. Placing her hands on her hips, she rubbed the toe of her boot up and down the inside of his ankle. "I want to go for a ride cowboy. *Get-e-up!*" She noticed the DVD in Brent's hand, causing her to stop her theatrics. "Is that what I think it is?"

"I was planning on giving it to you a while ago. I'm sorry it took so long." He held it out for her. "It's yours to start a new life. Everything is now history. I have no idea what's on it, nor do I want to know. Your future is clean"

She held it to her chest, and then leaned over, wrapping her arms around Brent. The tips of her fingers traced along his scar. "I love you."

Her hand smelled of fresh flowers on a spring day. She added a new dimension to his life—a life together without loneliness. He didn't want this roller coaster ride to end. Right now, the naughty girl standing in front of him wanted to play. "You're ...."

Amber touched her finger to his lips and quietly said, "Shh." She straddled his lap as if she mounted a saddle. "Close your eyes cowboy, you're mine tonight."

"I missed you—"

She leaned in and gave a light kiss to his lips. He felt her grab the front of his collar and pull back. Each time she came forward, she made her lips briefly touch his, and then as quickly pull away. Her hips rolled into him, rocking back and forth escalating the heat that built up inside. Grabbing her braids, he pulled her face to his. For a second their lips touch, tongues mingle. She tasted sweat, fresh. She shyly looked at him from under the brim of her hat and smiled.

Not waiting for her next move, Brent reached under her skirt, feeling only skin. His fingertips slowly trailed the inside of her velvety thigh and down along her bare legs. Before he could pull her to him, she intercepted his wrists and drew them up above his head. "The rules are, no touching, only watching. This is my gift to you."

Her movement lifted the sweater up her stomach. She leaned her chest into him and arched her back. *Fuck the rules*, kissing the softness that pressed against his face. Her rocking intensified, and he moved with her, forgetting about what he did—focusing instead on the girl riding him.

With the grace of a ballerina, she let go of his wrists and flung her hat across the room. "Yeehaw cowboy," she yelled. "Let's rodeo!"

He disobeyed her rules and pulled her sweater over her head, exposing her soft breasts. Pulling her body into him, they swayed back and forth under their mounting pleasure. His hands ... her hands explored each other as if this was their first time.

Brent's mind whirled with excitement, wanting this moment to last—wanting her! He felt himself beginning to climax. "Wait, not yet." Lifting her up, their mouths locked together as he carried her into the shower. "I hope you don't mind getting wet. I need a shower."

He set her down long enough to step out of his clothes—she pulled off her boots and dropped her skirt. After turning on warm water, he pressed her back against the shower wall, lifting her so he could kiss her stomach, breasts, neck then mouth.

She moaned—he thrust into her. The two became one as she pulled into him.

With their lips locked, she wrapped her arms around his neck and legs straddled his waist—squeezing him tight against her naked body. Relinquishing her hold, she nestled her face into is neck while beginning a slow bounce, increasing in intensity, then abruptly stop.

He felt her hot breath labored. Pushing her back to look into her eyes, a tear fell from along her cheek. "What's wrong?"

She said, "This is what I expected love to be like."

He pressed into her, allowing the warm shower to flow over them. This moment felt perfect. Between the two, as a gyroscope begins its spin, they began a rhythmic grind. They finally found themselves safe in each other arms.

***

Brent approached the base gate in his black Z. His thoughts became nostalgic—all that had happened behind this gated fence. He did not recognize the security guard checking identifications. The military is a continuous revolving door, when a person leaves, another enters by swearing an oath to serve. Brent showed his military ID to the guard, who saluted him as if nothing had ever happened. He drove by the Reaper Operations center, recognizing several cars in the parking lot. Another mission being conducted somewhere on the other side of the world, flown by a pilot sitting in the very room he once sat.

Brent parked his car in an open visitors parking slot across the street from the Wing headquarters building. He now felt like a visitor. Getting dressed for this day, he contemplated whether to wear a suit, formal uniform or his favorite—jeans and a flannel shirt. Technically still in the military, but as soon after he signed his discharge papers, he would again be a civilian ... and out of a job, but with the adventure of a new life.

Brent got out of his car and straightened the coat of his full uniform. A ribbon stack and silver pilot wings adorned his chest. He touched the mended sleeve and hole Amber stitched closed the previous evening. Crossing the road that led to the entrance steps, he noticed a Lincoln Town car parked in front of the building next to a sign that said "No Parking." A red Army flag with three stars fluttered from the car's front fender. *I wonder who could be visiting the wing commander.* He proceeded up the steps toward the building. Two men in khaki cargo slacks and dark windbreakers framed each side of the front entrance. Even with dark sunglasses covering their face, they both looked straight at him as he approached.

Brent overheard the man on the left speak into a collar microphone. "He's here." A couple steps away, the other said, "Lieutenant Parker, please follow me."

Brent followed him down the hall toward the same conference room he had been in the day prior with the classified sign still posted across the closed doors.

The man he followed knocked twice and opened the door. Brent entered the room, uncertain what to expect. The door closed behind him, but his escort did not come in with him.

Two men in business suits sat alongside the table where Vince and he had last sat. They were in an animated discussion about quarterbacks on NFL football teams. One said, "He might be old, but his arm is still a rifle." Causing the other to retort, "Wilson has youth and good luck catching him when he scrambles." It became apparent they had a long rivalry and friendship between them. Brent stepped into the room and waited for them to finish their argument. One of the men noticed Brent standing near the door and they both stood.

"I apologize for not hearing you come in. My friend here thinks the Seattle Seahawks are going to win the Super bowl this year. I'm rooting for Denver. What do you think?" Everybody looked at one another.

The other person broke the silence. "John, you shouldn't put Lieutenant Parker on the spot. General Shoemaker sometimes forgets his social graces." The man speaking reached out his hand. "I'm Admiral Grew." He shook Brent's hand. "My friend is your typical snake eater who's been out in the field too long. He's going to need to get his social graces down if he's going to survive Washington."

"Oh, don't pay any attention to him. He's been drinking seawater too long. I'm General Shoemaker." He also reached out and shook Brent's hand. "Please have a seat. Before we get started, we both want to thank you for your service to your country. What you did saved numerous lives."

Brent took a seat across the table from the two men. He noticed they both had a separate folder in front of them.

Shoemaker took the lead. "Brent, in front of me are your discharge papers. I'm sure you are aware your career in the Air Force is over. We both think it's in your best interest to leave this military branch."

"Yes sir. I'm ready to put this all behind me. What I did made a difference and I still hold to my decision."

The two men looked at each other, followed by a lengthy pause.

Admiral Grew took over. "We both think you should continue your military career. General Shoemaker and I have the authority and we want to present you with an opportunity. In front of me is a commissioning package into the Navy. Lieutenant Shook sustained some heavy injuries during his ejection. Thankfully, he is still alive. But I'm now a pilot short and I would like for you to join my Navy."

"What about everything I did?" Brent asked.

Shoemaker took the question. "If you take Grew's offer, any reference to what happened will not be retained in your service record—you'll start with a clean slate. That's the deal."

"And if I pass on the offer. What then?"

"I know you don't trust anybody after what we've put you through. Hell, I wouldn't either. I'm telling you we need men who think outside of the box. The war we're in is asymmetric—we're making up rules as we fight to stay ahead of a very formidable enemy. We both know you were instrumental in the discovery and the destruction of several crates full of SA-twenty-four missiles—let alone with saving twelve valuable men. If those missiles had gotten into the wrong hands, the ramifications would've been monumental!"

Brent's thoughts went back to the trucks in Benghazi and later the same crates offloaded in a Syrian village. "Have we recovered all the missiles?"

Shoemaker shrugged his shoulders. "There are four crates less, but quite a few are still missing. We have a good idea who has them, thanks to your involvement with two of my best men—Zender and Perez. They said he's the same person who brought the crates to General al-Obeidi. We don't have very much information on him other than we speculate he's Iranian. All we have is a grainy picture Perez took from a mini-mart security camera outside this base and your video footage. Which brings me to questions you might be able to answer. Do you know why he came to the United States and what purpose did he have here?" Both men stared at Brent.

"I'm still not sure. I killed some innocent people during a CIA mission in Yemen. Because of it, I became targeted by a foreign intelligence agency. I thought he came to kill me." Other than Amber, nobody knew how he and Sadegh's paths crossed. During the previous evening, everyone agreed certain events of his story would remain a secret.

"If not you, who was he after?" Grew asked.

"A First Secretary to the Pakistani embassy. His name is Sadegh. I think that was not his real position. He tried to set me up, but I got him instead."

This time Shoemaker spoke. "That must be why I got an interesting phone call from the Secretary of State. What you just said has connected the dots. I'm told he is being replaced."

Shoemaker broke their silence. "Homeland security has an APB out for both of them, but I've got a feeling they've vanished—halfway back to Iran by now. I'd sure like to know how they entered the US right under our nose. You saw this Iranian agent up close, which means you're the only person who can personally identify him."

"I would say too close. I do know this killer is smooth and calculated. He could have killed me, but didn't. He used me as bait to lure his intended target into the open. He appeared to have a sense of honor in what he believed in. I made a deal with him and he honored what he'd promised. *Nothing more, nothing less.*" Brent smiled on this last gibe.

"Is there anything else you want to tell us?" Shoemaker asked.

Brent wasn't sure how much they already knew. "I think the local police are looking at arresting me."

This time Grew spoke. "I'm not a lawyer, but my guess is the local prosecutor doesn't have a case. No witnesses and the victim, the First Secretary you mentioned, seems to have disappeared. I'm told he was a prime suspect to multiple murders of an escort service."

"I can guarantee he will not be showing up to answer any questions," Brent said.

Shoemaker broke into the conversation. "I'm planning on tasking Zender and Perez to hunt this Iranian agent down and find the remaining missiles. They're going to need some help. Would you be willing to join their team?"

Brent tried to absorb everything said. He needed time to decompress. Without waiting for them to ask further questions, he said, "Is there anything else you need from me?" He stood up from the table. "If I may, I would like some time to assimilate what you told me."

"We'll keep our offer on ice until you decide. Intelligence does have a shelf life. The longer we wait, the less likely we're going to be successful. From what I know about you, you're a man of honor. You've seen this Iranian agent and you think outside of the box, which makes you a perfect addition for this team. Before this meeting, I had a chance to catch up with my old classmate Vince. Along with what you told us, he mentioned a few things that will never be written in your service record. You have my word. Go have fun with your girlfriend. You deserve some time together."

Brent proceeded to the wooden door. Before he opened it, he remembered what the assassin had told him. "The Iranian told me something I'm sure you're interested in. He said for us to look at Abbottabad, Pakistan. I'm guessing our number one terrorist is hiding there." Without waiting for a response, he stepped through the doorway and out into freedom.

U.S. Special Operations units, on a daily basis, conduct clandestine military operations in over one hundred twenty counties. Their job is to remain a ghost.

Since the infamous events of Nine-Eleven, over 14,000 US military and American contractors have died while fighting terrorism.

CPSIA information can be obtained
at www.ICGtesting.com
Printed in the USA
FFHW02n1250101018
48772521-52864FF